Mauro Martone was born in Glasgow, raised in Edinburgh, and educated at schools in Fife and Perthshire where he boarded. Early fictional influences included Kenneth Grahame's '*Wind in the Willows*' and Robert Roosevelt's '*Br'er Rabbit*' stories. He began writing fiction at the age of eight when he produced a three-and-a-half-page prolongation of Grahame's riverside world. He got his MA (with honours) from the University of Edinburgh, where he read Ancient History and Classical Archaeology at Teviot. He also read Christianity and Social Christianity at New Collage, as outside subjects. Whilst a student, Martone worked as a nightshift taxi driver in the undesirable Muirhouse, Pilton and Granton housing scheme circuits of Edinburgh. He later began a postgraduate degree alongside volunteering as a classroom tutor to both young offenders and adults with substance dependences. He lives in Edinburgh and keeps rescue dogs.

Filomena, RIP.

Mauro Martone

KERTAMEN

AUSTIN MACAULEY PUBLISHERS™

LONDON • CAMBRIDGE • NEW YORK • SHARJAH

A CIP catalogue record for this title is available from the British Library.

ISBN 9781788483995 (Paperback)
ISBN 9781788484008 (Hardback)
ISBN 9781788484015 (E-Book)
www.austinmacauley.com

First Published (2017)
Austin Macauley Publishers Ltd™
25 Canada Square
Canary Wharf
London
E14 5LQ

Author's Note

I was working as a waiter in St Andrews during the 1990 Open Golf Tournament and would spend my three-hour afternoon break in the university's King James Library on South Street, reading George MacDonald Frazer and Jack Higgins novels, which I had purchased second-hand from the nearby bouquinistes' with my lunch-time tip money. I should credit those two writers above anyone else then, as my main fictional literary influences. All characters and events contained within this manuscript are a result of a very vivid imagination that has been fuelled from the outset by such outstanding story telling. Additionally, I must also thank my childhood drama teacher, himself a Glenalmond product – the 'Sapper'-worshipping Mr Watson, for apparently spotting an ability early doors and kindly nursing it along to the point of obsession. I still look back on those highly amusing re-writes of Stephen King's Shining with great fondness. I do not think I should have written Kertamen otherwise.

Ker'tamen in Ancient Greek, or Certamen in Classical Latin, refers to a game, competition, dispute and/or a struggle. The habit of giving titles to untitled Greek works was a Roman one, but the mention of 'Certamen' in the Roman period may also have invoked a reference to the brief ancient Greek account of a contest between Homer and Hesiod. This link is adduced by R. Hunter in his work 'The Shadow of Callimachus: Studies in the Reception of Hellenistic Poetry at Rome', Cambridge University Press.

Prologue

"Oh, what a tangled web we weave when first we practice to deceive!"

Sir Walter Scott

He headed east toward the walkway which flanked the northern edge of the Eastern Links. The Western Links were traditionally the busier of the two, zigzagged by pathways leading to Leith Central, Easter Road, and the main arteries of Restalrig and Meadowbank. The old red-brick school building was listed and had emerged intact from the mass regeneration and vanity projects that the local authorities had embarked upon years previously. Towering over the park like a Victorian workhouse, the building was currently occupied by a minor university, which was using it as a draughty drama campus.

The students were often to be seen up at the windows, dancing, talking, or watching the people walking below. These busy pathways, lined with mature elms, were linked in the centre of the park to form a huge Union Jack, visible only from above. The entities above noticed such things though; perhaps some recalled when there had once been a large pond with a neighbouring bandstand? Perhaps the park's original architect had been a unionist who believed in these beings?

The public used the Western Links to briskly commute between old and new Leith, though at weekends, there was a more leisurely vibe. The exception were the tennis courts and bowling greens, which were sprinkled across both Links. Today there were only a few people though, wrapped up in hats, scarves and gloves; who passed through hurriedly to limit their exposure to the icy afternoon wind. There was a cider drinker on a bench, politely asking everyone for "a pound for a cup of tea," but in general, the bitter weather deterred most folks from passing through.

Despite the cold, the kids play zones were still packed with well wrapped-up infants whose laughter was entertaining the watching crows. He wanted to smile and laugh with them too, but instead he recalled when the mothers' voices, as they nattered to each other in better times, had gone in tandem with their kids' laughter. That had been a healthy social outlet for housewives once. Today, he observed that these mothers were partly oblivious to their surroundings and sometimes even their kids. He was constantly disappointed by their addiction to their phones and as such, pitied them.

He approached two grassy mounds which had once been part of the French defence of Leith against an English siege of 1559. He could see the mounds in later times, too, as he passed them. Times without multi-channel television or the internet, when the kids had sledged down them in winter and then rolled their hand-painted eggs down them again in spring. Not so long ago there would also have been at least a dozen games of football on the go too, regardless of the weather. Not today, though. He ruminated that the youth of this era preferred to play their football upon sofas, with their fingers as opposed to their feet.

Just then, a fat woman appeared into his line of vision; one who may have been pretty if she were not so obese. Oh, his kind could appreciate the design and shape of a woman, but that was as far as it went. "They are getting fatter, too," he whispered to himself while opting to smile as he glided past. She did not look up from her text message though.

The Western and Eastern Links were also somewhat diverse in appearance and by frequenters. Separated from the West by a main road, the East had a fairly upper class vibe to it. It was a vast common greenway which expanded eastwards as far as Seafield and which hosted two cricket pitches and a clubhouse. It was also regarded by some local historians to be the traditional home of golf due to its former six-hole course dating back to 1619. No golf was played here now; instead, it was home to picnickers and the beloved dogs of the good, well-fed burghers who owned the Georgian mansions of Claremont Park.

These well-to-do residents tended to claim the East Links as their own, and strangely, the bums with cider bottles appeared to comprehend this. The wave of Polish migrants who had arrived in the city in recent times now supplied a new wave of bench drinkers, mostly skin-heads, attempting to set up court on the Eastern Links. That is, until the Claremont Park brigade had called in their police and council connections to end the occupation.

"They drink their cans of Polish lager, which they leave on the Links. They pee on the grass and even make fires to cook sausages. It is an intolerable state of affairs." He could hear the voice of one female caller who had gasped down the phone at her local MSP some months earlier. He knew it was unfair to leave empty cans and burn the grass – he could see the blackened patches dotted along the green as he passed by now. The Polish fashion of walking around drinking cans of beer was never going to be accepted by everyone in this town. He wondered why the city council couldn't just put in some barbeque areas instead, with warning signs and rules.

"Without rules, chaos reigns," he reminded himself. He was also aware that there was a subtle prejudice developing against the Poles and that their un-British habits such as not using bins, or saying 'thank you' when a door is held open for them, was the beginning of the end of common courtesy. In this case, however, the fierce opposition was hidden behind an apparent veil of concern for the local environment, as opposed to any disapproval of East European habits; for that was still in the post.

The main pathway which ran east toward the old Restalrig railway was quite long, and acted as something of a wind channel. It was flanked by allotments to the north which gave no protection from the winds arriving from the sea, only a stone's throw away. The track itself was now a walk and cycle route and home to foxes, badgers and a variety of birds. It then became a bridge swooping down a tarmac mound onto the Links pathway, which he was proceeding along. Normally the path would be frequented by couples and joggers but in the current weather, just like the West Links, only the occasional hard-core cyclist ventured along it today.

He had been called Bruno by men since France in 1793; for that had been when Uriel had introduced him to the puppet Robespierre. He had been ordered to direct Robespierre away from the fallen ones who had been influencing his lust for carnage. He remembered that old France well enough; the Reign of Terror still filled him with sadness and disappointment. They had failed bitterly with that quest, and it still hurt. As he took in the bourgeois Georgian mansion houses to the south side of the Links, he was reminded of the screams of the victims as they were attacked and dragged from their chateaus.

He recalled the sheer frustration his kind had experienced at the divine orders which had restrained them from intervening. Many people had died in France in properties very similar to these, long before any trial or guillotine. Thankfully this matter today was an entirely different ball game, he mused; pressing on toward the rendezvous, scanning the branches of the old oak trees for entities as he did so. The trees stood like sentry towers between him and the Links and he saw, despite the wind, many a starling and robin darting from the branches and hedgerow, like ballet dancers rejoicing at his presence. This caused him to smile to himself again.

He could hear their language as they played, and wished he had brought some bread crumbs. He often carried something for the birds and the foxes who now ran the gauntlet of people within the city because of the destruction of their natural habitat. Today he had no time, having been sent directly by a command from Gabriele to meet with one of the fallen ones. He was often regarded by his own to be more concerned with the welfare of animals than that of humans. This was not quite true; he simply felt obliged to help animals because he had the power to do so.

"That was all we were doing when we taught man a thing or two," a voice echoing now in his head had argued long ago. This was said by one of the original fallen, years ago, during a bitter confrontation over the nuclear question. Bruno had been present at the clash, which had occurred at the Metallurgical Laboratory of Chicago University in 1942. The Allies had been secretly researching plutonium and reactors by means of graphite as a potential neutron moderator; they were, of course, being guided by an elite team of fallen angels. The clash had been swift and had left the place in quite a mess which the humans couldn't figure out. It was those words said then, which would echo in Bruno's mind whenever he helped another being out.

When they dropped the bombs on Japan in '45, Bruno heard it again in his head all day long as he wept for mankind.

"Hardly the same thing though," he reminded himself again now, his warm breath hanging in the air as he exhaled. Propelled by a sense of righteousness, he quickened his pace toward the rendezvous point.

He was wearing a waterproof hiking jacket, jeans and brown leather ankle boots. He had chosen a Peruvian hat today to combat the bitter, sleet-filled wind which had persisted for a week or so since he had been in this particular iteration of Scotland. Over on the green to his right were several dog walkers, whom he kept his eye on as he passed. He observed the dogs to see if they caught his scent, or that of any other beings who might be within the vicinity. Suddenly, a heavily wrapped-up man jogged towards him with a small spaniel running alongside him. Upon passing Bruno at the wooden cricket club hut, the dog put its head down in respect and pulled slightly away from him. The owner failed to notice the strange behaviour of his pet, but Bruno noted it: instant respect and surrender of the path to a superior being, by a loyal and trustworthy creature. He regarded the action as a tribute and was well pleased.

As he approached the far end of the Links, he came to a small fenced-off orchard at the foot of the old railway. It contained young apple and pear trees, and some wooden picnic tables. He noticed that the old rope which held the entry gate shut was tied in an angelic knot. Humans would be quite unable to untie it, as Alexander the Great had learned at Gordian back in the day. Bruno swiftly untied it, entered the orchard, then shut the gate and retied it again. As he did so he noticed a woman approaching down the bridge with a Rottweiler at her heel that was eagerly onto the scent of something. Eventually, it jerked its master off her footing for a brief second, but she recovered and pulled the dog back into line quite well, Bruno thought.

"What is it, Alfie?" the frizzy redhead inquired of her hound, but the dog was more interested in the scent it had caught and began to growl – softly initially, in the manner that some dogs do when they look through a window and spy a cat passing in the garden. Perhaps they know through painful experience that they can't reach the intruder and that if they bark, the master will shout at them to be quiet. So, a quiet growl then.

Bruno saw that the dog began looking over the walkway embankment and down into the little orchard. He turned to see what it was staring at and spotted a smiling man in a long grey cashmere overcoat who wore a similar grey fedora hat. The dog's growl became louder now, as if it was sizing up the possibility of a jump down the 4 ft. embankment and over the fence. Thankfully, its owner was experienced enough to lead it away at a trot, verbally doing so at the double, like a drill sergeant. The dog turned to look back at the orchard a couple of times and had its collar jerked for its trouble. Bruno smiled at the beast as it passed him and it lowered its gaze. He had always appreciated their loyalty and faith in their masters' leadership, but it was their hatred for the fallen which earned them the friendship of his choir.

"Suicidal instinct, which once again proves the imperfection of the current seeds occupying this world," one of the fallen had once been heard saying to some angels who had learned about its fight with two dogs which had been protecting a child. The fallen one had tried to take the child, but both dogs had attacked him with ferocity. The dogs both died but the child was saved, and the fallen one had felt the hounds' teeth tearing at his flesh before he managed to slay them. The problem was that despite being capable of wounding a fallen angel, dogs would always die when they attacked one. Bruno had once witnessed a wolf pack tear one up quite badly on a battlefield before it mortally wounded most them. Even still, he had seen how the fallen angel had later been lifted up and away in considerable pain by two others. The enemy were made painfully aware then, that dogs would fight them to the death.

As Bruno entered deeper into the orchard, he uttered a basic spell in his own tongue, creating an unseen barrier which would discourage humans from climbing over the fence. This needed to be a completely undisturbed parley.

He approached the man in grey, who was sitting up on one of the wooden picnic tables with his feet on the bench. He was flicking a pound coin up in the air and catching it again, smiling at Bruno as he approached. The man was dressed in the 1930s style, but the fine cut of his clothes was clearly modern. He wore black brogues with grey-knitted socks which, Bruno noticed, had small red devils embroidered upon them. A neat little detail. The face was that of a handsome man, pale and cleanly-shaved.

"How are you, Brother?" the fallen one removed a black leather glove and offered a pale white hand for Bruno to shake, which was ignored.

"I'm very well, and I'll join you at this table if you do not object," Bruno smiled back at him.

"Somewhat parky today, old chap," the old Cacodemon mused in a clipped Oxbridge accent, as he replaced his glove and commenced flicking the coin again.

"Precisely. Appreciate it while you can, then," Bruno grinned, causing the fallen one to beam in appreciation at the apparent wit.

To a casual observer, the two of them would have looked like any other pair of middle-aged men, chatting away while their dogs exercised freely in the secure compound, except that there were no dogs in the orchard and these beings were quite alone together. One of them, perhaps the blonde Cacodemon with the handsome face and piercing green eyes which reflected so much resent and fury, attracted the interest of other random dogs beyond the fence who were not deterred by Bruno's spell. Other than that, however, both entities would remain undisturbed for as long as they chose.

They had chosen to meet in the appearance of men. This had been a tradition between the factions for some time now, though other forms were not uncommon either. Bruno found this beast's human appearance to be friendly enough on this occasion; though there was no mistaking his mischievous air. Both soon became comfortable enough and relaxed a little. Neither would abuse a parley meeting; there were rules and traditions. They had simply agreed to talk today, and Bruno had suggested the location. Both sat and stared out at the humans struggling by the fence, in the wind. They seemed oblivious to the two men in the orchard, who could see and hear everything within a one mile radius if they chose.

"It's the dogs I feel sorry for, brother," smirked the other. Bruno found himself chuckling at this and both of them turned to smile at each other in genuine amusement.

"Some humans buy them coats," Bruno replied delicately in the hope of more banter from this old Warlock, but the attempt proved futile.

"If only they treated each other with such affection, you and I would be redundant," sighed the other, the smile disappearing from his features.

His cue had arrived sooner than desired, but Bruno was on to it sharply enough, despite his disappointment. "Well, let's get down to it then, shall we?" he sighed.

"Capital, let's," the grin was back, but it was obviously forced now.

"You are warned to refrain from any further involvement in the Scottish Referendum." Bruno continued to look straight ahead at the people passing by the orchard fence, rather than turning to face him. He let this sink in for a moment,

"Furthermore, I am authorised to tell you that the Lord wants them to think for themselves at this stage of the game," he added. His companion remained silent.

"Thought he objected to that?" teased the other in Aramaic now.

"You must leave here and concentrate on whatever other poison you lot are brewing elsewhere," Bruno pressed the point regardless.

The other shook his head, then looked at Bruno; the cheerfulness in his sharp green eyes undercut by both anguish and anger. Man couldn't read their eyes – he had given that right up in Eden when he had also lost his understanding of the languages of the animals, but Bruno could see deep into them now easily enough.

"Rum notion old boy, but our other brews are not quite boiled yet. We have the US economy close to the brink and Syria is turning out just fabulously you know; however, it's here where we desire to make things easier for Russia when the time comes," the other shook his head once again.

Bruno stared hard at him now.

"Anyway, is it not their ability to think freely, or the lack of it rather, that is the very nature of our little game?" the fallen one whispered.

"This is a commandment, and that's that!" Bruno maintained the hard glare before adding, "I have had it straight from the top and there is to be no deviation from it!"

"Then why the fuck is it you're telling me this, Bruno, and not my commander?"

"That could easily be arranged – shall I report that you refused to accept? I'm sure your puppet master will appreciate being forced to command you himself, whilst giving you a slap in the process."

"Just tell me, why the late demands? Are you afraid of yet another defeat?"

"It is what it is. I am simply an enforcer of the commandment," Bruno sighed again.

"Ah… the proverbial cop-out," groaned the other one mischievously. "Once again, the goalposts have moved and it is not negotiable? This is a concerning pattern that renders the game uneven, and thus unjust, Bruno."

The first-time Bruno had ever encountered this being had been from a distance, behind the bobbing heads of several old men in ancient Sparta, where he was protecting the Athenian fugitive general Alcibiades. Although Bruno had been there with other seraphs for an entirely separate reason, their eyes had met. It had been clear to him that this old Warlock held influence over some nobles who were being asked by Alcibiades to involve themselves in another war with Athens.

Five centuries later, they had encountered each other again on the temple mount in Jerusalem. At that time, Michael and others fought a group of fallen ones led by this one, whose name was then Rumael. In the end, after Michael had knocked this one through a wall, the fallen ranks had broken and fled across the dusty Jordan valley and into Arabia.

Bruno recalled how Michael had warned the fallen not to influence certain Pharisees, and how they had responded violently to this request at the time. Oh, they were brave enough, but they had been scattered that day at the battle of the Temple Mount by the sheer power of the magnificent archangel.

Bruno later clashed with him on a somewhat more personal scale in 1942 in Russia. Angels had been protecting certain women and children in Stalingrad from the Nazi invaders as best as they could. They created easier access to food among the ruins, while also protecting children from the desperate soldiers of both sides by moulding hideaways. The whole affair had been a vast, bloody mess for both armies and it had been this creature here with the grey fedora who had orchestrated much of the bloodbath at Stalingrad. The fallen had infiltrated the German high command by late 1942 because Hitler was gradually losing the respect of his Wehrmacht officers. Many fallen had initially lent Hitler the hugely prized power to influence the thinking of others, but by late 1942 it had become less effective due to his demonic possession becoming more visual through his orders. At this point they changed tactics, and wormed their way into the minds of the senior Wehrmacht commanders in the field.

This particular Warlock had been whispering in Field Marshal Von Manstein's ear and urging his relief force forward to rescue the surrounded pocket within which the German 6th Army was disintegrating near Stalingrad. Angels had created problems for Goring's air supply line into the pocket and the Lord sent the worst winter conditions the under-equipped Nazis could have imagined. The 6th army was completely surrounded by recharged Soviets; as the soldiers huddled together, they were covered in lice, frozen near to death, and inadequately supplied.

Bruno had thought that the aim of stopping Hitler's blitzkrieg in the eastern Soviet Union had been accomplished by that point. However, out of the blue, this creature served up a handy relief force led by Von Manstein, which was en route to blast an escape corridor for the 6th Army. Von Manstein's force had made considerable progress too, despite fierce Russian opposition, so Bruno was sent to hinder them.

They met face-to-face in the kitchen field tent of Von Manstein's camp. Bruno was with Hasa, another Angel sent with him to slow down the relief force. The two angels had not been permitted to kill any Germans, but their vehicles and food were fair game. Upon arriving and walking around the camp in their true form, quite invisible to the Germans, they approached the soup pots with firm intent. Suddenly they were both aware of the Warlock's scent, before he appeared beside them. He screamed at them to leave in a Munchner accent, before drawing his golden sword. A quick clash ensued, with him parrying their cuts and thrusts before managing to slash Hasa across the forehead and then fleeing into the night.

The German relief force did not make it to the rescue of the 6th Army, and the fact that many of them went down with food poisoning soon after this incident contributed greatly to the failure of their mission. Consequently, well over 100,000 Germans fighting in the 6th Army surrendered to the Soviets at Stalingrad soon afterwards.

Bruno could also recall a tale of how this creature's friend had been slaughtered in a dingy flat in Brighton on the night before the IRA bombed the Tory Party conference in 1984. Apparently, there had been an unauthorised confrontation involving old Watchers, angels and the fallen ones, which went unpunished by the Lord. Yet in the end, Bruno knew this one was wasting his time with these trumped-up grievances against the Creator.

"It's not for us to question," Bruno whispered to him whilst continuing to gaze over at the humans on the Links.

"Ah now, once again my brother, our choir tends to disagree with such ancient thinking," the old Warlock winked cunningly at Bruno.

"It is never up for question," came the stern reply.

The other laughed, almost childlike, "Even when it is an error in judgement?" He used his hands in the Italian fashion, to emphasise the magnitude of his point.

"It is never up for question," repeated Bruno, with the beginning of a growl evident in his tone.

"Well, you're wrong there, brother, we have been questioning it for centuries. At least in being wrong, you can claim to have something in common with your pet monkeys out there," he snarled back with even more of a growl and a flash of his real teeth at the humans across the fence.

"Do you not look at how they have evolved scientifically over the last decade? If you have, then how could you consider them mere monkeys?"

"Vermin!" snapped the Warlock in reply, his pale face turning red in anger. He gazed deep into Bruno's eyes in search of his soul.

"...And yet, Thomas Allin would have wagered upon your lot being saved from such blasphemous thinking," mocked Bruno.

"Well, that thoughtful monkey, like the rest of his species, was also quite wrong, old chap," the other snarled in response.

"Just because your lot control the regulation of their education, does not mean that some are not developing efficiently." Bruno shook his head in disagreement. "And just because your human disciples listen to your bile and hide the cure to some of your recipes..." He continued to shake his head, but with disgust creeping across his beautiful features. "That does not mean that the species are not developing. That is precisely why it is not up for debate!"

The fallen one was silent a moment before then asking: "Are you chaps going to rig the referendum, then?"

Bruno ignored the bait and got off the bench as if to leave; at which point the fedora wearer dangled yet another carrot,

"For you are perfectly aware that we have turned them to our plans here, are you not?" he hissed through his teeth at Bruno, quite unable to control his anger.

"We are well aware of the division you have created – not only nationally, but within individual families and friendships, yes." Bruno assured him before slowly turning to leave again.

"He's surely no awa' tae chuck brimstaines doon upon Auld Reekie after we put oor jimmies in power, is he?" He was now testing the water, under an obvious veil of slightly forced banter.

Bruno saw right through it and did not turn around to parry the obvious sarcasm.

"No, the city itself is safe. But it isnae kent as the 'The Athens of the North' for nought, laddie," he said, mimicking the bad Scottish brogue. "You will no doubt recall how it all panned out for your chaps in the

Cylonian Affair?" he added in perfect Attic Greek before walking off and leaving the memory of Athens lingering behind.

"I was not in Athens until much later," the fallen one shouted in old Doric. "I had been securing our interests in Ephesus when your lot had that particular moment," he insisted with urgency at the departing angel. "But, if I had been there, chaos would have reigned like in Robespierre's Paris," he shouted, grinning. Bruno now turned around to meet his eye from a distance. "Ah yes, considerably later," the fallen one grinned, "but my handiwork, nonetheless." However, Bruno had already turned and left before he had finished the sentence.

One
"Young heads take example of the ancients"
Elizabeth I

Chuck Kean worked for Police Scotland at their Stockbridge HQ in Edinburgh. Having served with the Drug Squad there for over a decade as a Detective Constable, then as a DS, he slogged away under the supervision of his friend, Detective Inspector Grant Martin, who had poached him from CID. When Martin switched to Special Branch six years later, Chuck had waltzed through his Inspector's course in Ayr to become the new squad DI. He enjoyed working with the 'Druggies' more than his previous roles elsewhere, primarily because they were an honest, close-knit, and effective unit. He was not always sure that he could say likewise about the other branches he had worked in within the force.

Having heard the rumours about the squad's so-called arrogance before he was originally seconded, Chuck had been a little apprehensive initially. Yet he had experienced no arrogance at all. Compared with his previous experience in uniform and the CID, the Druggies were a joy to work with. He was often amused, however, at the belief among some of them, that they were the greatest masters of disguise since Sherlock Holmes.

"Some even fantasise that they are on *Miami Vice*; wearing white summer suits and all that crap," he had said with a grin to his wife Kim during his first week there.

"A pair of white espadrilles would suit you, dear," she told him with a wink.

Kimberly McBride had not fancied the young Charles Kean straight away when they had both worked at GEC-Marconi in Bothwell. She had worked upstairs in admin, while he was an apprentice radio engineer on the same floor. He had been involved in the Martello radar system project at the time and passed by her office most days. On Friday, when she handed out the wage packets, he would steal a glance at her, taking her in. He had fallen in love quite quickly but only tentatively revealed his interest after a while. Kim's working-class Catholic family from Carluke had raised her not to date Protestant boys. Consequently, Chuck made it his mission to teach her that, as a born and bred Leither, whose family were simply Protestant by inheritance, the Kean clan were neither Catholic nor Protestant.

Chuck's father Chic had served in the Black Watch in Korea, and had always insisted that everyone maintain a respectful silence during the Queen's Christmas Day Speech. He voted Labour, but that was as far as his politics went. Most weekends his expression of faith was standing upon the terraces of Easter Road stadium, supporting the Hibs. A place where Irish tricolour flags were occasionally flown, but where politics and religion did not apply as strongly as they did in the west. Leith was like that, you see; united by class, as opposed to anything else.

"Kean is an Irish name, is it not, lad?" Kim's pipe-smoking father had asked when Kim finally brought Chuck home for tea one rainy Saturday.

"I believe so, Mr McBride, yes, but we have no record of the link; there has been a suggestion by my Mother that the Irish spelling is Keane with an 'e'," Chuck replied, trying to engage him with a smile.

"Aye, well, that might explain how your family are all Protestant, son," the older man replied despondently as he refilled his pipe.

The whole house was muggy due to the pipe smoke, and Chuck was quite uncomfortable.

"Well we are actually not Protestant at all, other than my late grandfather, who was Church of Scotland," Chuck stated. "My parents married in the Kirk, yes; but if truth be told, we don't attend any church as a family and my sister married in a registry office," Chuck cheerily tried to defuse the theological concerns.

"Christ, are you all atheists?" Kim's mother exclaimed, hands on head in a well-worn routine of despair.

"No, well, we all believe in God and celebrate Easter and Christmas and so on; we just don't attach ourselves to any particular church or cult." He attempted to explain the new generation of British Christianity, which had been emerging since the sixties, to this sofa of devout Catholics.

"Well the Scottish Kennedys were all Protestant, you know," hissed Kim's old granny from a corner. Chuck found the old crone a bit strange, and did his best to avoid staring at her distinctly hairy chin.

In the end, despite their initial reservations, and after another eight months of courting between Leith and Lanarkshire, the McBride family agreed to the marriage. Shortly afterward, when lodging at Kim's parents' home, Chuck responded to an ad in the newspaper for Strathclyde Police. Soon he had quit Marconi's and gone to police college. After a period as a rookie in the Govan district of Glasgow, he proudly became a full-time police constable at Motherwell police station in December 1984; before transferring to Edinburgh, his home city, the following year. It had been a good Christmas that year for the new family as they also celebrated the birth of their son, Charlie. After Boxing Day lunch at Chuck's parents' house, with both his in-laws present, Chuck was somewhat merry from the wine he had necked that afternoon. He suddenly straightened up however, when his niece pressed his father to tell, "That old ghost story your papa told you, Grandpa Chic."

It was a story Chuck had heard many times before and which had not been altered over time. This brought an eerie sense of credibility to the tale, Chuck reckoned. The old soldier, who had been looking forward to this moment, smiled, took another sip of malt, leaned back in his chair and began telling his tale to a hushed table.

"My grandfather was Hugh Kean from Prestonpans, and he signed up for Kitchener and the Black Watch at the old Leith Academy in 1915," he began. "He went to the war in France and was recognised three times for bravery and for saving an officer's life under fire. By 1916 he had risen to the rank of sergeant at the beginning of the Battle of the Somme." Chic paused a moment and pointed toward an old mirror on the wall with an image of Hugh in his Black Watch kilt.

"He served with the 2nd Battalion in the 1st Division under Major-General Strickland's command. Anyway, one morning, on another insane advance across no-man's-land towards the Jerry positions, something strange occurred. The Jerry trenches were supposed to have been destroyed by a massive artillery bombardment beforehand, but this had obviously not been the case. Hugh was in the third wave of men who went over, only to discover this when it was too late." Chic sighed despondently at the folly of that battle and took another deep mouthful of malt.

"Apparently, some of the men in Hugh's section had started putting tins of Bully Beef in the chest pockets of their tunics in the hope that it may slow down a German bullet," he said with a shrug of his shoulders.

"My own grandfather joined the 10th (Irish) Division because both nationalists and unionists at the time in Ireland supported a war against Germany," Kim's father took the opportunity to pipe up now. "Killed at Gallipoli in 1915. They were dumped on a beach by the SS Clyde and were all gunned down within a few minutes," he said sombrely. Chic nodded sadly at this and silently raised his glass to both men.

"Yes, well, where was I?" he said, impatient to return to his story.

22

"Hugh was on the Somme in the summer of 1916, when his platoon was sent back from the front for a few days to rest at a farm. Here, the men found that they were sharing a barn with a group of Indian infantrymen. Now, he recalled that this was a good thing, because the Muslim Indians fed everyone with curried Bully Beef and chapattis. This was obviously a rare change for Hugh and his chums, and there was plenty of it because the Hindu Indians didn't eat the beef for religious reasons. Instead they apparently put Bully Beef tins in their pockets when going over the top, to catch a bullet."

Kim's mum appeared confused at this point and flashed a glance around the table in search of enlightenment, "The Indian Muslims eat it but not the Hindus?" she asked.

"I guess so, yes," Chic chuckled. "Apparently, a tin of the stuff had slowed down a bullet and saved a bloke's life. The Hindu lads all did it, but then again, one of the Muslim Indians told my granddad not to believe a word the Hindus told him." He shrugged again and everyone laughed at this.

"Well that old Hindu – George, at the Ganges restaurant," he continued with humour, now that he was on a roll, "keeps telling me a lot of crap about his curry being the recipe of some Maharaja or other," he laughed.

"They do a lovely chicken korma and garlic naan over there," declared Chuck's well-tipsy-by-now mother, which fuelled the laughter further.

There was a short silence after this as Chic sipped another slow dram of his drink before continuing with the heart of the story.

"Anyway, old Hugh decided to try it and the next few times he went over the top, he escaped any injury. So, very superstitiously, he understandably began to consider the old tin of Bully Beef to be a lucky charm. So, one day when he was in the third wave to go with his tin of Bully Beef in his pocket protecting his heart, he went over only to see all the men ahead of him being mown down by machine gun fire. He was soon shot in his thigh and shoulder, and went down only ten yards or so from his own trench. He crawled back and was shot in the arse in the process, but somehow still managed to grab a kid who had been shot in the throat and dragged him to the trench before realising that his tin of Bully Beef had come out of his pocket a yard or two earlier. The lunatic then turned around, crawled back and reached out for it, all while everyone in the trench were screaming at him not to be so stupid."

Everyone was transfixed, as always.

"He lost two fingers and a thumb to mortar flak, just as he reached out for the bloody tin. He came around briefly a few minutes later in the trench, lying in mud and surrounded by men from the King's Rifles who were lined up to go over the top. He was unable to move and passed out again. Sometime later he awoke to the vision of two officers, both tall, slim and with handsome faces, standing over him. He remembered their unnaturally casual pose and despite his condition, he noted that they seemed somehow out of place. They were talking about him and he could hear them despite all the carnage going on around him. They were debating whether he was dying or not, apparently."

"That's crazy!" exclaimed Kim's teenage brother Peter, who had overdone the Merlot somewhat and who struggled not to laugh at the bit about Hugh's fingers.

"Well, he claimed to have heard one of the officers saying, 'He's out of the game, so pick another pawn, as this one is ours'," Chic told him. "And then the other officer replied, 'He's still breathing, so we'll decide – not you!'"

"Then, both officers looked down at him as if considering him for a moment longer before one of them finally said, '*Fine, have him*' to the other. The same officer turned, with what old Hugh remembered to be an evil grin, and blew his whistle, sending more of the young men of the King's Rifles over into that turkey-shoot."

"Terrible bloody war, that," offered Kim hesitantly, but everyone quickly agreed with her.

"Hugh recovered fully after being sent to a dressing station and then an army hospital in some chateau or other 30 miles from the front, on a horse drawn ambulance. Apparently, the pain endured by many of the injured men on those old carts was quite brutal," Chic said thoughtfully before coming back to his story. "The doctors were quite astonished by the old boy's rapid recovery and the lack of infection in his wounds. They had done their best to clean out and repair them, but they thought he might die. A surgeon called him the luckiest man alive, while he was being wheeled away to get the train home to a British hospital; a month or so later."

Everyone smiled and agreed. Chuck refilled his glass and smiled at Kim, for they had heard the old tale before but knew how much Chic loved telling it.

"Then, with his blighty[1], he was sent home on the train to the coast, where he shared a carriage with two nurses and a blinded cockney infantryman. His arm was in a sling and he sat in pain, looking out of the

---

[1] A WWI term for a wound that earned the victim a journey back home to Britain, either permanently or until deemed fit for a return to the carnage.

window. Half an hour into the journey, the two nurses left to refresh themselves. Just then, the cockney removed his bandages and said 'Hello Hugh'."

"Eh?" gasped Kim's father in astonishment. Chuck wondered if he was exaggerating his surprise, as an excuse to refill his glass with a large double while his wife watched on unfavourably.

"Hugh claimed this bloke looked just like one of the two strange officers from back in the trench, too," Chic shrugged again.

"Apparently, he introduced himself as an angel and explained that when Hugh had been shot, he had called for God's assistance and debated his life with '*the dark ones*'. He convinced Hugh by reducing his pain somehow," the old storyteller shrugged yet again, before allowing a moment to pass as this sank in.

"Then, he told him to go home and marry, for he had a good heart and an ancient bloodline that should reproduce," he said finally, causing Chuck to chuckle and raise his glass high in a mock toast to the angel, while everyone merrily joined him.

"To family," they all declared.

"Did the angel say why he had intervened, other than that he was answering a prayer?" asked Kim with genuine interest.

"No, but he mentioned a game called '*cataract*', apparently," Chuck's dad replied, taking the opportunity to shrug his shoulders one last time.

"Maybe something to do with his eyes or his vision?" suggested Kim's mum.

"Well, we don't know, and I can't swear that the story is genuine. God knows my own father didn't believe it, but all these years I have remembered it."

"Why's that, dad?" Chuck asked, bang on cue.

"Right, you've told your story Chic, let's change the subject and I'll get Trivial Pursuits out," urged Chuck's mother, keen to reignite the merriment.

"How about a song while we wait?" Aunt Winifred banged her fat freckled hands upon the table and gasped like Miss Piggy from *The Muppet Show*, before bursting into a shockingly high-pitched rendition of *The Auld Rugged Cross*; which made Kim's mum squirm in her chair.

"It sounds like a plausible story, Chic. Well, most of it at any rate, and it certainly sounds like old Hugh believed what he claimed," Kim's dad leaned over and whispered.

Aunt Winifred then stopped for a blissful moment, having forgotten the words. "Och, how does it go again?" she asked the room, but everyone shook their heads.

Kim was on the Bailey's by then, so before she crashed out on the sofa Chuck stood up, took her hand and led her out into the adjoining lounge where he sat down with her at the old piano. He kissed her, whispered some gibberish festive tidings in her ear, before playing some carols. This lured Winifred and Peter through and before long, everyone was around the piano singing "Good King Wenceslas," with Kim's dad playing along on the spoons.

Chuck had not enjoyed the job in the early days at the station he was positioned at – Drylaw; it had been an entirely different world to what it is now. The beat walking in Thatcher's Britain had been murder on the feet – a beat cop was required to both think on his feet and to move quickly on them at any moment. Only Blair's lavish spending in the nineties provided the police with enough vehicles to do their job.

They had plenty of space in Chuck's parents' large home but by the summer of '87, Chuck's mother had to be moved into a care-home. She no longer recognised her family and would shout at them to leave whenever they visited. He couldn't handle that and the torture of watching her waste away. In the end, it was too painful, and he came to the realisation that if his family could not visit her without being shouted at, they needed to stop visiting. He stopped praying for an intervention by the time her physical health had almost expired and privately felt contemptuous and bitter about what he regarded as God's refusal to intervene. This obviously did not help her or himself in the slightest, but the anger helped numb his sadness.

Then, four months later, his father died from a stroke and Chuck knew his mother would never return to the home she had resided in since she was a newlywed. When she died of cancer, six months after her husband had been buried, her funeral took place on the south side. She was laid to rest beside him. There were forty-odd mourners in attendance at a service presided over by a Rev. Stephen Martin of the Anglican Church. Chuck's childhood friend Kenny hailed from a family of Anglicans and had offered to arrange things, since Chuck was somewhat lost.

Shortly afterwards, Chuck and Kim decided to sell the Restalrig house and buy a smaller place by the beach in Portobello. They soon found a main door flat with gardens on Marlborough Street, which was just off the beach. There was a sort of middle class, Cornish vibe to Marlborough Street which was heightened by a wine bar on the corner. It served wonderful swordfish and a popular herring stew, which provided heavenly aromas most evenings. For Chuck, though, it was the salty sea breeze and the sound of the ocean which provided a certain nostalgia, and which made him happy

On the Keans' new street, cycles with baskets were lined up, chained along the railings of the Edwardian flats that all had Greek-style blue and white window frames, and bits of driftwood and old lobster pots displayed outside. At the bottom of the street there was something of a French feel, where a plethora of creole cottages and French Quarter/New Orleans-styled villas with ivy-draped balconies stood behind tall walls and sweeping Australian ferns. It was certainly a rare location, and Chuck felt as though they were entering a golden period of their lives with their young family.

He was particularly chuffed about having avoided a placement at the Niddrie station, too. Niddrie was the arsehole of the city, and the station was a last-drop saloon for bad apple cops. Chuck would learn soon enough, however, that the Drylaw station was hardly the Little Sisters of the Poor. His shifts there began at 6 am, 2 pm and 10 pm and lasted for eight hours. Chuck was allocated to Green Watch and was often paired up with a fat constable named Pew, who was so obese he couldn't run a couple of yards without risking a heart attack. He was, like most of Chuck's other new colleagues, an Orangeman and a Hearts man through and through.

"There's only two things I can't stand, Chuck," Pew would say whenever they gave their feet a breather, "Fenians and Pakis." He would grunt this information between gulps of air, while wiping the sweat from his forehead with his tunic sleeve.

"Now, I know your good lady is Catholic and all that jazz, Chuck, but well, I think you and your family are different because you're a good Proddy, eh?" the cretin declared.

From then on, Chuck simply nodded and faked appreciation of this idiot's logic, patted the bigoted slob on the back and increased his pace the minute they returned to the beat, in order to punish him.

At a colleague's stag-do at Silverknowes Golf Club, Chuck was surprised to hear Hearts songs and anti-Catholic chanting as the night wore on. He left early and tried to put it at the back of his mind. His childhood friends were Hibs-supporting liberals who had no interest in the sectarian bullshit that these lads at the station embraced. There was also a Masonic clique among these cops which alarmed him slightly. He became aware of their antics early on, thanks to Pew's endless chat. A couple of Chuck's friends were Catholic and obviously Kim also was one, so from an early stage of his time at Drylaw, Chuck felt that he had no option but to build barriers between the job and his personal life. If this meant isolation from the growing clique of officers, then so be it.

Once, he had chased a group of men who had been throwing bricks at the Panda car he was driving, while fat arse farted about on the old car radio, calling for back up. By the time Chuck had chased the group along two streets, all of Green Watch appeared in cavalry fashion and three of the suspects were dragged into vans where they were beaten up by several officers. Back at the station, when one roughed-up suspect had sworn at the desk sergeant, two officers had him face-down upon the floor with his trousers around his ankles in seconds. They then dragged him by the hair into a cell and kicked the shit out of him until he begged for mercy. Chuck had to intervene to stop the brutality before escorting the prisoner himself, in a somewhat more orderly fashion, to hospital. Afterwards, he had asked his sergeant if the violence had really been necessary, but was told in no uncertain terms to forget what he had witnessed. Again, Chuck went straight home after the shift and tried to put these things at the back of his mind; after all, this was all part and parcel of protecting Joe Public from villainy, was it not? Pew had words with him when they were both back on duty and subtly pointed out that Masons look out for each other, and that he would do well to note that.

"The guys involved were brethren, Chuck, and the craft can be a wonderful friend, but a terrible enemy, mate," he had pointed out casually, followed by a chuckle to veil the threat.

In general, after violence, drug dealing and house breaking, petty crime such as shop-lifting and disorderly conduct were the bread-and-butter of the job. There was a shocking quantity of heroin in the schemes of Muirhouse, Pilton and Granton throughout the eighties. Chuck learned the impact of class inequality here but soon understood the usual process to be:

1) Unemployment,
2) Poverty, and then finally,
3) The dreaded booze.

Yet he also discovered that with heroin, there came a whole new type of fallout; one which saw uniform up against desperation, as opposed to traditional dishonesty. Often, there was a requirement to physically restrain teenagers, who were being removed to secure units or residential care. Chuck was always uncomfortable in doing this because he felt physical force was inappropriate. Not all of his colleagues tended to agree, though, because some of the kids had a tendency to instigate complaints. He had learned well from older officers, like his sergeant at Govan who had served for 37 years by the time Chuck had crossed his path. Or old PC Tulip at Motherwell, who had accidently put a young Rangers supporter in a coma at a match in Hamilton once when chasing him outside the ground.

Old Tulip had rugby-tackled him, and regrettably, the kid had cracked his head off the pavement. Tulip had come through a court case that had eventually collapsed, but Chuck had noted the dangers well enough. The force was like that in those days, full of wise older heads who would nick a villain and instinctively know when handcuffs were required. They were different days now, though, Chuck knew. Everyone was getting handcuffed, even OAPs picked up for non-payment of fines, and in full view of their neighbours too. It was clear that the new batch of recruits in the late eighties enjoyed the melodramatic Americanisation of Scottish law enforcement.

However, Drylaw officers did not simply police the council schemes, where they could claim danger was on the increase thanks to heroin. They were also expected to respond to the wealthy suburbs of Davidson's Mains, Cramond and Barnton. These so-called posh zones included another five pubs, two golf courses with bars, the hectic tourist beach, and the island and Roman remains at Cramond. One particularly educational call-out to these suburbs came when an old lady in Cramond Vale had thought she heard someone being strangled in the flat above her. Chuck and fat Pew were sitting outside the chip shop in Davidson's Mains when they were given the job. Pew continued to gorge like an alligator from his king rib and chips as Chuck flicked on the lights and sped off for Cramond. Upon arriving at the chic Cramond flats which stood at the end of an American-style procession of detached houses with driveways, a rare peacefulness was evident.

"They built this place in the sixties, and the houses are worth a few quid now," Pew said contemptuously as he heaved himself up and out of the car, wiping his greasy fingers on his trousers.

They were buzzed into the building by the complainant, an Eleanor Crawford, aged 71, who lived alone in a ground-floor apartment. The entrance hall and stairway were richly carpeted. There were paintings upon the walls and large, verdant plants everywhere. A door to the right opened and Mrs Crawford appeared in a white dressing gown and pink nightcap. "Come in," she whispered nervously. She halted them in a rectangular hallway which housed an Edwardian writing desk and, between two oak doorways, a framed oil painting of a Springer Spaniel. Chuck guessed that they were standing upon a genuine Persian rug too.

"I'm sorry about this, officers," she whispered in a crisp, posh Cramond brogue, which was classically new-money, but which may also have ideas of a vague descent from gentry.

"I was in my bed asleep at about 11 o'clock when I was woken by a loud bang on the ceiling," she pointed upward. "Then, I heard what sounded like a struggle, and then nothing; it just went silent."

"Right, Mrs Crawford, it's quite alright. Can you tell us who lives in the property upstairs?" Fat Pew stepped in before she had a chance to continue.

"Well. It was a Sikh family for years but they moved out to Dalmeny a few months ago, and said they would be renting it out to a professional couple," Mrs Crawford explained. She scratched her head and frowned, "but I had not understood there to be any new tenants."

"OK, well, we can go and try knocking and see if we can get an answer, but we can't kick the door down if there is no answer," Pew told her, with half a mind on a Caramac bar back in the car glove box.

"What if the killer has fled the scene, officer, and there is a dead body upstairs?" she asked. Pew was lost at that suggestion; he was close to laughing, but took a moment to compose himself, and turned to go upstairs.

"If we don't get an answer tonight, we can arrange for officers to try again tomorrow morning and throughout the day. Then, if we still can't get access, we can find out the address of the owners and compel them to grant us entry to investigate your report," Chuck felt obliged to explain to her.

She went quiet at this but nodded in understanding. Pew led the way upstairs, with Chuck following. Pew gave a traditional police knock: strident, overly loud, and somewhat alarming, for effect.

"Who is it?" a female voice asked from behind the door with a hint of concern.

"It's the police," replied Pew confidently. The chain went back and the door opened slowly to reveal a teenage female wearing nothing but a t-shirt with an image of Michael Jackson on it. It was clearly too big for her, hence it covered her modesty; but her nipples were visibly on display through it.

"Is something wrong?" she asked.

"Several neighbours have reported a noise coming from this flat, which they believed to be unoccupied," Chuck lied to protect Mrs Crawford.

"And they were a wee bit concerned," added Pew, wondering why Chuck had bothered – before mentally undressing the girl.

"Well, there's just me and my boyfriend here, and there has been no noise or anything like that," she assured them in a shaky voice.

"Is this your house?" Pew enquired with a creepy smirk that expanded gradually.

"No, it's my boyfriend's." The girl appeared to be proud of this fact.

"Do you mind if we look around to make sure everyone is OK?" asked Chuck softly.

"It's just me and Raavi, who is in the bedroom there," she pointed to a door behind her.

Pew led the way again, and Chuck followed into a large bedroom without any furniture. The light failed to come on when Pew flicked it, but several candles dotted around the walls served to dimly illuminate a naked Indian man sitting cross-legged on a double duvet. He had long hair, a beard, and a thick gold chain around his neck. Both cops noticed with amusement that he had been attempting to unlock a pair of pink fluffy handcuffs from his left wrist, but had abruptly stopped and dropped the key when they entered.

"Hello officers, would you care for a cup of tea?" he asked.

They scanned the scene. Chuck could smell marijuana, but the sight of several short ropes, a large pink rubber vibrator and a short leather whip caught most of his attention.

"Oh, I see," said Pew, in a manner not unlike a Victorian Workhouse Master who had just been asked for more. This appeared to have something of an effect upon Raavi, who immediately stood up to attention, after sensing the threat.

"It's not what it seems, Sir." He fell short of saluting Pew, but his privates were now swinging around in the flickering candle light anyway – so they might have missed it if he had.

"Uh-huh, and what's in here then, sunshine?" asked Pew as he opened the door to the en suite. Raavi remained silent but the girl chipped in from behind Chuck, "we're getting married, so we aren't doing anything wrong."

"Care to explain this, then?", asked Pew when he came back from the loo with a half-smoked joint, a small bag of dope, a half-full bottle of vodka and some empty cans of cola. Pew shook his head, then made eye contact with Chuck and raised his eyebrows in mock disbelief.

"Looks like possession of dope to start with," he grinned.

"Your neighbours thought they heard someone being hurt?" Chuck said to the girl.

"No!" gasped Raavi, all concern now.

"It was just me standing on his back with my heels... er... it turns him on," the girl began blinking and blushing now, but in the candle light, no one noticed.

"Oh, aye..." grinned Pew as he gently spun Raavi around by the head to reveal several red stiletto marks on his skinny brown back.

"Right, take her into the kitchen, Chuck. Do a person's check on her, give the other rooms a quick scan, then pop back through here," ordered Pew.

"Name and date of birth?" Chuck asked when he had checked to make sure there were no bodies in any of the other rooms.

"Carol-Ann Sharpe, 14/10/1968. Born in Edinburgh," she clearly knew the routine.

"That makes you 16 years old," Chuck sighed. He then put in a person's check on his radio. They both stood in silence while the check took place. Occasionally the dispatcher would reply by asking if the officer was alone or able to speak, particularly if they felt the information was confidential. Chuck watched the girl smoking and staring at her own bare feet.

"Known, not wanted," came the reply. "Shoplifting and theft, mainly," he added.

"Ah, Roger that control, out." Chuck then turned to the girl, "Wait here, Carol-Ann, and don't do anything stupid, alright?" He went back through to the bedroom to discover that Pew had Raavi up against a wall by the hair. He turned around with a vile grin and winked at Chuck.

"Chuck, meet Ravinder Singh Esquire, of 22 Barnton Park Gardens." He dragged Raavi around. "Ravinder here is the owner of this pad and he is married to a lovely wife who has given him four even lovelier bairns," Pew said and Raavi looked like he was about to cry.

"She's known, not wanted," Chuck said, desperately wanting to leave now.

"Raavi here is well-known, however, as he has just told me his father owns the Stag Wholesale Cash & Carry," Pew laughed, as a man who has struck gold might.

Chuck knew it; they had bought a bed and a bean bag from there for his son's bedroom recently and it was a huge place.

"Now, Raavi here would be in a helluva state if you and I were to bust him now for possession of dope, considering that Sikhs aren't allowed to smoke," smirked Pew. "Never mind a sexually-related breach of the peace which involved us dragging the wee perv home to his family in his current condition, eh, Chuck?" he winked again.

"Yeah, well, the girl is sixteen, Davie; so consenting adults and all that jazz," Chuck saw where Fat-arse was going with this and wanted no part of it.

"Aye, but this bugger is forty-two, Chuck, and he is at it with a girl who's not long out of the bloody school," Pew snarled before releasing Raavi, who dropped to his knees.

"Please, officers, I'll give you anything to prevent such shame. My wife would leave me and my father would disown me. I was going to give Carol-Ann this flat to help her get a start in life." He started pleading, talking fast, but Pew booted him in the side and sent him scurrying into a corner, groaning.

"Shut it, Gandhi. You're up shit creek and nothing is going to provide you with a paddle now," snarled Pew.

"Easy, tiger," said Chuck as he laid a hand on Pew's shoulder. It was obvious that he was enjoying this charade a little too much. Pew simply smiled, winked, and returned to his Mr Nasty bluff. It was working, Chuck noted, despite being inappropriate. He would remember the psychology applied here by Pew. It was obvious to Chuck that the technique might be utilised in dealing with real villains.

"Scumbags like you make me sick," Pew snarled at the poor bastard quietly, for only the three men to hear. "You've got the fucking lot, son: money, property, and a beautiful wife and kids, no doubt." Chuck wondered if there was some real resentment in Pew after all.

"I'm sorry, Sir," Raavi got up on all fours, clearly still in pain. Then he raised clasped hands, almost in an act of prayer, toward the great god of gluttony – Pew. Strangely, Chuck recalled an image of Alec Guinness in the film *Kim* for a second. Then he instinctively found himself thinking about intervening.

"And my wife is a truly good woman who doesn't deserve this," cried Raavi to fat-arse, who stood over his poor victim like an executioner now.

"Fucking shut up, you horrible wee shit," he eventually snarled down, but not before winking again at Chuck. "Pleading about your wife while you're abusing a wee white lassie who should still be in the school."

At this Raavi completely broke down, though quietly enough to prevent either the girl or Mrs Crawford downstairs from hearing. Chuck was startled by all this and froze like a proverbial rabbit in the car headlights. He was mortified by the racial abuse Pew was doling out, yet almost giggling at the madness of it all. He was also struck by a slight loyalty toward Pew. He sussed that Pew was probing for a cash bung from Raavi. This disgusted him and was against his professional ethics, yet he remained still, said nothing, and simply took it all in.

"I know the police are under-staffed, officer," Raavi suddenly gathered his senses enough to know he needed to play this smartly. Still sniffing and with his hands raised, he added, "Please don't destroy my life. I promise I'll never see Carol-Ann again and I know you officers don't need people like me wasting your valuable time. I have an envelope downstairs in my van with the afternoon takings from the cash and carry..." he paused and looked from Pew to Chuck nervously.

"And?" Pew asked more courteously now, in pretend puzzlement.

"And if you would be kind enough to accept it for what I have put you through today, I will gladly tell my family that I lost it in the casino. I often go there and they know that, so I will be punished but my wife won't know; please, I beg you, have mercy. I really respect the police. My grandfather was a military police officer at the D-Day landings. Oh officer, please have mercy..." He would have gone on indefinitely if Pew hadn't slapped him across the head – playfully, mind, now that the prize was within reach.

"Enough! How much is there?" he asked.

"Five grand, easy," Raavi looked up optimistically at his torturer now.

"Right you are then, lad. If you ever tell another living soul about this, we'll not only destroy your fucking life, but I'll personally strip search your fucking wife for suspicion of carrying dope up her crack, do you fucking understand?" Pew whispered his threats in Raavi's ear and his victim nodded eagerly as some Pew's sprayed saliva dripped from his cheek and ear.

It had been as simple as that. Chuck had tried to refuse his £2622 share on the drive back to Drylaw, but Pew made it abundantly clear that unless they both took it, neither of them could. He then banged on about trust, loyalty and the Masonic brotherhood's notion of secrecy.

"Like I told you once, we make better friends than enemies, Chuck. So come on board and enjoy an easy ride," he said as he stuffed Chuck's share into his tunic pocket. Chuck took the cash, and said nothing to his sergeant or the Duty Inspector. Instead, he went home, told Kim everything in bed, then endured her protests and insistence that he go to his commander and hand in the cash. He compromised in the end and anonymously donated it to the Police Widows and Orphans Fund.

There had been other incidents that crossed the line for Chuck; with Pew taking cash from various suspects, including one occasion when he taxed a small plastic bag of ten-pence pieces from an obviously broke taxi driver. Chuck had not argued about any of these incidents either, though he was thankful Pew had stopped offering him a share of the spoils.

"You see, Chuck," Pew said to him when they were on duty at a Hearts versus Dundee United match at Tynecastle one cold afternoon, "the boys are all a wee bit unsure about you because you have knocked two separate invites to the lodge at Longstone for a pint with us, over the last year."

Now, this line was obviously alarming but it had been anticipated by Chuck, so he played it coolly:

"I am beginning to sense it, Davie, but I live at Restalrig and Longstone's the other side of the town mate. You know the score, I just can't afford the taxis and besides, I've got young kids, you know," he pointed out.

"Och, I know. You're a sound lad, Chuck, but you're an awfy moany cunt about things, like Johnny Gilchrist punching that wee housebreaker in the cells the other week; that did not go down well with the other boys." Pew sounded concerned for him now, which was just another act, Chuck knew.

"Davie," sighed Chuck, raising his voice a little in order to be heard over the roar of the crowd, "the lad was only 15 years old. Yes, he was a little thieving shit, but Johnny is a grown man who plays rugby, for Christ's sake. He was lucky I didn't report him." Chuck resented having to explain the morality to this fat bully.

"That thinking is exactly what concerns us, Chuck. You see, we are on the front line, protecting the tax-paying public from low-life vermin like that wee bastard."

"Then I guess we can thank God that some of you guys are not working in the States and carrying guns, eh, Davie?" Chuck had had enough of this "friendly advice". Pew fell silent, glowering at the crowd and not addressing Chuck again for the rest of the shift.

Life at Drylaw became awkward for Chuck after that encounter. Guys would either hush up or change the subject whenever he appeared. The frequent invites to drinks after work in the Masonic Lodge soon dried up too, which he was thankful for. Pew had clearly put the word out that Chuck was not interested. Gone, too, were the golfing invites, and he was even erased from the Christmas party invite list. Instead, he took Kim to see *Highlander* at the old ABC on Lothian Road, where he was more than happy to embrace the spirit of Christmas with her, rather than that lot. By the following spring, he was finding working with Pew more and more uncomfortable. The man had stopped speaking to him completely on patrol, but still farted like a sewer in the car. At one point, he even threatened to "shove this pizza" in Chuck's face, which led to Chuck requesting a new partner. His sergeant was one of the good old boys; either that or he was an appeaser. He had been expecting this from Chuck.

"Fine, but I suspect you'll find that whoever I place you with now will have similar issues with you," the cheeky swine had remarked without raising his head from his paperwork.

When Chuck was finally paired up with another partner, it was with the oldest-serving constable in Edinburgh, a man who had not been considered for promotion and who had never sought it. Rather, PC Larry the Lamb had been approaching retirement, having walked the same beats for 30 years. Larry was another podgy-faced drinker, but he was permanently rosy with curly white hair. This combined to give him the appearance of a garden gnome. He was nicknamed 'Splinter-Arse', after having spent the last two years sitting on the station reception. Larry was a bit slow on the move due to his age, and had the least number of collars out of everyone at the station, despite his time served. To mark the occasion, Chuck was given a new Ford Escort patrol car. He intensely disliked Larry from the minute he got in the car, stinking of cheap grain whisky. After a while he realised that the old codger was drinking the stuff from the wee tartan tea flask he brought with him. One tell-tale sign, other than the fumes, was Larry's constant gibbering about his "fucking whore" of an ex-wife who had left him 10 years earlier. His voice usually became slurred after his sixth cup, and on one occasion while responding to a complaint in a tenement stair, the old piss artist was accused by the complainer of being: "absolutely reeking".

Chuck reported his concerns to his sergeant and was told to "fuck off and give the guy a break" for his trouble. Inevitably, it all came to a head after Christmas that year, when they were on a nightshift. There had been a stabbing at a party at a multi-storey flat off the Pennywell Road. A van from the station was already there and Chuck's was the third car to arrive on scene.

Upon exiting the lift on the eighth floor, a constable approached them in the corridor and explained that a party had been given by a local teenager, whose mother was drinking herself to death somewhere else. She had given her kid permission to have the party. Several local youths had been in attendance, and a smaller group from Broomhouse had shown up. Surprise, surprise, the cheap booze did its job, and one of the Broomhouse kids had been stabbed.

Inside the flat, there was blood all over the corridor. "Fuck's sake, did they not stem the bleeding before they carried him out?" whispered Larry, who had sobered up at the sight of it all sprayed across a white telephone and a magnolia-washed wall.

In the small lounge, two worn-out brown three-seater sofas were occupied by several teenage boys. Empty cans of cider and bottles of Buckfast lay strewn everywhere. Chuck noted the large homemade hashish bong on a bloodstained seventies-design carpet. At the window were the early arrivals, two plain-clothed detectives. One of them was Calum Clancey, a tall, good looking man. Clancey was holding a plastic evidence bag with a large knife in it. In his other hand was a radio. "Roger that, thanks," he spoke into it.

The other detective was the station snob, DC Ronnie Cunningham. Cunningham had nailed a local individual, once a famous musician, for child abuse when he was an acting DC. The case had been a nationwide headline and 'Cunny' had featured prominently in the press reports.

"Guys, can you keep an eye on this lot?" Clancey nodded toward the seated youths.

"Nah, Calum," Cunny shook his head without turning around. "The gaffer says to wait for the vans, detain the whole lot of them, and interview them all at the station."

"Yeah, but I mean until the vans arrive?" Clancey suggested.

"Nope, need to get them all on tape. I'm finished with this one, but those two," Cunny turned and smiled at Larry and Chuck, "need to take this one here back to the children's home she has absconded from – she's only fifteen." Cunny gave Clancey a shrug, took the girl by the arm, and led her over to Larry, all while ignoring Chuck.

"This is a runner from a kids' home in Fife. She pegged it while on a swimming trip three weeks ago, in Glenrothes. She is known and dangerous, so cuff her and get her back to the home," he ordered.

"Do you not want to get her statement?" asked Chuck.

"She didn't see the incident as she was too busy getting shagged in the other room," replied Cunny. "Get the address from control on your car radio. OK?"

"Er, aye Cunny, no bother son, and cheers," replied Larry.

As they descended in the lift afterward, Chuck turned to Larry, "What was the, 'aye Cunny, cheers son' all about, Larry?"

The girl was looking down at her trainers and swaying slightly on her feet, probably due to whatever she had been on. Larry took a second to check that she was out of it before leaning over and whispering, "That's what a fellow brother of the Lodge does for an old soul like myself, son. He excuses me from standing on my bloody corns all night, taking statements from those wee bastards; not to mention the endless bloody typing up afterwards." He winked knowingly.

In the back of the car, Larry sat with the girl who, despite her drugged state, kept asking to have her handcuffs removed. She was told that there was "no chance" of that by Larry the first time and then to "shut up" every other time. Chuck radioed in for the address of the residential care centre.

"Susan Black, born Edinburgh 1973. Absconded from Centre Court Children's Residential Unit in Glenrothes. One Children's Hearing appearance for breaking and entering in 1986. Another for smashing her neighbour's window with a brick in May 1987. Supervision Order was granted to the local authority. Her parental address is registered at 17 Gilmour Court, Inverkeithing. She is known to have a half-sister in

Granton, Edinburgh, and subsequently we were made aware of her potentially being in the area by both Fife Police and the Fife Social Work Department when she initially absconded," the female controller explained. Her basic description was then given, which included a "Fuck Mum" tattoo on her hand.

"Roger that, we're en route to return her then. Kindly make the facility aware, please," replied Chuck. "What on earth made you want to run away to this shithole, Sharon?" he then gently asked the girl.

"Sister stays here, boyfriend stays here, and anyway, fuck you two, like what do you care, like?" she shouted, but her speech was slurred.

She then leaned against the car window and closed her eyes. Chuck wondered what was going on at home that had prompted such a mad tattoo on her hand, and how he might find out more about her background. He quickly checked himself; he was not a social worker, after all. The forty-minute drive north was an eventful one because from Barnton to the Forth Bridge, the girl began a carry on by demanding things in a hysterical manner. Her main gripes were that she wanted to be allowed to smoke in the car. When told to forget it, she began screaming feverishly.

"Listen, hen," said Larry, who had been expecting an easier time of it, "you carry on like this an' I'll lay you down and sit on you until we get there, and you won't like that, will you?"

Sadly, the old cop had misread this new wave of juvenile delinquent, and she very neatly head-butted him on his nose in response.

"Ahhh! Ya fucking wee bitch!" howled Larry in pain before he slumped down towards the door panel, clutching his nose with cupped hands. Chuck put the siren and hazard lights on and pulled over. By the time he had run around to open her door and drag her out, Larry had recovered enough to grab a fistful of her hair, and to repeatedly smash her face into the headrest of the front passenger seat.

By the time Chuck had grabbed his wrist, Larry had jabbed her in the face with his blood-soaked right fist and knocked her out cold. He then came to his senses and began acting more professionally. "Right, Chuck, drag her out and make sure she doesn't swallow her tongue, for Christ's sake," he gasped.

Chuck reached over to her.

"She attacked me, Chuck and then she tried to strangle you while you were driving, right? So I restrained her and she banged her head; otherwise you would have crashed, right?" He was panting in order to amplify the damage.

Chuck didn't answer as he dragged her out of the car and sat her up against the rear wheel arch to examine her. She was going to have quite a black eye, but he was relieved to see her slowly coming around.

"Get the cuffs off her and get her cuffed from the front quickly!" Larry said as he appeared at his side.

Chuck knew why: that way, they could claim that she had tried to strangle Chuck whilst he was driving. They could hardly claim she had attempted that if she had been handcuffed from behind. Chuck looked up at him, then back at the girl.

"I think that deserves a fag, no?" she smiled at him as she spoke in a frail voice.

Chuck nodded. Larry lit up a Capstan, took a draw, exhaled, and then put it in her mouth. She dragged on it and exhaled through her nose as Chuck uncuffed her, brought her hands round to the front, and cuffed her again.

"Best call it in, Chuck, and tell control that we have her restrained and are still en route. Oh, and ask them to phone ahead and warn the staff that she freaked out on us," urged Larry.

Chuck knew well enough that Larry would be supported by his handshaking friends if Chuck informed control that Larry had just assaulted a child in police custody. There would be looks and whispers, and should he ever find himself calling for assistance on the job, he might well find that it does not appear. Feeling the pressure with Larry watching him through the window, Chuck did as he was told and lied to control.

The journey to Glenrothes took a further half-hour, and of course they then wasted another 20 minutes trying to find the place. It was set in the middle of a residential housing scheme consisting of a grid of identical grey blocks. Chuck drove up to the steps of the main administration block where two yellow Ford Transit minibuses were parked. A sensor light came on and three people appeared from a glass revolving door. Two were men, both wearing brown cords with matching new romantic, highlighted hairstyles. The other was a busty older female with silver hair and glasses.

"She has been a nightmare, and completely hysterical," claimed Larry, who got out and then gently ushered the girl out as if he cared about her not banging her head.

"What happened?" asked the older woman when she saw the blood on Larry and the girl's now badly-swelling eye.

"She was at a party where a youth was stabbed. She is on something without a doubt, and on the drive here she became hysterical because she wanted to smoke in the car and then head-butted me," Larry said sombrely.

"She then attempted to strangle PC Kean here," he nodded at Chuck, who stood motionless beside the car.

"Is she on drugs again?" asked one of the new romantics.

"We have no way of knowing, but she almost killed us, as we had an artic lorry behind us when she kicked off. She then required physical restraint and banged her face on the gear stick when she was lunging forward at PC Kean. She's made a right mess of herself." Larry spun it convincingly enough, and the staff accepted his account with an ease that concerned Chuck.

The two new romantics then took a hold of a wrist each while Larry uncuffed her. "Come on, Susie – let's get you cleaned up, and a nice cup of cocoa," one of them said as they escorted her through the revolving doors and into the complex.

"Don't worry about anything, officers," the female said to Chuck and Larry. "We are regularly assaulted by that little madam and forced to restrain her, so we know only too well what she is capable of," she smiled at Larry before adding curtly, "Thanks for returning her safely, and safe journey back to Edinburgh." She nodded in appreciation, then turned and walked back through the revolving doors and locked them with her master keys.

As Chuck stood there watching her, he felt an urge to say something about all of this; to discuss the child's real issues which had created these behavioural problems. He wanted to investigate the self-harm signs and the tattoo. Was her mother negligent in some way? He wanted to find out about all of this and help her to avoid the almost-inevitable road to prison or even death. At that precise moment, he felt as if someone or something was blowing softly into his ear, urging him to try. It didn't seem like the right time, though, and he bowed his head, feeling defeated and cowardly.

"Right, Chuck lad, let's get the hell out of Dodge and back across the river," Larry said with uncontained relief. There was a silence on the return journey. Larry tried to chat a couple of times, simply to sense if Chuck was going to stick with the story or not, but he got monosyllabic responses.

"What's wrong, lad? You're not going to say anything silly when we get back, are you? She attacked us, Chuck, probably would have killed us if she could," he stressed, eyes wide, but Chuck said nothing and simply drove and thought. When they finally pulled into the station car park, Larry suddenly found a spine and growled, "You try and destroy my pension, you cunt, and you'll lose your entire career."

Chuck ignored him, got out and walked into the station. The dayshift was starting and the shift inspector, Eddie Lavrock, confirmed he knew about the radio report of the incident by telling Chuck to go home and get some sleep, all without making eye contact. Clearly, Lavrock was too weak to question a cover-up. Chuck did go home, where he slept on it and then dreamed of it. When he awoke, he knew he just couldn't let the matter go. This dark clique within Drylaw was covering up crimes, and Chuck just couldn't stand by and do nothing anymore. To do so would be tantamount to being a *Kapo* during the holocaust, he believed. To go with the flow meant self-preservation and various benefits, it was true. He might even be invited to become a Mason one day, but for Chuck this did not sit well. The next day, he drove to Fettes to raise the matter with his divisional Commander, Chief Superintendent Ross 'Rosco' Lang.

"I'm here to see the Chief Super, please," he asked the two old boys in reception.

"Do you have an appointment? What's your name?" asked the one who was a doppelganger for the late actor Terry Thomas.

"PC Charles Kean out of Drylaw Station and no, I do not, but it is a matter of the utmost urgency." Chuck tried not to stare at the large gap between Terry's front teeth.

"Take a seat then, and I'll find out if he's in," nodded Terry.

Shortly afterwards, he entered the office of the Chief Super. He found himself in a relatively small room, with white walls covered in black and white frames of the man himself graduating police training and the army over the years. In the corner, beside a plant that touched the roof, were a set of expensive-looking golf clubs. The man seated before him was an ex-Para officer, and the Heart of Midlothian engraved whisky decanter on the small book cabinet was shadowed by a frame of him parachuting from a plane in full combat fatigues. Chuck told him all about the Fife job with Susan Black and how he felt he could not report Larry to his superiors at Drylaw due to the clique there.

"Did you discuss this with your Duty Inspector at all?" Rosco asked.

"No, Sir, because I was quite sure that Inspector Lavrock would bin it. I suspected that a cover up would occur after PC Lamb spoke to him anyway. This made me think that perhaps it was wiser to bring it to your attention," Chuck told him.

Rosco eyed him over his glasses for a moment, then went back to his sporadic note-taking.

"Well, you did the right thing, Constable," he eventually said.

"Thank you, Sir." Chuck nodded sombrely.

"If your allegation is correct, then that is not on at all." Rosco shook his head. "So, I will look into this, you can rest assured." These words were said somewhat over-enthusiastically as he scribbled down a note, and Chuck consequently smelled the faint odour of bullshit.

There was just something, a darkness perhaps, about Rosco's demeanour. Chuck could not quite put his finger on the unnaturalness. In fact, he had never really analysed what it was in his senses that detected both good and bad vibes about a person; he ignored such thinking due to a vague fear of discovering that he was, in fact, quite mad. Yet here it was again, this sixth sense, telling him not to trust Rosco. His thoughts were soon interrupted as Rosco spoke again.

"I'm going to call up Inspector Eddie Lavrock at home just now to find out what exactly happened, and whether or not the cameras on the bridge caught any of this. Can you take a seat outside while I look into this, Constable?" At that, both men stood up and Chuck went and took a seat in the corridor.

After a while, an attractive woman in civilian clothing glided past, carrying some papers. Chuck caught a whiff of her perfume as she knocked and entered the Chief Super's office. He still had to take baby Charlie for their weekly swim in the afternoon, he remembered. He had been taking him to the infant section of the Royal Commonwealth Pool for a while now. Eating the impressive cheesecake they served in the canteen upstairs was their favourite after-swim tradition. He resented spending his day off here in a corridor, waiting to find out if the risk he was taking with his career was worthwhile.

Half an hour passed, which Chuck could only fill by twiddling his thumbs and allowing his thoughts to wander. Finally, Rosco popped his head out and called him back in. Again, he motioned for him to take a seat as he leaned back in his chair and flicked a pen through his fingers so skilfully that Chuck reckoned he could have been a casino croupier in another life.

"What was it you did at Marconi's before you joined Strathclyde Police?" Rosco asked, a firmness evident in his tone now.

"Well, I was a Technical Assistant to the product support and trials team," Chuck replied, wondering where this was going.

"So, a handy chap to have around the house, or indeed with motorcars, I suspect," probed Rosco.

"Well, I take an interest in car mechanics, yes Sir; but I'm certainly no expert."

"Well anyway, Constable, I've looked into things like I said I would." Rosco leaned forward now. "I'm hearing reports which suggest that you're a bit of a loner who doesn't get on particularly well with the other men. Is that fair, hmmm?" He made an exaggerated sad face as he spoke, which looked ridiculous.

Chuck smirked at the absurdity. "I'm not part of their wee clique, Sir, no, but I wouldn't say that makes me a loner," he replied.

"Enlighten me, constable; what do you mean by 'their wee clique'?"

"Most of Green Watch, Sir," shrugged Chuck.

"And they are all are involved in some sort of dark covenant, you say, is that correct?" Rosco was dissecting the claim as a good barrister might.

Chuck had to tread carefully here. "I don't know about any covenant Sir, and I'm not saying that; but yes, they conspire to protect themselves from any spotlight being shone upon their activities," he confirmed, then wished he had not when he saw Rosco's flippant smirk back at him.

The senior policeman then took a deep breath, and crossed his legs. "You are aware, no doubt, Constable, that modern policing has to deal with those who want to steal from, and hurt, members of the honest, tax-paying public like you and I?" he asked, his face now blank.

"Last night was a classic example of this," he continued. "That brat you escorted over to Fife was poisoned at birth by her junkie parents and has had her chance at living in proper society. She has been placed with various community carers and shown time and again that she needs to be in a secure unit. She could have killed both of you last night with her tantrums and antics, and despite what you claim, neither PC Lamb nor the delinquent herself back you up, I'm afraid to say," he stated in a flat, matter-of-fact tone.

"Then, there is the fact you called it in on the car radio and reported it exactly as PC Lamb says it happened?" He raised his eyebrows to let the weight of it all sink in, before adding, "And you did not approach anyone with the version you are now presenting to me, when you returned to the station, either?" Chuck was about to explain that he had needed to sleep on it, but he hesitated and missed his chance.

Rosco shook his head now. "We are on the front line here. That means if one institutionalised little delinquent hurts another delinquent, some might regard that as a bonus, or at best of little interest to anyone; but if any of them intends to hurt either our own officers or Joe Public, then we must deter them one way or another. On which note, I am of the view that both yourself and Constable Lamb did a fine job in dealing with what was a profoundly awkward and volatile situation last night." He appeared more placatory now, but sounded smug and vaguely threatening too.

"It's both immoral and criminal to assault a child, Sir." Chuck suddenly realised he was smiling at the man's smugness. He pushed his chair back and stood up to express this point, again quickly wishing that he had not.

"Get your fucking arse back down, Constable!" snapped Rosco, unable to avoid swearing in tense moments, as most of the army lot tended to do. "Look, I've learned that your Inspector thinks you're unsuited to general police work and that there is a consensus at Drylaw that you're having a negative influence on the other officers; especially the younger ones."

"Bollocks!" snapped Chuck, unable to remain silent at this injustice.

Rosco jumped off his chair and slammed the palm of his hand upon the desk, causing the contents to spring up and down again,

"What did you say, you little...!" he snapped in regimental style. "You'd better rein that right in, Constable, because if you ever speak to me like that again, I'll put you through that bloody window," he promised.

"This is all shite, Sir." Chuck spoke softly now and shook his head.

"Well it can easily get much worse, pal," guaranteed Rosco, sitting back down now.

"In the name of Christ, when did we start taking oaths to protect the public with no intention of doing so, Sir?" Chuck found himself asking.

"Who? 'Christ'?" growled Rosco. "The redundant God who does nothing about this city's heroin epidemic? The so-called God who leaves you and I to carry dead teenagers into ambulances? Who starved all those Ethiopian kids recently while the British taxpayer tried to feed them? No son, there is no Christ on the front line, only our boys in blue, so spare me your amateur dramatics. Your problem is that you're hot-headed, Kean. You simply couldn't let sleeping dogs lie, and had to come in here and have your say against several long-serving officers." It was clear that Rosco was justifying whatever it was that he was about to do, Chuck sensed.

"Like I said Sir, it's all shite!" Chuck commented, defiant.

"Right, get the fuck out of this building right now. As from this minute, you're suspended for disorderly conduct toward myself and facing a potential breach of the peace, do you hear me?" Rosco was back on the military parade ground again.

Chuck stood up, saluted, and briskly walked out. By the time he left the building, he felt hopeless. They could throw the book at him now and simply destroy his career, as old Larry had warned. On the drive home, he thought about this. On reflection, he still felt that he had done the right thing, and did not regret it since he honestly couldn't imagine living with himself doing nothing anymore. He was not sure Kim would agree though, so he went home, ate lunch with her and told her everything.

"They can't sack you, Chuck, don't worry. I'm really proud of you for doing the right thing," she said, hugging him.

After a long five days without any contact from Fettes, during which he found it hard to relax or concentrate on anything, Chuck received a call from Inspector Lavrock at Drylaw asking him to come in for an informal chat. When Chuck arrived, Lavrock struggled to look him in the eye as he greeted him.

"I was invited to investigate your verbal report regarding PC Lamb, Chuck. In doing so, I personally spoke to him, the individual who was on dispatch, and the residential Senior Social Worker, a Mrs Pat Dalhousie, who received Susan Black into her care from you and Larry," he began, talking in a measured and professional tone, but still without making any eye contact.

"Larry gave a different account from yours, and suggests that you are mistaken, as you know," Lavrock went on.

"Naturally, if you were to take this matter further and instigate an internal investigation, the force would find the differing accounts of its two officers not proven either way and would, as you know, require corroborating statements. Now, initial informal research has indicated that Susan Black would, firstly, have zero credibility as a witness, and secondly, she is in any case highly likely to concur with Larry's version of events." He frowned, leading Chuck to think that he could detect a glimmer of sympathy, but also that there would be no good news here.

"Research, Sir?"

"I spoke to the residential social worker who took custody of Black from you; she says that Black admitted she was bruised in the struggle with yourself and Larry, and that nothing untoward took place. She also has a history of making various complaints against staff anyway." He smirked now, but continued to keep his gaze upon his notes. Chuck felt his stomach churn as Lavrock continued.

"I also spoke to her field social worker, an Isobel Lawrie based at the social work department, who informed me that Black has a record of self-harm going back to the age of ten." At that, Lavrock appeared to rest his case, as it was apparently established that she had no credibility whatsoever.

"What should that tell us, Sir?" Chuck was increasingly frustrated at the man's apparent prioritisation of protecting bent coppers.

"What it tells me is that Black is telling the same tale as Larry, but also that if she told a similar tale to you in the future, Fife Social Work Department would say she is a cry-wolf delinquent who prostitutes herself to old men in public conveniences for enough money to buy a bottle of cider."

Chuck exhaled a loud sigh. "So what happens now, Sir?"

Lavrock had been waiting for this, and rubbed his hands together. "My finding is that I consider your allegation to be without substance. If you take this further, an investigation into your conduct in the Chief Super's office will see you hauled in front of the beaks where your issues with your colleagues will be revealed. Your guess is as good as mine as to whether or not you will stay in the force at that point, but if you do, you will be transferred to another station where you will find you are considered *persona non-grata* by your new colleagues." Lavrock displayed a smarmy confidence now, for he had Chuck over a barrel and had just revealed his winning hand.

"Or, you can stand down, withdraw the allegation against Larry, and accept a transfer to a station of the Chief Constable's preference. This is the best option, because you'll get a few more days off while it's all being processed," he added curtly.

"OK, I'll take a transfer," Chuck said with a sigh of surrender. 'Knowing when to retreat' was how his grandfather had described the British collapse and evacuation at Dunkirk. Chuck remembered that now as he recognised and understood the power that opposed him here, not to mention his lack of options in the face of it.

"Good, I think that's the wisest course of action for you. Right, take these and fill them in." Lavrock looked at Chuck directly for the first time in the meeting, and handed him an application form for the Police Taxi Examination Centre, an administrative backwater known as the "Cab Office" by taxi drivers and the rest of the constabulary.

"Just fill that in here and state that you have applied for the position because of your experience with motor engines. Oh, and state your Marconi background in engineering, too."

"The Cab Office, Sir?" Chuck knew very little about the place except that they enforced the licensing regulations of taxi cabs. He guessed that this would be a dull, ditch-water, form-filling, file managing job. In other words, it was as far away from his notion of police work as it was possible to be.

"It's a nine-to-five, Monday-to-Friday role; you can't do much better than that," Lavrock maintained.

"Hardly policing, though, is it, Sir?" Chuck replied as he began filling out the application. He was aware that they had checkmated him here and was beginning to plead. Regardless, as he went to sign the form, he dwelled on the silver lining for a moment. A nine-to-five would mean a normal family life, he told himself. It also meant he no longer was at risk of getting pricked by a used syringe or smashed in the face by a pint glass.

He signed.

Driving home that day, he went over it all again in his mind. He had slipped up, and had been naive to hope that the disease had not spread its ugly tentacles into the brass. He had believed virtue to have been the key; that morality would always triumph over evil. In short, he had assumed that justice occurred automatically and that he, as an honest policeman, would be believed.

Something had to be learned from this folly, then. There was clearly a dark force striving to oppose justice, as justice was a threat to their lust for power over everyone else. These power seekers were Chuck's keepers now, as long as he took their coin. They had forced him to his knees here and could have finished him off. Yet somehow, as Hitler had done at Dunkirk, they had let him off the hook to go and lick his wounds and, he thought, to regroup and come at them again one day.

Two

"When men are full of envy they disparage everything, whether it be good or bad"

Tacitus

Kim was more relieved about her husband's transfer than he was as they shared a bottle of Shiraz in the kitchen, with some Corey Harris Blues guitar playing lightly in the background. "It's a normal day job, and it gives us a normal family life, Chuck," she pointed out for the fifth time as he slouched on the table, swirling his wine around in the glass. She could see that he was disappointed; in a huff, even. "Charlie will get a bedtime story now." She tried to make him smile, and it half worked. "Plus, it's the same wage and you weren't sure you would still have a job this morning, sweetie," she laid the bright side out again.

"It's evil, you know?" he said, sitting up and emptying his glass.

"It is certainly unfair Chuck, granted." She nodded and put her hand on his.

"No, I mean their clique," he said. "It's a force, of sorts, and it's powerful, it's not good." He looked in her lovely brown eyes. "It flourishes within the very fabric of the service," he maintained.

"Like the one my Dad says has polluted the church?" she asked softly.

"A similar cancer of sorts, yes," he agreed.

"A cancer that lurks in the shadows too?"

"Doesn't all cancer?" he took a deep sip from the refilled glass.

"Yes, until discovered and challenged," she mused.

"Oh, I don't know." He shook his head. "This is more an engine of personal advantage and aggrandizement. I think it no longer seeks to hide." Chuck was thoughtful as the wine turned him toward contemptuousness. "It's a covenant with secrets, but one with some influence over the rest of society," he explained. "I suspect their agenda is to wield power in all departments. A so-called Privileged Order whose very title reflects their lust to dominate," he insisted.

"Such as?" Kim asked.

"Sovereigns, Masters, even Grand Kings and Grand Priests, they call themselves," he was becoming angry now but continued to sup deeply at the wine.

She was trying to comprehend the nature of what he was alleging. "Are they even Christians, Chuck?" she asked.

He got up and went over to his bookshelf, found what he was looking for and returned. Kim didn't ask the name of the book; instead she remembered that "Eastenders" was on shortly.

"Did you know, for instance, that four popes issued papal bulls condemning Freemasonry and outlawing it for all Catholics with the threat of excommunication, and that the current Pope still denounces it? So, no hun, they are Christians at Christmas, I bet, and nothing more," he said, engrossed in the book now.

"Well, whether they are or are not up to something, Chuck," she glanced back at the clock on the kitchen wall again, "they decided not to destroy your career, so can I suggest that you just grab the opportunity they have given you and go with the flow." She raised her glass to either him or them; he could not tell.

"It always comes down to money," he sighed.

"Money puts food in your stomach and it provides the wine you're drinking. So, what if you have to tolerate things you don't like in order to achieve that?" She smiled at him.

He watched her saunter off through to the lounge. "I can expect similar antics at this new post, Kim, but this time I won't give the bastards the ammunition to fire at me," he called after her.

Chuck recalled the words of a Procurator Fiscal – Mark Dailly, who had sent down a small-time thief, whom Chuck had caught and charged with the burglary of a Masonic lodge in the Trinity area. He could picture the scene at court very clearly now.

"Did you hear that key holder's evidence?" Dailly had moaned to the four cops in the witness room after the accused had been sentenced. "Slavering on about the lodge being a house of good Christians?" He smirked. "Show me one of the buggers who actually goes to church on a Sunday. Christians my arse, it's about wealth and power. Anyway, didn't Kipling[2] say that Freemasonry was full of Sikhs, Hindus, Muslims and Jews?" he teased, whilst being well aware that they were all likely to be brethren themselves. Chuck had only offered a silly confused smile and a shrug of his shoulders.

---

[2] Rudyard Kipling.

"Kipling… didn't he write the *Jungle Book*?" one of the uniforms asked.

Another of the officers, a youngster who had assisted in the original arrest, loquaciously perked up then. "That's England maybe, but my own grandfather is a Mason who goes to the Kirk most Sundays, Sir," he declared proudly.

"Interesting Constable, I'm quite sure he will be the first to blackball you for your open honesty," replied the ever sharp Dailly.

"Perhaps you could remind your relative that the Church of Scotland General Assembly, recently found there to be, and I quote, "very real theological difficulties" with any of its flock who practiced the ancient craft of Freemasonry," smiled Dailly at the now-confused young officer. Dailly then promptly shook all their hands and waltzed off down the corridor murmuring something. Chuck had admired the man's style.

"I think that's 'Absent Brethren' he is reciting," said the befuddled youngster, but the others were all leaving too, by that point. The Cab Office was in the west of the city near the infamous Wester Hailes housing scheme. The buildings themselves were enclosed by a 12 ft. barbed wire fence. The buildings within had metal shutters with alarms on them, and a plump security guard with 'friends' in the police and a secret desire to be a commando patrolled the complex in the evenings. The office building had been attacked in the past; it had been burgled and had even, on one occasion, been burned down by a Molotov cocktail that was thrown onto the roof. No person was ever charged with these crimes, but the cops suspected associates of a ghost-owner of a certain private-hire car firm, who went by the name of Bertie McManaman.

Chuck started his new job on a Monday morning. As he drove into the heavily-secured compound, he noticed two metallic shutters opening. After a few normal handshakes and one or two friendly introductions, he was handed two polo shirts and a bright yellow waterproof coat similar to those worn by traffic wardens. He was told by a tall, balding guy, who introduced himself as 'Dixie the mechanic' and offered him a coffee, to take a seat outside the Inspector's office.

"There are two choices here," said Herriot, the Inspector, when he finally turned up and had been served a strong black coffee for his obvious hangover. His room stank of cigars and he stank of the previous evening's boozy session down at the golf club. "Work responsibly within my system and no one try to steal my thunder," he let this sink in a second. "Or you'll be sent back to Fettes with a *'Kick my Arse out the Force'* note pinned to you; is that clear, Constable?" he asserted.

"Crystal, Sir," Chuck feigned the obedient enthusiasm of a rookie seeking to obey, and learn from the older, wiser cop. It was clear already however, that this clown would not be teaching him anything other than self adoration and envy.

"Good," Herriot seemed satisfied. "I see you offered your expertise with car mechanics," he said, reading from a report. Chuck suddenly realised how they had pushed this through: by championing his Marconi history, which had nothing to do with bloody cars at all.

Herriot was an observant man and detected slight concern on Chuck's face. "Don't panic, I know why they binned you, but the staff here do not. Regardless, I do not give a monkey about what happened at Drylaw, it is all about what you can do for me. Got that?" he coldly declared.

"Right, Sir." Chuck was not impressed, nor was he supposed to be; Herriot was simply seeking instant compliance.

"You have landed here because we need a second officer. We were in the middle of a clean-up project which has now become something of a cold war," explained Herriot.

"A cold war, Sir?" Suddenly, Chuck had hope that this might not be as monotonously intolerable as he had anticipated.

"Yes, and it's all systems go, Constable."

"I was prepared for an arduous tenure, you know," Herriot took gulps of coffee between sentences and looked Chuck up and down. "But let's just say this is a problem that has grown, and which requires all hands on deck. I couldn't care less that you're a troublemaker, nor that you claim your station was full of corrupt Masonic officers." He eyed Chuck now.

"You'll find brethren here too. No matter, we are all working together to ensure that licensing legislation is enforced so we can shield the public from an onslaught of crooked taxi drivers... burglars, rapists and drug dealers. The enemy are getting sneakier and stronger, so we are required to fight back along similar lines." Herriot was clearly a wannabe Patton[3].

"Anyway, go now and Brucey will get you started. In a month or so we will review your attitude." With that, Herriot abruptly stopped talking and flicked a finger toward the door, like how a Pharaoh might have dismissed a scribe.

---

[3] US WWII General: George S Patton. Patton's military philosophy was on leading from the front, which often brought him into debate with Allied High Command. Additionally, his vulgarity-ridden speeches earned him further frowns from Allied commanders who disapproved of his methods, including his slapping of men who were suffering from battle fatigue, then ordering them back to the front lines.

Chuck could tell that Herriot was simply another obsessive cop who wanted to make a name for himself in the taxi game. Another Inspector relegated to the subs bench by the gods of Fettes, forced to live out his career as the almighty Cab Inspector and quite willing to beat up all and sundry to mould a delusional legacy.

Gordon 'Brucey' Bruce was the only other police officer based at the Cab Office. He was a 53-year-old local from Sighthill who had joined the force thirty-odd years ago. He was constable-rank through and through, like old Larry the Lamb. Brucey had done his national service with the army in Korea, joined the police afterwards and walked the Clermiston beat for several years before joining Traffic; where he had enforced the law upon offenders with a merciless vengeance.

He had a pink face with a drinker's nose and a rough complexion. He also had a 1950s American flat-top haircut. His grey hair was turning white and he now had a plump belly and pair of droopy man-boobs.

Dixie approached with a friendly smile, "That's your desk there beside Brucey's," he said, pointing to a spare desk with a pile of files upon it. Brucey hung up a phone call in which he seemed to be organising a lads' holiday, and engaged Chuck with a friendly smile.

"What do we call you then – Charlie? Chic?"

"No, my father's Charlie and sometimes Chic, my son is Charlie too. I'm Chuck."

"Right you are, Chuck," he said. Dixie and two other mechanics – who were seated, tapping away on typewriters, were eagerly listening in.

"Did Inspector Herriot tell you that none of us here know about your situation at Drylaw?" Brucey asked.

Chuck merely shrugged his shoulders.

"Cos, we know everything." Brucey stood up and motioned for him to do likewise. "Let's you and I go get ourselves a cuppa and I'll fill you in on that silly old drunk through there." He thumbed in Herriot's direction. Chuck nodded and followed him into what appeared to be a classroom with several desks, but without any blackboard. Instead, there was a sink, a kettle with brew material, and some bottles of red and brown sauce on a counter against a wall.

"This is where we do the monthly exams for the Hackney Carriage Drivers' Licences, Chuck." Brucey waved his hand towards the desks as he headed on toward the brewing corner. "This is where you and I decide who gets the good houses and the two holidays a year in Spain," he grinned, as he began rinsing a couple of mugs.

There was a newspaper cut out of some Hearts players visiting the Cab Office, and beside it was a framed picture of Her Majesty the Queen. "Do you support the Hibs then, Chuck?" asked Brucey as he prepared the brew.

"Always," replied Chuck firmly.

"Well, we are all Hearts men here except 'El Cid' – that's what we call the Inspector; he is a Teddy Bear[4] and a rugger man."

Chuck turned to look at Brucey, who was still smiling but shaking his head in dismay.

"We heard on the grapevine that you're married to a Catholic, hate Protestants and went to the brass to report your colleagues at Drylaw for being evil members of the freemasons. Is that about right?"

"Is that what you heard?" Chuck smiled back; understanding now what Herriot meant when he had said that his staff didn't know everything. Brucey was fishing for the finer details only.

As it turned out, Brucey was a decent enough guy; at least towards Chuck and the glorified mechanics they worked with. There was clearly a sort of clique established at the Cab Office which was based upon an appreciation of the role being a cushy number for them. The common link between them, was that they were all Hearts supporters, Protestants and at least some of them were freemasons. It did not take Chuck long to realise that Brucey and Co were probably receiving backhanders from aspiring cabbies, which perhaps cemented their little pact.

In order to obtain a black cab licence in Edinburgh, a large sum of money has to be paid to enrol at one of several taxi schools. Several months of study follows, until the candidate is deemed ready to sit the exam at the Cab Office. The topographical exam they were required to sit was designed and updated regularly by Brucey, with monthly exam sittings in the Cab Office. It was famously regarded as the hardest taxi exam in Britain and had more failures than passes every time. If an applicant failed to reach the rather harsh percentage required to pass, that individual could not re-sit the exam for a year.

There was also a stiff fee for the exam itself, and another hurdle in the form of a subsequent decision by the Cab Inspector on whether or not he would oppose a particular application, even if that applicant had passed. A legitimate reason for opposition would be an individual's criminal record and a fair assessment of his/her threat to public safety. Chuck couldn't understand why any opposition was not raised before an applicant had to pay for studying and then sitting the exam. He soon learned that opposition

[4] Slang in the Cockney fashion for a supporter of Rangers Football Club.

often depended upon whether or not an applicant was regarded 'suitable' by Brucey and Herriot.

If applicants wished to contest any Cab Office opposition, they had to hire a civil solicitor and attend a farcical and intimidating meeting at the City Chambers on the Royal Mile and argue their case in front of a panel of councillors. In most cases, Herriot himself would present his objection to the committee, with either Brucey or Chuck alongside him as his PA.

"Anyone who argues against an objection by us is made to wait till after the rest of the day's business is done, so that their lawyers can charge them by the hour," explained a grinning Brucey to Chuck on one rare occasion when they had both assisted Herriot at a regulatory hearing. Due to the legal costs, and also partially because of the fact that the council nearly always sided with Herriot, most applicants simply accepted an objection and wrote off their chances and their cash. This in turn gave the Cab Office at that time, considerable power.

Although Chuck was initially well-watched and treated with general caution when he started there, he slowly grew to be accepted by the team. Initially he was assigned endless piles of paperwork related to vehicle inspections and testing, and he did this thoroughly whilst also making an effort to get along with the other staff. He gradually did himself a few favours by laughing at their shit jokes and going for the odd drink with them at the prison warders' club down the road. Fortunately, his strategic assistance in the planning of an operation to take out Bertie McManaman's unofficial minicab firm – Fringe City Cars, turned out to be a massive contribution. The team had all worked late into the night with an intensity which raised any barriers between them and which resulted in McManaman's arrest for the supply of cannabis through his taxis. Thankfully, his input gave Chuck considerable respect from his new colleagues.

Still, Chuck had observed convicted criminals obtaining licences without Brucey batting an eyelid at their application forms which, Chuck presumed, was down to the applicant being a Mason or having a Masonic connection. One guy even had convictions for police assault and burglary which were only a year old; yet again, no objection was raised. Whilst a poor man, without the right connections, received an objection simply because he had been convicted of stealing a lawnmower, twelve years previously, when he was just a kid.

There were other strange happenings that Chuck had been able to witness from a distance. Every Monday, various complaints from members of the public who claimed to have experienced an unprofessional service by drivers of both black cabs and minicabs would be received. The list would be left on Herriot's desk and he alone would determine who got a pass and who would end up at the city chambers, costly legal representation in tow, to appear in front of councillors and defend themselves from one of his suspension applications. From the calls Chuck took, the loquaciousness of Dixie, and the subsequent list of suspensions, it was obvious that brethren often received passes. Chuck's understanding was that the complainer was always right, regardless of a driver's claim that the complainer had been drunk, or violent, or had attempted to avoid payment. Whether a driver was given a handshaker's pass or, in the cases involving repeat offenders and friends of friends, a tribute payment, was all down to boss-man Herriot.

Those not deemed to be of the right sort; such as non-masonic drivers, former villains who conceivably should not have a licence anyway, ethnic immigrants and Roman Catholic supporters of Glasgow Celtic, were often on the official suspension lists Chuck would have to compile for regulatory committee hearings. Three times, Chuck saw brown paper bags being slipped over to Brucey and then Brucey taking them through to Herriot. On one occasion, he saw that the name of the driver who had handed the envelope over was erased from the list. Dixie was also overheard saying that the going rate was £500.00 and that was why the flush Herriot gave every member of staff a bottle of malt at Christmas. Sounded like Herriot got the better end of that deal, reckoned Chuck – who opted to keep all of this to himself.

There was certainly a thriving enterprise going on at the Cab Office and after a few months there, Chuck reckoned several thousands of pounds were changing hands in return for licences, vehicle certificates and the sympathetic management of complaints. Chuck became highly aware that there could be no hope for anyone considered to be unworthy of friendship or who could not provide favours. There had even been indications that certain brethren with interests in the black cab industry had gifted Herriot £30,000 to support a motion that the city council create greenways for buses and black cabs, which strictly excluded minicabs. Chuck never saw evidence of this, however he did note the growing conflict between the two cab industries and Herriot's bias in favour of the big black cab firms owned by his brethren.

In that summer, the cab war began in earnest. Chuck was eating his lunch one day when Herriot was heard screaming at Brucey about, "fucking minicab drivers," and it being his "job to destroy the bastards once and for all." Minicabs were new to Edinburgh at the time. Licensed by the council, they were not appreciated by the black cab industry and therefore had quickly found themselves without any friends at the Cab Office.

Known as 'private hire cars', to hit home the fact that they were not driven by exam-tested cabbies, these vehicles were simply four-door cars which were licensed to chauffeur anyone who phoned to book them. They had no taxi plates on them in those days, and no on-off lights or advertising to distinguish them for the public. This was because under Herriot's management, the Cab Office fought intensively on behalf of the Masons at the pinnacle of the black cab industry to restrict these private hire cars from breaking their monopoly on street fares.

Chuck reckoned that this stupidity made it easier for non-licensed vehicles to operate without being easily distinguished, and thus resulted in more danger to the public. Herriot did not care, however, and instead committed himself to his masters within the black cab industry, who urged him to commit his resources toward enforcing the perks they had established for themselves. It would be a war that would break many individuals but fortunately for Chuck, he was on the verge of escaping back into the world of real police work.

Around this time, a tall, suited senior CID officer had turned up unannounced at the office, looking to recruit someone for an ongoing CID operation that was apparently taxi-related. He had come across Chuck as he passed through and started up a conversation with him about his role within the Cab Office, before proceeding to Herriot's office. A few days later, Herriot called Chuck in at lunch time.

"That was Grant Martin who was talking to you the other day." Herriot sighed and looked up at Chuck to search for any recognition. "He's a Detective Inspector at Leith and my former sergeant at Dalkeith back in the day," he explained with a hint of jealousy in his tone.

"Can't say I've heard of him, Sir." Chuck shrugged his shoulders.

"Right, well, he was just popping in on his way to Leith. Lives in Currie, you know." Herriot looked uncomfortable now and his face became somewhat flushed. Either the old fart had been on the sauce again, thought Chuck, or he was pissed off about something.

"Leith have been investigating Roger Hartley at Sunshine Cabs, and they fancy the bugger has been hijacking," he made a face as if he had been served a turd in a restaurant, "hijacking lorries filled with booze and cigarettes from supermarkets." He spat these words out with considerable distaste.

"What?" Chuck could only mouth the question; he was shocked too. Who would have foreseen that Hartley, the smelly little Geordie owner of Sunshine Cabs in Leith, would be doing anything as dramatic as that?

"Martin wants to go in this evening, arrest Hartley at home and then simultaneously raid the Sunshine office and pull in all their vehicles for all-night searches." Herriot was looking stunned now too.

"All-night examinations?" Chuck heard himself say. Hibs v Rangers was on the TV later but he sensed where this was leading.

"Correct. He wanted someone from here to go along with him as our representative. Obviously, Brucey and I will be in the bloody court trying to destroy that bastard McManaman until silly o'clock and Grant wants to gather his team at 4 pm." He paused to see if Chuck was smiling. "So, what I'm coming around to saying is – you're going to do it," he told him.

"OK," Chuck continued to look bewildered.

"He said he has checked up on your background and thinks you'll do." Herriot looked puzzled as to why that might be. "Right, anyway, stick it out here until 3 pm, then head over to Leith. Take Dixie and all the files we have on Sunshine Cars and Home Jeeves Cars too," he ordered.

As Chuck turned to go, Herriot spoke again: "Don't get any delusions of grandeur, Kean; you're here because the brass say so, and I won't ever be endorsing you for your CID exam unless I'm told to do so by the brass, right?"

Chuck did not turn around. "Right, Sir," he muttered, as he closed the door gently behind him.

"I'm not a bloody Mason, Chuck, and I recognise a good cop when I see one. I won't turn my back on him simply because some secret-keeping twat tells me that I should," Martin said, as he patted Chuck on the shoulder early the following morning after the bust on Sunshine Cars. Chuck would sometimes feel that there was more to Martin's sudden support and protective arm; however, he couldn't quite put his finger on what it could be.

An £18,000 haul of cocaine had been found behind a false wall at the office of Sunshine Cars on Junction Street, and it had been Chuck who had spied the fake wall during the raid. The homes of three of the firm's registered drivers were then raided; turning up stolen electronic goods which had been hijacked from a Tesco lorry in Coatbridge earlier that summer. The lorry had been full of widescreen televisions on their way to Aberdeen. The three drivers had all sung openly under Martin's questioning, and in the end, they and Hartley received twenty-four years between them.

"I told that pen-pushing wanker, Herriot, the other day in his office that I wanted you to join the investigation when I heard you played a big part in capturing that other taxi rogue – McManaman, Chuck," Martin explained over a fry-up in a greasy spoon.

"That prick Herriot had years to do something about vermin like McManaman and Hartley who operated on his patch, yet he achieved nada; then along you come and pinch the bastard straight away," Martin laughed warmly.

Chuck presumed that this brief secondment would be the end of the matter, but Martin had other plans. "Do you fancy coming in again and helping us tidy up a couple of other cases, as we are a few men down at the moment?" he asked with one eyebrow raised, vaguely reminiscent of Roger Moore. He had not had to ask twice, because as soon as Chuck had removed the grin from his face, he had agreed instantly.

"You'll come in as an acting DC, then. The hours are irregular, mind, and there is plenty of overtime on the go; but anyway, I'll deal with that jealous wanker Herriot and get it all sorted, lad," Martin had assured him, and the rest had been history, as they say.

A year served as acting DC led to a permanent position for Chuck at Leith, under Martin. Martin then moved on to lead the Drug Squad. Shortly afterwards, Chuck transferred to Gayfield station, where he worked the city centre. There he learned much about corporate white-collar digital crime before Martin poached him again for his new-look Druggies in 2003. At first, Chuck had found the shifts long, and he particularly disliked the 'surveillance shift', as it was referred to (which stretched from 5 pm-1 am). There was certainly a more frenzied vibe to the Druggies than there had been in CID, but Chuck settled in quickly and soon discovered that he savoured the war on narcotics.

Three

"For you see, the world is governed by very different personages from what is imagined by those who are not behind the scenes"

Benjamin Disraeli

The warm summer of 2014 saw Edinburgh's office people strolling around at lunch time as though they were in Cannes; eating al fresco, wearing designer sunglasses and indulging in that extra glass of cold wine. Some picnicked in Charlotte and St Andrew's Squares in the New Town, with French cheeses and Mediterranean nibbles. Even the benefits brigade lapped up the international vibe in Princes Street Gardens by drinking Irish cider and munching on Mexican tortilla chips. Tourists passed them on their way to the many outdoor fringe shows, while the local thieves prowled around their prey; much as the Sahrawis do to holidaymakers in the Canaries.

There were fewer students around in August, but many of those who had stayed in the city could be seen walking around in surfers' vests and cut-off jeans, handing out flyers for the evening shows. For some Edinburghers, then, the Fringe month provided a taste of the Riviera; while for others it might have been Benidorm. Beneath the surface, however, the festival veiled a bubbling brew of political unease and increasing division among the natives and regardless of class.

Many jobless youths lounged around the city centre with panting pit-bull terriers at their heels, often better conducted than their masters. In the mornings, the city paid an army of East Europeans to clean up, while these bums remained in their beds. Come the evenings when the heat relented, the cops had their hands full with the violence which spilled out of the pubs and onto the streets. The Drug Squad spent the summer pitched up against a growing cocaine epidemic. It was said at the time that it was easier in Edinburgh to obtain cocaine than cannabis. They had nicked several large local suppliers between Easter and the Fringe, but had still not made a dent in the overall problem.

Chuck had begun his career with the squad in a coke bust during the Festival in 2003, when two middle-aged married women from Surrey were reported by hotel staff for snorting white powder in the bar. Uniform arrived, and when they detained the pair, they soon discovered a few grams of cocaine in their room. Chuck and the squad Chief-Detective Superintendent Grant Martin had attended, as they had been passing in Martin's car at the time. The fact that the two women had recently flown up from Gatwick, and gone through airport security to do so, convinced Martin that the coke must have been supplied locally.

They were also to discover a pornographic DVD involving the two women and two teenage boys. Subsequent inquiries led to Guildford CID discovering that one of the boys had been underage at the time of the recording. The investigation then developed further, and the squad ended up charging into a licensed sauna on Albert Street in search of drugs. Here, they found an assault rifle and a cowering group of Thai girls who pointed them in the direction of a flat in Joppa, where £50,000 worth of cocaine was stashed in a shower. For Martin and his squad, it had been a great result. So, from the word go, Chuck's career with the Druggies had been highly successful.

Now, as he got into his car, the afternoon heat hit him like a blast from a baker's oven. Subsequently he drove with the windows down, often sticking his head out as he headed over to collect the squad DS, Chris Forsyth, from his Newhaven flat, to prepare for a surveillance operation. He half-expected Forsyth to turn up in flip flops and a pork pie hat, going by the rest of the squad that summer. They had all embraced the heat wave by turning up to work in creamy cotton summer suits and dark shades, just as they imagined their Miami counterparts would wear. Even the catering staff at Fettes were prancing about in cut-off slacks and sandals.

Forsyth was waiting outside his flat, wearing a Hawaiian shirt and khaki cargo shorts. Chuck regretted not wearing shorts himself now and wondered where he could pick up one of those little hand-held fans Kim always took on holiday with her. Forsyth was a little younger than Chuck, and hailed from Kilsyth, near Glasgow. He was slim, with mousey short hair and warm brown eyes. He looked like he should have played guitar for the Stone Roses, and had once been a winger with Raith Rovers' youth team before joining the Fife Constabulary. He had transferred across to Edinburgh seven years previously and settled down with a local lass. Chuck liked and trusted him as a fair and honest cop.

"Fat people hate the heat too, guv," Forsyth teased as he got in and noticed his boss' obvious discomfort.

"I don't hate it, Chris. Christ knows I've spent thousands on holidays seeking it," Chuck sighed as he drove off. "I just hate how the air coming out of this bloody air-con is not freezing cold on days like this," he argued glumly.

"Volvos are Swedish, guv, perhaps they are already cold enough over there?" The bugger was overly perky, and as sharp as always.

They had the windows down as the traffic came to a halt for the umpteenth time at Goldenacre, on the parkland beside Stewart Melville Rugby Club. There were several people picnicking on the grass. Forsyth spotted two women sunbathing in bikinis on beach towels.

"Take a look at those two, guv," he urged. Chuck leaned forward and saw that both females were lying on their stomachs, with their bare backs receiving the sunrays.

"Fire!" roared Forsyth out of the window, which caused the two women to sit up and look around for the emergency. Both had plump breasts which bounced about like jelly on a bus, for all to see. Both men chuckled as the line of traffic blasted their horns in appreciation.

Chuck got along with everyone on the squad, mainly because none of them were bent, nor, as far as he could tell, signed up with the Handshake Brigade. Since Grant Martin's arrival and his leadership of the Druggies, the squad had regularly produced results. Chuck believed this to be down to Grant's honesty and his insistence that the team play fair.

The other resident DI, Karen Adams, was as efficient as her mentor had been, and when she arrived as support for Martin's command, Chuck was the DS assigned to help her settle in. They had gotten on famously right from the start, and no one was happier than her when Chuck was promoted to DI upon Martin's departure. Having previously investigated corruption within the old Tayside constabulary, Adams had been the leading inspector on the investigation. She had been appointed to the post after whistleblowing on several of her own colleagues within Grampian Police, who had conspired to shield an oil industry tycoon from a diamond-smuggling investigation.

Adams then nailed more bad apples in the anti-corruption inquiry into the professionalism of certain Drug Squad officers stationed at Dundee's Bell Street station. In the process, Adams scalped a DI and a DS who had framed a suspect and extorted several others. Afterwards, she stated to the press that she had no qualms about bringing any old boys' networks down. She was then a DI with CID in Aberdeen for a while before joining Martin's new look Edinburgh Drug Squad. Chuck respected Adams for her obvious talent as a detective, and, more importantly, for being a clean one. She possessed that funny working class colloquial humour found in cities such as Aberdeen, Dundee, Glasgow and Leith, so Chuck found it easy to laugh with her. She was the type to piss herself laughing at old Billy Connolly videos. Chuck was not convinced that outside Leith, the rest of Edinburgh appreciated that legendary craic.

Forsyth, however, was Chuck's closest colleague and a sort of friend. He often had the younger sergeant and his Mrs over for dinner, or for a drink in the Baillie Bar. The Druggies all drank together once a month with their families, and the Baillie was their haunt. Chuck frequented it from time to time because he recognised that the squad needed to maintain their bond. It also helped some partners appreciate and understand the unsociable demands of being a Druggie.

When he parked outside Fettes, both men hurried up the little mound which led to the entrance of police headquarters, where the Squad office was located. Chuck had originally been seconded here from Gayfield CID, as an acting DS under Martin. The initial switch had been to assist Martin in an operation involving Strathclyde's Special Branch. Chuck obtained a permanent placement with the squad shortly thereafter, thanks to Martin's influence.

Martin had taken a liking to Chuck when he had first been seconded to his CID command in Leith from the Cab Office back in '87. When then brought him into the Druggies in 2003 it had been only temporary, but Martin scrounged a permanent transfer for him 14 months later. Chuck saw straight away that intelligence gathering was a key element of the Drug Squad detective's role. Thankfully, he had some experience of playing this game quite well whilst with CID; where he had produced results that had pleased his superiors. He had shown little inclination towards promotion or any form of leadership, as he believed that by allowing others to claim the glory, he had found the safest way to avoid being dragged back into serfdom at the Cab Office.

It had been the consistent results though, that had enabled Chuck to sit his Detective Sergeant's exam. By the time Martin went over to Special Branch as their new chief at the tail end of a rather impressive career, Chuck had worked under five DIs and three Chief Supers. He was promoted to squad DI, partly because he had become the longest-serving officer and Martin had recommended him. The new Chief Super, Colin Wong, specialised in bureaucracy, however. He was another splinter-arsed pen-pusher who once claimed to have been racially abused by his colleagues, when still a young uniformed Cantonese translator.

The son of a Hong Kong cop, Wong gradually climbed the police ladder and was promoted to a bigwig position in counter-terrorism, where he soon adopted the role of a splinter-arsed luvvie. Eventually he was made head of Liverpool's Drug Squad where, for five years, he directed operations against a Triad-controlled marijuana supply line which operated from Glasgow to Torquay. He came to Edinburgh soon after he had ended that particular enterprise and took an over-paid role with the then newly-formed Police Scotland. Initially Wong had been content to extend his settling-in period as DSI and encouraged the squad to run itself, while he did the odd lecture at the Tulliallan police college and toured Scottish golf courses.

In this period, the squad busted a heroin ring running between Edinburgh, Birmingham and Bruges. Various other forces also became involved, including the Belgian DJC, in what developed into a Europe-wide investigation. An excited young PC from Tayport had instigated the whole shebang when he rang up Edinburgh with a tip-off which was put through to Chuck. He insisted that he had information that there was a small yacht leaving Tayport harbour on the River Tay for Granton Harbour in Edinburgh with 'a few nine-ounce bars of cannabis resin' aboard. Chuck told the cop not to alert anyone else on the Fife coast, particularly not St Andrews police, while he personally rang the coast guard and charmed them into standing down. Chuck had been optimistic that, despite the supposedly small amount of contraband on board, the fact that it was being transported by sea would make his report read more dramatically, and so it might open up other avenues of investigation.

In the end, Chuck, Forsyth and four other officers were sitting in wait for the little yacht as it bobbed into Granton harbour. They discovered forty ounces of heroin on board, along with a very talkative and compliant skipper. The end result was big – twenty-six individuals were jailed in both the UK and Belgium on the evidence of the skipper and one or two others. Wong took the plaudits on the local television news. The fact that both Chuck and Adams had insisted upon this showed Wong that the Druggies were an effective and loyal unit who pursued results rather than glory. This was the polar opposite of Chuck's previous experience in CID, where some slimy bastards had competed for glory at a bloodthirsty rate. Self-glory was a habit that was supposedly being weaned out under the new national police service, but in reality, it was rampant among many officers. Chuck had noted how it fractured a team's effectiveness: "schisms create shit results," he would tell new detectives.

Racism had also been rife in the CID in the eighties and nineties, including among a few hate-filled officers who regularly attended Hearts games. These men had openly passed out bananas to each other in the office, to throw at the new Rangers signing Mark Walters. He was the first black professional footballer in recent times to appear in Scottish football. For Chuck, it had been a sad state of affairs for the Scottish game, not to mention a sign of a rotten constabulary in crisis.

"It's the beginning of the New World Order, all this single currency, one set of European laws, and now us here with our new state police; what next, a European army or passport?" Chuck's elderly neighbour had complained back at the time when the new Police Scotland had been announced in the papers.

Presently, Gav Caine, a DC in his mid-thirties, sauntered toward them with a beam across his freckly face while entering the Drug Squad offices. It was grin not unlike one a parent might have displayed when watching their child unwrapping presents on Christmas morning. "Wait till you see this, guv," he said as he eagerly handed Chuck a photocopy of a recent charge sheet. It was in the name of a Lionel George Frazer, who had apparently been charged with indecent behaviour of a sexual nature with a minor in a public place. The minor was a Stacey Williamson of 14 Magdalene Gardens. Frazer's address was given as 99 Grange Avenue. Chuck had to think for a moment.

"Is that Leo Frazer, the lawyer?" he looked up and asked the still-grinning Caine, who nodded enthusiastically and seemed on the verge of doing a jig.

Chuck glanced around at Forsyth, who was standing silently as this exciting news sank in. Frazer was a lawyer who practiced as a Solicitor-Advocate. He was currently representing a big-time property magnate named Leslie Cairns, in a much-publicised divorce case. What was interesting here was that Frazer's client was about to be put under surveillance by the Druggies that very evening. Chuck suspected that Cairns was involved in a cocaine cartel with, among others, former rogue Northern Irish paramilitaries. So, this was a very interesting development indeed.

"There's more," insisted Caine, tapping the sheet with a pen.

Chuck read on and then gasped, "Well, well, well, he was only over the alcohol limit too, AND, they found a half-ounce of coke on the little shit," Chuck chuckled now.

"You're kidding, guv! Let's see!" Forsyth grabbed the sheet.

"I've been talking to the uniform who dealt with it, guv," explained Caine.

"And?"

"They have him in custody, but he isn't going to court today as it's a bank holiday. They said CID aren't interested in him, so we can interview him if we want." Caine, still grinning, gave a mock salute. Chuck saluted back and turned to wink at Forsyth.

"I'll go see Frazer myself, with Joe," he said. A curly-haired DC, Joe Roxburgh, who was seated nearby talking on the phone, waved upon hearing his name.

"I'll interview the bent little bastard myself and squeeze his nuts about Cairns," Chuck nodded at Caine. "You bash on with organising tonight's surveillance, Gav; that's still on," he insisted. "Chris, you run things here." He gave Forsyth another mock salute.

"Joe, let's go," Chuck shouted over to Roxburgh who promptly finished up, grabbed his coat and proceeded to follow his DI out.

At St Leonards station in Newington, Chuck flashed his ID at a portly WPC.

"DI Kean, Drug Squad. This is DC Roxburgh. We've come to interview a prisoner, Lionel George Frazer," he told her in a friendly manner. They waited while she went off to find the Duty Inspector. She duly returned with a ginger-bearded chap who shook Chuck's hand.

"Hello there, I'm Rod Coulthard," his handshake was not abnormal, Chuck noted.

"Hi, Rod – Chuck Kean – Drug Squad. We're here to interview a prisoner, Lionel George Frazer," Chuck flashed his card again.

"I thought that case was all sewn up, but OK. I take it the investigating officers have told the custody sergeant that you're expected?" Coulthard scratched his beard.

"I certainly hope so, my office informed them that we wanted to speak to Frazer on a separate matter," Chuck kept up the niceties for this pen-pusher.

"Right, I see. Tom, can you take these officers down to an interview room and I'll see that they have Frazer ready for interview?" Coulthard asked a tired-looking officer who was returning to the control room with a cup in one hand and a packet of chocolate chip cookies in the other. Tom looked nonplussed at this, but downed tools and led the way through a door and along a short, carpeted corridor. He was silent as they then descended a small flight of stairs and went through the security door of the custody suite. The smell of disinfectant from the cells hit them instantly, and the echoes of female prisoners shouting through their cell hatches completed the penal atmosphere.

"Came in first thing this morning for shoplifting, the whole lot of them," commented Tom as he motioned them both to sign their names in a book. When they entered the booking room, the custody sergeant was just coming off the phone, no doubt with Rod Coulthard. "Do you boys need a room with tape recorders?" he asked them with a strong Australian accent.

Chuck shook his head. "No thanks, but you can call me Sir, thanks Skippy," he replied.

"Sorry Sir, I'll get you an interview room."

"Much obliged."

"He's been crying like a bairn ever since they charged him and got even worse when he realised he was being kept in over the bank holiday," Skippy said as he walked them down another corridor, towards an interview room. Chuck found the Australian's effort to use the word 'bairn' amusing and exchanged a knowing glance with Joe.

"Didn't even want his wife informed, and he also declined a lawyer. We have the bugger on a suicide watch just in case, but he ate breakfast and asked for a book, so we reckon he should be OK."

"Did you give him one?" asked Joe curiously.

"Think the turnkey might have, can't be sure; but we have some books, it just depends on the mood of the turnkey and how the prisoners are with them," Skippy explained as he showed them into a bare room with a desk and three chairs.

Leo Frazer was soon brought in and ushered, uncuffed, into a chair on the side of the desk opposite to them. He was a small and chubby man, with prickly brown hair and a little pointed nose which made him look somewhat ratty; Chuck thought as he eyed him curiously. He saw before him a short-legged man wearing a shirt which hung out over his suit trousers, and a pair of thin black socks.

"Well, I'm Lionel Frazer, gentlemen." Frazer leaned across and offered Chuck his chubby little hand. Chuck shook it and felt what he believed to be a Masonic handshake. Frazer's thumb pressed hard between Chuck's second and third knuckles, but Chuck could not be sure, nor could he have identified Frazer's Masonic rank even if he had been sure.

"I was wondering when the Drug Squad would turn up to threaten me." Frazer leaned back in his seat and exhaled deeply. He looked quite dejected and exhausted. His eyes were red, presumably from crying, and he had stubble across his face.

"Did the turnkey tell you who we were?" asked Joe.

"No, he didn't know." Frazer closed his eyes and inhaled deeply now. "It's the casual clothing which gives you away," he added, nonchalantly.

66

"I'm DI Kean and this is DC Roxburgh from the Drug Squad," confirmed Chuck with a wink and a grin. "Why would you be expecting us, Leo?" he asked cheerily.

"Well, Inspector," Frazer lifted his beady little face now, "I reasoned that if there is any competence within Police Scotland, then my legal representation of a certain person should bring an inquisitive Drug Squad sniffing around," he said, massaging his head with his fingers as he spoke.

"Well, here we are Leo," smiled Chuck, "let's have some craic, then."

"Hangover?" Joe asked mischievously.

"Hardly, I only had two glasses of wine," snapped Frazer, jerking his head up at this audacity.

"Still too much for driving though, Leo," said Chuck. "You're looking at a trial for the coke where you might get a Not Proven, but it will take some lawyer to argue that anyone other than yourself could afford to pay for such a large bag of coke." He sat back, folded his wrists and shook his head hopelessly.

Frazer was quick to reply, "It was in the glove compartment. Like I told those uniformed idiots, she must have put it in there," he insisted as he rapidly flicked his eyes from Chuck to Joe and then back again. He was fully alert now, like a zebra which has caught a whiff of the lioness.

"Still," smiled Chuck, "with the kid giving evidence against you regarding the sex part," he flicked two palms out over the table, "the drinking and driving, and of course, your well-known high-profile coke-dealing client, well... I wouldn't fancy your chances with a jury, mate," he warned ominously, still with the grin.

"Then there are the circumstances in which you were captured, Leo," put in Joe. "She is only fifteen, and that makes you a beast. The problem is, a beast has no credibility."

"Oh, I know that." Frazer dropped his head into his hands now and his elbows knocked upon the desk. Chuck winked at Joe while Frazer messed up his own hair as though he were clearing it of insects.

Chuck and Joe exchanged another glance; it was clear that they had a cornered animal here which now realised that everything it had previously valued in life was close to vanishing. The question was, was Frazer sane? The prisoner began to emit a whining groan while shaking his head at his situation. He was at the acceptance stage of his position still, Chuck judged, so he pressed home for the kill.

"I am in the process of obtaining a warrant to search your home," he revealed to him.

"By George, what the hell for, man?" Frazer suddenly snapped out of it and looked up at Chuck with an expression of utter horror. He quickly realised that his reaction had been beyond his own control, and would only encourage the Druggies to search his home.

"Something to hide, Leo?" asked Chuck.

"No, of course not. It's just that I don't want my family to know about this yet. Anyway, the girl told the police that she saw me buy the cocaine from a chap in the bar, so nothing to do with my home, officers." Frazer's legal instinct had clearly not deserted him.

"That doesn't matter to me, Leo," Chuck told him firmly. "I still want to search your home as I think your client potentially supplied that coke, and if you don't tell me everything right now, I'm going to send a team right through your house. They will alert all your neighbours and tell your little wifey the whole sordid story," he promised with a gentle nod of the head.

Frazer began sobbing at that. He gave a long sniff in an apparent attempt to compose himself after a minute, then mumbled, "There's nothing there, I swear to you, my family are innocent... please, I beg you Inspector."

"OK, here's the deal, then, Leo," replied Chuck, taking no pleasure from the man's emotional disintegration. "You're going back to your cell for half an hour to consider your options." Frazer gaped at him like a terrified child now, waiting to hear more.

"Those options are as follows: one, you refuse to help me, and I raid your home and your office while broadcasting your sins to all and sundry. I might even leak your name to the press today and have the word passed around the legal fraternity that you like shagging kids." Chuck allowed this threat to sink in before continuing.

"Or, two: you can tell me everything I need to know about your client's shady business and I'll consider having a word with the Fiscal about your current mess." Chuck sat back with his hands behind his head. He had offered the carrot by letting Frazer know a deal may be possible. Whether one actually was or not was a different matter, because Frazer really was in a mess regarding the underage sex allegation.

Joe called the turnkey, who returned promptly and escorted a slightly stunned and disoriented Frazer back to his cell, while he and Chuck went up to the canteen for coffees and a quick conference. They both agreed that Frazer was a potential suicide risk, so they would press home their advantage to see if he would bite or not. Chuck suggested that the CID may have turned their backs on raiding Frazer's home as a Masonic favour to him. Then Joe suggested that potentially, the uniformed officers who had captured Frazer may not have both been of the handshake persuasion, otherwise they probably would have let him go. When they returned downstairs, they had Frazer brought back, looking even more red-eyed.

"I know nothing about Cairns other than that I asked him to get me the coke for the girl. She wanted it as payment for sex," Frazer calmly told them.

"Then we are done here, Leo." Chuck pushed his chair back to stand up.

"I can offer you another deal entirely if you would indulge me with half an hour of your time, gentlemen?" Frazer spoke quickly to stop them from going. It had been the sudden appearance of new optimism in Frazer's eyes which intrigued Chuck. He didn't know why, but he simply believed Frazer. It was as though some divine power had just clicked its fingers. Chuck now knew for sure that Frazer could do very little, if anything, to help them nail Cairns, although he didn't know how he knew this.

Joe also experienced this resounding realisation. He stared into his notepad a moment as he understood that it was indeed pointless to work on Frazer regarding Cairns. Instead, both detectives were, within a brief instant, compelled to listen to whatever else this guy had to say. Joe felt drawn to the scent of treasure within Frazer's offer. He studied him for a moment, scribbled something down, and then looked at Chuck to see if he too had caught the scent. It would be madness to mention it either way, of course. Chuck also stared at Frazer a moment, trying to understand why it was that he intuitively suspected that he could offer absolutely zilch with regard to the Cairns investigation. He then put Cairns to the back of his head. "Go on?" he finally replied.

Frazer shuffled in his chair for a moment before taking another deep breath. "What I'm alluding to is something considerably grander than anything you could ever have imagined, officers," he spoke slowly now, almost at a whisper.

"It might mean my life if it ever came out that I have spoken of it here." Frazer looked at both men with genuine concern, verging on fear.

"Go on," Chuck said as he crossed his legs.

"When I do talk and you act, I will need a new identity," Frazer pointed out.

"Go on?" repeated Chuck.

"I'm offering treasure." Frazer paused and met the stares of both detectives before nervously looking over toward the door and lowering his voice again. Joe raised his eyebrows, as he had had that precise word in mind just a moment before. "In return for which, I want all charges dropped, and I also want to walk out the door with you two guys today," he nodded at them both nervously. "New identities for me and my family, an income, and it has to be an overseas relocation such as New Zealand," he insisted, his beady little eyes darting towards the door again.

Joe snorted at this and looked at Chuck, who remained quite unmoved. Chuck knew that what he had on his hands here was no ordinary criminal; far from it, this pervy little lawyer may well have an ace up his sleeve and should not be written off. Something urged him to listen to what Frazer had to say. So, he smiled at Joe for effect, and turned back to Frazer. "It had better be sensational then, Leo, if these are your demands," he grinned. Then, with his hand, he bade him to get on with it.

"OK. I will give you nothing less than information regarding a clandestine network across the city whose operations relate to regular crimes far worse than that which I am charged with." It looked from his facial contortions like Frazer was going to choke, but he quickly recovered himself. "Who... do things which the entire nation would be shocked to discover," he said with a slow, knowing nod of his head.

He continued, "I will help you to obtain the convictions of prominent individuals who participate in organised child sex and narcotics abuse."

"Child sex? Narcotics?" snapped Joe, before looking at Chuck to confirm that he had asked an acceptable question.

"What types, Leo?" Chuck confirmed that it was fine to ask this. He knew the sex claim might potentially be massive, even at this early stage. He would also need to find out if any children were in any danger currently, before potentially liaising with Social Services. The drug question however, was bread and butter stuff to a Druggie detective.

"Yes. Cocaine, Heroin, and Rohypnol," sighed Frazer, "And I will tell you of two locations where large amounts can be found today," he promised.

"Are any kids in danger as we speak, Leo?" asked Chuck.

"Not that I know of, or could tell you about." Frazer shook his head with an air of finality.

Chuck looked long and hard at him now. He usually prided himself at identifying a false smile or a storyteller. He was right to do so, since he had developed this ability slightly more sharply than most men. As he scanned Frazer's ratty features and posture here, he could not detect any trace of dishonesty. He was aware that many people would say anything to prevent the loss of their career, family and liberty, yet Chuck still instinctively felt that Frazer was serious about what he was telling them.

70

"Tell me everything – we're Drug Squad, but of course, the child sexual abuse is probably of even greater gravity – and if it's good enough intel, I'll have you out on a Fiscal's release, but I can't categorically guarantee that the charges against you will be dropped," Chuck finally said after a moment's thought.

"I want the charges dropped and to be relocated for what I give you," Frazer insisted again. "Otherwise I'm a dead man."

"You're a fucking dead man in jail," offered Joe with a faint grin.

"I can get you a Fiscal bail order today with a summons in the post for you to appear at a later date. Your family will remain in the dark about your antics as long as they don't see the summons, of course, and you will have your liberty with which to break the news to them privately at a time of your choosing." Chuck shrugged his shoulders but maintained eye contact to display his sincerity.

"I'll need Drug Squad protection if I talk. I can't go home until you have smashed the group." Frazer displayed his frustration that the detectives did not grasp what was at stake here.

"Look, I hear what you're saying," assured Chuck, reading his concern. "I would need to go to my superiors to authorise that kind of thing, and relocation takes a lot of work. I can't just magic it up instantly, but I will do my best to arrange it and I know who to talk to. So, tell me what you have first."

"But you would promise to try to do that for me?"

"What I guarantee is that you will walk out of here today if what you have to say convinces me to make a deal, and that I will press as hard as I can on your behalf for the charges to be binned," Chuck assured him firmly. "I'm a man of my word. If your life is in danger as a result of what you tell us, I will speak to my boss about placing you in protective custody while the matter runs its course, and potentially in the long-term," Chuck nodded encouragement. "That's the best I can offer, Leo," he added, as though to close the deal.

Frazer nodded hesitantly, and a single tear rolled slowly down the man's cheek. "This will be hard for you both to hear officers, and I know this as neither of you are Freemasons, judging by your failure to recognise the signs I have displayed to you both here," he said, as he wiped it away.

"I detected the handshake," Chuck corrected him.

"Well that is by-the-by, it's going to be hard, but I have no choice now; I am going to tell you about a group of people whom I shall forthwith refer to as TIC – The Internal Circle," Frazer began.

Joe started taking notes again.

71

"I myself am a Freemason of a particularly old craft, as my father and his father before him were. I am of the second degree by order. My craft are of the Ancient Oak of Fairmilehead Lodge," Frazer failed to hide the pride in his voice as he spoke.

"What number is your lodge on the Grand Lodge of Scotland roll?" asked Chuck.

"We are not on the roll. The Grand Lodge only dates to its founding by a confederacy of Scottish Lodges in 1736. We, like some others, did not recognise the new constitution and declined to involve ourselves in their schism." Frazer shook his head. "So, let's just call them the TIC."

"Our order can be traced back to our founding father – Adam de Gordon, a grandson of a Norman knight. He established our craft during the reign of David I of Scotland in 1130 AD. As explained, our order did not attend the gathering of the new Grand Lodge in 1736 and rejected the standardisation of the crafts. Subsequently, we retain our own procedures, regalia, distinctive rituals, and we keep our craft secrets to ourselves." His tone was calm and focused now, Chuck noted.

"To be quite clear here, gentlemen," Frazer paused, took a deep breath, then went on, "I am conscious of how this may sound, but nevertheless, our lodge practices what some would regard as Black Magic."

Chuck just stared at him. He could see that the guy was serious, and believed what he was telling them.

"Are either of you gentlemen familiar with the term Nephilim?" Frazer asked.

Chuck remembered enough Old Testament readings from Sunday School to have a half shot at it, once he saw that Joe didn't have a clue, "Weren't they supposedly drowned giants or something, when God flooded the earth?"

"Quite so. In Genesis 6:4, the Old Testament tells you that fallen angels screwed human women, and that the Nephilim were their bastard offspring," Frazer confirmed. "It describes said offspring as legendary men of power," he continued his pitch.

Chuck was interested and saw that Frazer was looking down at his feet now. Chuck's experience was that if a person looks down when recalling an event, they are often genuinely remembering; whereas those who gaze upwards while telling a story are usually inventing it as they go along. Frazer was not showing any hint of bullshit here.

"Well, the power they possessed was not simply that of physical strength, but also one of wisdom given them by their fathers. An inheritance from the angelic realm, as it were. One they themselves call 'Arcane

Knowledge',"" he revealed while looking down, as if through a momentary portal that was visible only to himself.

"Are you telling us that these Nephilim are in existence today, Leo?" Chuck asked, trying not to appear amused.

"An abomination, some say." Frazer was now punctuating his sentences with sombre shakes of his head and long penitent sighs.

Joe stopped writing, and instead listened.

"But no, they do not exist as Biblical man-eating ogres, but the bloodline itself persists. Albeit not in as pure a form as they might desire, but yes – it most certainly does exist today within what you might consider to be a hybrid bloodline," Frazer seemed to consider it all a further moment before continuing.

"Their paternal bloodline can be found within the Septuagint of Deuteronomy 32:8, and their ancestral claim to rule mankind in the pseudepigraphal *Testament of Nephatali* 8:3-6. Though Psalm 82 gives more detail on those who were once allowed to administer God's will on mankind but who then broke from heaven. Indeed, Psalm 82 also confirms that these corrupted beings were behind all pagan traditions of worship across history and that their offspring were many and powerful. Today, the remaining hybrids claim that they are the guardians of the old Arcane Knowledge," he told them in a very quiet voice.

"Spirits and Hybrids?" Chuck was wondering if this strange sensation of being relaxed while eagerly focusing upon this insanity, was partly because he did not quite disbelieve this extradimensional tale just yet.

"Daniel 10:13-14, refers to the Archangel Gabriel fighting with the fallen angels who control Greece and Persia, as spirits" Frazer explained while Joe continued to write the references down.

"Hybrids today, are the descendants of these spirits' offspring – the biblical Nephilim that have repeatedly reproduced with humans until the genetic linking became something of a stretch at best, in my view," replied Frazer, quite matter-of-factly.

"Arcane Knowledge?" Joe asked, "Spell it." He began taking notes again.

"A-r-c-a-n-e," sighed Frazer. "I am referring to nothing less than the knowledge of all the mysteries of nature and science," he said. "Of technological skills and occult magic."

"And so, this knowledge is passed down from father to son?" Chuck wanted to know. In that case, the angelic bloodline claim was just a myth.

"In the TIC, it is often referred to by its metaphorical term, 'Witch Blood', and it is a hereditary asset," claimed Frazer as casually as though he were discussing car engines.

There was silence for a moment as Frazer allowed Joe to catch up. Chuck sat silently and considered what he was hearing here. Frazer's monologue had certainly gotten rather far off the drugs-and-child-abuse track. Yet Chuck instinctively felt that despite the entertaining nature of the subject matter, this might be going somewhere. He knew instinctively that he should explore this unusual prospect further.

"Are you saying there are individuals within this TIC who believe they are related to Nephilim and are keepers of black magic?" he asked.

Frazer thought for a moment. "Perhaps, I can talk to you of their crimes instead now, Inspector? As I'm quite sure you wish me to do."

"Answer the question, Leo," Chuck sighed impatiently.

"All I can tell you is that the governing body, or the highest council of Masonry, are known to some as the Illuminati. They most certainly have Nephilim secrets," he nodded.

"Such as the cure for cancer?" Joe looked up at him, poker-faced.

"Sorry?" Frazer seemed surprised.

"This Arcane knowledge?" Joe stared hard now.

Frazer nodded with a smirk, "Yes detective, B17, for example."

"B17, Leo?" asked Chuck.

"Google it," said Frazer, and he dismissed the question with a flick of his wrist "It's a vitamin found in apricot kernels. I take 5 a day."

Chuck and Joe exchanged a glance between them, still unsure as to what the other was making of all this.

"It's a secret that came out somehow, but which is kept under wraps as far as possible," Frazer admitted.

He could see that they were somewhat stunned by all of this, but also that they were listening and not dismissing the context he had set out for them. "Look, its content is recognised as attacking and killing cancer cells, but it also contains cyanide. All the cancer authorities here and the FDA accept this, but argue that the cyanide content makes it impossible to prescribe," he explained.

"Watch the Lecturer G. Edward Griffin's video, 'A World without Cancer', which I believe is on YouTube. It reveals certain doctors' beliefs that the disease is down to a deficiency of an essential food compound – B17, which is sometimes missing from the human diet. It also explains why the cyanide content is harmless and is only released upon contact with the cancerous cells," he continued while Joe scribbled frantically.

"The Illuminati chaps within the cancer industry have rubbished his claim, mind, and called it quackery." Frazer grinned at them both and it was obvious that he believed himself to know better.

"This, gentlemen," he went on, "is only an example of a fraction of the knowledge held by the Illuminati, as in the 'Enlightened Ones'. You have heard of them, presumably?"

Joe nodded while continuing to write. Chuck, on the other hand, also nodded and revealed his personal interest in all this, without thinking. "Yep, who hasn't, thanks to the internet, but do go on," he said.

"Well, they are often portrayed as a secret society who aim to establish a New World Order, a Luciferian age, where pantheistic monism obscures Christian thinking, and when mankind is offered the significance of a religion but without the moral restrictions that God imposes. In the process, the order is required to destroy the national identities and powers of all nations. The alleged members are sometimes quoted by investigative writers as holding ideas such as freeing the world and saying that, "All humanity who cannot identify itself by our secret sign, is our lawful prey", and so on," Frazer explained.

He was encouraged by a nod of interest from Chuck and by the fact that so far, he was getting a fair hearing without any scoffs. A less intelligent DI, or one without a shred of faith in these biblical tales, might well have walked away by now. Joe was interested too, but was also wondering if what Frazer had on sale here was going to be somewhat out of the Druggies' realm of investigation. He knew that Chuck had no time for masonry, and he also knew very well that it had once flourished within the police. This fact raised some alarm bells as to where they could be headed with all this if they did investigate it, he considered.

"OK, well, beneath the Illuminati is a worldwide umbrella network of Freemasonry. Working, in most cases, for the revival of the ancient crafts, but more so nowadays, towards this New World Order that rejects the commands of scripture and their author. Most Freemasons are oblivious to this, as they only embrace the craft to increase their personal power or wealth. Again, powerful individuals within local politics, commerce, industry and finance lead the umbrella lodges, including here in Scotland," revealed Frazer.

"These are usually third-degree Grandmasters, and few second-degree Freemasons have any inkling about the real secrets possessed by those above them. The Grand Lodge here, which you mentioned, has thousands of members who join the lodges as entered apprentices of the craft, but who never progress up the ladder to second-degree." Frazer shook his head now.

"Only little snippets of the actual knowledge held by the supreme order are made available even to the highest Master Freemasons. This applies particularly among the brethren of the Scottish Masonic confederacy, who are regarded as somewhat unimportant in the larger scale of the worldly organisation."

"The ladder?" asked Chuck.

"At the apex of the worldwide pyramid are a select few who know the full agenda. The clear majority of masons, regardless of the lodge or craft they belong to, are only on the first three rings of a thirty-three-tier hierarchy. These low-levellers swear an allegiance to the Grandmasters who in turn swear likewise to the elite bloodlines. Despite the linkage, however, your average mason knows very little, and your highest craft elder knows only a little more than that," smirked Frazer now.

"Does that mean you know bugger-all too, then, Leo?" Chuck smirked back at him.

"The TIC, my lodge, is old, Inspector, and quite different from the other Scottish lodges." Frazer immediately lost the smirk and spoke with pride. "Our craft has an awareness of certain things without having to rely upon the supreme council for said snippets. However, we have kept our secrets very safe over the centuries, and do not generally mix with other brethren. We are Luciferian by nature, as are those Illuminati at the top of the worldly pyramid." Frazer paused for a moment now, still looking down. "That is why we swear allegiance to them," he hesitantly conceded.

"Other Scottish lodges have their own crafts, which I would say are not always credible, and their own forms of worship to go with them. It's a bit like Greek mythology in terms of the variety of individual deities being worshipped," he explained. Neither Joe nor Chuck interjected, so he continued.

"The ancient Greek deities originated from tales of fallen angels and Nephilim who have been worshiped by men for thousands of years. Indeed, many are still worshiped by some crafts today under their Phoenician and Babylonian names such as 'Baphomet' and 'Rahu'. Within my own craft, the TIC, it is the Dragon himself whom we revere," he revealed with an unpleasant grin.

Joe was thinking as he took notes, while Chuck dissected every single sentence in a pointless search for bullshit. Still, he could detect none, but that did not mean that Frazer was telling the truth; only that he himself might truly believe that he was. The distinct possibility that Frazer was both morally and mentally flawed had not escaped Chuck's thinking at all here.

Frazer continued his overview. "These elites are obviously not like us, detectives. As I said, they have unique bloodlines and unusual abilities." Frazer sighed once more. "It is important that they enforce their position at the top of the ladder, and the release of clues and promises of wonderful arcane knowledge to others is a continual part of that process."

"Promises, as opposed to the sexy stuff?" Chuck asked while noting a faint trace of resentment from Frazer.

Frazer did not bite, though. "The actual knowledge revealed remains encoded and only serves to whet one's appetite, yes, you are correct about that," he conceded. "No one is ever given the full scenario, only small pieces of a picture of the most awesome significance. As more and more is shown to those who climb the ladder, the better the perks become, and doorways open in terms of income and esteem," he said, and Chuck gestured for him to continue.

"The global brotherhood enjoys vast amounts of wealth and esoteric knowledge, so they have flourished and developed into a worldwide network. Power, affluence and control have been achieved and maintained via warfare, exploitation, and especially in the last century, control of the world's economic systems. Collectively, the brotherhood has flourished under this system. Naturally, worship is required of us, and it is the dragon who is the patron of TIC. Our founder, Adam de Gordon, was of a Templar line, but before that his line was that of the *Celtae* Druids[5]," Frazer revealed.

"Prior to that, the line had been Pythian, and so on." Frazer waved away all this with his hand... "At the very outset, the 'Shining Light' himself; Satan, that is, instigated this blood lineage; therefore, my own lodge redeem him as our creator and Lord," Frazer said, surveying them for their reactions; a potential backlash was half-expected.

Chuck was surprised by this open acknowledgement of satanic worship, yet it made perfect sense in relation to everything he had read and experienced over the years. Why would anyone want to abuse a privileged position, if not for wealth or glory? And what, or who, could tempt a person to pursue materialism over morality, if not Satan? They were not so much a secret society, then; rather, they were a cult with secrets that had never been thoroughly investigated due to the influence of the cult themselves. Yet it was still hard to believe that satanic worship was ongoing within a so-called liberal, democratic and peaceful society. He quickly reminded

---

[5] Wood-dwelling, pagan and animist soothsayers of ancient Celtic Gaul and Britain. Described best by Julius Caesar as a human-sacrificing, elite religious cult who influenced tribal politics.

himself that this was, however, the territory of conspiracy theorists with little evidence.

"Satan is very misconceived, you know," Frazer coolly informed them. Joe kept writing and did not look up while Chuck smirked contemptuously and motioned for Frazer to elaborate.

"Today, entry into the various sects that form the large pyramid is regular and quite simple," maintained Frazer. "Potential freshmen are spotted and pursued by another member. Big businesses, which are merely a front for the pyramid, often point out targets. Potential candidates are obviously tempted by the notion that, once accepted, many doors will open for them. Obstacles to wealth will disappear and a self-perpetuating sense of superiority is quickly established. In other words, this mutually beneficial old-boys' network takes care of its own. In the TIC, we have much stricter membership regulations and processes than other British lodges."

"Three questions before we move on," insisted Chuck. "Firstly, what is the overall Grand Plan of this pyramid?"

Joe raised his eyes from his notepad and looked curiously at Frazer, who seemed a little surprised at this, before he replied. "Well, world dominance, Inspector, clearly."

Joe spoke up now, instantly irritated by the arrogance of such a presumption, but also because it was all such a rabbit warren of information. "OK, but are you saying that everyone in the entire Masonic fraternity across the globe has this agenda, Leo? Or just the TIC? And sorry..." He checked himself by giving Chuck a look of apology for interrupting, before slowly turning back to Frazer. "Are you also saying that the TIC is a rogue lodge from the roll of the Grand Lodge of Scotland?"

Frazer recognised where Joe was at, and quickly offered clarification.

"Well, the Illuminati are at the top, and they have various factions under them who all unite to form the rest of the pyramid, or brotherhood." Frazer shrugged his shoulders and then licked his parched lips. Chuck guessed that he hadn't taken a sip of anything since he had first been detained. He had probably chucked his breakfast in the loo, like most other detainees. What with the booze and coke, it was little wonder that he was dehydrated. He was still eager to continue though.

"Which includes the world's Freemasons. All of them in Scotland adhere to the 33rd degree of the Scottish Masonic Rights," Frazer added.

"This degree indicates that the majority of Freemasons are controlled by a centralized worldwide body who govern all the Masonic Grand Lodge

Councils, and thus, that all of Freemasonry worldwide acts in a unified direction."

"Under an elite group at the top who seek power and dominance on behalf of the devil and his bastards?" Chuck heard himself flippantly ask, despite his willingness to believe what was said. He was testing the man by pressing him to convince him further. He was also testing his own comprehension of the whole thing.

"Quite, and no need to be facetious, Inspector." Frazer forced a smile at him and Chuck nodded back, halted proceedings and had a turnkey bring in three bottles of Highland Spring water for them. Frazer greedily accepted his and emptied it down his neck in seconds, so Chuck gave him his as well.

"As for the TIC being unattached to the Grand Lodge of Scotland," Frazer turned back to Joe after he had gasped some air, "we can hardly be 'rogue' as you put it, seeing as we were never part of the initial schism of the crafts in the first place," he told him in his best Glenalmond School Housemaster brogue.

Again, Chuck detected sincerity in the manner with which Frazer was legitimising his group's position; the bastard believed in it, was proud of it, and if he was prepared to defend it here, he could well be telling the truth. If he was really a Walter Mitty type, then Chuck could find no trace of it in his demeanour.

"What I'm asking, Lionel, is whether the members of the other Scottish lodges are all supporting the supposed agenda of those elites, who you claim pull the strings?" Chuck tried again.

"Not all of them, I'd wager," came the confident reply. "Like I say, there are various claims, predominantly made by conservative protestants, mind, that the Freemasons at higher degrees are deceiving the lower degrees," he told him.

"Back to my second question, then," Chuck interjected. "What is the agenda of the TIC, how does it involve narcotics and kiddies, and do you take orders from an Illuminati contact?"

"That's three questions, but OK." Frazer closed his eyes a moment and nodded. "Our brief is simple, we maintain the control we have established and try to establish more. I would argue that this has been a vibrant enterprise in my generation," he said cockily before taking a breath to gather his thoughts and then continuing.

"For centuries, there were different agendas for various crafts, most of which involved establishing sufficient power with which to protect and strengthen the elite. Go back to the *Alta Vendita* document, for example; you can find it online easily enough due to incompetent recruitment within some mainstream lodges, and give it a read if you doubt me. It reveals that the brief of all Freemasons, from the reign of Charles I onwards, has been to engage and defeat the Catholic Church." Frazer rubbed his head again before clearing his throat slightly. "You have to understand that the Roman Church was once deemed to be the true Christian church, and thus a serious threat to Satanism," he insisted, looking Chuck closely in the eyes as he spoke.

"And, I quote, *'Our ultimate end is that of... the final destruction of Catholicism, and even of the Christian idea... The Pope, whoever he is, will never come to the secret societies; it is up to the secret societies to take the first step toward the Church, with the aim of conquering both of them'*," he recited, nodding to reinforce the point.

"So, are you saying that the only brief you guys have in the current era is to creep into the corridors of power and defeat the Catholic Church through infiltration?" asked Joe, who was a non-practicing Catholic through his mother.

"Yes, I am. Though I might argue that the Catholic Church has been 97% infiltrated and is therefore ours now," insisted Frazer.

"But the Church is not defeated. Lionel, the Pope, visited Edinburgh in 2010 and had a massive following – and that's the point of the church, I would say." Joe put his pen down and sat back.

"Oh, my dear detective." Frazer grinned at him, "I congratulate you on your ignorance, as of course was intended, mind; but no, the Church is mortally wounded. We dominate it today. Have you not seen the video of the spider crawling over Benedict's shoulders on his TV speech recently? Did you think that the perversity within the priesthood was godly?" Frazer sat back at that too, but his pose, unlike Joe's sceptical one, was like a spoiled little school boarder refusing his porridge as he folded his little fat arms, before continuing in a defensive manner.

"The brotherhood made it cool to swap the altar for the registry office, then replaced that with 'common-law' partnerships, and thus attacked and profaned the sacrament of matrimony in only half a century, detective. Then, with demonically-controlled priests championing our cause, the church was on its arse by the late eighties. Have you not seen the images of the new Pope displaying both the horned hand signal and the hidden hand symbol?"

"Well the horned hand signal also means I love you in sign language," said Chuck.

"Yes indeed, Inspector, but one must also remember that the individual who designed a hand sign system for the deaf, Helen Keller, was herself an occultist," Frazer retorted before turning his gaze back to Joe.

"In 1974, Pope Paul VI made the following mega-statement. I have it by memory, as I have read it many times: *'The darkness of Satan has entered and spread throughout the Catholic Church. Apostasy is spreading throughout the world and into the highest levels within the Church, even to its summit'*." Frazer shrugged his shoulders as though to rest his case.

Joe lowered his gaze and simply began writing again.

"So, the focus now is on political power. The only way for the Brotherhood to prosper is to keep the world in ignorance of who they really are. By convincing people that they are little more than robots, they can use them to perpetuate their powerbase. I myself have represented big business in Scotland, achieving fine legal results, including the supermarket takeover of our food chain," Frazer continued.

"Food chain?" Chuck dreaded to hear the elaboration of this claim.

"How many butchers, fishmongers, cobblers, greengrocers or newsagents are left on the British high streets?" shrugged Frazer. "Or even British-owned manufacturers of soft drinks, crisps or chocolate?" He spoke between slower sips of water now. "Few. That is the answer. Soon the big supermarkets will be incorporating dentists, doctors and vets and maybe even – schooling."

"Then there is the net – who owns the newspaper websites you're using, Detective?"

"Big business," mouthed Joe.

"Big business is a front for the progression of dominating the world food chain." Frazer flicked his hand again to indicate how effortless this process was. He then shook his head and met Chuck's gaze as he came to his point. "They say that mankind is only three meals away from chaos, Inspector, so if the brotherhood establishes a hold of the supermarket food chain, then they could create chaos very quickly, yes?"

Chuck nodded in reply.

"We saw the riots in England back in 2011; imagine if they had been fuelled by hunger, or racial hatred, even? Well, whoever has the power to do so, could then step in and sort out said chaos."

"Whilst securing the appreciation of a relieved public, and all under the rule of law?" sneered Chuck.

"History reveals this to be a recurring reality, gentlemen. It's difficult to accept, I know, but it's as simple as that, frankly."

"You haven't yet answered my earlier question, Leo. What I need to know is whether there is a narcotics wing to your 'Big Businesses' that I should know about," Chuck queried.

"Not officially… well, not that I'm aware of in my own experience, no. My own view, and I'm only a Fellowcrafter myself, is that individuals use the protection of their craft to enable them to profit from independent drug enterprises." Frazer shook his head despondently as if to suggest that he disapproved.

"What about your client – how does he come into this?"

"Leslie Cairns is a member of TIC now, but he's only been a member for two years. He was elsewhere as an Apprentice and was obviously brought in due to his successful property portfolio. I didn't know him, and I even blackballed him once. I have been representing him in his divorce but he provides both drugs and pets for the gatherings I am going to tell you about. Like I said, I can do no more for you regarding his drug business, and shall instead help you get him for the other stuff," Frazer now assured them.

"Pets?" asked Joe.

"Teenagers, and younger ones occasionally." Frazer closed his eyes and rubbed his temples wearily.

"Will you wear a wire with Cairns?" Chuck moved closer and indicated that this suggestion was something Frazer should agree to if a deal was to be reached.

"Indeed, yes, and phone calls if required," Frazer assured him.

"And you will reveal to me the identities of all the members of your lodge as soon as any deal is agreed between us, Leo?"

"Yes, I shall," he promised.

"How many members are in the TIC, and are there any cops?" Joe had to ask this question straight out. He was thinking of self-preservation now and was half expecting Chuck to declare that he thought the whole thing was nuts, before abandoning Frazer to his fate.

"One hundred members. I don't know who they all are, but I will give you the details of the main players and of those participating in the child sexual abuse," Frazer promised again.

"And cops?" Chuck pressed Joe's question again.

Frazer appeared nervous again and took another sip from the bottle. "One or two of senior rank," he finally admitted. He was clearly apprehensive about Chuck abandoning him to his current predicament, and it showed now.

"Only two?" Chuck looked sceptical, as he was far from convinced.

Perceiving the doubt, Frazer explained further, "rest assured that there are other TIC members who are powerful enough to influence the other leaders of many influential Scottish lodges," he responded.

"Who have plenty of cops among their brethren?" smiled Chuck, who now nodded slowly as it dawned on him that the TIC were the potential puppet masters of the other Scottish lodges and their armies of cop members.

Frazer nodded. "Unlike those lodges aligned with the Grand Lodges of Scotland, the TIC is only open to those of the second-degree level of Freemasonry – the Fellowcraft, as we refer to it. All the other Scottish lodges accept initiates at Apprentice level who may work their way up. So yes, there are cops who are members of ordinary lodges, but as I have explained, ours is quite unique and privileged, gentlemen."

"Write some names down as a goodwill gesture, Leo?" Chuck urged Joe to offer the pen and paper to Frazer.

"I'll tell you who they are when I walk." Frazer was fiercely cautious and shook his head.

There was a silence between the men for a few seconds and Frazer fought a faint desire to spew up the water. Chuck was staring at the little lawyer now. He was no longer trying to figure out whether the guy was telling the truth, for it was clear that Frazer at least believed his own story, and that was sufficient for now. Instead, Chuck was considering whether or not the little rat could actually serve up Leslie Cairns in the process of grassing up this alleged posse of high-ranking establishment players. Getting Cairns on child exploitation was, as Elliot Ness may have agreed, better than not nailing him at all.[6]

Frazer, meanwhile, took another deep breath, then sighed and lowered his head. He was as depressed as a guy who had just lost everything upon a roulette wheel, even the taxi fare which would have seen him avoid the ten-mile walk home in a torrential downpour to explain what had happened to the wife.

"I'll tell you who is in the TIC, and by that, I mean councillors, politicians, peers and judges," he said as he raised his head again. "Then, I'll prove that some of the supposedly happily married heterosexual ones

---

[6] Elliot Ness: US Treasury Agent 1927/31. Ness enforced the National Prohibition Act of 1919 in Chicago, Illinois. His small incorruptible team tried desperately to take down the Mafia boss of that city – Alfonso Capone, for violations of the act, but struggled. In 1931, Ness prompted the IRS to prosecute Capone for tax evasion instead, and this they did successfully, Capone going down for 11 years behind bars.

have gay sex with each other, as well as regular gang-bangs involving susceptible under-aged teenagers who they may also occasionally rape. I'll show you their special gathering places, wear a wire if required, and you can arrest them with a considerable pile of narcotics."

Chuck knew now that if all this was true, and considered to be a runner by his boss, it would be a big result which would echo across the UK. Despite this fact, there was unlikely to be vast amounts of drugs. The allegations suggested that the whole case could be massive, and this was what would count in the end. Proving it all would be something else though, and as Chuck was well aware, any attempt to do so could result in him losing his job. He also needed some more information while Frazer was on a roll. "Tell me more about the child rape," he demanded.

"Well Inspector, messed up kids are often groomed and provided by various sources. If requested, they can be under 16 years old and I have known of them being runaways from Leeds who were brought up here and then sent back with cash in their pockets. I have..." Frazer paused for a moment now and looked concerned, both men noted. "I have known of the murder of, well I was not present, but heard stories of murders of babies. In my time." He squirmed slightly, out of reach of them now.

Chuck and Joe exchanged a glance, then both stared hard at Frazer. "Wait, hold it there, pal," Joe growled. "Are you telling us that this TIC murders babies?"

"Yes, or at least, I have heard rumours, as I said, but I could only prove this by getting those who know about such things to talk, and that might not be easy or even possible," replied Frazer.

Chuck could tell that Joe was getting angry from the drumming of his pen on the desk, and decided that it was a good moment for them to stop and compare notes.

"OK, Leo." Chuck placed the palm of his hands on his thighs. "We are going to take a short break for refreshments, and then we can restart," he declared.

Joe then went out and called the turnkey back. Chuck very nearly instructed the officer to keep Frazer under constant observation, but checked himself. It would not do to alert Frazer to how important he had just become to them; at least, not until they had closed any deal.

"We'll see you in a wee while, Leo," he said casually to Frazer as he left with the turnkey. As soon as they were away, Joe turned and grinned.

"Well, guv what the hell just happened there?"

"I don't know, Joe." Chuck shook his head in confusion. "I had intended to put a full squeeze on him, but somehow it just happened that I believed him from the off."

"Me too, guv," confirmed Joe. "I'm glad you say that because that was strange, and I thought it was just me." Joe quit talking until two new turnkeys walked past them.

"I mean, it's massive stuff, guv… is it bullshit or what?" Joe asked quietly, when they had signed out of the custody suite and were exiting the building.

"There's no way he just made all that up, Joe," said Chuck as they headed for the car.

"He has had all that bottled up inside him and looked like he was experiencing a cathartic release when talking to us. I mean, did you not see his face, the expression of a man overcoming bloody constipation; either that, or an Oscar winner?"

"Weird," Joe thought aloud.

"Let's nip over and chat with Sharon Adams about this first, Joe; we have time. Then we can decide how to proceed. You're right, it is massive and I'm inclined to investigate, and that would mean a deal to get what he knows out of him." Chuck was still figuring out how to deal with this part and planned to seek a wise second opinion before approaching his boss for any deal. "I'm sure Special Branch would also wish to know about this intel, too," he mused as he quickly rolled down his car window.

The Volvo was like a sauna as usual. "Right, you find out who the duty Fiscal is and don't tell anyone why. I'll ring Chris," Chuck instructed. Both men got their phones out, searched for contacts and then put the phones to their ears.

"Chris, it's me" said Chuck. "Where are you?"

"In the office, guv."

"Right, get yourself over to Sharon Adams' house at Baberton, where me and Joe will RV shortly."

"Why? What's happened?" Forsyth instinctively replied.

"Nothing, and don't tell anyone where you are going, right? Oh, and bell Sharon and tell her we are en route with new intel on Leslie Cairns, and explain that we need an urgent word," Chuck ordered.

"Right then guv, but what about tonight's op?"

"Tell Mulligan or Gav to keep on that, and say that you're en route to join me at St Leonards, at my request. Once we see Sharon, we can decide whether tonight goes ahead or not, OK?"

"OK, I'll see you up at Baberton then, guv," Forsyth complied.

"Good man." Click… the line went dead.

Forsyth slid his untouched cappuccino over to Mulligan, stood up to leave, but helped himself to a chocolate biscuit to go.

Chuck drove through the Meadows which, as usual, was packed with people enjoying the sunshine. There was a large pink circus tent where the Ladyboys of Bangkok performed every night during the Fringe. Around it, the place resembled an overcrowded pop concert campsite. Both men were already perspiring in the sweltering car as the long line of traffic ground to a halt underneath the beautiful cherry blossoms, which still lined the parkway strip. Joe was still on the phone, tracking down the duty Fiscal's details when Chuck began to need a pee. He despised sitting in traffic in such heat, but his insistent bladder made it all utterly torturous.

"Right, thanks." Joe wrote down a landline number, then hung up.

"The duty Fiscal today is apparently some wee lassie called Greta McAlistair who isn't long out of law school, guv," he declared. "And at court tomorrow morning, there will be several of them on."

As they approached Marchmont, they could see that the reason for the tailback had not been a Fringe performance or a pop concert, but a political rally by the Scottish Liberation Party. The great Scottish Referendum lead-up was in full flow across the nation with all the political parties campaigning vigorously around the city and, of course, across the media. The country had never seen such a calling, and people who had never voted in a UK general election were now spilling out onto the streets to attach themselves to one side or the other. Thousands of supporters of the party, displaying pro-independence flags and banners, crowded together, singing and chanting in the gaps between megaphone speeches.

Chuck thought it was a sight akin to crowds on their way to a Scotland v England football match; such was the size and passion of the crowd. The SLP, though, were just another scrubby little fascist party who had piggy-backed onto the independence debate simply because they felt they could potentially achieve more within an independent Scotland.

"What prick at the council granted this in the bloody Meadows right in the middle of the Fringe?" snarled Joe in contempt at the crowd.

"Some twat from Auckland or bloody London, no doubt."

Chuck had not really devoted much time to the referendum debate. He, of course, knew that Alex Salmond, the leader of the Scottish National Party and First Minister of the Scottish Parliament, was the darling of the domestic voters. His party had initially risen as an alternative to Labour, who had dominated north of the border for decades. But Labour had fallen from grace due to the party's terrible economic handling of the UK and for taking the country into two wars, in Iraq and Afghanistan, which so many ordinary people had marched against. They had also amassed a long list of tabloid headlines on subjects ranging from seediness to fraud, which had turned a new generation of voters away from them. The SNP had taken their chance and sailed into office on a wave of discontented opinion. Chuck considered that they had done a decent job so far, but he did not trust their agenda.

Street kids, the famous local 'neds', and overall levels of violence had been reduced simply by placing more cops back on the beat alongside a judicial zero-tolerance approach. These were the things a cop who had family cared about more than bloody trams or wars. The other main options in the previous parliamentary elections had been the Tories, but they had lost any footing they once had in Scotland thanks to devolution and a series of leaders who looked like men in drag. The sudden rise of the SLP then, was alarming to Chuck, but understandable too. They were hard-right of centre and, to Chuck, were as abhorrent as UKIP.

The SLP were campaigning vigorously for independence. The SNP had kept their distance from them, of course, but could not avoid their common agendas for national independence. Pundits were even predicting that the SLP would do well in the 2015 UK elections, possibly finding themselves in a position to lead a coalition against the SNP for government.

Their stickers and flyers were on every lamp post and bus stop, and they had large numbers of vehicles driving around the country with loudspeakers and bunting, campaigning their blunt message on their behalf. It was their alarming focus on stirring up anti-English hatred and resentment toward Polish migrants which raised initial concern. Yet their numbers were growing, and the fact that a group of trouble-making, right-wing anti-Islamists who craved to relive the street brawling days of the 1980s football casuals had started attending party rallies and providing unofficial security, appeared not have raised many concerns among the party's growing band of middle-class supporters.

"Bunch of Nazis, that lot, guv," hissed Joe as the Volvo pulled away and onto the Marchmont Road.

"Pretty much, Joe, but like Hitler they have identified certain concerns among the people which they twist for their own agenda. I mean, look at their stupid TV advert about a kid not being able to find porridge in the Polish supermarket aisle; it's cunning, if not very subtle."

Joe began to laugh, "Or the halal chicken being where the haggis should be? I know, guv, but surely most people won't fall for all that pish."

"Looks like many already have, mate." Chuck surveyed the crowd in his rear-view mirror; there were plenty of them, that was for sure. "Right then, let's go talk to Chrissy boy and Sharon about what is to be done about this offer of Frazer's."

"Right, guv. I'll get that B17 cancer video he was on about, up on my phone as we drive." Joe then began fiddling about with his phone.

Four

"Disciplining yourself to do what you know is right and important, although difficult, is the highroad to pride, self-esteem, and personal satisfaction"

Margaret Thatcher

Joe parked right across Adams' small driveway at Baberton and Chuck shook his head at the rudeness. Kids were flying around the middle-class estate on bikes and roller skates while a few residents washed their cars and hosed their lawns. As pleasant and peaceful as these semi-detached and somewhat pricey estates were on Sundays, they did not appeal to Chuck. He loved his old property and much preferred the Edwardian feel to Portobello. They both got out. Joe waited for Chuck to walk round and lead the way down the little path, towards the glass porch.

A couple of lawnmowers – one close, one somewhere else on the estate, buzzed in the background as they approached. The porch door was slightly ajar as Chuck rang the bell. A few seconds later, Forsyth appeared and nodded for them to come in. They followed him through to the kitchen, where bacon rolls awaited upon a plate for everyone, filling the room with their tempting smell. Forsyth smiled as he sat down and got stuck into a roll, out of which ketchup gushed onto his plate. Chuck took a seat and helped himself to some coffee. Adams appeared shortly afterwards in shorts and a vest, eating a roll of her own and chatting on the phone to a woman who may have been her sister about how to make a beef stroganoff.

She gave Chuck a wink and went over to open her kitchen window, which looked out upon the cars, to let her cat in.

"Right, Jackie, I've got to go; that's the neighbour waving for me to give her a hand with something, so I'll call you back in a wee while, right?" she said.

"Right doll, chat soon," she put her phone down on the worktop and took a seat beside Forsyth, who was drowning his third roll in ketchup while Chuck reached for a second.

"So, what's happening with our friend Leo Frazer then, guys?" she asked as she refilled her coffee cup.

Just then, her husband walked past the kitchen door on his way out. He stopped and stuck his head in to say hello before leaving. He was wearing an Aberdeen football strip, and had a bottle of water in one hand.

"Away for a game?" asked Joe.

"Fives, nice to see you all, but got to dash; my lift's here," said Mr Adams as he left.

"Any excuse for a pint on a Bank Holiday for most married male GPs then," laughed Joe.

"Most men, even," grinned Forsyth.

Adams laughed but then turned to Chuck again, who sipped some coffee first and gathered his thoughts before speaking softly.

"Well, this is massive and will only proceed based on any collective decision we all make here today," he stressed to them all. Forsyth stopped chewing, then slowly began again, though with less noise now.

Adams was shocked and immediately thought that the case was going to concern bent coppers, so she nodded warily and spoke slowly, "I trust everyone sitting here," she confirmed plainly, her eyes flicking from face to face.

"Good, because this might be too big, too risky for us but if it is not, then we are going to need to be united in order to do anything about it," Chuck assured them.

Forsyth put his food down now and stopped chewing his mouthful of bacon for a moment, his eyebrow raised.

"What's happened?" he rudely mumbled, before taking a swig of coffee to wash down the food.

"Frazer is offering us a paedophile ring involving the fucking crème de la crème of society." Chuck looked at them all.

Forsyth felt overjoyed and clapped his hands, "Do tell?" he grinned mischievously.

"He won't give names until he has a deal, but he promises high-up figures in the judiciary, big business, and even Holyrood," Chuck told them.

"Cops?" Adams looked at him directly in the eyes.

"That's why we are here; he mentioned that one or two of the top brass were in on it. He offered to set them all up for us and promised that a high quantity of drugs would additionally be found. Obviously, bail requires work at our end, dropped charges even more work… and, of course, if we instigate anything we might shaft ourselves based on what Frazer reveals to us about high-ranking cops."

Adams stood up and went to over to the coffee machine. "Right, I'd better make us a fresh pot of coffee. Tell me everything from the start."

Forsyth turned to Chuck for a moment and said in an uncertain voice: "Are you convinced that the little bastard is not just pulling your chain, guv? He's probably a bloody good court lawyer and may have thought this up?"

"But why make up such a demented defence unless there is something in it?" asked Joe.

Chuck gave Forsyth his 'we're good friends' look, the kind that often came with an arm around the shoulders, but replied inflexibly:

"I think it's good, Chris."

There was considerable discussion regarding Frazer's charges, his credibility and of how the Druggies alone could take this on and not be squashed like ants by the brass, if the intel was genuine. Adams listened and stood a while, gazing out of the kitchen window. She thought about her boss, Colin Wong, and whether or not he would support them – should they decide to act on the information they had. She snapped out of her thoughts and spoke.

"I think we should spring him, get the charges binned by the Fiscal, and get him to deliver the goods. He can also make some calls to Leslie Cairns that we can wiretap, surely?" she suggested.

"We would get a tap on Frazer's phones and Cairns, based on his intel, but I doubt that Cairns would take a call from Frazer once we spring him," Chuck pointed out.

"And he has demanded protection if we spring him, so potentially the intel might be useless within a day or two of him getting released?" Joe put in.

Adams turned around to face them all. "The charges will need to be dropped and he will need a bloody good excuse for how that happened, or no clique involved in such filth would ever let the little shit back in again, would they?"

"Couldn't we just bullshit him that a deal is on and get the list of names from him, get a recorded statement say, then bump him? Then, we stalk all the names on the list until we get something firm? After all, he wouldn't dream of telling them he had cooperated with us, would he?" This suggestion came from Joe, who knew this was not how either of his two Inspectors rolled when making deals, yet it seemed viable considering the alternative.

Chuck shook his head but said nothing and was not surprised, for he had already considered that option and dismissed it. Not for any moral grounds, but for the simple fact that it was a gamble. Gambles must always

91

be excluded from any plans the Druggies instigate in this matter. What if Frazer committed suicide inside prison and informed the TIC of what he had done, out of spite at the betrayal?

"Might not be a bad idea, guv…" Forsyth began, but Chuck cut him off,

"No, because he might alert them out of spite, anger or fear, Chrissy," he shook his head.

"Correctamundo!" agreed Adams. "Either he is our star witness in a major criminal petition, or he helps us catch them bang to rights by making calls, wearing wires and generally coming across with the crown jewels," she insisted. She sat down again and continued to think. She knew they were all watching her. Half for an insightful lead, and half because the warm weather had encouraged them to appreciate her shapely legs in her shorts. She watched what she ate and did plenty of walking with her cross dog, 'Radar'; nothing more really. She enjoyed the watching but was wondering whether she could trust Wong with this information now.

"Chuck, we could try going to Wong on this one but if he is connected he might tell us to fuck off and concentrate on that ecstasy intel from Causewayside instead," she said.

Chuck knew this already and looked at everyone's eyes in turn as he considered things. Joe had been hiding the fact that he needed a crap for the last ten minutes and it had started to punish him somewhat. The last time he had been here had been Adams' squad dinner a while back, an occasion upon which he had pissed all over her loo and wiped it up with her towel. She had presumably found out the hard way because she had roasted everyone who had been there, so he fought the urge now.

"Sharon, if we don't get the DSI involved, then we won't be able to get the charges dropped. Nor for that matter will we be able to arrange to have Frazer back to work tomorrow as though nothing has happened," Chuck pointed out.

She shrugged her shoulders, "So, we are between a rock and a hard place, Chuck."

"Plus, CID are suspect and clearly aware. They refused to get involved in something which they should have, so if we don't get the DSI behind us …"

"They might come at us with senior rank anyway," Forsyth warned.

"Not on a fucking drugs matter, Chrissy," replied Joe.

"Aye, on a drugs matter Joe. Rank is rank," Forsyth reminded his colleague.

There was silence amongst them again for a moment while an ice cream van passed outside, playing the Popeye theme. Chuck remembered the ice cream van from his youth. It was brightly painted and called 'Papa Caffulo'. Usually he had bought a cone with raspberry sauce and a Nutty bar for his mother.

The Scottish childhood memories were booting up now. "I used to love an oyster," smiled Forsyth and they all smiled individually within their own branches of nostalgia.

"Mind, they gave you two ice poles for a Barr's juice bottle." chuckled Adams.

"Perhaps that's a good point, guys?" Chuck then asked.

They all looked confused now; even Joe, whose urge had slightly eased for the moment, but he suspected that it would return with a vengeance soon.

"Well, the DSI is the son of a Hong Kong cop, right?" and they nodded.

"Raised in London and relatively new to Edinburgh, yeah?"

"Yep," Adams was hopeful.

"Well, he lacks history or common ground with the old boys' brigade who have been brought up in Auld Reekie. He doesn't care for Hearts, football or hanging around with cops in smelly clubs; in fact, didn't he run some marathon in the desert a while back in aid of tsunami victims?" Chuck asked.

"I think it was an orphanage for kids whose parents were lost after a tsunami," Adams confirmed.

"Well, my point is that we can't be sure one way or the other whether the DSI is connected to Frazer's 'Cops' – he made little quote signs with his fingers as he spoke.

"But maybe they haven't been interested in him and vice versa, simply because they are unsure of him," he offered.

"Don't know about that, but yes, I think we should take it to him, boys," she told them.

Chuck knew she was right, and eventually nodded his agreement.

"Right, agreed. How about me and Joe go over to his place now and I'll give him the pitch as best I can?" She made this suggestion with a warm knowing smile that none of them could resist.

"Fine, go for it. I'll go over and tell Frazer he has a deal. I'll extract the names from him at the very least, and await your text," he told her.

"I'm going with you then, guv?" asked Forsyth, and Chuck nodded. This meant that Joe wasn't best pleased with the arrangement, as he had hoped to go to the loo somewhere, but now he had no option but to nod and force a half-smile.

"If Wong backs us, I'll go and see the Fiscal myself at home today. Then I'll track down the uniform who nicked Frazer and give them some crap about the charges being dropped for Frazer to assist MI5 or Special Branch in a matter of national security," said Adams as she found a jogging suit to chuck on from a pile of clothes on her washing dryer. She then turned to Joe, "Actually, Joe, can you get all the details and addresses now, please?"

Joe nodded and started to call the office to get the info from a computer.

Chuck took a deep breath and then stood up, "Mind – text me, don't call," he reminded Adams

She nodded. They agreed to arrange 24-hour surveillance on Frazer and his family through Gav at the office, if Wong gave the go-ahead.

Forsyth gave his squad car keys to Adams and patted her on the shoulder. "Good luck with the DSI, guv."

Twelve minutes later, as Chuck and Forsyth drove up Lothian Road, they saw two guys hanging an SLP banner from the window of a four-storey tenement for all the traffic to see at the Western Approach Road.

"Bet Frazer votes SLP," said Forsyth as he leaned out of his window to catch a breeze.

"Tory, I expect, Chris; aren't his family cattle farmers from the Boarders?" suggested Chuck.

"Well, no matter what he gives us guv, he doesn't deserve to get off with shagging a minor."

"Nope, and I suspect he will find things tough going for the rest of his life, because he will be on the witness protection list and his kids might never forgive him," Chuck observed.

"Better of two evils and all that jazz guv, but still unpleasant for us to have to deal with his type of scum."

They soon pulled up at St Leonards and went through the same routine with the female as before, then stood around waiting for the return of the uniformed inspector. As they stood in the busy control room, they listened to the commands and grasped the city's summer drinking problem first hand. It was only 1 pm, but Chuck reckoned there were four separate booze incidents being addressed in the Bridges area alone, by the sounds of the uniformed telephonists. Then, they both heard it:

"Roger that, a shooting incident… do not approach any suspects: simply stand off and observe until the ARV arrives."

They both looked at each other. This is what Edinburgh had become, a violent hot spot in the American tradition, where people are openly gunned down on the street.

"Roger, two CID cars from St Leonards and Tango 22, who is en route to you from Cameron Toll. Armed Response are en route from Meadowbank."

The woman reappeared soon afterwards,

"I'm sorry, but Frazer was bailed half an hour ago," she told them.

"What the hell?" Chuck was confused and rubbed his forehead. "Police bail?" he eventually gasped.

"No, a Fiscal release," she said, helpfully.

"Ah Roger, there are paramedics en route regardless and there's a traffic vehicle going to drop off some tape for you, OK?" said the telephonist behind them again.

"So, it is a fucking miracle that he suddenly gets Fiscal bail, considering what he was nicked for," Chuck growled at the female.

Forsyth was already on his phone, texting Adams to find out whether by some magic she had convinced Wong and seen the Fiscal in the space of a few minutes.

"Give me the Fiscal's contact details right now, please," Chuck snarled at her.

"Wait," Chuck called her back, "Where's his car?"

"It's been impounded because it was a hire car and the rental firm wanted to collect it later this afternoon, sir," she informed him softly.

"So, was he walking, then?"

"Well, as far as I know he didn't call anyone from here to arrange a lift, but he may have done so when outside of course. He may even have jumped in a taxi, Sir," she suggested, trying to be as helpful as possible.

The telephonist was now barking loudly in the background about a helicopter being requested to search for suspects, who were believed to have sped off into Queens Park on a motorbike.

"Right, so make sure you put the cones at that bit, then start taking the names and details of those people at the Commonwealth Pool – but first tell me that name on the card, please." the telephonist confirmed overly loudly.

"I'm surprised you can handle that," Forsyth joked with another officer, who passed them while carrying a box of tissues.

"Roger, ok, so that is F-R-A-Z-E-R, Frazer, Mr L., is that correct?"

Chuck and Forsyth looked at each other, then bolted out the doors and jumped into the car like men possessed, "It's him – they sprung him and shot him down straight away, I'm telling you!" gasped Chuck as he drove off at a wheel spin toward the Pollock Halls, which were just around the corner. Traffic cops and two vans had sealed the street off from the Scottish Widows office to the swimming pool, as they arrived.

"Drug Squad Inspector coming through," Forsyth told two uniforms while flashing his badge, before crossing over. They both then began jogging down the road past the Armed Response Vehicles and CID cars in the middle. At the entrance to the halls of residence were more uniforms engaged in taking statements from stunned students, and further down were CID and two ambulances gathering around the body. Chuck and Forsyth proceeded down towards it and were approached by an AR guy carrying an automatic machine gun.

"Can I help you guys?" he asked, in another Aussie accent.

"Drug Squad Inspector," replied Chuck and flashed his badge. The marksman nodded and stepped aside.

There was blood on the wall, which ran around the parkland enclosing the campus halls. They looked through the crowd and saw Frazer lying face down on the pavement with a section of the rear of his head missing. A plain-clothed officer looked around, turned and spotted Forsyth.

"Who are you?" he sharply asked.

"Drug Squad, and that's a DI over there," Forsyth grinned and pointed towards Chuck, who was listening to the paramedics talking about fragments of skull having been found stuck to the wall.

"What happened?" Chuck asked the plain-clothed guy.

"Just as you see sir, not gathered any statements yet but apparently, there are people who saw it and say it was two guys on a motorbike who then sped off through the park."

"A shotgun, then?" Chuck asked.

"Looks like it sir, pepper shot everywhere."

"Are the witnesses all corralled up at Pollock Halls?" Chuck asked.

"Yes, but we will need to do door-to-door over there," he said and pointed over toward an opening where private flats were located. "East Parkside," he added.

"Right Chrissy, let's get at the witnesses before some head honcho turns up," Chuck said to Forsyth and they started to jog back up towards the campus entrance. At the entrance to the campus, a uniformed group of officers stood taking witness details. They jogged right in among them. Forsyth approached a sergeant engaged in supervising his constables while they took down all the names and addresses.

"DI Kean, Druggies," Chuck gasped, trying to catch his breath as he flashed his badge at the officer, "How many witnesses are there so far?"

The sergeant nodded as Forsyth appeared, also out of breath.

"Two who saw the shooter, and then between the university and the pool, maybe another twenty," he guessed. "The security guy here has a camera on the road at the entrance so he's away with CID to seize it in the main building," he told them.

"Who saw the shooter?" Chuck asked quickly.

"Erm, two female students coming out of the campus, Sir," the sergeant said.

Chuck stared down at the man. "Give me their details, mate, as I am investigating the victim for suspected cannabis importation and think this may be one of his own lieutenants staging a coup d'état," he politely commanded, before turning to Forsyth.

"Chris, pop over there and see if we can find out what it is that CID are away to seize," he pointed to a barrier with a small security cubicle, which had various cameras sticking out of it.

Chuck turned back again to the sergeant who was obtaining the information from a WPC's notebook. By the time Chuck had the details stored in his, Forsyth had returned with a wry grin across his face.

"Come see, governor," he motioned.

As Chuck entered the little kiosk, he noted the four mini camera screens above some sort of alarm system that might have been connected to the barrier itself. The place was empty of people but was furnished with two seats, a table, and an old paraffin heater. Forsyth went over to a small electronic switch panel, then turned to one of the small screens.

"This one, guv," he pointed and Chuck saw that it was paused. It played for ten seconds and did not show the hit, nor the road or any bike. However, it did show one of the CID cars parked up on the road outside, a new blue Mondeo packed with suits, coming out of the barrier 32 minutes previously.

"Get the registration," Chuck nodded.

"Done, guv," Forsyth nodded.

"Well, CID are away to seize the tapes with whoever was in control here earlier, so check the plates of the cars parked outside and let's get the hell out of Dodge, Chris," Chuck said as he made to leave.

"There's nothing in there as the cameras don't cover the road," Chuck told the sergeant who was now further into the crowd itself. He was listening to a request to leave by a family from Guildford who had just dropped their son off to begin a degree in chemistry. Quite a welcome to the city for them then, considered Chuck.

"Thanks, Sir." The man nodded, then rudely returned to the Guildford mother; who sounded more Cockney than Surrey, Chuck noted. Just then, a PC started passing something on to his sergeant by whispering in the man's ear amongst the crowd. As he did, Forsyth returned and together he and Chuck walked out of the chaos onto the outside street and west along the pavement, toward the baths. Forsyth noted the vehicle plates as they crossed the road towards the police cordon at the Scottish Widows building. There were more uniforms around there now and they had to flash their badges to cut their way through the gathering of a squad. Chuck guessed it might be about to be sent into the Scottish Widows offices for potential witness names and addresses for CID to follow up throughout the murder investigation.

"That's the press here already, guv," Forsyth noted two men with cameras.

Just then, a black VW Passat sped past with a flashing blue light on the dash, full to capacity with men. One male in the rear was wearing a denim jacket and a yellow baseball cap. Neither Chuck nor Forsyth recognised anyone, nor was the car familiar, but Forsyth watched as they entered the kill zone and headed across to the campus entrance.

"They haven't set up a murder squad that fast, so who are they, guv?" he asked.

Chuck didn't reply because he was too busy watching the forensic van passing as they approached the Volvo. They exited the vicinity and headed for Jim Barrett's pub on the Southside. It was a little historic building with room for no more than 30 heads, but which was reliably peaceful and only frequented by one or two Grange locals and friends of old Barrett himself. Chuck had met him years earlier at a wedding, and the two of them had hit it off straight away. Barrett was a retired Station Officer of the Fife Fire Brigade. He had opened the pub 25 years ago. Of course there was the Lanarkshire connection, Jim hailing from Holytown and Chuck working at Marconi's, but in general Chuck trusted the man and would pop in every now and again with or without someone from the squad, for a pie and a pint of Guinness.

Barrett's offered a friendly little corner where Chuck could be left alone with work or enjoy the craic with Barrett himself, underneath the old black and white images of Ken Buchanan and Jim Watt; which hung everywhere. Barrett was behind the bar as Chuck and Forsyth entered. He was wearing a cream Guinness sweatshirt with a checked shirt underneath and was standing proudly upright, drying glasses.

"Aye aye, here comes trouble," he smiled.

"Good to see you Jim. I see you started early?" Chuck smiled at the half of Guinness on the bar, and Barrett nodded,

"Medicinal compound for health purposes, son," old Barrett laughed.

"Four pints of fresh orange and lemonade please, sir. I'm afraid it's shop talk today but good to see you mate," Chuck apologised and took a seat in a corner. The place was almost empty apart from two old blokes watching horse racing on the TV. Barrett served up the drinks, chucked in some crisps, and re-joined his two pals for the 4 pm at Ayr. The fan blowing on them from the bar was refreshing and as the two cops drank, Forsyth asked directly:

"Do you think our lot did the hit on Frazer, guv?"

"What do you think, Chris?"

"Timing was quick, guv; the fast bail suggests his lot sprung him, which also suggests they killed him and at the end of the day, it all seems to point to someone at St Leonards, or even Fettes."

"But did they know he was offering us the crown jewels, and is that why he died?" Chuck asked.

"Good point, guv," Forsyth agreed as he opened a packet of crisps.

"And who were those fuckers in the blue Mondeo, on the video monitor going through the barrier?"

"Shall I call in and get the lowdown on the registration?" Forsyth suggested.

"No, not yet Chris: we don't want to set any alarm bells ringing anywhere until we can establish whether or not anyone even knows we were sniffing around the scene. Let's go canny and not show our hand just yet," Chuck advised.

Soon afterwards, Adams arrived with Joe. Chuck went over it all again as he had tried his best to do in the brief texts he had sent earlier.

"Someone at St Leonards made a call, then?" Joe was convinced.

Adams seemed shocked and sat, looking worried.

"What did the DSI say about it?" Chuck wanted to know.

"He was really good, Chuck; he just listened then told me he was 100% behind our department investigating Frazer's evidence on an incognito basis. He only answers to the Assistant Chief Constable once a week so he has no direct involvement with any of the other brass," explained Adams.

"Thank Christ for that; so how did he seem when you broke the news?" Chuck pressed.

"Disgusted, that was my take on his face and posture," she said with a wry grin.

"What is he saying now?" asked Forsyth.

"For us to keep out of the murder investigation and to direct our resources toward Cairns, because if we can pinch Cairns, we might get him talking too," she replied.

"Doubt it; he could handle the time, no?" Forsyth speculated.

"Anyway, he wants you and I to meet him at 2 o'clock tomorrow with an update and to discuss things, Chuck," Adams confirmed.

"Fine, that sounds like the only thing we can do at the moment. I suggest we all just leave it and go home and get some rest."

"Well I'm on the back shift, you prick," smiled Adams, but with a slight prickliness from knowing she still needed to get back home first to get some rest.

"Can you do me a favour, Sharon?" Chuck asked gently, "can you tell Gav to postpone tonight's business and that there will be a squad briefing at 3 pm tomorrow, when we have spoken to the DSI about everything?"

Adams nodded with some relief, "Can you drop me off at Barberton again, Joe?" she asked.

Joe nodded, "Mind if I just take the squad car home guv as I'm not far from yours?" he asked Adams.

She told him that would be fine then added, "If we were to inform CID about the child sex claims against Frazer, they would do no better than us in any investigation now."

"They wouldn't have a chance of finding out those names now either," agreed Forsyth as he got up to go to the loo.

"Unless they are in on the whole cabal thing, of course?" Joe mused as he sipped his fresh orange and lemonade.

"And if that were the case, they would bury it, but they have nothing because we have nothing." Adams was riddling now but smirked knowingly… "It's impossible now and we may well be attacked just for repeating the hearsay from a paedophile junkie; and that is with Wong behind us." Adams was clearly a realist, but the loss of faith from his counterpart did not deter Chuck.

An Irish racing commentator could be heard from the small mounted TV on the end of the bar where Barrett and the two old men were watching. Chuck mused that the slow drawl of the man's accent suggested that the commentator was from the south, somewhere like Waterford or Cork, and as he did so, an idea came to him.

"Is there some sort of gala event at Musselburgh next weekend, with the mayor doing something with that chap from the radio?" Chuck asked them.

"Don't know about that but apparently some rich Arabs are going to be in town, watching their horses running. One is apparently royalty, so it is going to be busy getting in and out of Musselburgh," Joe replied.

"That is where we would find some of Frazer's cabal," Chuck said, straight-faced and looking up at a black and white photo of the boxer Lloyd Honeyghan on the wall.

"What?" Adams asked.

"At the racing, with all the fat cats and royalty present; we just have to see who turns up from the Edinburgh establishment and I'd wager we'll come across a few of them," he replied as Forsyth returned.

"Good point, Chuck, but I think now you should head home and get some sleep. We can see what the DSI wants us to do about this intelligence and whether or not he is even going to mention it to his Guvnor – the Assistant Chief Constable," she urged.

"Yeah, I could do with a decent sleep – I'm turning my phone off. I'll see you and get a coffee with you before we meet with him, yes?" he asked.

Chuck drove Forsyth to his Newhaven flat, having talked about Jim Barrett and boxing most of the journey. At the flat, Chuck turned to him. "Chris, I don't think we can do anything now except pursue Cairns and catch him – we're out of other options." he said.

Forsyth got out of the car and sighed as he straightened his back.

"I know Guv, but never say never. See you tomorrow."

On the way home through the traffic, Chuck flicked the radio on; hoping to hear some local news about the shooting, and he got it right away.

"What we do know is that the people we would like to talk to then drove off on a motorbike at a dangerous speed into the park, and we think they may have driven it onto the back of a van somewhere and exited the park or nearby area in the van," said one voice that Chuck presumed to be a senior investigating officer.

"Why do you think there may have been a van?" asked the journalist.

"Well, there were a lot of cars on the various main roads exiting the area and so far no witnesses have come forward to report having seen a bike with two men on it. We also had a helicopter out looking for a bike," the officer surmised.

Chuck, sweating in the heat of the car, was no longer listening. Instead he kept seeing the hole in the back of Frazer's head and wondered why the man would have walked that way in the first place, when he lived in the grange?

When he arrived home, the house was empty, so he decided to grab a snooze on the sofa in the lounge until someone came in and woke him up. He often did this and woke up to the distinctive smell of Kim's cooking, which he found comforting. However, this time when he woke, slightly dazed from the heat and exertion of the day, he realised that it was only 8 pm. He felt a strong urge to go back to sleep but hunger dragged him up and to the kitchen. All the lights were off and he was alone. On the fridge was a torn-out piece of paper from the diary Kim's cousin had sent for her birthday, under a Cyprus souvenir magnet. He remembered now that he had walked passed it without reading it.

She was around at her Alpha group in the local church which ran from 7-9 pm every Monday. She had been going for ages and often talked about it, which Chuck had found interesting enough; but as much as he approved of the idea of a theological debate between those of faith and those without, he couldn't help reminding himself that in his line of work there was no space for anything else. He poured himself a glass of water and checked his phone. There were two texts waiting, one from his wife telling him to go to the chip shop for his tea and another from Forsyth, "Heard on TV that the shooters escaped by driving the bike into a van and fucking off?"

Chuck quickly replied: "Don't text me again, you drunken bum." Forsyth read this to mean that Chuck believed that their phones could be or had been compromised and that the subject of Frazer was taboo via text or phone chat until further notice. The two colleagues had been able to understand and read into things that each other said or did from the beginning; this was not rare in police partnerships but even a sudden change in mood or sentence was usually always correctly interpreted, as had just happened now.

Chuck put on a cardigan and walked up onto Portobello High Street to Paolo's fish and chip shop. He ordered a spring roll with chips, which looked like the only thing on offer that was fresh. He had the little Italian woman put plenty of salt on the food and headed back home again with it. A female roller-skater zoomed along the pavement in front of him as he crossed over on to Marlbourgh Street. The warm evening air was slashed by her curly brown hair which cut a breezy perfumed trail behind her and along the pavement. It was too sweet a scent for Chuck's taste; more sickly than sweet, he thought as he walked through it. French perhaps, like Loulou?

"It was the little selection box of miniatures your auntie got one Christmas," a friendly voice suddenly spoke as Chuck tried to remember where he had smelt Loulou before. He smiled and turned, expecting to encounter a friend or family member – he felt that he recognised the comforting voice without quite placing it straight away.

"I think it had Anais Anais in the little bottle with the flowers, and of course Loulou in the little blue bottle which you were trying to place – do you remember that Christmas?"

"Who are you?" Chuck was a bit taken aback and quickly looked around him to see if someone he knew was with this guy; he saw no one else, though. Nervousness set in and he eyeballed the man to explore his face, searching for a threat.

"Who the fuck are you pal, and how do you know these things?"

The mysterious man stared a moment, before waving his right hand in front of his own chest in the way a window cleaner might wipe a small glass panel. The instant he did so, Chuck became relaxed and comfortable with the man's presence. This impressive change in sensibility was not lost on Chuck, who took a deep breath in contemplation.

"I'll tell you everything, Chuck but please don't swear at me or I may have to hurt you," the man promised.

Chuck felt the warning hit home directly within his inner soul, and immediately understood that he should not doubt for one second that this individual could and would back up the threat. Yet additionally he sensed that the stranger was naturally compassionate and did not wish to carry out his threat unless forced to do so.

"I apologise for swearing, but this is surreal; surely you see that. Just don't threaten me pal, can you... well, can you tell me who you are?" he asked before looking up at his neighbours' windows to see if anyone was witnessing this. He then stared at the man again. He was around 6 ft. tall, with soft brown hair and friendly brown eyes. He was wearing simple enough clothes: jeans, trainers and a thin black fleece, but he looked well-built, fit, handsome, and even cool.

"Good," smiled the man. "I know that I shall need to convince you of who I am, but I prefer not to beat about the bush. So let us walk now, Chuck; past your house and down to the beach for a chat. Before long, we can both be on our way." He nodded to indicate that Chuck should trust him, then led the way confidently.

"You can eat as we walk my friend, for I despise seeing food being wasted," he said, just as Chuck was thinking of chucking his food in the nearest wheelie bin.

"Are you telepathic?" he asked the man.

"Yes, but I consider it an outdated and uncouth practice," the man replied without speaking.

"Uncouth?" Chuck then attempted to ask without using his tongue and the angel nodded.

"By always doing, thinking and speaking righteously, there is no need. If there is no need, then the process is, like the Latin tongue, dead. Yet it is still used for mischief and as a tool to be used against someone or something by a few, and thus it is vulgar," the angel explained as the stroll became a march.

This all impressed Chuck greatly and his face lit up as the pace quickened. He had just communicated telepathically too, and he was excited.

"See, I just explained all that to you but you choose instead to be impressed and pleased that you can practice reaching out, regardless of me telling you that it is nothing of worth. That is your selfish side controlling your wisdom. Sadly, this has been the story of your species so far, young man," the angel sighed.

"Oh well, excuse me for being overwhelmed – but it is not every day that I meet a random and telepathic stranger. Who are you, then? What's your name?" he asked as they walked shoulder-to-shoulder towards the promenade.

"Can you guess first, just out of curiosity?"

"Are you some kind of magician, or something to do with what I heard a dead man talk about today at a police station?" Chuck played along.

"Ah, disappointing. No, young Chuck; you are quite wrong, for if I were one of Lionel Frazer's puppet masters, those chips you're carrying would be lying on the ground covered in your blood instead of ketchup," he suggested calmly. Then Chuck saw a bright yellow light flash across his vision and a clear image of himself face down on the pavement beside a red Fiat; the spring roll and chips fallen everywhere, while a slow pool of blood formed under his head on the pavement. The yellow flash was repeated and he found himself gazing into the angel's face.

"They do not know anything about you yet, Chuck, so do not despair. I, however, do." As he spoke these words he had put the brakes on, turned back to speak, but now continued walking again at a somewhat slower pace. Chuck didn't speak and soon they arrived at the promenade railing. Chuck remained silent, but he felt so drawn to this man that he hadn't noticed that he had been eating his chips. The angel descended some steps down onto the beach and walked out towards the calm evening sea where two canoes were passing on their way towards Leith.

Chuck offered the stranger a chip and to his surprise the man accepted, took one then threw it up in the air, where it was instantly caught by a magpie, which flew off into a nearby garden.

"A magpie," smiled the man. "Scavenging in the territory of the overly hysterical gulls for any scraps of food left by men," he chuckled. "Now there is bravery for you Chuck, and their situation is somewhat similar to yours." He looked at Chuck as he spoke with a gentle yet anxious expression,

"For you too are soon to be surrounded by enemies, like the magpie is," he warned.

"But like with the magpie, I am here to help you out," he winked – this felt reassuring and calming to Chuck.

"Yes, but who on earth are you, then?" he gasped, with the heavy food turning in his belly at the sudden worry over what this character wanted from him. "You said you'd explain?" he asked again softly, whilst munching away on a spring roll through a new fear of wasting any food.

The man smiled. As he did so, his eyes lit up like candles and projected a warming glow, which Chuck felt engulf his whole being like warmth after a bitterly cold hike on a winter's day.

"I am an angel, Chuck, and I have been commanded to present myself to you here tonight and to talk to you about certain matters." With these words, he gently put a pale, smooth hand upon Chuck's shoulder and smiled at him so warmly that Chuck felt the need to cry, then did so. Ever so softly the angel hugged him and it was as if all the weight in the world had been lifted from Chuck's shoulders. He instantly stopped weeping and began to smile with joy instead.

"I feel it," he admitted to the angel, and dropped his chips.

"Yes, but let us dispose of any remaining doubts quickly, Chuck," the Angel smiled and lightly patted him on the shoulder.

"Well can you show me some other evidence without scaring me? Also, don't worry, the gulls will get the chips." Chuck gamely pointed out as he dropped his food.

"What you feel is the holy spirit. It radiates through me and is present now because my boss chooses it to be," the angel explained whilst looking out at the still sea and the Fife coastline beyond.

"God?"

"Well done! You are improving already." The angel turned and smiled, and as he did so, Chuck noticed that he had white teeth and pink gums, like all men. The angel spoke in the calmest manner, though; Chuck had never come across such a style of expression before in anyone. He realised he was staring but it was like looking at fire, something holding the eye longer than normal while the cornea soaks up the light.

"Anyway, I have thought of the best way to prove to you that I am an angel of heaven sent to talk to you," the angel paused a moment as if thinking, then turned back again.

"You have heard of Jesus' mother Mary being informed by the Arch-Angel that she would give birth to a child?" There was sarcasm in the tone, yet humour in the facial expression. Chuck thought he was beautifully baby-faced and young looking, while also being sure that the angel must be very old in reality.

"What am I on about, reality? This is utterly insane," he shook his head in more disbelief now.

"Answer the question, Chuck," the angel urged. Chuck felt such warmth toward this creature that he simply nodded to indicate that he had heard the nativity story.

"Gabriel was the messenger, I think?" he said softly now.

The angel's face beamed at that knowledge, and nodded for Chuck to walk with him along the beach a while. There were one or two bonfires dotted around and a few dog walkers, but the beach was quieter than the famous old promenade with its many lovers and skateboarders.

"Don't be scared – just trust me," the angel said softly, and Chuck not only believed him, he was not alarmed by this instruction either. After all, any time someone had said something along those lines in the past, it usually meant doing something he instinctively wouldn't normally want to try. This time, the angel suddenly placed his wrists under Chuck's armpits and firmly carried him up, off the sand, at an approximate speed of 140 miles per hour into the sky. He then stopped and adjusted his grip while they just floated there, at a height somewhere just above the roofs of the 5-floor Victorian tenement blocks which ran along the promenade.

Chuck felt butterflies exploding in his stomach at the sudden lift off, but now he found himself dangling in the cooler air above the beach. He thought he might piss himself. He had had vertigo since he was a child. The current situation was awkwardly similar to a childhood fairground scare, with the familiar sound of the gulls and the smell of the sea. Yet the fact that he was only secured by the grip of an alleged angel weakened his bladder more.

"What are you doing? No, God, I'm sorry," he managed to get out just before the angel swung to their immediate right in a manoeuvre that would have placed a helicopter out of control. Chuck could hear the angel laughing but he did not speak; instead he scrunched his eyes up and actually prayed to God to get through this unscathed. At one insane moment, he dared to look down. The dark blue sea below, with tiny white surf patterns dotted across its surface, was like something out of a Van Gogh painting; they had obviously climbed higher and the view below was like that seen from an aeroplane window. A few seconds later, they began a slow descent onto what appeared to be a large cruise ship at the mouth of the Forth estuary.

"Oh my god, what the hell?" Chuck mouthed as the angel released him on deck, but he was in cold and in shock, and in need of a second to grasp what had just happened. Fear began to set in and he stood shaking, as if subjected to extreme cold. The angel had taken him to the corner of a lower deck of a ship of some kind, where they now stood completely unseen by the crew, beside a wooden door and an old clock on a green metal wall.

"Are you convinced now?" the angel asked. Chuck saw the warm and essential compassion in his eyes and knew he was caring and good.

"Yes of course, and please... I'm sorry I doubted... please don't do that again," Chuck continued to shiver until the angel waved his hand again and appeared to dispatch a warming calmness which descended upon Chuck's body and mind and instantly relaxed him.

"And that is the Holy Spirit again," the angel smiled.

"Thank you," Chuck nodded, relieved to have calmed down; though he instinctively took a step back and leaned against the wall, where he let out a great sigh of astonishment.

"So, is more evidence required, Chuck?" the angel wanted to know.

"Well, no, Sir," Chuck was mentally terrified of the power he had just witnessed and was beginning to focus now on exactly what this entity wanted from him.

"We're not going back the same way we came, are we?"

"Yes, unless you want to end up in Norway with no passport or money and a lot of explaining to do?" smiled the angel. His face was remarkable and kind. He was beautiful too, and because he was now deliberately adopting a gentle pose, Chuck could look into the indefinable eyes for a moment; eyes which sent out a calmness and tranquillity that Chuck's fear could not breach.

"Are you my guardian angel?" he guessed.

"No, but would you like to meet him?" came the amused reply.

"Ok?" Chuck wasn't sure again and cringed slightly in anticipation but suddenly he sensed that there was another man standing to his side beside him. This guy was different; he had green eyes and blonde hair tied back into a ponytail. He was somewhat older-looking than the first angel.

"This is him," smiled the first angel.

"Hello Chuck. I'm quite honoured to meet you this way, as I have been around you since you arrived in this world," the guardian angel said in a similarly soft, and familiar, yet unidentifiable accent.

"Hello, I'm Charles Kean," Chuck whispered, then slowly reached his hand out as if being told at gunpoint to answer a phone 'slowly'. The two angels looked at each other and smiled at this gesture. Then, in an instant, the guardian angel was gone. Chuck didn't see him leave, because he had looked out to sea again, as if to confirm that this was actually happening and that he had not accidently been given an LSD mushroom supper from the fish & chip shop.

"Let us return now, Chuck," the angel said, before gently taking hold of him and smiling warmly to reassure that all would be well.

"I shall move faster this time as I wish to talk to you before you need to go home," the angel warned, before they rose into the cold and icy sky again, then slowly descended onto the beach seconds later and with much tummy butterflies. It had taken them only a moment to return, with Chuck holding on like an infant langur monkey. Now they were firmly on the beach again and this time, they were alone without anyone looking at them. Chuck stood shivering on the sand, trying to comprehend the speed he had just been propelled at. Again, the angel waved his hand to relax him, and the effect was instant.

"How do I know you're not one of those Nephilim things that Frazer talked about?" Chuck asked once he had regained his breath and composure.

"Because there are none of those left, just fanatical disciples of hell with dark magical energies; don't you read the Bible at all?" the angel inquired curiously.

"Well… I haven't in a…"

"It is on the top bookshelf at home, so why not?"

"OK, fair enough; I had lost my faith, as you probably already know," Chuck admitted somewhat wearily. The angel smiled and looked at him in the way a brother or father might.

"Will that change now?" he asked.

"Yes, but I need to ask you something," pleaded Chuck.

"Stop trying to find answers and let me tell you what you need to know. That has always been the problem with your species," the angel said, while looking out to sea again.

"Do you expect me not to ask anything?" gasped Chuck.

The angel turned back and smiled, "You can call me Dai; that was your first question, was it not?"

"Is that your real name?" Chuck was immediately unsure as to why he had asked this.

"I will answer a couple of questions before I leave and you can ask me more when we meet again tomorrow," Dai suggested, and Chuck nodded in agreement.

"Chuck, you stumbled into a nest of vipers when you met Lionel Frazer earlier today, and that is why I am commanded to talk to you about certain things. Tonight is just the introduction for us, and so far you have responded well," the angel told him.

"What Frazer told you was correct, but it goes much deeper than that," he warned.

"Were you at the interview?" Chuck wanted to know.

"No; let's just say I read the minutes, but don't ask questions Chuck. I shall tell you when you can ask me things, understand?"

Chuck mouthed his assent, then looked down the promenade to see if anyone else was watching, a group of teenage girls walked by without as much as a glance in their direction.

"They won't notice us, Chuck, it is just us here until I say otherwise," Dai assured.

"Remember that story about your great-grandfather at the Somme?" he then asked.

"Yes... I...? Well, yes," Chuck nodded now, refusing to be surprised any longer.

"His bloodline ties this Frazer situation into your life and the Lord, your God, has authorised myself and others to advise and protect you," Dai revealed.

"What does the Lord want from me?" Chuck was in a daze at all this.

"To anticipate the moves of the enemy and to devise and direct the counter measures."

"But how can..." The daze did not dull Chuck's sense of being unqualified for the position.

"Like I said, you can ask me things when it is time, but all you need to know at the moment is that you are blessed by God, Charles Kean, and that regardless of the fact that you face great danger and huge challenges ahead on earth, you are on a mission that will be supported by angels." Dai cut him off as he was about to interject.

"You must prepare yourself to lead your department in the right direction regarding all of this Fraser stuff, but we shall discuss this after your meeting tomorrow. Don't worry about Sharon Adams; you can trust her and she is waiting for you to lead by putting forward a realistic plan of action. Rest assured too that your boss Colin Wong is not your enemy, at least he has not been to date; I cannot promise that that situation will not change though," Dai said as he raised a finger knowingly.

"They might infiltrate our squad, you know?" Chuck protested. Again, he was not sure why he was arguing, except that he was scared of working for angels or God.

"Yes, fair point, but it is all about character and leadership. You do not want to accept this divine quest because you're scared that you're not competent, I know. Yet, ask yourself why on earth you have been chosen by us? Because we know that you can provide the cunning and leadership for this particular task," insisted Dai.

"They shafted me before career-wise, Dai, and could take me right out of the game with a flick of their finger, if they're powerful enough."

"Yes, they did, and it was my boss who stopped them eating you up; look where you are now? A DI in the Druggies with security, luxuries and authority. You got that for a reason Chuck, because of your good soul and your bloodline."

"Bloodline?"

"No matter. Frazer was correct about the things he told you, the pollution of civil society. This systematic poison within society must be confronted, Chuck, and you have been chosen to help out," urged Dai.

"Why me? Don't you know that I'm up to my neck in stuff at work as it is?" Chuck wanted to know.

"Since when did the affairs of the Drug Squad take precedence over the affairs of God?" Dai calmly asked him.

"Well, why does God allow this to be so, then? I just don't get it," Chuck knew his tone was stubborn, and wished he had not been, but Dai was not angry at this persistent questioning. On the contrary, he recognised this legitimate question and nodded.

"The physical sensors of men are unable to see or comprehend the higher dimensions and the entities who operate within. Men only see a three-dimensional universe, so it is perfectly normal that you cannot understand."

"But surely, fundamental to any solution is an understanding of the issue?" argued Chuck.

"It is what it is, Chuck. I'm not going to discuss the rules with you now, or at any point in the future. It is like a dog; a dog must trust its master not to leave broken glass in the garden and to observe the traffic, otherwise it is a disaster waiting to happen," Dai told him firmly.

"Perhaps that is why people lost faith, I think," Chuck thought but Dai merely smiled at him in response.

"Yet the alternative is quite horrendous, I assure you," guaranteed Dai.

Chuck wanted to hug him for some reason and to laugh and to ask many more questions, but knew this was a serious and momentous situation that would not only change his life but potentially his afterlife, too.

"Now that we have met and you have been given a little understanding of the actuality of the laws within this cosmos, I am telling you that you have been selected to assist us in a mission." Dai put an arm around Chuck's shoulders and the soothing relaxation was both instant and assuring. "And to answer your question about why you, well your bloodline is known to us as one which produces a strong moral code, bravery, astuteness, and a philanthropic tendency that we appreciate," smiled Dai.

Chuck nodded. He just knew that the angel was to be trusted and relied upon.

"A mission that you will soon understand, but first you must go home and come to terms with your experience tonight, Chuck. It won't be easy – it will be confusing and you will doubt it at times. You could be up all night pondering this, but try to sleep and tomorrow we shall talk again after your meeting with DSI Wong. There, you will of course argue for a secret investigation into the claims recently made by Frazer."

"I was doing that anyway, Dai," promised Chuck.

"That is why it must be you Chuck," beamed Dai knowingly.

"Am I allowed to discuss it with Kim?" Chuck asked.

"No, not yet Chuck, don't tell a soul or we shall end up like Lot," chuckled the angel, whose laughter was both infectious and astounding.

"Who's Lot?" laughed Chuck.

"Oh, old Lot, you can find him in your Bible; he was a decent enough chap I think. I met him once or twice and found him to be quite unselfish. His wife, however… well, best left unsaid," said Dai thoughtfully.

"Kim's a good person," insisted Chuck.

"I know, and that is becoming a rare thing in a world of greed and exploitation, but please do as you're told and listen," Dai replied.

They stood face to face smiling at each other, and Chuck sensed that the meeting was ending.

"OK, I said earlier that you can have two quick questions," Dai nodded whilst slowly started taking a step backwards towards the promenade.

"Fine. Can you show me the face of Jesus Christ?"

"Have you seen a picture of the shroud of Turin?" Dai sharply replied.

Chuck sighed by means of a protest but nodded that he had. "Is that really him?"

Dai nodded, "Yep, they even tried cloning it and creating an abomination, but they failed."

"OK, well, next question: when you said you would hurt me at the start if I continued swearing, what would you have done to me and why would an angel hurt a man?" Chuck asked.

"That is two questions so I will answer the first one only. I would have given you a 24-hour migraine that no drugs could numb, then relieved you of it myself and tried talking to you again." Dai winked, turned, and casually walked away.

Chuck watched him go, surprised at the abrupt ending to the conversation, and turned in the other direction, walking back up to the promenade. He looked back a couple of times without breaking his stride, but there was no sign of Dai. During the rest of the walk home he went over everything again and again and wondered where his guardian angel was; was he with him now?

"What did you do for tea?" Kim asked as he appeared in the kitchen, where she was taking bedding out of the washing machine to hang outside overnight.

"Never mind all that Kim, have you ever heard of Lot?" he asked, as he swiftly moved towards his book cabinet.

Five

"Talent wins games, but teamwork and intelligence win championships"

Michael Jordan

Kim sleepily sensed him getting into bed; it was late. She opened her eyes and stayed awake until she heard him snoring, before drifting off again.

"What time did you come to bed, dear?" she asked as she buttered toast in the morning. Chuck, however, was sitting at the table in his boxer shorts, sipping coffee and reading the Bible.

"I don't know; around five-ish, maybe," he replied as he dragged himself from the book, then quickly returned to it again.

Kim said nothing for a moment while she took his egg and toast over to him. He was spooked by something and engrossed in the Bible, which was very unlike him.

"What's this about, then?" she said in a 'don't bullshit me' tone as she sat down to her cereal.

"It's nothing, just a lead at work which may also give me an insight into that story about my great-grandfather at the Somme." He was sharp enough to give her a hare to chase, which she bought instantly.

"Wow, did someone mention him?" She was even more interested now, so he put the book down and seasoned his eggs.

"No, it's more like a similar scenario which someone is claiming, with Biblical ties."

He disliked lying to her, but having read all about Lot and his wife throughout the night, he reckoned he had little choice: the trick was to divert her suspicions and then drop the subject. The back door was open and despite it being only 11 am, Chuck could already feel the heat of the day coming in and touching his feet. The washing would be dry, he would get up and bring it in if she did not back off, he mused.

"I think I'm going to just buy a new car, Kim," he said, trying another tack.

"Because of the air-con?"

"Well, look at the sun outside; I feel like I'm going to faint sitting in the endless bloody traffic jams every day." He shook his head while he chewed his food.

"I end up getting cranky with other drivers as well as at work," he said, inviting her to latch onto the carrot.

"Well, you are moody right enough, but the job contributes to that too, I'd say."

"Yes, obviously, but regardless, I'm fed up handing the car in to get the job done, paying for it and it still needing more work. In the end that will cost us more than the bloody car itself," he smiled.

Kim nodded. "I guess we all get crankier with age," she smiled back.

"Anyway, I'm away with my group, what time will you be home?" she asked as she left her half empty bowl, leaned over, kissed him on the lips and then put on her sunglasses.

"Not sure; I have stuff going on. I'll text you if I'm wanting supper," he replied.

She nodded, slung a mint sporty bag over her shoulder and left via the back garden with a little wave. She had recently begun an all-female swim group at Portobello's old Victorian baths and had made some new friends, who would be waiting on the little wall outside for her by now.

Chuck had joked once that they would all be perving like "Manhattan hags at all the talent on the beach" as they walked along to the baths. Kim didn't go via the promenade though, and told him this with a wry grin, but he still teased her about it from time to time.

Chuck was tired; it had been a long night and the light was uncomfortable. He had read Genesis Chapters 11-14 and then 19 throughout the night. The angel had mentioned Lot's wife from the Bible, and although Chuck knew a bit of that story, his memory had been rusty; he wanted to explore Lot and understand how this had been relevant to Kim.

He now understood and for the first time in his life, he truly feared God's long reach. The thought of Kim turning into a pillar of salt was perhaps amusing in jest, but had this angel threatened her in the same way as he might have threatened Lot way back then? He even said that he had met Lot, didn't he? Chuck was very tired, but there was no way he could go back to sleep, as his mind was racing. He wondered if the angel was in the house with him. Could he make himself invisible? If so, could he be watching as Chuck went for the crap which he now needed? Oh, this was intolerable. He groaned, closed his eyes and rested his head in his arms on the table for a moment.

Slowly, he pictured the people who would soon be passing by the house with their beach towels and inflatable lilos. He remembered doing the same on trips to Portobello as a kid. He would swim out into the waves on an inflated inner tyre tube and let himself be washed back onto the beach with the other boys. He was almost asleep now as he recalled the warmer turquoise waves of Mallorca. He would float so still on them, without sinking, that he sometimes fell asleep under the sun. He dreamed that the water rose up and fell back down, but that he floated in harmony with it until he seemed to be caught on something. He raised his head to see what it was, and found himself caught within a net. Immediately, he was being pulled out of the blissful slumber by a faint, dark face which was not a face; it seemed like a faint, swollen face but only an imprint of a man's face. He realised that what he saw before him was the Turin Shroud, talking. Other men were pulling Chuck upwards in the net, and with great effort too. "Come, follow me and I will send you out to fish for people," said the voice from the shroud.

Suddenly there was a touch on his arm, and Chuck awoke sharply to the heat of the sun. He got up and closed the kitchen door to try to cool the room down, then he made some fresh coffee, which he took with him into a cold shower. He sent Forsyth a text while dressing in a suit and tie for his meeting with Wong. When he drove over to pick his DS up 30 minutes later at Newhaven, the sweat had begun to trickle down his temple again due to the lack of air-con in the Volvo. At a traffic light, he loosened his tie, chucked his coat in the back and rolled up his sleeves.

The Drug Squad office was relatively quiet when they arrived with half the duty shift at lunch and only two DCs present, typing up reports. Sharon Adams was in the briefing room, talking to Gav Caine about putting other investigations on hold until her and Chuck had discussed both targets and the use of the squad with the DSI after lunch. Gav Caine appeared to sense that something was brewing, as the squad began swinging away from active operations.

"It's alright, Gav," Chuck said as he and Forsyth entered. "Cairns is still a priority but the DSI wants to talk first before we strike. So, don't worry, we should fill everyone in before the end of the day," he assured.

Caine left the room with a nod and headed off for lunch himself. "Shall we get that coffee then, Chuck?" suggested Adams.

The pair of them were soon sitting, supping lattes with double espressos in them, in an empty room. They had been sleeping less over the last few days, and both were nervous and somewhat jittery.

"Personally, I think if Wong tells us to forget it then we arrange our own wee unofficial investigation into Frazer's claims," she declared.

Chuck nodded, forced a smile and raised his cup at her. "Agreed," he said. He was still thinking about the face of Christ on the shroud which he had dreamed of earlier. He had Googled it after a few hours spent reading the Bible; perhaps that was why he had dreamed of the image? One thing was for sure, just like the song; every move he made was being watched.

Adams seemed pleased. "I'm glad you agree, as it will take both of us to make it happen, and someone might grass us anyway," she considered as she sipped her milky caffeine.

"He will back us, Sharon; we just need to press a good argument in his face now and let God do the rest," he found himself saying what he believed out loud.

"Since when has God given a toss, Chuck?" Adams sighed at him reflectively, but quite without any contempt, he believed.

He didn't reply. Who the hell did he think he was if he thought he could argue God's corner? No, he couldn't even contemplate trying, yet he was bursting to tell someone about everything he had witnessed. Still, he had no choice but to drag his concentration back to the job at hand.

"Anyway, I think you're right, I'm sure he will want to do something about this without involving anyone else," she pointed out.

"Even when it involves the sexual abuse and murder of kids?" Chuck suddenly raised an eyebrow at her, despite having been encouraged by her optimism. In general, Chuck felt that he needed to trust Adams' judgement, and he did. If he had not, he would have carried on regardless and argued the case himself to the DSI, because the angel had told him to.

Adams looked down and gave a slow nod while swallowing a mouthful of coffee. She took a deep breath before replying, "Particularly because of the allegation about the kids; yes, I think so." She nodded again in belief that Wong was a good man and not yet anyone's puppet.

They talked further about how the squad could even try to investigate Frazer's claims without either Frazer or any evidence other than total hearsay. They agreed that proving Frazer correct might well be a draining process and weaken the impact the squad had on the drugs industry. When the time came, they talked as they walked along together to the DSI's office, both unsure of how the squad could handle this matter adequately.

Wong rarely frequented the building, what with his ongoing summer lectures at the Police Academy in Tulliallan, but the firm Lutonian accent which replied "Enter!" after Chuck's friendly, light knock on the door, confirmed his presence today.

They went in, ladies first. Wong sat at his desk using a small silver laptop, the typing ceased.

"Right, in you come guys, sit down and tell me your thoughts on this intel, off the record."

The office itself was small and had nothing indicating any kind of connection with its occupant. A small cactus plant and a fan sat on top of typically grey filing cabinets, and the whole effect was one of complete anonymity. Chuck thought Wong seemed a little discomfited, but that could be down to any manner of reasons; starting with whatever he was working on the laptop.

"It's like I said yesterday, guv," Adams began. "We can't just turn our backs on this type of allegation." She pleaded with her eyes widened, and Wong grinned at her because he fancied her, like everyone else. He closed his computer and spoke quietly.

"Right. I thought about this overnight, and during the drive here today." He raised his right hand. "So, here is where I am at with this Frazer intel, guys. I agree it cannot be discarded. The question is, can we investigate it?" he asked the ceiling as he leaned back in his chair. "Could we spare the time and manpower or should the intel go to CID, or Special Branch even?"

Chuck listened intently, feeling tension throughout his being as he waited to hear more. Wong dragging it out longer by pausing in thought a moment before continuing.

"And, if we do keep it to ourselves for a short interval to gather our bearings and sniff around in the hope of increasing the intelligence we have, which could potentially just turn out to be the cover story of a desperate man in Lionel Frazer; well that would leave us wide open to attack," Wong reasoned.

"Fact is, Frazer has told you that there are top brass officers involved in this thing, so that is why none of us are surprised by what I have just said, and also why I am going to move this on now and ask you both for your thoughts." He looked directly at Chuck and nodded to him to speak.

"We can only pursue evidence as far as we are able to in a clandestine way, and hope for the best... And if we get nowhere sir, as may happen given the circumstances, at least our consciences will be clear – particularly in this time of scandals like the Jimmy Saville one."

Chuck subtly pressed the case. Wong raised an eyebrow at his cockiness; he hadn't seen that one coming. Yet, after then listening to Adams, who concurred with Chuck, he agreed and stated that he was pleased his two leading officers wanted to have a sniff at it.

117

"Right guys, let's be clear," he spoke up again, "If other officers are involved, and we must assume for now that they are, anything you do must be deniable, unless there is decent evidence for me to hit my boss with when he comes calling," he pointed out.

Both Adams and Chuck nodded eagerly like school kids being offered a day out to the zoo. Chuck relaxed slightly and found himself liking Wong due to his apparently clean demeanour.

"You'll have to keep the squad's day-to-day stuff separate. Those who are going to be involved must not get in the sight of the murder squad assigned to Frazer's murder," he warned them with a Clint Eastwood stare down the barrel of his pointing finger.

Both remained silent, just nodding back, because this couldn't have gone any better as far as they were concerned. Sure, it looked like Wong was the type of guy for whom self-preservation was the strongest instinct, but at heart he was clearly a decent copper who didn't want to cross the good ol' boy brigade, while at the same time being prepared to go fishing for evidence to take the bastards down with.

"Now, as you are both well aware," he continued sternly, "I report on squad business only to the Assistant Chief Constable. He in turn reports on me, not necessary the squad itself, to the Deputy Chief Constable. I won't forgive being made to look like the height of nonsense, so don't ever put me in that position," he firmly warned them.

"I report to him weekly in person and am due to meet him tomorrow for lunch at the academy," he added.

"By the time I meet him next week, you will either have established a bloody strong lead or you will bin it and we shall move on without mentioning it again, is that understood?" he demanded.

"That's fine sir, we'll give it our best go within the timeframe," Adams assured with a grin the size of a Cheshire cat's.

"Just remember, the whole process is deniable and if anyone makes drama or gets caught hiding in the bushes of my boss' home with a camera etc. without evidence, they are going to be back in uniform, walking the beat out in the southern sticks in a place like Bonnyrigg or Dalkeith," Wong added with an almost cartoonish seriousness and some strange neck manoeuvres, which wouldn't have seemed out of place on a hen.

Chuck nodded and went on to explain how the squad would select a team to look at certain targets under the guise of a fictional narcotics investigation. This met with Wong's approval, as what he feared most was having to deny to anyone that the druggies were secretly investigating outwith their particular remit. This plan of Chuck's also indicated some logical planning. Wong desired to remove vermin from society, but he certainly couldn't authorise an official investigation and unless evidence was available, he felt he could not authorise more than a week of unofficial investigation; in order to manage the risk involved.

"Right, well, careful how you go, people, and touch base with me as soon as you get anywhere on this. Otherwise, good luck and I'll see you both back here in my office at the same time next week, OK?"

"Yes, sir," nodded Chuck. Adams smiled while handing Wong a file on the squad's activities over the previous 7 days, minus anything regarding Lionel Frazer.

In the corridor, Chuck high-fived his counterpart and decided that he would offer to lead the team to hunt down the bastards. Adams only agreed because she knew she would do a much better job than him of holding the fort 24 hours a day in his absence.

"Fuck knows what we will do if another job comes in, as I have too much on as it is; I take it you are going to pass me some of your stuff too, now?" she gave him a grave look.

"Only the Snooker hall thing that has a deadline on Thursday," he said gently.

Adams sighed despondently as she opened the squad office door, her elation at the off-book investigation suddenly evaporating as she thought of the need to keep everything else going in the meantime.

"What needs to be done on it?"

"It's all in the file, Sharon. I've done it all; you'll just have to finish the report I dictated and get a statement; then fire it up to the Fiscal by Thursday."

They walked silently through the office to their small shared office at the end. "Busy old me while you get to be the Milk Tray advert guy," she whispered as she held the door open for him. Once inside, they could talk freely again.

"So, my cover is that I'm investigating Frazer for claiming to buy cocaine from a Nigerian group in Manchester," Chuck said.

"Targets?" she asked curiously.

"Initially the two girls who saw the shooters, and then a look at who is on the murder squad," he suggested.

Adams nodded, but looked concerned. "Mind, you and Chris were spotted by CID in the kill zone, so be careful there, Chuck. If you go out too deep, the DSI will cut the rope, yeh?" She looked like his mother used to when warning him to eat his greens.

"I know. I'll need Chris, Joe and Debbie," he said.

"You can't have Debs; she'll have to stand in for Chris here, and besides, you're over-using her as the honey trap." She shook her head.

"Gav, then, and get that Jamie the photographer bloke on 24-hour stand-by in case I need him."

"There will be no overtime money unless you come up with something, so take it easy, Chuck, and keep me posted regularly," she urged.

"I get that, right that's me away for a week on this, you might see me; you might not, but I'll phone you every day," he said, standing up again.

"Right, good luck and like I said, be careful."

"I will... Listen, can you do me a favour and find out why Frazer walked all that way round to Pollock Halls, without hailing a taxi sooner?" he asked.

"Is it a busy place for taxis, St Leonards?"

"Very, and why walk? Was he expecting a pick up?" he thought aloud.

"I'll look into whether his wallet or bank cards were released with him or not."

"The Sheep's Heid," he thought out again.

"Eh?" she was confused now.

"Was that an inn he frequented? Or where else could he have been headed? It's deep in the park, Sharon," he smiled.

"OK...," she said slowly.

"We need to know why he walked that way in dress shoes instead of jumping a taxi home to get cleaned up," Chuck considered this further. "Right, tell those three to meet me in Speirs Bar in ten minutes," he gave her a cheeky, confident wink as he left.

"I'll contact you on a clean number later today, so log it," she whispered.

Six

"Instinct is a marvellous thing. It can neither be explained nor ignored"
Agatha Christie

When Gav Caine entered Speirs Bar, he clocked Chuck sitting in a corner sipping a pint of Irn Bru, and reading a notebook. "Sit down, Gav; do you want a pint of juice?" he asked. Gav asked for a fresh orange and lemonade and wondered again, as he had throughout the drive over, what exactly was going on. When Chuck returned with his drink, he sat down and proceeded to enlighten him about it all.

"Well, it was clear something was up, guv, but I really couldn't have made this up if I tried," Caine chuckled as he came to terms with the insanity of it. Illuminati, potential police top brass, and secret cabals who could all be after us in due course?

"Yep. It's some game we find ourselves in here, Gav and it may get messy, but are you happy to proceed?" Chuck wanted to know.

"100%, guv but if it's going to be silly hours for the next week I'm wanting overtime if we ever find the fuckers." Caine confirmed cheerily.

Chuck nodded and shook his hand, "Well look, we'll give it our best shot and if we fail miserably, I'll take the four of us out for a slap up meal instead," he promised.

Soon, Joe and Forsyth arrived and two more pints of juice were purchased.

"Right, boys, Gav's been briefed. The four of us are on a deniable investigation that will run almost 24/7 for the next week," explained Chuck.

"Can I propose that we all get some pay-as-you go mobile phones, registered in bullshit names of course, and use these as our coms?" Forsyth suggested.

Chuck looked sharply at him, "If you just let me finish, you'll find that I'm going to send you to do just that in a minute Chris," he snapped jokingly.

"Sorry guv."

"That's the problem with us blokes, too eager to ask questions and make suggestions rather than listening for five minutes," Chuck said. This fucking angelic stuff was affecting him, he realised with a smile, before continuing the briefing.

"Now, Gav and Joe, you two go buy phones and sort out your good ladies, then turn up here at 7 pm to shadow him all night," Chuck handed Gav a bit of paper from his notepad with the following scrawled on it:

'Sinclair Ellis-Naylor, 12 Whitehouse Road, Barnton.'

"Who is it, guv?" asked Joe while he stretched his neck to see.

"Frazer's partner in the firm of Nairn Archibald, and the main man now, obviously," said Chuck.

"Whitehouse Road? Weren't they the big money properties where the Hearts owner lived? What's his name again?" Joe grabbed his own curly mane in frustration with his fingers and pulled slightly as he tried to recall.

"Yes, yes, Wallace Mercer lived nearby back in the day, I think," Forsyth grinned as he placed a hand on Chuck's shoulder, "But the older DI here from Edinburgh could correct me," he said, and they all laughed; which released the edginess that each of them felt.

Chuck thought the origins of his own apprehension were down to his experience with Dai. He couldn't stop himself from peering at the faces of car drivers, or at people sat on packed buses, and wondering if any of them were angels now. Even here in the pub, he wondered if the 'enemies' Dai had mentioned were sitting around him drinking too?

"Anyway, there will be support at base through Sharon only, so don't mention this to anyone. Get new phones now, keep the receipts and we can all exchange numbers at Gamekeepers Road, around the corner from Whitehouse Road, at 19.00 hours precisely," he concluded. Each man also had a two-way radio to keep the team in contact with each other.

"Don't use coms unless I say so: we'll just use the phones, right?" Forsyth warned.

"We could look into why Frazer was bailed and why the fuck he was walking into the Queen's Park when he lived in the opposite direction in the Grange, guv?" Forsyth suggested.

"Sharon's checking something out there, and I'm going to give her our new numbers later" he winked. "Under the circumstances – if what Frazer said was true – there could be all sort of evil observing us, so don't talk shop to each other unless you're on the new blowers," Chuck emphasised.

"Right, let's get moving, and we'll see you two with your new phones later."

Gav and Joe nodded and drank up. Gav did look particularly confused though, but gave one of his mock army salutes which confirmed to Chuck that he had chosen the best team possible for this mission.

Chuck and Forsyth then left and got in the Volvo outside.

"Right, let's go talk to the two birds whose address we took at the murder scene. Then we can pick up phones at Argos, and nip home before meeting those two at seven," Chuck handed Forsyth his notebook.

Forsyth flicked through until he found where Chuck had written down:

"Valerie Erskine and Poppy Eastwood, 8/5 West Preston Street, guv," Forsyth grinned at the names. "Sound like typical yahs[7]," he said, trumpeting an upper crust Edinburgh burr.

"They were visiting a younger sister in her first year, who resides on campus, but they are fourth year honours students, apparently," Chuck mentioned as they slugged on in traffic at Inverleith Row.

"Meaning?" Forsyth didn't get it. He was never sure with Chuck whether a point was being made or not.

"Well, you know, by third year they want autonomy, don't they. So, they team up and get party flats instead of having to endure campus rules," explained Chuck.

"Right, and then struggle to keep the flats running after graduation due to everyone fucking off out the country to get jobs, but hey, are you saying you reckon those two are dykes?" grinned Forsyth.

Chuck laughed, "No idea Chrissy, but let's pay them a wee visit."

The rush hour had begun and would worsen soon; it took them half an hour to cover the 3 miles there. The car was sweltering again and Chuck could feel the sweat trickle through his shirt. Outside, the SNP and SLP were both highly visible throughout, with supporters of both parties everywhere campaigning for independence. There was no sign of people or vehicles trumpeting on behalf of the Tories or Labour, but they did notice a small gathering of Green Party people handing out fliers on Hanover Street.

"Greens jumping on the nationalist bandwagon, eh?" said Forsyth disappointedly.

"They see how the closet Nazis have all come out in support of independence through the mask of the SLP and thought, yeah, an

---

[7] 'Yahs' being the plural. The term possibly originating from posh Edinburgh University students with English public school accents and the judicious use of, "Yah darling, yah, yah, oh we are in Edinbraa" in general conversation.

independent Scotland means fewer voters, so let's try and get some power that way too," Chuck argued.

"Do Nazis care about the planet?" smirked Forsyth.

When they arrived at the address, Chuck parked up and flashed his card at the traffic warden, who had stopped dead on the pavement, reading his machine.

"Police. Do you understand not to book that motor, pal?" Chuck got out and pointed at the Volvo.

The guy didn't care much for the police and was more focused upon his daily commission, but replied sarcastically in an Eastern European accent: "I obviously understand English, *pal*," before walking on past them.

Chuck pressed the buzzer and a female voice buzzed them in as soon as he declared his profession.

"Hi officer – we thought you were finished with us now?" said a pretty young redhead standing in the doorway; wearing shorts, flip flops and a vest which revealed an attractive figure.

"Sorry, just a few more quick questions, my love," smiled Chuck. His body language urged her to stand aside, which she duly did,

"Fine, come in then, we were just cooking." As Chuck entered the large Georgian hallway, an inviting whiff of garlic frying in butter filled his nostrils.

"Smells lovely. I apologise for interrupting, but are you Valerie Erskine or Poppy Woods?" he asked nicely.

"Yeah, I'm Poppy and Val's in the kitchen with my boyfriend, Gordy," she replied in a husky yah twang.

Forsyth shut the door behind him and some Edwardian chimes rung above his head. This was a typically spacious, high-ceilinged and well-built Georgian flat, but the carpets and torn wallpaper hinted that it had probably been rented out to students for a considerable period. In the large kitchen was another young woman in her early twenties in a worn grey cardigan that was two sizes too big for her, pulled over a t-shirt and shorts, with flip flops on her pale feet, which were painted with Indian henna. She was chopping up ginger on a wooden chopping board and her nose stud sparkled upon the professional-looking blade.

"Have you forgotten something?" this one asked as he entered. There was a black male there too; Chuck thought he looked younger, perhaps in his late teens. He was sitting on a stool, making a roll-up cigarette. There were three glasses on the counter between them and a bottle of cheap supermarket wine.

"We are from a separate unit actually, and are investigating the background of the murder victim," explained Chuck. "We just wanted to ask you a couple of questions about his death." He went for the kill without declaring which unit he represented, assuming (correctly) that the young people wouldn't ask any detailed questions from him.

"Fine – have a stool, guys." Val motioned with the knife, so the three of them sat down. Val offered some chilled cherry juice which they both accepted, grateful to cool down after the car journey.

"I hope you don't mind me cooking here, guys," she smiled and they both shook their heads. Chuck then took a swig of the cold sweet juice while Forsyth asked her what she was making.

"It's a spinach dish from Nepal," she smiled slightly at his apparent attention.

"Can you talk me through what you saw happen please?" Chuck then asked.

Val sighed and looked at Poppy. "OK, well, myself and Poppy were over visiting my sister Anthea who boards at Pollock Halls. We went over to give her some cash as my mother had put it in my account. We hung around for a while and had a cup of tea then we had to leave as we both work," she explained.

"Oh right, where do you work?" pressed Chuck.

"Well, I work in the Blind Poet pub and Poppy works a couple of doors along at the Pear Tree Inn," Val replied as she placed the chopped ginger into a hot pan of oil, filling the room with its exquisite scent.

"I see; OK, please go on," Chuck said above the sizzling.

"Well, as we were approaching the barriers to go out on the street, the man walked past, heading toward the Queen's Park," she explained.

"How did he look? Was he strolling, or stressed?" asked Forsyth.

"Well I didn't notice, but Pops…," and she casually pointed the knife at her flat mate, while placing her other hand on her hip and leaning back against the sink.

"Yeah," Poppy came in now, "I thought he looked behind him for something as he passed."

"Did he wave like he was hailing a taxi?" Forsyth asked her.

"No, just looked."

"OK, and then what?" Chuck wanted to know.

The silent young man finished rolling his cigarette, which he tipped with a torn business card. Chuck noted this and took him for a pot smoker. The guy then lit up and smoked away beside the food being prepared, which Chuck found disgusting. He suddenly wanted to grab any intel these girls had and then leave before the murder squad turned up or he caught cancer from the smoke.

"A motorbike pulled up slowly from the left side where the Commonwealth Pool is, and there were two men on the bike," Val paused and seemed a little scared as she recalled what she had seen, her lip quivering as she exchanged a look with Poppy, "the one on the back of the bike pulled something out which looked like a carrier bag and shot that man," she said.

"Careful," Chuck nodded at the chopping board, which she was using again to chop onions, a little too fast for his liking.

"How do you know it was two men on the bike, and not two women?" Forsyth asked.

"Well, we just instantly hit the ground and heard them drive away. We told the other officers this but they said it was best to say it was men as they seemed to be in bikers' clothing," Poppy spoke up again.

"Eh?" Forsyth looked at Chuck who pretended that this was normal procedure, by nodding knowingly.

"Can you tell us anything else about them?" he then asked.

"No," insisted the other female. "They were just a blur, dark perhaps, with helmets of course, but the officers who took our statements wrote down that we thought the bike was red and the riders had jeans and trainers, which we never said, did we, Pops?"

"No, they suggested they were sized like teenagers but we said we couldn't tell; only that the riders had helmets and wore dark clothing and looked like they were carrying an orange carrier bag," Poppy confirmed.

"Did the bike beep a horn at the man?" Chuck checked. He was now of the opinion that the CID at the murder scene were covering something up.

"No," both girls said together.

"Right, that's fine girls, thanks. We're interested in the victim's legal business and we thought we would follow up from our colleagues who spoke to you earlier," Chuck said before smiling at Forsyth to make a move.

"Do you want me to tell the officer coming around tomorrow that you were here?" Val asked innocently.

"No, don't bother – he will be up to his neck in this awful crime and our investigation is going nowhere, so thank you for your time. We'll be off," Chuck stood up and waved as he walked out of the kitchen behind Forsyth.

"Well?" Forsyth asked as they descended the stairs towards the street.

"They're not lying, Chris, but the bit about the CID pressing them to finger a pair of teenagers definitely hints at monkey business," Chuck chuckled contemptuously.

"I pity the little rodents who are going to be placed in the frame then, guv."

They then drove down to the Cameron Toll Sava-Centre on the south side, where they picked up cheap pay-as-you-go mobile phones. The phones annoyingly took almost 30 minutes to charge and register while they both sat in the car park, on the bonnet of the Volvo under an elm tree, for shade. Chuck texted Adams' phone on the number she had given him when he called her from Speirs Bar and soon got a reply:

"Our friend had his wallet, car key and cash seized for forensic examination as part of his release agreement. That was why he was on foot. Keep me posted."

"So... Frazer is bailed, and instead of going straight home, he decides to walk into the park. Then he is seen turning around behind him looking for someone or something as he proceeds past the university campus. Now, we can safely say that he wasn't looking for a taxi as his wallet was seized. No doubt they will claim to be testing his card and notes for cocaine," Chuck said, though he knew it looked more and more like a police conspiracy.

"Fuck's sake guv, do you think the fucking Fiscal and the brass masterminded his execution just because he'd been banged up for naughtiness?" Forsyth asked.

"Or because they knew or suspected he was offering us the crown jewels, Chrissy."

"If that's true, they probably told him to make his way into the park to meet someone he knew? Why else would he walk into the Queen's Park on a day like yesterday; when it was mobbed with people?"

"Unless he was going to walk to the other side, the south side down to Duddingston Loch and the village pub there, what's it called again... the posh place?" Chuck clicked his fingers as he tried to recall, while Forsyth's face looked pained as he tried to remember.

"The Sheep's Heid," Forsyth eventually snapped, as if on a quiz show.

"Right Chrissy, let's go see the staff there," Chuck said; then he texted Adams, asking her to send him an image of Lionel Frazer back in a text. He received it by the time they had driven the long way around to the loch to avoid the police presence back where Frazer had been shot. The image was from his firm's website, and showed him in a tuxedo and bowtie at some award ceremony somewhere; it would do just fine.

Duddingston Village is situated in the heart of the city, at the south-eastern point of Arthur's Seat; the volcanic hill which towers over both the Scottish Parliament and Holyrood Palace. Duddingston Loch flanks the southern crags of the hill and the village itself, snuggled along the crags, covered by a canopy of ancient woodland behind the park road. It is relatively quiet compared to the northern flank of the hill, with its government and historic buildings. The land and the loch itself had a recorded history reaching back to when Celts owned the land prior to 1066. King Malcolm IV of Scotland gifted it to an order of monks in 1128, who cashed in around 1150 when they flogged it to a Norman Templar named Dodin de Treverlen. The foundations to the buildings in the village itself have been traced to a William de Dodingstone over one hundred years later.

"Bonnie Prince Charlie apparently spent the night in a council of war here before the battle of Prestonpans," Chuck said, pointing to a large white house they were passing in the old village.

The Sheep's Heid Inn was supposedly the oldest pub in Scotland, and local Edinburghers would travel from across the city to enjoy the restaurant within. Yet tourists did not really venture here, and Chuck wondered why as he pulled up outside. He thought that the tourist-besotted city council should capitalise on such historical gems as this and the Roman ruins at Cramond, which lay derelict and overgrown.

They walked into the inn and up to the bar where an old guy was reading a paper beside a younger barman, who was drying glasses.

"Now, you two gents are iver whiskey men or here fur dinner," said the Brummie bar man, a comment which raised a frown from the older man seated at the bar.

"Neither, we're solicitors, here to meet a friend," Chuck said as he got Frazer's image up on the new phone and showed it to both the men.

"Yeah, he's been in here a few times for supper with Mr Trevelen, I think, Sir," said Brum, but the older man interjected:

"Isn't he the guy who was murdered yesterday?" asked the older man.

Chuck immediately flashed his police card at them both with a smile.

"And who might Mr Trevelen be then?" he smiled.

Ten minutes later they were driving into Leith again, armed with the knowledge that Frazer was known to the staff in the pub because he had eaten dinner there a few times in the past with a certain Mr Philip Trevelen. Chuck had in his possession an RBS Visa card receipt for £122.00 in Trevelen's name, made out to the pub. Forsyth texted over the details to Adams with a request for further info.

By the time Chuck arrived at Forsyth's flat, it was 4:10 pm and he received his reply:

"Philip Trevelen, not known, other than someone of same name reported a theft of a rowing boat from the white house with the jetty at Duddingston Loch last year. Address he reported it from was 6 Duddingston Loch Mews."

Chuck and Forsyth looked at each other after they had both read it,

"Do you reckon he was going to this guy Trevelen's house then, guv?" Forsyth asked.

"God knows, Chris. It would explain why Frazer walked into the park. Let's take a look at this Trevelen guy."

Chuck arranged to pick Forsyth up again in three hours so that they could get sleep if they wanted to. The rush hour drive from Newhaven to Portobello was slow, however, and Chuck knew he wouldn't get much sleep. He thought about Dai while he sat in a tailback which stretched almost from Seafield to Newhaven, then googled the name on his phone.

"Dai – an angel of the Powers, as well as the Zoroastrian angel of December."

Chuck then searched for the 'Powers', and discovered that they are second sphere angels and warriors who directly oppose evil spirits in the universe. He also noted that they are known for never falling from God's grace. Their job is to manage the distribution of power among mankind, hence their name. The traffic was not moving, the car hot and Chuck felt time was being wasted.

"What the hell?" gasped Chuck, utterly stunned as Dai appeared in the passenger seat beside him.

"I'm sorry for surprising you but I thought you now comprehended things." Dai grinned mischievously, but again Chuck began to feel that there was no threat. Hence, he relaxed slightly.

"It's not about understanding or believing Dai, anyone would get a bloody fright if the car door opened and someone they know as an angel got in." Chuck exhaled, then unwittingly leaned back against his door anyway.

The angel liked the answer and nodded with a smile, "Yes, you are quite right, and I apologise profusely. Know this, Chuck: that is how this thing works, and as your faith improves you will accept it as simply as you would accept your change from a shopkeeper."

He wore the same clothes as before, but he smelled pleasant in the way a man may admire another man's aftershave. The smell reminded Chuck of something pleasant, perhaps a holiday somewhere; but he couldn't quite place it.

"It is not I, but rather the place that I have come from, that you smell." Dai mind-read him again.

"Do angels wear deodorant?" Chuck asked casually.

Dai laughed, a dry but genuine chuckle that was infectious enough to make Chuck follow suit.

"I shall tell you one thing: we love humour, even the bad variety, and don't let anyone tell you differently," Dai said as he continued to laugh.

"Are you a Power angel, Dai?" Chuck tried another question, seeing Dai was amused. To his surprise, Dai nodded with a smile,

"Yes, Chuck. You looked up the name earlier – that was wise, but how did you know I was not the alternative answer that the internet gave you?"

"As in a Persian angel associated with December?" Chuck asked.

"Quite," the mischievous grin had returned as Dai awaited the truth.

"Because of God, as in Christ, no?" Chuck didn't know himself.

Dai seemed happy with that, "That, Chuck, regardless of how it is later perverted, is instinctive faith." He leaned over and gently put his arm around Chuck's shoulder and nodded. Then, he leaned back in the passenger seat, took out two small cartons of milk with straws and handed one to Chuck, who was surprised enough to ask:

"Did you buy them?"

Dai looked surprised for a second and replied sharply: "what do you think?"

Chuck didn't know what to think, so he said nothing, took the milk, and started drinking it. To his surprise, it was as cold as it had been when in the fridge.

"So, you guys eat then?" he asked.

"We can eat your food if we want to – and yes, it can be quite pleasant – but we don't need to. It is a personal choice," revealed Dai.

"OK, well... if you don't mind, please tell me about the differences between an Archangel, a Seraphim, and these Powers?" Chuck asked.

"Well, Seraphims are higher spirits who can heal and are incorruptible. They surround God's throne and constantly sing his praises, though occasionally they can be sent as messengers or even enforcers. They are above my choir and sometimes command the Powers, and…" Dai explained between sips of milk.

"My celestial choir are known as the Powers because, as you read today when you looked us up, we police the distribution of power amongst mankind. We also act as intermediaries between God and humanity. We work closely with the Ishim choir, better known to men as the guardian angels. They labour incessantly to guide humans, and can be called upon to support those of us who are charged with defending humanity and enforcing God's will upon evil spirits," Dai explained. He sipped again and then continued his summary in a mellow voice.

"Being warrior angels, we Powers violently oppose evil spirits, and prohibit them from doing as much harm in the world as they seek to do; usually by casting them into holding zones. We take commands regarding humanity from Seraphims and Archangels, who are the princes of the angels, and the commanders of the choirs." He smiled again.

"I see. Thanks, Dai. What can you tell me about the threat of these evil spirits, then?"

"Plenty," said Dai firmly. "That is why you are being addressed by a Power now, which I can assure you is quite a rare thing, young Chuck," he said, sounding quite convincing.

"Does Jesus know you're here talking to me now?" Chuck asked, burning with curiosity.

"Perhaps," nodded Dai, "If he desires then yes, as the Lamb is all-knowing," he confirmed.

"Have you met him?" Chuck knew he was pushing against his better judgement with all these questions, but he found it very hard to resist while Dai seemed amenable to answering.

"Of course, Chuck" Dai began chuckling again in amusement. "Luke 2: 8-20 Chuck, I was there at his first coming. He is always around; why, you yourself smelled the fragrance of faith upon me simply because you understand a little about the truth, and to understand is to know him, Chuck. 2 Corinthians 2:14," Dai waved his finger knowingly as he sipped on his milk.

"Does he eat too?" Chuck wondered as he took another sip.

"Well, he ate and drank when he was last here, didn't he? Look, let us return to your question about evil spirits, shall we?" Dai suggested politely.

"Of course, sorry," Chuck had been drawn like a moth to a light, but snapped out of it.

"Ephesians 6:12, 'For we wrestle not against flesh and blood, but against principalities, against powers, against the rulers of the darkness of this world, against spiritual wickedness in high places'," Dai quoted. "Have you heard it before?" he asked cheerily. Chuck shook his head, took his notepad out and wrote down the reference.

"Well, you heard Frazer elaborate, at least on some of it, and how some of it operates, I believe?"

Chuck nodded.

"Well, let me start by telling you that I am only authorised to help you by influencing and guiding your instincts." Dai explained. "It is not often that a human has contact with my kind, never mind a Power, so do not waste this great honour by doubting or questioning me. Of course, I shall answer and explain as best I can in the permitted time I can give you, but I must warn you that you might find yourself in a situation where I ignore a question or simply do not give you help with an answer, do you follow?" he asked merrily.

Chuck agreed with another nod and a sip of his milk. Dai went on. "Well, this may prove to be exceptionally frustrating for you as you progress in this matter, alas there is nothing whatsoever you can do to change that. So, do not get angry or tear your hair out. Have faith and follow my lead rather than delaying matters with anger or frustration," he advised.

Chuck briefly mused that he himself might not be a divinely empowered angelic warrior, but he was a decent DI and had reached an acceptance of things a while back.

"What I can tell you is that your paternal bloodline runs back to its emergence in Cyprus in the reign of the Roman Emperor Trajan. The lineage was blessed, Chuck: blessed to carry out the work of the boss," he revealed.

"Cyprus?" Chuck had been there in Pafos, on holiday with Kim.

"Yes, and that was what drew you to the place. Athenian philosophy mixed with fifth generation Persian blood, which was then merged with Tuscan, to create a new line; a family line that is unique for its goodness and which is loved by us all," Dai said. He paused to let this sink in before continuing to speak, softly but firmly.

"That was why your kin was pulled from the arms of death at the Somme, for it was an angel who saved him as the boss commanded, and why you grew up hearing about it through your father's watery account of it. That is also why you have been chosen here, because of your exceptional methodology, we know you can do the job, Chuck. Your bloodline is, in itself, an example of fully functioning human loyalty and morality, and you will naturally oppose the dark hordes of hell which seek the destruction of the human seed."

"Why must a man go up against such evil? Why don't you guys deal with it?" Chuck asked with some justification.

"Because it is about men, or it is supposed to be," Dai shrugged his well-shaped shoulders.

"It is the nature of the *Kertamen*, that humans play out the scenario and neither angels nor evil get involved other than by, say, whispering in an ear or the creation of the odd obstacle. However, that all changed in the 1960s and now the enemy are killing, infecting and torturing as often as they can get away with[8]. Often the boss has to issue edicts; in the last few years, even these have been challenged to the point where angels have brawled with fallen angels," he revealed.

"Fallen angels?" Chuck knew from Frazer who they supposedly were, but the more information he could get on it all, the better.

"Yes, fallen angels, Chuck. They once dwelt in the kingdom of God and then they fell. They are here now; plotting, killing and molesting mankind."

"So, what – do they have angelic power?"

"Very much so: power and magic, my friend," Dai nodded.

"Why?" asked Chuck.

"That is one of those 'can't answer' ones, Chuck; all I can say is that that is the nature of *Kertamen*."

"*Kertamen*?" repeated Chuck.

"Yes, the game. Old Hugh knew the word but by the time the story got passed down to you, it had become 'a game of Cataract'. Dai chillingly impersonated Chuck's father as he had last told the story. "It's *Kertamen*, Chuck, not Cataract," Dai chuckled at this.

"What does it mean?"

"It is a struggle, one in which mankind holds all his own calls." As he spoke these words, Dai's stunning eyes glistened and Chuck suddenly realised that it was all a game, and that the pawns were human beings.

"Not pawns as in the plural," Dai read his thoughts, "Man has the greatest gift of all: freedom of thought, and he can either obey and worship his creator, who loves him very much, or he can stick two fingers up to the boss and follow the pied piper to hell; but every individual is unique and regarded as such."

"Yes, but people in general are still pawns, Dai; otherwise these evil bastards who want to ruin everything would have their powers seized, wouldn't they?" Chuck disagreed.

"No, Chuck," smiled Dai, "And quit the profanities!"

"Sorry," Chuck lowered his head.

"It's OK, Chuck, its normal to shout out when you're frustrated, but understand that man himself is not a pawn. The question is more about

---

[8] Perhaps a reference to the assassination of President John F Kennedy in 1963 or Rev Martin Luther King and Robert F Kennedy in 1968?

whether man will choose darkness over light, but also whether or not he can, due to his selfishness, be persuaded to reject his instinct or not."

"Why are man's instincts in doubt?" Chuck asked.

"Instincts are an angelic sense. Man possesses both good and bad ones, Chuck; as you know from your police work. The primal emotions are checked by morality in some men, and the desire to kill can be checked by law and order in others," explained Dai.

"I have no desire to kill anyone," said Chuck, defending his species now.

"Yet you have read a couple of obituaries and experienced deep satisfaction and pleasure, no?" Dai was grinning again.

"Perhaps," Chuck thought aloud, "Some people deserve it though, don't they?"

"And there we have it..." Dai flicked a hand at Chuck, as if he had proven a thesis to an imaginary audience.

He sighed before winking at Chuck, who could not resist a smile either.

"Anyway, in this instance, you have conveniently landed upon a battleground, Chuck, and a conspiracy within that, by investigating the late Lionel Frazer."

"A battle that I myself am involved in, related to the Scottish referendum," he then revealed.

"The referendum?" Chuck had not seen that angle coming.

"A dark power has gathered in this land Chuck, and it has an army of disciples who hope to control the power after Scotland votes for separation from the UK."

"The disciples you mention being the handshake brigade and all the poisoned media outlets they own?" Chuck asked.

"Indeed, and a lot more, including evil entities which are disciples of Hell. Fallen spirits who despise mankind, Chuck, and who wish to induce the destruction of man," Dai continued.

"They are rebels who use black magic to influence the order upon this planet, and very often they are prepared to break the rules set down by the boss," he continued.

"I and others are committed to a regular cold-war type conflict with them that lies beyond your comprehension. At times this has escalated into violence and killing between us. On occasion, it has resulted in the murders of human beings and the killing of animals. There have been occasions when the boss has raged at them; well, you know of the great flood and Noah etc., don't you?" Dai teased again but Chuck nodded.

"Yet in the main, they have focused upon mind control, and the magical infiltration of governments and national security units," he continued.

"There were quick penetrations into the minds of Roman imperial families and things really heated up in the conflict at that time. It was not until the emperor Trajan that we managed to cleanse the Roman corridors of power, yet we lost it all again with Hadrian. So the struggle progressed until the fragmentation of the churches, and the penetration of evil into Rome and Spain, and the torturing of souls in the name of the boss."

"In WWI, we entered the fray in the manner with which Homer sang of the fallen angels influencing the battles on the bloody plains of Troy: fighting, saving, directing. Yet Satan himself had already won the souls of too many commanders, and we lost heavily on the soul front. In WWII, we were faced by the Morning Star himself."

"Morning Star?"

"Satan. He has many names: he is the prince of chaos and he leads the fallen spirits. He has favourite commanders among them, whom he sent into the senior corridors of power in Germany. We managed to smash them in the end, but at severe cost to the angelic choirs."

"This sounds like a huge panorama of worldly affairs, Dai, but what on earth do they want from the Scottish Referendum and me?" Chuck laughed nervously at the madness of it all.

"Well, strategically they are fighting on various political and military fronts at the moment: Iran, Iraq, Syria, Israel, Palestine, Libya, Egypt, Ukraine, America and even Argentina, but do not think that the UK is not another vital piece in the jigsaw for them," the angel warned with such chilling effect that Chuck actually shivered.

"So, breaking up the UK is what Satan wants?" he had to ask.

"No, but civil strife, being cut off economically from the EU and a rise of fascism due to the lack of European legal restriction may create chaos. In which case, the uncertainty regarding Trident and the cost of transferring the weapons south may lead to disarmament, as the SNP want," Dai replied.

"And?"

"And, if no weapons of deterrence are left in the UK, then the instinct we were talking about – that instinct within other more aggressive peoples – will make this land a target for conflict and political manoeuvring."

"I never really thought that anyone would attack us," Chuck said quietly as the realisation of this hit home.

"If aggressive states carry swords, non-aggressive states require swords, Chuck," insisted Dai before adding, "Russia has just taken Crimea and there is violence in eastern Ukraine. She is also in Syria without a UN resolution," Dai urged him to realise the point.

"But the Russians wouldn't invade Britain, would they, Dai?"

"No, but they might nuke it to bring Washington to the negotiating table regarding a new World Order that involves Russia, China, North Korea and Iran," Dai radiated truth and Chuck believed him.

"What was it Russia said recently? 'Britain is an inconsequential little island'?" Dai grinned at him again.

"So, is Putin one of them?" Chuck sought straight answers.

"Again, I can't answer that one: you need to judge from any truth you can find in the media, Chuck. Did he lie about his troops being in Ukraine?" Dai looked quizzically at him and then shrugged his shoulders.

"Even good men lie though?" Dai shrugged. *He was riddling now*, thought Chuck.

"Does he act any differently than anyone else with power?" Chuck questioned. He preferred Putin to, say, Bush, or the far-right in the states who had not gained power yet. Russia had always been a firm opponent of fascism and extreme racism, he believed.

"Currently the mechanics of infiltration of the far-right into football supporters in Russia is being orchestrated by the Kremlin, Chuck, so don't kid yourself about that," Dai read his thoughts again.

"Well, I always thought North Korea would target us if they ever had the reach and capacity," Chuck now began to see his personal belief in abandoning Trident falter.

"Trust me my friend, Pyongyang is indeed working on targeting America and her allies, but that is another pressing matter in this great game; best addressed on another occasion," Dai confirmed.

"Or, *Kertamen*, even?" Chuck asked.

Dai nodded, "Quite, Chuck. Consider this a moment: even Pakistan is closer to the UK and they have India, Iran and Turkey surrounding them – are they only a couple of years' away from reaching UK soil with a missile or plane? Is that so far-fetched? Only last week Russian long-distance planes capable of carrying a nuclear bomb probed British air space, in order to time the RAF response," Dai pointed out.

Chuck looked out of the car window as he realised that the picture Dai was painting was a case of safety in numbers, and that having a nuclear deterrent would protect against being picked off by the greedy, bullying nature and theological insanity of rogue states.

"Look, Chuck, it would be the perfect scenario for the world to disarm and this, of course, forms part of my daily struggle, but the fact remains that at this precise moment there are too many armed states apathetic to the notion, thanks to Satan's hordes and their human disciples. It would be folly to drop swords in the face of clear and present danger from other sword-carriers. There must be arms that can be used as a deterrent to Satan's human disciples, whose instinct first and foremost, is to stay alive. So it is important to play upon weakness, by being able to deter them by the threat of mutual destruction."

"Is that because they fear death and going to hell?"

"Quite. They serve Satan because they want him to become a god, but they are also human, and as humans they instinctively fear destruction and defeat," nodded Dai. "Instincts are divine gifts from the creator, Chuck. More valuable than rationality, which is why you were drawn to investigating the route Frazer took after he was released from custody. They are also the reason why you ended up in the Sheep's Heid, and why you are drawn to investigating Philip Trevelen," Dai had what seemed to Chuck to be a proud expression across his beautiful face. He was pleased that Chuck was onto Trevelen, then?

"And like I said, that was clever," he patted Chuck on the shoulder again.

"So, he is involved with the group Frazer told us about?"

"I'm not allowed to say certain things, but well done. Now, stay on the trail, forget about Barnton and always follow your instinct, Chuck," Dai said lovingly and yet firmly enough to remind Chuck that he should be obeyed.

"Follow your instincts, Chuck. There can be as much value found within a flicker of an eyelid as one might discover from a long lucid investigation. Being able to manage this sense may require either learning or experience. Yet you have a more refined version; as did your relative Hugh, of the Black Watch," Dai assured.

"Yes, I think that is why I became a decent detective, Dai," Chuck considered.

"Indeed, but the problem you have had is that you jump the gun and act impulsively before initially having a quick think through of things," Dai chuckled again.

"Such as?" Chuck couldn't help smirking back at the delightful personality beside him.

"Such as your revealing yourself as a police officer to the staff at the Sheep's Heid pub," Dai was frowning now.

"Have I triggered alarm bells?" Chuck felt his heart sink as he realised that his visit to the pub may have potentially alerted members of the dark force to his investigation.

"Time will tell."

"Can't you help with that?" Chuck asked.

"The enemy's influence has seen to it that most dogmatic religions owe more to the perversion of basic truths and fundamental knowledge than to scripture itself, so yes, I can do the same to their flock."

"So, do you mean that religion on earth is corrupted, then?"

"The enemy seeks to corrupt everything and everyone; take the film 'the Omen', for example."

"Yes, what about it?" Chuck had been terrified of the soundtrack as a kid.

"They whispered in someone's ear somewhere, which resulted in certain dogs being considered 'devil dogs' to this day by those without wisdom," the angel said as he sighed contemptuously at the media hacks who would threaten the existence of animals in order to achieve a snappy headline.

"I like rottweilers. My friend has one; a rescue called Charlie actually, and he is a perfect gentleman," Chuck agreed.

"Yes, and they are the sworn enemies of Warlocks and dark spirits, which is why the enemy targets them, of course," Dai shook his head again.

"These Warlocks, are they fallen angels? And what exactly am I up against here?" Chuck sought to hear the reality of the crisis; then quickly leaned forward again and added, "I'm only a DI with a week to look into this and hardly capable of fighting Satan and his minions, Dai!"

"My dear Chuck, I know enough about power, remember? And try to also keep my earlier point in mind, that you have a support team of angels by your side. Though you are right to ask about the threat to yourself and our cause, which is a grave one indeed."

"Yes, I gathered that much, but what I'm asking is... well, is God going to protect and help because..."

Dai raised a perfectly-shaped, olive-skinned hand and instantly relaxed Chuck, who sighed and sunk back into his seat.

"God instigated the command that sees me here with you right now. I am only a breath away from you at all times throughout this matter, Chuck," assured Dai in the most effective and calming way, which relaxed Chuck's body and soul further.

"And if black angels attack me or mine?" Chuck calmly offered a possible scenario to the entity beside him, to find out what might happen.

"They are not allowed to kill you. If they try to hurt you, your guardian angel will fight them, and then myself or others will slaughter them: you just get out of it, boy, do you understand?" It was gentle, logical, even and firm enough to have been a command.

"Yes Dai, I promise I'll run."

"Besides, it's more than likely that if we progress to that stage, they will want a parley with the boss, so never fear." Dai was smiling again, which always brought hope and confidence to Chuck.

"Now. We are at war, Chuck, so you can expect anything at any moment; how else can one avoid the enemy's cunning?" Dai shrugged his shoulders. "I will seek authorisation to issue you with a man-club," he added.

"A man-club?" Chuck didn't like the sound of that in the slightest.

"Oh, it's a weapon beyond human comprehension, designed to blend into normal human life without raising an eyelid. I'll tell you more if you are allowed one for self-defence, but in the meantime, stop worrying." *Which was easy for him to say*, thought Chuck.

"You're going to hurt them, Chuck, scuttle their plans, and they will know that good men will oppose their evil plans every time. Sadly, those good men are targeted for their reputations: men like Jack Kennedy, Mahatma Gandhi and Martin Luther King."

"Gandhi was not Christian though, Dai?" Chuck was curious again to understand why an angelic being would include a Hindu on that list.

"Perhaps Mr Gandhi was more Christian, at least from an ethical perspective, than some so-called Christian clerics. That is not for me to say, but JFK was hardly considered Christian for many reasons. The point is that those three men possessed instinctive reasoning and a sense of social morality based upon the teachings of Christ; their own reputations merely followed their instincts."

"And they were all killed for it?" sighed Chuck knowingly.

"Yes, they were. Hmm… what was it Plutarch said again? Ah yes, *'what dangers threaten a great reputation'*, I believe."

"I take it Gandhi didn't get a man-club then?" Chuck was despondent.

"No, as they did not have divine intervention squads made available to him nor Jack Kennedy – and don't be facetious Chuck. I'm here for you, so kindly have respect while we talk," Dai smiled warmly despite the mild telling-off.

"Well, I certainly think it's debateable whether you are here for me, for mankind, or for yourselves, Dai; but forgive me for not being enthusiastic about being attacked by blood-sucking beings from hell in a bizarre game of thrones." Chuck was careful to watch his tone, but he pressed on and felt he needed to be as assertive as he dared.

Dai admired the stance, "Yes it could be debated, but moving on, if you don't mind?"

Chuck nodded, glad to have gotten away with it.

"It's time for you to drive home, eat, then sleep for a while before you go back out and put your squad on the target whom your instinct directs you towards," Dai said cheerily. "And don't worry, I shall come to visit you tomorrow and may have more to tell you. In the meantime, be careful, Chuck," he said, as he turned to get out of the car.

"Wait," Chuck said, "Can I ask one more question, please?"

Dai turned and smiled warmly again, "Of course."

"OK, well, it's a big one: I want to know why Jesus doesn't intervene in catastrophes and terrible situations, and allows them to happen?" Chuck asked.

"The short answer is that he is obeying his father, as you and I are doing here, Chuck."

The implication hit home as Dai had intended and Chuck understood this to be the root of the whole game: are men capable of devotion to their creator in the manner a dog might be to its master?

"The longer answer is that before leaving this world, Christ realised the need for ongoing support. So he not only left an intelligence manual for man to follow, he also regularly intervenes in matters we angels do not intervene in," Dai insisted.

"My point is, or was…"

"I know the point you wished to make. It is the argument which evil feeds to its human slaves and individuals like yourself; who hang in the balance between belief and doom." With those sterner words Dai cut him off before driving the point home.

"You need to get it into your head that regardless of whether or not you agree with the nature of the game or the rules, you are playing it Chuck, and you must either accept the tactics of your manager or go on the transfer list, pal," Dai's sudden recourse to football metaphor was made in Kenny Dalgleish's voice, easily recognizable to most British men of Chuck's age.

"By giving me free thought and speech, there will always be a tendency to question everything, though?" Chuck smiled as he realised that obedience to the Ten Commandments was surely the most effective display of loyalty to the boss.

"Well, loyalty to your creator, who will not ask you to do anything but act in the spirit of goodness, is, as they say these days, a 'no-brainer', my friend. But there are people on this planet who do not use their entire intellectual capacity, and that is truly the nature of this struggle." Dai's face expressed a deep sadness.

"Salvation is not for the righteous, Chuck. It is a gift from Christ on behalf of the boss to those who fail to use their minds, or those who have them controlled by others," he sighed.

"Such as what? Prayer, I know, but you don't make it very easy for us, do you? I mean, the Bible is all in code, riddles even. Faith has been removed from schools and family lifestyles thanks to those scumbags who pervert everything from education to sexuality, which makes it inaccessible to many." Chuck immediately wondered why he was now developing into a believer who was criticising the leadership of Jesus Christ and God Almighty to an angel of the Lord, when faith in the high commanders were all that he had been required to consider.

Suddenly Dai waved his hand over the dashboard and what looked to be a round screen appeared to be hovering just above the dash.

"Oh my God," Chuck gasped as he pressed himself back into his seat again.

"Don't be alarmed, Chuck, it is simply a screen, with which I will show you why the riddles you mention are far easier to decipher than to moan about." Dai waited to see that Chuck was able to relax and focus.

"OK…" there was no need to worry, Chuck knew. However, his heart was pounding with trepidation, anticipation and excitement.

"Now, I know what you're thinking – this is not a miracle, Chuck. It is simply a screen projected upon air; something man will understand in due course, but not today," Dai smiled.

An image appeared on the circle – it was a book; a page. "Matthew 23:33," Dai said. Chuck read the highlighted part which confirmed it to be the New Testament,

"You serpents, you brood of vipers, how will you escape the sentence of hell?" it read. Chuck looked to Dai for guidance.

"It is an account of Christ verbally attacking the Pharisees within the old temple, wherein he referred to them as serpents who pretended to worship the Lord, when in reality they simply interpreted his words for their own purposes."

The screen then changed to a plain white background with blue writing across it in the form of a web address. Almost immediately, a news report on Pope Francis performing mass in Paraguay began on the small projected circle, like a TV or computer screen. The newsreader declared that several snakes had appeared seemingly from nowhere, and bitten some members

141

of the Papal congregation. It lasted a few seconds, then stopped just as the screen disappeared.

"So, you're saying that what Christ is recorded to have said to the head Jewish priests in the old temple in Jerusalem is a guideline for how we can interpret the present Pope?" Chuck understood the point, which of course was 'read your Bible', but he was still dubious about any argument which said the riddles were simple.

"Well Chuck, one wonders if they were viper bites." Dai said with that mischievous glint back in his spectacularly piercing eyes.

"Well, I get it; most people know the Catholic church is questionable in many ways, but it still feels like we need to experience and solve a riddle in order to understand this 'manual' left to us by Jesus," Chuck pointed out.

"What the video shows is that if you know your Bible, you would understand what to look for a lot better. In this instance, if you understand the points Christ made in the temple to the corrupted clergy in Matthew 23:33, you will find the evil within other religious institutions to be somewhat more identifiable," Dai coolly pointed out.

"Fair point." Chuck knew the Bible to be a wealth of information, and also that it purportedly holds a set of secret messages encoded within it. He remembered just then that he had read a bit about the so-called geometric code in Michael Drosnin's 'Bible Code', a book that had been confirmed by cryptologic mathematicians to show a genuine code of ingenious proportions; a code that Drosnin himself believes was placed in the Bible by an extra-terrestrial intelligence.

"Ok, I shall read it more," Chuck stated.

"Moving on, then," Dai continued happily. "What you need to know is that Satan and his Warlocks control certain old masonic crafts that are unconnected to the main list of world-wide lodges. They have established themselves in many corners of society, and regularly make bids for power through their human puppets. That is how our enemies line up, Chuck, but I'm not allowed to help you more, as you need to be the one to stop the Scottish problem and I can only do so much," said Dai as he sighed again.

"At least tell me what I'm looking for?" Chuck protested lightly.

"Remember that Trevelen is of a Templar line on his father's side; I can point that out at least," smiled the angel as he turned to leave again.

"And?" Chuck was almost begging.

Dai stopped a moment, "The Templars were infected with all the errors of the Fraticelli[9]; despising the church and holding contempt for such sacraments as penance, and so they feigned compliance to the church to escape detection," he sighed again. He let this sink in and studied Chuck's face briefly.

"For denying the divinity of Christ and attempting to establish themselves as a worldly cult of the ancient Pagan priests, not to mention their desire to rule the world on behalf of the fraudulent pious claims they professed," said Dai, going into further detail for him.

"They controlled the temple in Jerusalem long enough to excavate and remove certain items from the soil such as the Holy Grail, which they claimed contain certain powers, but the truth is that they are deceivers who long ago welcomed the fallen ones into their order. In fact, I am permitted to tell you that this line is active even now on and continues to labour on behalf of Satan, who originally approached them at their base in Cyprus soon after they were defeated and ejected from the Holy Land by the Muslims in 1291. He established control over them at that point, sending them out across the world with abominable claims to be spread in accordance with his agenda."

"Where did they hide these relics?" Chuck was primarily thinking of the Grail now.

"At land near here, at the village of Rosslyn, where they built that little replica of Herod's Temple and stored the stolen scrolls they excavated at Jerusalem, and where their fingerprints continue to remain evident within the stone masonry."

"Is Rosslyn where I will find this group Frazer spoke about?" Chuck asked.

"No, Rosslyn is irrelevant today, though the stonework and carvings do reveal the Templars' attempts to use the shroud and other relics as tools with which to gain power," Dai pointed out as he briefly recalled the period momentarily. Re-focusing swiftly to the task at hand, he then urged Chuck to: "Concentrate upon Trevelen; understand who he is, and trust in your God-given instincts; for that is all you will need, Chuck."

"I will speak to you tomorrow," he said again warmly, before giving the car roof a couple of taps with his fingers and walking away in the direction of the sea.

---

[9] The Fraticelli were a Franciscan sect who were declared heretical in 1296 by Pope Boniface VIII.

Chuck sat for a few moments to try to take in what he had just heard, enormous in its scale and consequence, before then driving home whilst listening to Radio 4, which was broadcasting a debate on the referendum. Kim wasn't home yet, so he took a shower before lying on the sofa to doze for a while. When he awoke afterwards, the time was 7:22 pm on the fireplace clock. He heard Kim in the kitchen and went through to find her serving up lentil soup into a couple of bowls; the smell of crusty French bread warming up the oven made his mouth water as he fetched butter from the fridge. There was a briefly comforting sense of home and love, he was aware.

"Have you got time to break bread before you head off, dear?" Kim asked keenly and without seeing the butter in his hand.

"Yes, that would be nice, thanks," he smiled as he instinctively closed the kitchen door, just as a large fly appeared and smacked into it so loudly that Kim looked over.

"That was lucky," she smiled.

"Mmm." He was not so sure.

Seven

"Oh, divine art of subtlety and secrecy, through you we learn to be invisible"

Sun Tzu

The Bistro de L'oulette sits between two tenement buildings in the Old Fishmarket Close in the old town. It was a rustic little French number which specialised in the signature dish of the Marseillais owner – bouillabaisse – and was surprisingly busy, despite being tucked away off the main drag. Outside, Gav Caine could smell shallots being fried in butter, and despite having eaten, felt his appetite whetted as he crouched awkwardly within the hedgerow of an opposite tenement building. He and Joe had been instructed to stalk Trevelen at his Duddingston home by Chuck. Fortunately, not long after they arrived the man himself appeared, jumped into a black Land Rover, and drove off into Holyrood Park.

They had discreetly tailed him into the Fountainbridge district, where he suddenly jinked out of the traffic, parked outside the old Meat Market, and seemed to disappear into the Standard Life building. The detectives were unsure exactly, as the traffic had begun moving again and they found themselves quickly stuck at the lights between two double-decker buses. If they had pulled out and parked too, Trevelen would have seen them, and once the traffic had begun moving they could not turn the car around again until they reached Grove Street. However, upon burling around and speeding back up to Fountainbridge, they observed Trevelen placing an object which looked like a case of wine in the back of the Land Rover. Gav slowed down and sat behind a taxi, which conveniently slowed down to let the Land Rover out.

"Must have a fare, otherwise the wanker would never have let him out," commented Joe on the taxi driver's strange selflessness.

"He does: look at the heads in the back," Gav pointed.

"I hate the bastards, you know," Joe shook his head in disgust.

"Just making a shilling, lad," smiled Gav, whose eyes were locked on Trevelen's Land Rover beyond in front of the cab.

They had followed him up to Parliament Square, where he then walked away with the case of wine. They had quickly tossed a coin between them; Gav lost, so he followed, while Joe sat in the car with his phone on. After half an hour, Gav texted to say:

"He's in the French restaurant down the close. I am in bushes watching, but can't see inside."

Joe responded with, *"And the plonk?"*

"Took it in, obviously, do u think he would leave it in the close, Kermit?"

Joe leaned back in his seat with a packet of onion rings, listening to a CD drama about a busker and his cat. An hour and a half later he received another text from Gav:

"He's coming, follow him. I'm following the guy he was hugging as he left. Will call when I see where he's going."

At that moment, Trevelen appeared on the Royal Mile, walking back to the Land Rover. Joe observed him while crouching down into the foot well. Trevelen was a smartly-dressed, medium-sized man in pleated grey trousers, a shirt, tie, and a dark blue shiny buttoned blazer, like a ship captain's. He had dark straight hair and a circus ring-master's moustache. Joe wondered if he had been drinking as he got in and drove off.

"Was he drinking, as he's driving?" Joe texted Gav back again as he began to follow Trevelen at a distance.

The reply came a while later as Trevelen was pulling back onto his gravel driveway at Duddingston, *"Couldn't see and we can't go in and check as he must have given the owner the wine, so there must be a connection there, it would set alarm bells ringing if we did."*

"OK. He is now home, and I'm waiting here," Joe typed back.

Chuck and Forsyth had briefed both of them earlier and established Trevelen as the new surveillance target. Chuck was keen to see if anyone came or went from Trevelen's house, and told his men to keep a firm vigil until he and Forsyth relieved them in the morning. Instead of heading home, however, he drove over to the Magdalene estate to speak to the underage girl that Frazer had been caught with. Adams had provided her home address and warned him to be careful, otherwise the dark force might discover the Druggies' involvement.

"We'll imply that we are following up the Frazer inquiry, and use false names," Chuck said to Forsyth as they drove.

"A quick flash of our badges then, with thumbs partially covering our names?" Forsyth knew the score.

It was a lovely evening, and with the windows down, less traffic and a few green lights, it was a cool, pleasant drive over to the south-east. Chuck passed the New Yorker pool hall at Jock's Lodge and spotted a known hash seller named PJ Skegg walking in the direction of Peirshill. He briefly recalled the time years before, when he had been a DC back in Leith CID and had pinched PJ for housebreaking. Those days seemed like simpler times to him now.

"Here we are," he sighed, when they arrived shortly afterward at the Magdalene estate.

The place was a typical council scheme, but not yet a completely run-down one. The main concrete blocks of flats with balconies dominated the place and Chuck could recall coming here as a teenager for the odd party or sexual encounter. It had been quite the shithole then, of course, and was regarded as the east-end version of Broomhouse. *It was somehow slightly better now and more cared-for*, Chuck mused, as he looked up the balconies with flowers on them and the well-tended gardens along the flanks of the buildings. There were a few immigrants too, blending in with the locals who were obviously now a very different community from the spray-painting, sofa-burning mob of the 1980's. *A little masterpiece of gentrification*, thought Chuck.

"I remember the wee Pakistani shop that was over there in the late seventies," Chuck said as he pointed to a cream-coloured building with a sign above it which now read:

"*Smile Dental Care. Dr Ching Wu. BDS, DDSc & Nadia Khalid BDS.*"

"Who says immigration is a bad thing, Guv?" joked Forsyth.

"Yes, well, that place was once a shop covered in racist graffiti across it and an almost permanent police presence protecting it. I used to wonder how the wee owner managed to run the place back then, but it's changed days now for the better, obviously."

"It's funny how it's always the scheemies[10] who shit on their own doorsteps guv, and who are so stupidly racist that they would attack the only shop for miles," Forsyth contemplated as they crawled around to the eastern side of the estate.

"Not only scheemies, Chris. Just because they publicly display their bigotry does not mean that there are not others who choose to be subtle about theirs," Chuck opined as they drove down a street with terraced houses and well-kept gardens, looking for number 14.

---

[10] Edinburgh term for residents of council housing schemes.

"You're right guv, it's better days now." Forsyth pointed at a mixed-race couple walking hand-in-hand along the pavement.

Chuck thought back to the SLP rally and considered that it was possible that things may change yet again in the future. "This is it, Chris; just follow my lead, right?" he pulled up outside a hedge with two green bins standing like sentries at the gate. As he got out, a man walked past with a small dog that Chuck reached down to pat after closing his door behind him. "I'm thinking of getting a dog, you know," he said as Forsyth joined him and they opened the gate. As they walked up to the door, a man with grey hair and a moustache could be seen watching them from around the edges of a curtain in the downstairs window. The door eventually opened and a big, tall bear of a man with a week's stubble and a food stained t-shirt appeared.

"Aye?" he snarled at them. Chuck saw the grey-haired man from the window lurking in the shadows behind and could hear whispers and a distant TV.

"I'm a senior detective with the police and this is Detective Sergeant Forster," Chuck said as both he and Forsyth flashed their badges just long enough to not appear too hasty, but too quickly for their real names to confirmed.

Chuck was gambling that the man wouldn't have enough intuition or confidence to challenge and demand to see them again. If he did, Chuck would insist he had meant Forsyth but that it had been a slip of the tongue due to having recently interviewed a Mr Forster earlier that evening. Fortunately, the man simply nodded and appeared to withdraw his defensive stance, now that he realised that it was the police doorstepping him.

"We need to have a quick word with Stacey Williamson please. Are you her father?" Chuck cut to the chase now.

"I'm her dad, aye. She's in the kitchen with her aunties; come in," the man smiled nervously now and stood aside.

They emerged into a small kitchen with a large circular glass table at which the girl was sitting with two older women, all eating Chinese food in their dressing gowns. With the grizzly father behind him and far enough away from the table to prevent embarrassment, Chuck felt safe enough to give them a brief flash of his badge, finger still covering his name.

"Police. Sorry to have to bother you again while you're having your dinner, but we'd like to clarify a couple of things regarding the incident, Stacey," Chuck said to the blonde teenager who sighed but then nodded her consent.

"Let's go into the living room, then," suggested the dad, and Stacey quickly obeyed while the two aunts remained at the table. There was no sign of the old man now.

"Stacey, we are looking into different angles of this matter on behalf of the investigation team, so could you confirm to us exactly how you met Mr Frazer again, please?" Chuck asked gently.

"The other lot have already asked her all this and she told them again on tape," the dad said quickly.

Forsyth spoke. "Mr Williamson, we are a separate unit who are making sure the investigating officers are doing things correctly," he lied.

Dad fell for it instantly, "Aye, hopefully to make sure there are no cover-ups to protect cops, eh," he snapped. Chuck simply fuelled his suspicions by smiling as opposed to denying, thus establishing a connection and securing tolerance.

"Right OK, go ahead hen, tell the officers," dad then smiled at his daughter.

She looked tired, her dirty blonde hair coarse and tousled. Chuck thought she had recently woken up as there were still traces of sleep in her eyes and she had a drained look to her. *She nodded too eagerly*, Chuck thought.

"I used to smoke hash in a flat in Musselburgh with a guy I was sort of with, if you know what I mean?" She looked at her father nervously, then back at Chuck. *She was just a child*, both officers thought as they watched her nibble at her nails.

"Go on Stacey, it's OK," Forsyth gently helped her along.

"Well, it turned out he was a bit of a bastard and my dad had to get the police to let me go home in the end," she explained. Her father growled and then forced a smile at her.

"He was a wee rat in his early forties who sold dope, nothing much, just enough to entice young lassies like Stacey here to idolise him," the man explained.

"Did he rape your daughter?" Chuck decided to press again now.

"Well, he mind-controlled her." He looked at them to see if they understood and both Chuck and Forsyth nodded for him to proceed. "To tell you the truth, he's off his head, a Walter Mitty fantasist who bullshits to young lassies like Stacey that he's something special. Once he got control, he dominated her like a dog," the dad went on, clearly more concerned with getting across the nature of the situation than protecting his daughter's feelings.

"OK," Chuck nodded slowly, hiding his eagerness to press on.

"Anyway, she ran away from him and came home but the wee shite followed her and started stalking the house and putting silly wee notes through the door professing to love her and stuff," he told them. "Like him buying a boat and cruising the world. He couldn't afford a car, never mind a bloody boat."

"And what did you do?" Forsyth asked.

"Well, I got the police involved and he was arrested, but nothing came of it as Stacey denied most of it when she was questioned and so did he. A while afterwards I heard he got done in by a group of masked men outside his flat," he smiled, clearly delighted about that.

"Do the police know about that?" Forsyth asked.

"Of course, not only was he a coward, he was also a grass. I was even detained and questioned, but I had been at my work at the time," the man added, continuing to smile proudly.

Neither officers returned the smile but Chuck asked, "So, no one has been charged with that then?"

Both Stacey and her father shook their heads but she failed to control a grin that broke out across her face.

"So, how does Leo Frazer come into it, Stacey?" Chuck asked again, nice and gently.

"He owned the flat and sometimes came down for his rent and to talk with Irvine or Alby," she said.

"Who?"

"Irvine Stroker and Alby Dudley," she repeated.

"Stroker was the one who preyed on my Stacey," her dad snarled.

"So, Frazer met you there and you left Stroker and became Frazer's victim, then?" Chuck asked.

"Aye, victim's the word, like. My Stacey was the smartest in her class a few years ago, you know," dad put in.

"Right," Chuck nodded at him before addressing the daughter again, "How long ago was this, Stacey, and did Frazer ever introduce you to any other people?"

"I haven't seen Irvine for maybe a year and a half," she said, thinking aloud. "There was a place out in the sticks near the big IKEA store at Straiton where Leo took me once," she said.

"Can you remember where, exactly?" he asked.

"No, it was dark and Leo had given me some pills, so no. But I remember the woods and that there was nothing there except a white cottage with logs piled up outside it." She scrunched her face in a failed attempt to search her memory, but she had been out of her head on LSD by the time she had arrived at the place.

"How far from IKEA, roughly?" Forsyth asked.

"Not far. Close, I think, but I don't know."

"How long ago was this?"

"Maybe a couple of months after we started meeting," she said softly.

"And you met his friends there?" Chuck pressed.

"I told the other cops that I can't remember anything as I was drugged and drunk, but that there were a few men there and another girl about my age," she said.

"Could you ID any of them if you were shown a photo?"

"Well, the other officers said she was too drunk to remember and that it was best to forget about that part as she could get charged with drugs offences and underage sex," dad interrupted.

"I see. So, you slept with people there that night, Stacey?" Chuck nodded coolly. Stacey took a deep breath and for a moment Chuck and Forsyth thought she might start crying before she replied, but she rallied and took another deep breath before speaking.

"A few men raped us. Leo didn't, but a few did; one with a grey moustache kept giving us Chinese burns on our skin. That's all I can remember, sorry." At that, she was overcome and covered her face with her hands. She was obviously ashamed to do this in front of her father and within earshot of the women in the kitchen. Chuck noticed that her fingernails were chewed to the bone and there were home-made tattooed letters spelling 'LOVE' on her thumb.

"Stacey, you've done really well. I know this must be really hard for you. Do you have a mobile number we can contact you on, to fill you in on our progress?" he asked, without looking at her father, who looked up at him then conceded the issue without a word.

"Sure, it's…" and she proceeded to read it out from memory. Both Chuck and Forsyth logged it down.

"Right, well, thank you for giving us some more of your time, especially when you were eating. We'll let you return to your tea and get out of your way. Sorry for upsetting you, Stacey, and again Sir," Chuck then nodded respectfully at her father, who appreciated that and stood up to shake Forsyth's hand, and even patted Chuck gently on the back,

"I hope you manage to get all the scumbags involved in all this," he said as he walked them out.

Back in the car, Forsyth looked puzzled. "Guv, why didn't you get Stroker's address and description?"

"Don't need it. I know the little shit, Chris, and you and I are busting him tomorrow."

"What for?" smiled Forsyth.

"Anything. You get Sharon to give us the lowdown on him tomorrow morning and confirm his address, as he has a record," Chuck couldn't believe his luck.

"Ok guv, but what's so funny?"

"Stroker is a grass," Chuck sighed as he pulled away from the kerb. "I've done him for minor gardening[11] in the past," he revealed.

Forsyth was quiet for a moment as Chuck drove out of the scheme. On the right, a gaggle of teenagers were sitting, chatting on bikes beside a taxi loading up with suitcases, outside a block of flats. The gardens looked particularly well kept, they both reckoned as they passed. Chuck wondered if the lucky buggers were en route to a beach holiday, and he smiled at the thought of sitting outside by the little harbour in Cala Bona at the strange Italian American's restaurant with Kim, sipping fruity Sangiovese and enjoying the evening sea breeze. He sighed again: "Look, let me tell you his story and then I'll drop you off."

He told Forsyth how he had first come across Stroker a good few years ago when he was with the Gayfield CID. Stroker had first come to the attention of uniform when he was in his early twenties; his girlfriend had called the police to have him removed from her parents' home, after he turned up for a meal and belittled her so callously in front of her family that the mother asked him to leave. Stroker had not been aggressive but had snapped in that unfortunate voice of his which Chuck thought of as a cross between a feminine tone, and that of a bloke suffering from a burst gallbladder. "No, Bette, I'll finish my dinner that you invited me here for," he had told the mother.

"Description?" Forsyth wanted to know the physical threat by then.

"That's the most bizarre thing about this little egomaniac control freak," smirked Chuck as they cruised east along the Duddingston Park Road, "He is nothing at all. In fact, he's a skinny so-and-so, I mean one slap and you'd break him."

Forsyth smirked but shook his head and exhaled a breath of knowing despair, "I know the type guv, a nasty little parking attendant wannabe, like that bus conductor fucker from '*On the Buses*'?"

"Eh?" Chuck pretended he wasn't impressed at this reference; "have you been sitting up late again, watching UK Gold?" he chuckled.

---

[11] Unofficial police term for the maintenance of marijuana plants.

Forsyth laughed too, "Yep, it's on after Porridge, guv."

"Well, Irvine Stroker is no Fulton MacKay [12], Chris," Chuck shook his head.

"More like Gollum from '*Lord of the Rings*'; at least that was what my old guvnor at Gayfield christened him," Chuck recalled.

"He's about 5'8, with a rugby-ball shaped head on a skinny little neck and frame, and he crouches his back incessantly like Gollum, presumably due to spending his life on a sofa playing an Xbox, smoking dope and fantasising that he is one of the characters on his Xbox."

"Sounds like the bastard love child of Gollum and Walter Mitty, Guv?"

"Oh, he is a complete Walter, Chris," Chuck insisted. "Very much so. Like most autodidacts, he has acquired a fraction of life experience and now thinks he knows it all better than the rest of us. He was apparently like that from an early age; I met the parents once while looking for him," Chuck replied.

"So, what was the story, then?" Forsyth was eager for the intel now.

"Right. Well, at the time, uniform attended and removed him from the house. He was cocky towards them, saying things like did they know his father was a sheriff who dined with the Chief Constable, blah-de-blah... I mean, this guy had begun to believe his own delusions, Chrissy. He had apparently been coming out with that all sorts of waffle since he once persuaded a traffic warden to rip up a ticket by convincing him that he was an undercover cop," Chuck smiled as Forsyth smirked too at this audacity.

"Anyway, uniform ended up doing him for a breach of the peace and he was slapped with a restraining order, which he broke by writing and emailing the girl daily thereafter."

"Saying what?"

"Same as Stacey said she received from him, just repetitive demands that she return to him and see things his way. In the end, he broke into her flat and hid in a wardrobe, hoping to catch her taking a bloke to bed."

"Dear, oh dear," chuckled Forsyth again. "And did he?"

Chuck nodded as he pulled up at the lights at Seafield. The view out to sea was a pleasant one; a mixture of mint and royal blue all swirled together. Beyond, on the Fife coast, white dotted caravans were visible. Chuck decided that he preferred the denim blue of the sky but turned back to Forsyth regardless. "Her parents found the bastard and the old boy knocked him clean out and rang 999 as Stroker lay sparkled on the deck. However,

---

[12] A Scottish actor who played a fair but hard senior prison officer opposite Ronnie Barker in the 1970s TV sitcom 'Porridge'.

by the time uniform arrived he was up and on the run, so we were called to find him," he explained.

"The joys," Forsyth commiserated.

"So, we went to his parents' place in Craigentinny, only to learn that they had thrown him out for spending much of his teenage life trying to bully them too. He failed utterly with that, mainly because his father was much of the same. In the end, the father saw that Stroker was a chip off the old block and much more, so he kicked his lad's arse out onto the street," said Chuck.

"How old was he, again?" Forsyth asked as they drove on.

"Early twenties, no education, living at home smoking dope and playing the guitar along to Floyd, while the old man worked away doing 9-5 as an army recruitment officer in Haymarket. A domestic struggle for the alpha-male role was obviously ongoing and the father simply had had enough," reflected Chuck.

"So, young Stroker simply turned his attentions to seeking out a weak-minded female, whom he could create a new family with, while exerting his control," he added.

"The ultimate control freak, then," stated Forsyth.

"Exactly. The only thing was, he continuously failed, thanks to God," Chuck said, and Forsyth blinked and looked at him; for he had never heard his governor mention God before.

"Anyway, we eventually picked him up and he got three months for the break in. The Social Work Inquiry Report recommended to the court that he receive counselling for his, and I quote, 'self-glorifying ego'. Sadly, the Sheriff ignored that recommendation for a reason best known to himself, and opted for a short sharp shock." Chuck said with a hint of despair.

"Still, a nice whack on the wrists is better than probation or counselling, guv?"

"Detention in the looney bin for at least a year, instead of a few weeks in the nick, would have been the better option," Chuck shook his head.

So, how did Gollum like the nick, then?" Forsyth grinned mischievously.

"Hated it, all cowards do. He was placed on suicide watch for the entire sentence, as he was terrified of showering or coming out of his cell."

"You said you pinched him for gardening, guv?"

"Yep, not long after I joined the squad, actually. We were watching a rodent heroin dealer called Billy Rutherford in Wester Hailes and lo and behold, we discovered that he had a regular mini cab driver driving him around. We decided to spy on the cabbie to see if he was potential grass-to-keep-your-licence material, it turned out that Stroker was the registered keeper and driver," Chuck laughed.

"Surprise, surprise, playing at being a gangster then, was it?" Forsyth had a grin wider than a Cheshire cat's by now. He loved hearing back-stories like this one from Chuck, the more experienced man whose memory for past cases always impressed him.

"Well, think of the altar boy characters Edward Norton has played in his films who turn out to have secret manipulative streaks, and you have Stroker's character. Then think Gollum... now you have his appearance." Chuck paused and grimaced, clearly recalling his interactions with this unpleasant character.

"Anyway, we paid him a visit at his flat on Northfield Broadway and found that he had twelve plants on the go. We nicked him and his eccentric flatmate Alban Dudley. Dudley, now he was harder to read because he was more intelligent than Stroker. A real fruitcake though, and the Rodney Dangerfield of the two," Chuck recalled.

"Dudley had been living in a cocoon of self-banishment from society ever since his partner left him for another woman and took his daughter with her and stopped any contact" he explained.

"And?"

"And she had tried to have him committed I seem to recall but failed and enter Mr Stroker...etc. etc." said Chuck.

The odour of the sewage plant at Seafield had departed the air a mile or so back, and now came the pleasant replacement of the smell of Fish and Chips as they drove down through Annfield toward yet another set of lights.

"Did he put his hands up then, guv?" asked Forsyth.

"Yes, Stroker was terrified of being in a police cell, never mind going to prison, so he consented to us putting a wire in his cab, as well as the dingy wee cab firm office in Tollcross he worked out of," Chuck recalled.

"Oh, Cameo Cars? I remember them, weren't they owned by that old fence[13] – Tierney, or something?" Forsyth recalled reading something about a stabbing over some petty villainous stuff which had occurred within that firm's office once upon a time.

"Tattler, not Tierney. He was an opportunist, nothing more. We took him down for reset and credit card fraud in the same investigation. The firm

---

[13] 17th century slang term used in several regions of Britain. A fence acts as a middleman between thieves and the eventual buyers of stolen goods. An infamous fence may be Charles Dickens' fictional character 'Fagin' from his 'Oliver Twist' novel.

was eventually sold on by his wife; I think it's a wine shop now," Chuck mused before adding, "Old Tattler himself died in some state-run home a while back, I think?"

"What happened to Dudley and Stroker, then?"

"Christ knows. We let them go as promised, and I sort of resented that, by the way. I learned a fair bit about them over the course though, including the fact that Stroker kept multiple Facebook accounts with which he stalked his prey – who were, of course, teenage female targets," Chuck explained with a castor oil expression.

"And?"

"And that prior to all that, after he had been booted out of his parents' house and pissed off to the Bristol area with a circus."

Forsyth smirked in anticipation.

"Yep, well, turns out he waved his wicked wand with some school girls before then getting a 16-year-old up the duff," Chuck took a breath.

"As you do." Forsyth looked out the window at a group of Festival performers cycling along the pavement on old-fashioned cycles, wearing the hooped pullovers and black berets of 1940s French onion sellers.

Chuck didn't look at them twice, having lived in Edinburgh too long to be impressed by the half-baked political dreamers who flocked to the city in August, in the self-absorbed expectation that were indeed as talented as their friends had promised them that they were.

"Stroker soon abandoned the circus to set up a flat with the school girl, and she and her parents endured his predictable mind games, then struggled to escape the little bastard's control. This resulted in him being cautioned twice by Avon and Somerset's finest for stalking and harassment before eventually being frogmarched onto a bus back up the road."

"And?"

"And, it was much of the same up here when he returned: usual stuff, preying on girls who were mentally unassertive, and impressed enough by him to allow him to dominate them for a period before they inevitably bolted."

"Presumably having sold them a Mitty-esque fantasy about himself from the outset?"

Chuck nodded. "The tough guy from the wrong side of the tracks routine," he scoffed. "One who would be a cool boyfriend to have as he has done and knows everything etc. An intelligent academic who claims to have quit university and conventionality for a life on the road, et cetera et cetera."

"Did he go to university?" Forsyth was surprised at this.

"Don't be silly, he just claims that. I mean, he was an unpopular school drop-out Chris; one who convinced himself that all the boys at his school disliked him because all the girls secretly fancied him," chuckled Chuck.

"Oh dear."

"Anyway, we discovered that he had pounced on some twenty-year-old with a young son soon after he returned to Edinburgh. Same routine, then when she runs, he stalks and bombards her with daily letters and texts. She gets uniform involved and when they pay him a visit, they find him with two runaways from a local children's home. Two 15-year-old girls, whom he was feeding and sheltering. The girls revealed that they met him on a bus and asked him for a fag; then Bob's your uncle and Fanny's your aunt!"

"Brutal, guv. What happened next?" Forsyth was hoping in vain now that the story's climax involved extreme violence against Stroker.

"Nothing; he got a caution because he said they had told him that they were sixteen," Chuck shrugged.

They both considered things a while without speaking. Chuck wondered whether or not Stroker and Dudley would still be flatmates.

"So, what are we thinking then, guv? The fucker's now fencing young blood for Frazer and maybe even this so called 'paedo cabal' of his?" Forsyth had the scent now.

"Hmm, well that would tie Frazer into a more hands-on involvement, Chrissy, and it might be where he was heading to when he was shot as Stroker and Dudley lived in Musselburgh."

Forsyth wasn't convinced about the latter part of his boss' thinking, so speculated aloud:

"Could be guv, as we can't trust that fucker Frazer either, but I can't see him having been up for walking to Musselburgh. I mean it's what, a good six miles?" Forsyth shook his head in disbelief, "Not in brogues, guv, he was either told to wait for a lift or was heading to meet this Trevelen guy in Duddingston, surely?"

"Correct!" Chuck smiled as he pulled into Newhaven. "Tomorrow morning, you and I are going to pay Stroker a visit, so get onto Sharon when you get home and tell her to get those persons checks on both Stroker and Dudley, tonight" he said.

"OK, guv." Forsyth had heard him the first time.

"Then ring Joe and Gav and tell them we will relieve them both at 9am," Chuck added.

Chuck's drive back along the coast to Portobello was a pleasant one. The breeze from the sea cooled him and the positivity coming from a Radio 2 discussion between a minister, an imam urging for Islamic liberal reforms, and an American rabbi, offered hope. The imam's idea of reforming his religion was to argue that alcoholic beverages could be used in cooking as the alcohol evaporates with heat, leaving only the flavour of a good wine in a sauce. Such changes may integrate the future generations of UK Muslims, he believed. The rabbi was promoting peace through tolerance and the minister was offering encouragement to his counterparts by recalling how old church reformers had found it difficult to argue for modernization in bygone days. Chilled and peaceful bubbles like this were a rarity within Chuck's hectic life that was obviously developing into an overheated stew. This routine journey would have been suffocating a couple of hours earlier, but was enjoyable now due to the evening sea breeze and it being home time. Chuck gazed out to sea and the stunning view of the Forth which to him was often worthy eye candy regardless, and he cruised toward Portobello in calmer traffic and with a refreshed optimism.

As he turned onto Marlborough Street and parked up outside his home, Dai suddenly appeared on the passenger seat smiling affectionately. "You're right," he said.

Chuck had sensed him for half a second before he heard the voice, and as he turned to see him, he was amazed not to feel alarmed or even partially surprised.

"About what?" he smiled back, genuinely pleased to see him again.

"That old church is a beautiful little building and makes a fine home," Dai nodded, looking out at the couple preparing dinner through a kitchen window, in an 18th century building which he had always admired.

"A sad sign of the times Dai, and another example of the deterioration of the Christian faith... the fact that it is a house now for an unmarried couple," Chuck mused as he looked out at them busying themselves.

"Yes and no, Chuck," Dai sighed. "Marriage is not as popular as it should be, but the building itself was too small to influence the matter of faith. If anything, it was just another example of a fragmented faith... of course, we can trace that particular mischief back to the schism of the church and to the pollution of both by the Old Dragon."

"Well, regardless, it's good to see you," Chuck smiled as he turned the engine off.

Dai turned to face him; the angel was pleased by this comment and showed his pleasure through a dazzling smile which radiated across his beautifully smooth face. "Ditto my friend, ditto," he said softly, before assuming a more business-like tone again,

"So, you went hunting the Stroker trail, then?" he half-asked, half-told Chuck.

Chuck nodded with a timid anticipation of the response. Dai nodded, opened his door slightly and suggested that they take a stroll down the street to the beach again.

"Stroker was interesting; that was an instinctive move, was it not?" asked Dai as they set off slowly along the pavement.

"Guess so; he is a horrible little man, as I know from past dealings with him," replied Chuck.

"It's good thinking. And totally of your own mind," Dai patted him on the shoulder very lightly. "I'm pleased. So, presumably you think the scent will increase once you get on Stroker's back?" he asked, somewhat cheerily.

"Well, Frazer was his landlord, the girl was a pass-on job between them, so Stroker might be able to help me get onto this paedophile ring," mused Chuck.

A couple approached, coming from the direction of the beach. The man was large and muscular with a cropped head, and was wearing dark sunglasses. The woman was pretty, with a sweatband over her short blonde hair. The guy was talking in a Geordie accent about someone whom he had helped but could not help any more, and he appeared to be seeking her approval. The woman, however, simply stared at Dai, Chuck noticed. They both slowed down almost to a standstill, their eyes interlocked. The Geordie bloke noticed this too and stopped talking. Dai turned away eloquently and walked on, and they were all on their way.

"She was a disciple of hell, Chuck," Dai eventually said.

"Eh, what… is she, is she a fallen angel, Dai?" Chuck found himself whispering despite the couple now having walked on out of earshot.

"No, she's just human with Nephilim lineage."

"Right…" Chuck looked back, but the couple were still walking, "and the bloke?" he asked.

"Her puppet," Dai said, stopping to observe Chuck. "She was not sure about me but she was scared; I smelled her fear. She was confused and when she realises that she encountered an angel, as she will do soon, she will understand the feelings she experienced."

"But what was she doing here?" Chuck needed to know.

"Don't worry, she wasn't involved with us, and she won't bump into you again either. They have travelled up here from Newcastle and were just stretching their legs before moving on," Dai told him.

"And you just know this?"

"Precisely."

"What makes her puppet, as you call him, want to side with her lot then Dai?" Chuck felt it was a logical contention to presume that humans would instinctively choose light over darkness, so he sought to understand.

"In this instance, they serve hell because they are firm in their belief that the promised rewards are glorious."

"Rewards?"

"Varied things from wealth to health. What was it Dylan said about the powerful song lyrics he had produced? He said he could not have produced such lyrics."

Chuck shrugged his shoulders, he wasn't much of a Bob Dylan fan; preferring the Stones for their blues style instead.

"Then look into what he said about the earthly rewards," Dai smiled back at him. Just then Chuck felt a text come through to his phone in his pocket, which he politely ignored.

"Regardless, they are required to pursue the destruction of any authority, in any state, that enforces moral law and order that is originally grounded in scriptural ethics. Often they are violent and very obvious but in the main, and due to the Kertamen, they operate more subtly in their pursuit of social secularisation."

Chuck could see how this had developed considerably since his own youth. He passed his old Victorian school almost every day and only recently had noticed that the stone masons were chiselling away at the old 'Boys' and 'Girls' entrance signs. "They are even make the school toilets unisex I think I heard?" he thought aloud.

"And all under a subtle appearance of acceptance and spiritual diversity" said Dai sadly; "A ready-made alternate reality where all can do as they wish and be rewarded for it by a self-appointed prince of this new world" he shook his head despondently.

Chuck sighed, touched his toes and cranked his neck. His back creaked and he wanted to ask Dai if he could magic up a massage, but thought better of it.

"Chuck, I know this is a hard project to run, and I know that despite the strides you have made today, you remain quite concerned, am I right?" Dai asked with an overwhelming sense of compassion in his voice that Chuck had ever only previously felt from his mother.

"Well, yes, I am a bit concerned about the deadline at work, not to mention the chance that I might be attacked by a variety of monsters and half-breed Nephilim," he replied, half in jest.

"Naturally."

"Not to mention the tentacles of the cabalists which reach among my own employers. Men who will have similar sentiments toward myself and my team, should they discover what we are up to," Chuck protested now.

"I know, and that is why angels are protecting you, remember?" Dai smiled at him, and he completely relaxed again.

"You have been chosen because you are able to anticipate their moves and outfox them. Anyway, I have been authorised by upstairs to issue you with a weapon," Dai murmured reassuringly.

"Oh yeah?" Chuck beamed with interest, "a light sabre, something like that?"

"I'll tell you after we talk about your two leads – Trevelen and Stroker. I want to tell you Chuck, you have done well with Stroker. I know you're now hoping to press-gang him into playing his part for the team, but you have no idea of what you are sitting on with this one, so fasten your seatbelt." Dai had a serious expression now and his stunning features displayed a firmness that worried Chuck.

"Oh Christ, what the hell are we up against?"

"Don't take His name in vain, Chuck. Besides, there really is no need. Remember the old football adage instead: The game is played on grass, and not on the team sheet," Dai said, again, gently putting his arm around Chuck's shoulder. "Let's walk on, as I'm now authorised to fill you in a bit more on Trevelen and his ghostly presence, for he lurks in the shadows, does our Trevelen," he said.

"Ghostly?"

"Yes, it's his *modus operandi*," Dai confirmed that he was not referring to physical appearance.

"His Masonic-ness, then?" Chuck smirked contemptuously.

"Indeed," replied Dai as he quickened the pace.

Portobello beach was pretty this time of the evening. A handsome military type jogged past the two of them as they arrived at the old promenade, pursued by a pack of toiling women, whom he was presumably coaching toward bikini graduations. Once they had passed, the beach ahead was almost empty except for a couple walking away hand-in-hand. They walked down onto the dry sand and to Chuck's surprise, Dai motioned for him to sit down upon it. Chuck did so slowly, and was appreciative of the cooling breeze coming from sea. The soft sound of the sea massaging the shore relaxed his mind, perhaps partly because of a sense of nostalgia formed from frames of summer holidays in his mind. Among them were memories of sitting on this same beach as a child with his family.

"Yet the laughter and donkeys hoofing along the prom don't accompany the melancholy, do they?" Dai looked at him dreamily, as if reminiscing also.

"Eh well... no, they don't," Chuck realised that he had not really noticed, but something had been missing from his reverie, like a good song being replayed without the bass or piano.

"Or the smell of the fish and chip shops which had once flourished here in better times," Dai looked out at the sea as he spoke.

"Yes," Chuck nodded in agreement. He had always bought chips when he came out of the sea as a kid, and the smell of vinegar had formed part of the whole sensory experience.

"You see Chuck, everything is there to be seen, smelled and heard; the trick is to use your capabilities fully," Dai told him.

"I understand," Chuck really did when it was explained this way. "Pickled onions still remind me of this," he smiled.

"Well, our objectives can be fulfilled in the same manner: you will need to apply your full range of instincts, subtlety and discretion whilst always remaining mentally sharp, if we have any hope of out-thinking the foe, Chuck."

"Yes, and I am onto something with Stroker, aren't I?" Chuck felt confident enough to say so.

"Stroker would have come to you through Trevelen, lad. Oh... that's the other thing you need to do..." Dai looked at his face with a glint of humour in those piercing eyes. "Listen to me when I throw you a tip," he said before that infectious chuckle followed.

"I followed my instincts, Dai, isn't that why you guys are using me on this?"

"Indeed, young Kean, indeed," Dai looked back out to sea again, but with a glowing smile now, which forced Chuck to do likewise.

"Let me tell you about Philip Trevelen." Dai patted Chuck on the shoulder again, ever so softly. Chuck sat cross-legged and let grains of sand pour from his fist like an egg timer as he listened.

"The Trevelens are kin to a Templar who took his wealth and retired from the order to the land around Duddingston loch, precisely where Philip Trevelen resides in his boat house today," explained Dai.

"A Templar?"

"Quite. He retired after the fall of their version of Camelot in 1312, when Pope Clement dissolved their order and gave their enormous assets to the Knights of Malta; in a bid to save them, I might add."

"Save them?"

"Yes; they were answering for their evil in France by facing arrests and persecution, but elsewhere in Europe they were found innocent of any wrongdoing thanks to Pope Clement's administration, who were sympathetic," Dai told him.

"A few were able to join the Knights of Malta and others held onto their wealth and retired out of the spotlight in the east, in Africa, and in this case – Craggenmarf."

"Craggenmarf?"

"That's the old name for the land between the crags of Arthur's Seat and east to where the Magdalene estate sits today."

Chuck nodded to show that he understood the geography.

"In 1140, King David I of Scotland gave the land to the church. Then, in 1311, just before the Templars fell, one of them going by the name Traefor Lyn arrived at Rosslyn, where one or two other Templars had already acquired land, seeking to establish himself. He was obliged by the church, who sold him the land at a pittance. Eventually, Traefor Lyn became Trevelen and the family were closely connected to a Norman family already established in Scotland by Adam De Gordon; who, I believe, Lionel Frazer mentioned to you."

"Sorry, but... so, Trevelen is connected and probably a member of Frazer's TIC lodge, then?"

"That is for you to discover, Chuck. Moving on," Dai smiled again. "Philip Trevelen is now the head of that little family and, as you know, lives on the Loch side in the same spot his descendants have occupied since 1311."

"So, he's our Master Mason?" Chuck raised an eyebrow, hoping to find some sort of acknowledgement.

"You tell me... Anyway, stop interrupting. Trevelen is an ambitious man, I can tell you that much. He believes that he has not fulfilled his potential."

"Don't all men?" Chuck asked, because he did.

"No." Dai shook his head, ending that notion. "He seeks power; not a huge amount, but like his ancestors he feels he deserves at least a little bit. His father Giles was worse, but he wasn't half as cunning. You see, Giles was a Satanist, as was his father before him. The last hundred years' worth of the family were all fanatical about the staged eccentricities of the Scottish upper crust."

"Privilege and wealth convinced them that they were royalty, then?" asked Chuck.

"I wouldn't quite go that far, but their education, occasional titles and family traditions ensured that they certainly fancied... and still do... themselves, as the crème de la crème of tartan society."

"Gordonstoun?" This was the only posh Scottish school that sprung to Chuck's mind as having any royal connection.

Dai chuckled at this, "What was it your namesake the Prince of Wales said about Gordonstoun? 'Colditz in kilts', that was it, no; the last few Trevelens went to Rugby, and Giles Trevelen was obsessed with boarding school privilege and grandeur. From what I can tell, his son is somewhat more adventurous about how to increase power, however," he explained.

"Giles was smart, educated and confident, but he was hardly bourgeois. He was an ambitious socialite who, through his Satanic worship, desired political power and failed a few times, before giving up and hanging himself at his Fife estate."

"His Fife estate?" asked Chuck.

"Yes, The Melville family had been the Foresters of Falkland in Fife and held titles, including the Barony of Monimail. They had a medium-sized estate in Monimail by Letham, and once held a strong presence at the courts of Charles I and II, who used Falkland Palace as a summer hunting lodge," Dai revealed.

"The Trevelens won the Melville estate over a game of cards in 1809 and, of course, your target, Philip Trevelen still owns the place today."

"Right, I see; and what goes on there, then, Dai?"

"It is a family business now. Bramble wine, that's their thing nowadays, and Philip only goes there occasionally to authorise paperwork."

"What, like raspberry or strawberry wine?"

"Nope, just bramble. Giles produced gooseberry wine for a while in the 1960s but it is just bramble today. Philip doesn't make much on it actually; just enough to run the estate; and even that is down to his French in-laws who sell it under their label as a dessert wine in Canada."

"So, he runs the estate to pretend to himself that he is a real wine man like his wife's family?" Chuck was beginning to feel that he had Trevelen half-sussed.

"Indeed, Chuck. He calls it the *Melville Brig Bramble,* and has failed so far to persuade the British public to go for it; in fact, he even had a tantrum at the last Highland Show at Ingleston when his marketing pitch was placed beside a popular Orkney rhubarb wine tent. He only produces 10,000 bottles per year and has been adding more and more loganberries due to a decline in his bramble supply, so it is on a timer and he knows this."

Chuck was no wine expert. "Do you like wine, Dai?" he asked out of curiosity.

"Yes, earthly wine… yes I do on occasion, Chuck, usually with honey; but moving on," Dai produced that loving smile again which created so much welcoming comfort and relaxation. Chuck found that despite the gravity of the subject matter, he was coming to love these exchanges, which could take him almost anywhere in time or space. Dai resumed his briefing with the gentle smile fading as he became more serious again.

"Philip Trevelen is quite a different proposition compared to his father, Chuck; he is similarly well-connected, but he also has a much cooler understanding of how to utilise his connections in the pursuit of power."

Chuck nodded, "Go on."

"Whereas both father and son were/are laissez-faire businessmen and socialites with burning ambitions, Giles worshiped Satan because his father before him had; he was an irrelevant worshipper rather than someone who offered leadership qualities. In the end, he gave up his pursuit of power and drank himself into despair and suicide. Philip, on the other hand, is very much someone his peers can use for his organisational cunning."

"Can you elaborate on the matter of 'peers', Dai?" Chuck asked.

"No, that is for you to research, Chuck." Dai smiled again before appearing to catch a scent on the breeze and looking over at a window somewhere. Suddenly, he turned back to Chuck and gave him another of those delightful smiles, which once again illuminated the soul.

"I take it the family all went to Edinburgh Uni too?"

"St. Andrews and the military actually, though one of the Rugbeians[14] attended Cambridge; where he was an associate of Ramanujan[15]," revealed Dai cheerily.

"Ramanujan?" Chuck wasn't familiar with the name.

"Another Mozart, sadly" sighed Dai, "Not important anyway, just note that your particular Trevelen is from sharp stock," he insisted.

"What else can you tell me about him, then?" Chuck felt that he needed to squeeze as much as he could out of his angelic source while there was an opportunity.

---

[14] Term for former pupils of Rugby School in Warwickshire.

[15] Srinivasa Ramanujan (1887-1920) was an office clerk in Madras India without any formal education, who wrote to mathematicians in England with his new analysis and number theories. He was brought over to Cambridge by excited experts, given lodgings at Trinity, a formal education and a degree. He is regarded by some academics to have been the finest mathematical mind in history.

"Well, he went to Cambridge, then did a Masters in Sydney, where he absolutely shone. After that he turned down some exciting internships in Hong Kong before returning home and working for Giles. He inherited the Melville estate in 1980 along with some Georgian properties in Edinburgh, which he developed into flats over several years. He has managed to create a lucrative high-end rental portfolio."

"Not short of a bob or two then, so is he the financial leader of our wee cabal?" Chuck whispered now.

"What makes you think that wealth is relevant?" asked Dai with a mischievious grin.

"Isn't it always with these types?" replied Chuck.

"Depends whose agenda is pulling their strings, Chuck, remember that." Dai tapped his nose as humans might.

"What else can you tell me about him?"

"This one plays the long game," said Dai as he allowed a bug to rest on his hand a moment before it flew off again across the beach.

"He cares not for the Bramble estate, nor for his flats. He runs the wine business to link him to his wife and her family, whose connections with the French elite he lusts to foster. Yet he has struggled in that particular design so far for obvious reasons, so he now focuses upon another game, which is closer to home and currently invisible," revealed Dai.

"Invisible?"

"Yes, as it is being played out in the shadows, of course," Dai urged him to keep up. "His properties are used to spy on the tenants he considers to be of interest, as opposed to being business tools, as such."

"And if they are Georgian properties, we are talking footballer-type lease-holders then?" Chuck saw the picture and Dai confirmed it with a nod.

"Unlike his father he is not fervently ideological. Though he is Mosleyite when pressed, he tends to keep it all in the closet. He is hardly cavalier; rather, he is the type to wait at the poker table until he really fancies his hand. He can be ruthless in business, of course. He may not have inherited his father's detestation of Jews, blacks or plebs, but he does have the assured personality of the Edinburgh upper crust and an their benign tolerance for everyone else. At school he liked to make himself look good at the expense of others, and this is still how he operates today. He is a cool customer Chuck; I can't stress that enough, and he may be a real challenge for you, if and when you duel with him. Regardless, he still should be the focus of your attention at the moment, trust me." These last words sounded very much like a warning to Chuck.

"So he is bent, satanic and highly ambitious… Well, he is going to have to slip up big-time, Dai, because the clock is ticking and if he feels the heat we are putting on him, he could cause a shit storm by calling in his connections." Chuck felt he had to point out the obvious.

"Certainly, but the fact that we know he doesn't play a straight bat means you might get somewhere with him, so be focused upon him tomorrow, OK?" the angel insisted.

Chuck nodded. He deeply appreciated the intel from his otherwordly companion, but he had sussed initially that Trevelen was potentially a lead, so none of this was exactly groundbreaking information.

"You wouldn't be able to trust him with directions, Chuck," Dai assured, "but that very fact means that now that you are observing him, the likelihood is that he will do something naughty and hand you a lead." Dai's words were insistent and delivered with another warm smile that projected confidence all over Chuck, who believed him instantly.

"So, I'm hoping this fascist sinner has an agenda this week which is sufficiently naughty enough to help me discover the names of all those involved in this paedo cabal," Chuck told himself, and Dai nodded at this thought.

"Precisely. Trevelen's avocations would make the weasels around his boathouse blush, so it is quite likely, young Chuck, never fear," Dai assured.

"You have an opportunity now to fufill your own potential to become a good man, Chuck. Don't let Trevelen and his clandestine mischief leave you behind," Dai urged, gripping Chuck's shoulder and transmitting a strange kind of solidity and confidence.

This was somewhat different to the previous conversations, Chuck considered. He was left in no doubt of the importance of Trevelen, and that Dai wanted him to investigate and take the man on somehow, but he also instictively wondered if there was more to all of this than just a paedophile ring involving some pwerful men. Was this immediate struggle simply a small piece in a bigger jigsaw?

"No problem, I'm on Trevelen 24/7. The boys are watching him tonight and I will get on his case in the morning after I hit Stroker," Chuck said to Dai, with what he hoped sounded like a steely resolve.

Dai chuckled, "You know, Chuck, I watch you struggling for faith; not in us, but in your own ability. All is well, I assure you; we are on track and preparing well for the tests ahead. Your Lord has granted permission for you to be issued with this," he said, as he suddenly produced what for all the world appeared to be a yellow plastic ball launcher for dogs, which he handed over to Chuck with two hands as if it were Excalibur.

"What's this?" Chuck wondered out loud.

"Hold the handle…" Dai pointed to it.

It was about forty inches long, and Chuck slowly did as he was told. It was flexible plastic with a tennis ball in the cup.

"Now, press your thumb on the thumb print," Dai pointed again at a small thumb print which had been melted onto the back of the holding part. "Yes…it is your fingerprint, Chuck," Dai said, reading his thoughts.

The second Chuck pressed his thumb on the print, the curved part of the launcher shape shifted into an obviously sharp rim like that of a machete. When he released the pressure, the sword edge disappeared and the smooth plastic rim returned.

"That blade is spell forged and will cut through the steel door of a bank vault, Chuck. If any fallen ones or Nephilim confront you in your task, you will defend yourself with this divine tool. It is, as you probably realise, shaped like a ball-thrower for dogs because no-one would ever consider it strange to see you carrying it; indeed, that's why the little price tag is still hanging from it," he explained.

"But I will be carrying it without a dog?" Chuck raised his lip into the beginning of a smile before asking, "And does the ball do anything?"

Dai laughed, "I'm not 'Q' from James Bond, but if you launch it somewhere then yes, every dog within 50 yards of it will attack whoever happens to be standing within a foot of where it lands, with all the strength they can muster," he confirmed.

"Right, well, thanks," Chuck said, wondering if he was going to have to learn some sword moves on the internet before getting to bed that evening.

"Don't lose it, Chuck; no one else can use it for violence, but don't lose it because I want it back, alright?" Dai warned and Chuck nodded.

"And remember, you're never alone."

Again Chuck nodded.

" *The only thing necessary for the triumph of evil is for good men to do nothing*'," Dai quoted Burke to him as they both got up, Chuck feeling the strain in his leg muscles as he did so.

"I know," he said, forcing back a little groan as his hamstrings tightened.

"The question is whether you are going to be a good man or not, Chuck," Dai said before turning and walking swiftly away, up the stairs then along the promenade, with Chuck trying to keep pace.

"Thanks for the sword," Chuck called.

"Collydean Golf Club," came the reply. "Research that when you're looking up Ramanujan and Dylan tonight," chuckled Dai knowingly, but then he was gone.

As Chuck walked up the road, he checked his text messages. There was only one but without any number, which was earily strange; "https://www.youtube.com/watch?v=3qI-Koffmpk" it read.

He watched the two minute video of Dylan being interviewed and then deleted it.

Eight

"You are a den of vipers and thieves. I have determined to rout you out, and by the Eternal, I will rout you out"

Andrew Jackson, US President (1829-37)

Colin Anderson-Forbes finally found a moment to chill out in front of the television with his partner and a bottle of wine. They were cuddled up on the large Swedish sofa, watching the Scottish teatime news on the television. A squeaky-voiced female was reporting on the Edinburgh Fringe.

"We should take in a show the next time you're at Holyrood, Colin," his lover whispered in his ear before teasing its rim with her tongue.

"Won't be much time for that with my schedule, Pat, not with the referendum run-in," he said before supping at his glass of rosé. "Besides, there isn't anyone good on, I'm told; all Johnny Foreigners and poofs," he teased in his bad Churchill impersonation.

"Crap! There's some great music on. Anyway, I've ordered the listings online and will let you know what I choose, right?" She gave him a little more flickering, which aroused him slightly. He took another sup before turning to look into her eyes, but then the house phone rang and she jumped up barefooted and glided pleasingly into the hallway to answer it.

"It's a Graeme De Sailes for you," she called through.

Forbes pulled himself up from the sofa and marched through with his usual catwalk strut. He took the cordless phone like a ballerina, winked and then strutted on through to the billiards room of his 19th century Italianate mansion.

"Good evening, Graeme," Forbes spoke crisply into the handset.

"Not so here in Cape Town, Colin, I can tell you that much, Sir. Thunder and lightning with hailstones the size of meat balls," came the distinctly southern American accent. Louisiana, Forbes guessed.

"What are you doing there?" he had to ask.

"Oh, I'm at a convention for the Sub-Saharan oil and gas industry, and we just landed into this weather," De Sailes explained. "The Western Cape was much nicer, I don't mind saying."

"Really, well I have never been much fussed about visiting myself, particularly the south where it appears to have all gone quite insane in the last few years," Forbes said curtly.

De Sailes gave out a well-worn but staged laugh before swiftly getting down to business: "Colin, you start your sponsored cycle on Monday, am I correct?"

"That is correct, Graeme." Forbes wondered where this was going exactly, and why it warranted an international call instead of an email.

"That is highly commendable, I must say, which clearly highlights the enthusiasm you bring to your party," De Sailes was crawling now and Forbes knew it.

"Well, thank you Graeme…"

"Would you be able to find time thereafter to meet some of our friends from Akadion?" De Sailes asked ever so sweetly.

Forbes knew he could hardly say no to this request; the oil company which De Sailes represented had, alongside Akadion, very discreetly donated £2,050,000 to his political party over the last six months. A few months earlier, Forbes had met with financiers from Akadion on Robin Handy's yacht in Menorca. Handy was a camp Scottish wannabe with a mother from Clydebank and a shifty Scouse accent. He was well-regarded as a celebrity chef and had two TV shows, one in London and the other in LA. Consequently, he was the darling of society on both sides of the pond and sucked up perfectly to the showbiz personalities.

Cooking for the private pleasure of various media moguls and showbiz luvvies at their private functions, Handy had wormed his way into the handbags of the rich and famous. Consequently, he had been encouraged by one or two sources to pay more homage to Scotland. So, in 2012 he brought out an eight-part cooking show set in various Scottish regions, in which he researched traditional recipes and then cooked for random Scots, including some celebrities, in their own homes: *The Auld Scran Tour*. A Christmas special followed from a cosy-looking home in Edinburgh which was popular not only in the States because of the Bing Crosby vibe and the three singers who turned up, but also in Scotland, where his ice cream Christmas pudding went down well.

When Forbes' two younger advisers, John Logan and Vernon Keith, were gifted £50,000 each to make their boss attend a party aboard Handy's yacht under the pretence that to do so would make him seem cool and classy to the Scottish people, both Forbes and his partner had flown out to the Balearics for a weekend aboard the '*Natalie Wood*'.

"Why on earth did you call her that?" A purple-nosed drunk, who owned a hair transplant surgery in Newton Mearns with his blonde secretary from Castlemilk upon his knee, asked Handy.

"She was already named that when I bought her; it seemed disrespectful to change it," Handy smirked as he helped himself to some more champagne sangria.

The morning after the party, Forbes found himself in a large room below deck with Handy, a so-called Canadian security expert, a man named 'Jim' from the oil industry, and the media mogul Pollock Hamilton. They had been playing billiards when they were joined by a certain Bill Garneau, who was apparently from South Carolina. It turned out that Garneau represented the arms industry giant – Akadion. It was here, in what turned out to be a three-hour boozy question and answer session, that generous offers to donate to the SLP first appeared. Handy had been called away to prepare food on deck, leaving Forbes among a party of SLP admirers. Initially, the figures offered were £25,000 each from Garneau and 'Jim', but a few weeks later these donors upped this to a further £1,000,000 apiece.

Everyone who was present at the time had been at great pains to express their accordance with the party's stances on immigration and economics, on which Pollock Hamilton was surprisingly well-informed. "My paper has an interest in the removal of ethnic minorities from the UK taxpayers-funded comfort zone, which they currently take for granted," he declared whilst watching the billiards.

"In the end, and quite off the record here, would you change Scottish law within an independent Scottish state, so that second and third generation immigrants could be forcibly removed from the country?" the old hack asked with a playful smile.

Everyone stopped in their tracks and the room fell silent as they all looked at Forbes for his reaction to such a dangerous question. Forbes had been sitting at a card table drinking orange with champagne and watching the billiards. This was a surprise but he considered the question a moment; he did not quite trust Hamilton and immediately imagined a '*Menorcagate*' headline running in Hamilton's tabloid rag, *the Mercury*, or even within his weekly political mag, *Manifesto*. "You first, Pollock," he grinned at him, causing the others to laugh, and look at Hamilton, who also smiled and nodded.

De Sailes was the representative of the oil cabal whose generous donation would later become so secretive. He had instigated talks regarding

SLP policies toward North Sea oil and gas within an independent state, soon after donating. So, this request for a lunch meeting was hardly unexpected; indeed, Forbes rather suspected there may be some more capital to be gained if he played this right.

De Sailes had cut him short on the phone and Forbes awaited a follow-up call, wondering how the guy got his home number. Just then, the doorbell at his comfortable home rang.

"Chinese is here," she smiled as he returned to the lounge.

As they ate the food, the inevitable return call from De Sailes came in and quickly Forbes agreed to meet with Bill Garneau from Akadion at 1:30 pm that Wednesday in Stirling at the Meeraj vegetarian restaurant. Forbes then quickly texted his PA and spin paramedic, John Logan, telling him to fit this appointment in for Wednesday.

"We are due to attend the schoolkids' performance at Stirling Castle at 2 pm, so it's almost impossible, boss," had been the irritating reply, just as Forbes had picked up another gooey spare rib. He tutted as he replaced it upon his plate and wiped his hand on an embroidered napkin before replying,

"It's 2 seconds from the castle, so a quick word, then away again." Forbes knew that with the majority of his lunch appointments, he got no lunch at all; and both Logan and Keith knew that on the campaign trail, sandwiches or bakery bridies were a necessity.

The following morning, Forbes got up and had a breakfast of porridge before taking his first call from Logan at 07:16. Logan went over the schedule while Forbes listened on loudspeaker and ate his meal. First, he would cycle to Johnstone, then to Elderslie, Linwood, and then Paisley, where he was to have lunch with staff and clients in a drug addicts outreach centre. Then, he would cycle to Renfrew and campaign for independence outside a Tesco store for an hour with a soap box and a loudspeaker. After that, he would cycle home via the B790 and get ready to travel to Hamilton for a radio discussion about his party's manifesto.

"You can expect to be home around about 9 pm, boss, do you want me to arrange for something to be in the oven, or do you want to eat out?" asked Logan.

Forbes had a cook who would be contacted and instructed on what to prepare and when to prepare it, but tonight he had other plans. "I'm meeting Ewan for a drink and some food later," he said. Ewan Lawrenson was a city financier who had offices in Glasgow, London and Singapore. He had been at university with Forbes and the two men had been close friends for years. Lawrenson had donated a fair sum to the party and worked hard on its behalf, quietly and without much public recognition, as he preferred to remain unknown outside of Forbes' 'clique'.

Forbes' clique, as it was known throughout the SLP, had drawn some criticism from one or two grumblers within the core of the party because of its exclusivity and opacity, as well as its silencing of critics. It had become known among some members as the 'Forbes Mafia'. Forbes' response was to remove the origins of the dissent and then hunt down any remaining bad apples, thus living up to that epithet. This worked perfectly until one person, a budgeting specialist, had been sacked, officially for refusing to share a referendum stage with a Scottish/Indian Labour shadow MSP from Dundee.

"Bloody Coolie should know her place," [16] he had said publicly on the radio, before proceeding to call the poor pro-unionist a "Tanned Myra Hindley."

Forbes had to sack him, though privately he was sympathetic, as the bloke was usually more discreet with his contempt, and had been an excellent fisheries expert. Following the cull, it became even harder for outsiders to enter the exquisite sphere of the preferred few. City man Lawrenson had, however, successfully instigated cash for access dinners with Forbes by whispering in the ears of his sympathisers both in Scotland and London. A boozy dinner in St Ives with various people, including a shipping magnate and some Eastern European businessmen, gained the party £312,000 in anonymous donations.

Despite Forbes, as a new energetic leader, not allowing a wider circle at the top, there could be little doubt that he had provided exciting new assets to bolster the party's totalitarian views and aspirations; that of charm, energy and much-required finance.

Forbes often credited Lawrenson among his inner circle as being "our unofficial head of strategy," and once to his mother as "The bloke who is going to help me drag our little party from centre-right to far-right." In reality, Lawrenson was just well-connected to certain money people ranging from centre-right to beyond contempt, and that was what he did best: promote Forbes as an intense, energetic, good-looking 46-year-old leader as the new cool face of the party. Forbes' rhetoric had been well-judged right from the outset, concentrating on climate change initially, before making a subtle argument for withdrawing all funding to ethnic minorities in the voluntary sector and proposing Scottish-only projects that

---

[16] Coolies were unskilled labourers who worked in British India, New Zealand and Mauritius. Train station baggage handlers in India today are still referred to as Coolies.

would be open to all instead of just minorities. It had a certain kind of logic, since Labour had been throwing millions at this sector in the hope of securing successful multiculturalism, while all they had achieved was to segregate minorities who had established separate lifestyles outwith mainstream communities.

Forbes' central argument was that this funding promoted separate religious communities and that these were the root cause of the UK's production of Islamic terrorists. With an undercurrent of racism emerging since 9/11, many Scots felt that Forbes was making strong points without the crude barrage of silly racist doctrine that other fascist parties produced.

"We were happy to have people come here from our former UK colonies because we are a fair and tolerant society. Many immigrants to Scotland have been successful and their descendants are an important part of our demography," Forbes pointed out. "However, unlike the Chinese, Italian, Caribbean and Persian communities, who work hard, integrate and embrace our culture, and who in turn are perfectly free to worship, be educated and capitalise on the laissez-faire traditions of our grandfathers, the Pakistani Muslim community prefer to live within a 6th century bubble," he argued on a live television debate with the flu-ridden and coughing Labour leader Josie McMurdo the previous year, where he received a standing ovation from the audience.

"American Muslims consider themselves as Americans, yet many Muslims here, even third generation ones from the Pakistani community, consider themselves Muslim first, then Pakistani and then as Scottish," he had told a rally in Perth, arousing rapturous applause.

"I see there are even Muslim Scout groups here in Edinburgh. An institution designed to bond and integrate boys from a young age, being used to create ethnic and religious diversity, must surely be considered a root cause of this social cancer within our land," he argued to a huge crowd of 14,000 at a party rally in Edinburgh. A rally where there was also some violent disturbances as thugs chanting racist slogans created a brawl with protesting students.

"Under my leadership, the funding that is, in effect, promoting the fragmentation of community, will end. For I believe that the most important possession our great nation has is our people. After all, we are the people who invented aviation. Who invented the marine compound expansion engine, the first passenger steamboats, roller printing, the motion picture camera, the telephone, the television, radar, the first textbook on surgery, the first ebook, modern economics, tropical medicine, the light bulb, the world's first oil refinery, colloid chemistry, and of course we discovered transplant rejection, the MRI body scanner, insulin, penicillin, general anaesthetics, and the X-ray machine." The crowd roared to this and even the impartial and unconvinced amongst them had found it difficult to find fault with him.

"We, the pudding race, are a unique people and we are rightly proud of ourselves. You are welcome to join us, but please do as we do. For we do not welcome barbaric 6th century cultures either being forced upon us or practiced within our society. Stoning women to death, genital mutilation and forced marriages will not be tolerated under an SLP government in an independent Scotland. Only if we become an independent state can we make the changes necessary to protect our great people from the evils of terrorism," he told the BBC breakfast studio recently in London.

"So, do you argue for the deportation of third-generation Pakistanis?" a student asked him one night, live on a Q&A TV broadcast from Arbroath being screened across the UK.

"No, certainly not. However, I think immigration should be carefully controlled and certain undesirables who were not born here could potentially be removed, should they flaunt our laws," he had replied softly, earning another round of applause as doubts were confirmed.

"So, you would simply chuck out a person in their 70s for speeding, despite the fact they had lived in say, Blantyre, for 65 years?" an irate Tory panel member had gasped in response.

"Hardly, Hazel," replied Forbes, without taking his gaze from the crowd. "Each case would require a professional review; however, I am talking about a person who commits an honour killing or who takes part in the gang rape of vulnerable children. Not to mention terrorist offences." Forbes spoke with a cheeky grin and a wink which again reached out even to many liberals watching at home, for he was handsome, endearing and manipulated very well indeed.

"Our liberalism has been our weakness in recent times, and if we are to end this problem of a deep multicultural divide, we must treat everyone the same and ask everyone to embrace their Scottish-ness. In an independent Scotland with the SLP in government, I will force this home and create an undivided people who are proud to call themselves Scottish first, and anything else second," he then told Holyrood. Afterwards, a high-profile Scottish Conservative MSP, James Snelgrove, jumped ship and was shown on the news embracing the SLP alongside Forbes on the Edinburgh Castle esplanade.

'Divided by Tradition and Wealth' had been the SLP's motto for their big independence push then, and Salmond's SNP point-blank refused to work with them. "The SNP under my leadership would never work with fascists, so the answer to that question is a resounding no," he told a reporter asking whether the SNP might ally with the SLP in the push for independence.

"We are not fascists here at the SLP," Forbes had chuckled when the press had asked for his response, coolly adding that "we really must take these reports with a pinch of salt, especially considering that one of his predecessors is reported to have held very contrary views and was also said to have conspired with Nazi Germany against these isles." Forbes dealt with the SNP in the same manner that he did Labour; he took the fight to them and did so by ordering his aides to issue daily statements across social media. This insured that he reached huge numbers of people who avoided the news. Due to his natural wit, he was also quite able to dictate fluently and without notes, which helped him to gain the audiences' trust via radio broadcasts.

As he cycled from Houston to Johnstone that morning however, the sun was out bright and early. He was wearing a shirt, a cycle helmet and jeans as he flew along the road. Behind him were two security men on Vespa scooters and a mini bus with Logan, Keith and three PR dollies, affectionately known by the national media as "Col's Dolls." By the time he arrived in Johnstone, a small Fiat was flying along the road beside them with a photographer leaning out from a window, taking snaps.

"Fuck off, you cunt!" shouted one of the security men as they entered Johnstone, but he went silent and wound his neck in when another car arrived from Scottish Television and began filming Forbes' push up the high street toward Elderslie. As he laboured along, there were some jeers and an egg flew from somewhere and hit the mini bus, but Forbes proceeded unharmed. As he passed Johnstone train station, several people with saltire flags cheered the passing procession, and as he exited the town he saw a huge electronic screen displaying his party's pro-independence statement. Forbes was impressed and told himself that he now knew where the money was going.

In Elderslie, he noticed two men unloading cases of fizzy drinks from a silver Mercedes Vito van. Both men looked in their thirties; one was Asian and the other white, and Forbes cycled up and pulled over beside them. He asked them if they were delivery drivers and they shook their heads. The Asian male spoke firmly, "shopkeeper, and he is my worker." Forbes guessed that neither man had recognised him,

"My name is Colin; may I shake your hand? I am a politician fighting for the rights of small businesses," he lied. Suddenly, as the two cars pulled up alongside to film and take photos, Forbes reached out a gloved hand and shook the shopkeeper's hand. The confused-looking man would be on the following day's front pages. Forbes then reached out for the other man's hand but the chap quickly pulled a hood over his head, then jogged off up the street. Forbes smiled calmly and began cycling again. The car with the television camera filming him pulled alongside him somewhat recklessly now and a male shouted out the window.

"Why do you think that guy bolted off like that and refused to shake your hand, Colin?"

Forbes turned in feigned confusion. "Perhaps the shopkeeper is doing what many others have done over the last twenty-five years and is employing individuals who are in receipt of sickness benefit?" He had been glad both of getting the photo, but also for having gloves on when shaking the Asian gent's hand.

In Elderslie, the birthplace of that champion of Scottish independence, William Wallace, there was a 'Yes' picket with several pro-independence locals gathered and handing out leaflets for the SNP. A smattering of boos rang out as Forbes cruised past towards Linwood, but the assembled SLP volunteers across the road soon drowned them out with cheers for their hero. After a long stop at a butcher's shop, wherein he accepted a gift of two fillet steaks and passed them to the girls on the bus, Forbes spent some more time talking to a paperboy who was halfway through his round. Forbes asked whether he would consider doing two years' national service in the military if it were available. Much to his delight, the kid replied that he wanted to be a mechanical engineer, and that if the military could help him do that, he would be glad to join up. Forbes gave the camera a trademark wink and spoke directly to it,

"All our youth require is direction and discipline in order to avoid the temptations of drugs or a benefit lifestyle," he told the camera. The camera man, a seasoned Labour voter, thought for a brief moment that it might be an option to consider the SLP in the elections next year.

That night Forbes was driven to a hotel near Loch Lomond, where he met, wined, dined and conspired with Ewan Lawrenson. They rejoiced in the fact that the SLP had greatly widened their base of support in recent times and that some political analysts were hinting that the party was not only going to blow both Labour and the Tories out of the water in any post-independence elections, but that in the long-term under Forbes, the party may well give the SNP a run for its money. Lawrenson was an outspoken Euro-hater, but for the moment he reined this in to focus on ensuring that the broadcasters adored Forbes.

"Once they sense how the tide is going, they will get on board with us," he promised, though the wine had got to both men by the time the cheeseboard was served.

"Well, we can get the plebs' votes by bigging up the downgrading of certain drugs and then focusing all our attentions on the farmers," Lawrenson insisted between mouthfuls of cheddar and oatcake.

"I really sense we're close to making some great strides," Lawrenson continued, a glint of imagined success in his eyes. He had always been a pragmatic centrist, but had turned to the hard-right in recent times whilst embarking on this mission toward Camelot with his old friend. The two men had bonded politically years ago, when they had been in trouble for burning Tony Benn's "*Arguments for Democracy*" in a mock KKK-styled ceremony in their university lodgings, causing the Fire Brigade to attend.

Currently they ordered port from the Polish waiter, who lacked class they both felt, as he clumsily told them that he himself preferred a brandy after dinner. The fellow was only being friendly and many diners would have welcomed this cheeriness, however Forbes looked at him as if he had farted while Lawrenson curtly replied: "Well that is by the by, young Igor, and we care not for your preferences, thank you very much. We also enjoy brandy after dinner, but we are still eating as you can clearly see and the port is an accompaniment... goodbye."

The waiter was not entirely sure if this was rudeness, for Lawrenson had cunningly displayed such a polite expression that the chap's grasp of English was not strong enough to detect the sarcasm. Forbes considered complaining but then smiled and said, "It is quite alright, thanks," and thought it would be good to be photographed with the waiter. He resigned himself to the fact that this was unlikely, and decided instead to leave a very large tip in the hope of some press leak by the hotel. If not, it could easily get leaked to the Mercury.

"Food for thought," he smiled as he washed his food down with a sip of water while they awaited the arrival of their port.

"Portuguese or Spanish?" Lawrenson tried to guess, when it arrived and he sampled it.

"All the same, Ewan," Forbes smirked contemptuously. "Dago bastards," he hissed through his teeth, and both men laughed.

When Wednesday arrived, Forbes made sure that he had been photographed by the press striding into the Meeraj restaurant in Stirling. He looked sharp in his grey Prince of Wales checked suit and pink shirt with blue polka dot tie. The meeting was short, but went relatively well. The Akadion representative discussed the concerns of the arms industry within

Scotland and the potential for a standing Scottish army and air force, should independence be achieved. Forbes listened to the man, but was careful not to commit to anything, nor even to smile or nod in assent, when the chap discussed his company's export focus over the last few years and how this could change with the need for a Scottish military defence force.

"The English won't show much interest in defending Scotland, should they leave the union," he had warned.

"You're working on some sort of missile defence dome for Israel at your Surrey base, are you not?" Forbes asked between mouthfuls of coffee. The man delayed his response as a rather attractive female wearing a hijab, and what Forbes thought might have been Chanel scent, served them some pakoras. Both men glanced at her obviously shapely breasts, which were well-covered under a tight blouse, but which pushed firmly against the material as she leaned over.

"We propose moving all our UK productions to Scotland within the next couple of years, should the situation be assessed as a lucrative one," the pink faced little man said as he began eating his pakora.

"I see; well, we should definitely explore whatever it is you have in mind. Let us arrange a meeting in due course, where we can examine your proposals and be clear about our relationship," Forbes smiled to give him some encouragement before then making his excuses and leaving.

"How was it?" Logan asked as they walked over to the car. He had been in the restaurant too, sat beside the team's media head, Darren Reid, but their table had been out of earshot beside the door.

"Fine, John," smirked Forbes. "That was Bill Garneau from Akadion Arms, who has the drone contract down south," he told the two of them as they walked over to the cars.

"Pakoras were nice then, boss?" Logan asked as Reid informed a journalist on his phone that Forbes would be at the castle in "a minute or two."

All three men then got into one car and, looking hard at one of Col's Dolls who was sitting waiting, Logan mouthed at her, "Do we smell of curry?"

"Not really," the redheaded PR officer smiled as she passed Forbes a mobile phone. "It's Dr Lesley Sheridan for you about Sunday's presentation at Ingleston," she whispered.

"Who?" Forbes mouthed back.

"The chief executive of Midlothian Regional Council," whispered Darren Reid from the front seat.

"Hello Dr Sheridan, how are you?" Forbes accordingly spoke into the handset with what he deemed his Sean Connery flirty voice.

"Uh-huh, I completely concur with that particular notion, yes," he said.

"What did she want?" asked Logan once the brief call had ended.

"To inquire into whether or not certain undesirable councillors are removed from the invite list to the Ingleston thing," smirked Forbes. "Anyway, to Camelot!" he cried as they approached the castle.

Later that evening when back at home, Forbes did not make love to his partner when he entered their bedroom at around one in the morning. Instead, he half-woke her and immediately forced her into aggressive sex wherein he closed his eyes, and squeezed her nipples and cheeks whilst imagining himself raping the hijab-wearing waitress from the vegetarian restaurant...

"Biiitch!" he yelled as he quickly ejaculated into her womb before drooping his head, rolling over, and lying limp with his tired eyes closed. She remained lying beside him, in tears and pain.

Nine

"To silence the puppeteer, you need only destroy the puppet"

Val Edward Simone

With a sudden, deep gasp for air, Alban Dudley awoke upon his bunk bed, facing the ceiling and still rather stoned. The sound of repeated banging cut through the dark still, as fists pounded upon the timber door. It stopped and then began again; this time, his heart skipped along to the thumping beat. Then a bellyful of dread arrived and extreme cowardice prevented him from moving a finger. This darkness engulfed him as he remained as still as a corpse, smothering his face as an embalmer might have bandaged a pharaoh. His shoulders suddenly shivered into uncontrollable life and he felt acute fear streaming throughout his body as he desperately tried to find some bearings. The fear slowed him down, and he struggled to see in the dark; he needed a light, but fear was alive and kicking within him now. He knocked his lamp over... it must be the cops... only the cops relished this type of pandemonium.

He now knew that he needed to go to the living room and hide his grass and joint-making stuff, but wait, no... what if it was the landlord? They were £800 behind on the rent. No, the landlord was sound and never behaved like this. It couldn't be the benefits agency either, as they only ever did housing spot checks during working hours. What time was it, anyway?

Bang... Bang... Bang.

Dudley realised now with certainty that the cops were here to do mischief, so he sprung up from his bunk, landed perfectly upon his feet and darted out along the corridor towards the living room, only to find Stroker also half asleep in his boxer shorts and with a look of absolute terror upon his bony unshaven face. He was urgently attempting to stuff a large Tupperware container full of grass into the soil of an exceptionally large, browning yucca plant that had not been watered in weeks. Consequently, he was spraying dry soil all over the place in his desperation.

"Don't fucking do that, they'll see your hands and look at the mess!" Dudley gasped. The combination of his whispered cockney accent and

182

frantic hand movement made Stroker stop and think of Monty Python. He burst out laughing, farted so loudly that whoever was at the door must surely have heard, and then continued his frantic burying regardless, before suddenly giving up and chucking the box under the sofa. Dudley stared for a moment, before then looking down at his brown and mustard 1970s Y-fronts and sinking onto the bright green leather sofa. There, he calmly proceeded to make a roll-up cigarette while humming 'Yellow Submarine'. The bangs at the door continued so loudly that the whole stair would be awake by now and probably out on their landings, Stroker thought, so he ran into his room to find a t-shirt to cover his undernourished frame.

When he did finally open the door, he got the fright of his life to see Chuck and Forsyth standing there. Chuck was the last person he had expected to see at that moment. "What the fuck are you wanting?" He snorted up a throat full of smoker's phlegm and kept it in his mouth as he stood there in his second-hand eBay t-shirt that had an image of the children's TV series 'Rainbow' on it.

Stroker felt tough now that the realisation that it was not someone who wanted to kill him at the door, kicked in. Displaying the large piano key gap between his teeth, he growled at them. "Well?" He then snorted up some more mucus.

"Morning Irvine, I'm afraid you're in a spot of bother, sunshine," Chuck said as he placed the palm of his hand upon Stroker's tiny chest and lightly pushed him back into the large Edwardian hall with high ceiling. This caused him to swallow the bile in his mouth, as Chuck stepped in behind him.

"You're right, guv, he does look like *Gollum*," said Forsyth as he too followed suit and gave Stroker the once-over.

"Where is Rodney Dangerfield?" Chuck growled at Stroker, who was beginning to recover.

"Who?" he began cringing now.

"Albarn Dudley," snapped Chuck before then turning to Forsyth, "He's a ringer for *Gollum,* isn't he," he said, intentionally playing upon Stroker's ego.

This of course stung Stroker, who flicked his gaze between both of them, like an Action Man[17] toy, while thinking up a response. He then decided to protest. "No, I bloody don't!" he snapped before returning to the panicky fusion of fear and affront, whilst sizing up of his predicament.

---

[17] British-made action figure toy; known for a scarred cheek and mechanically operated moving eye gaze - back and forth.

"I mean, what the hell do you think you're doing, banging at my door and barging in here? That's against the law, officers," he said, his arrogance back in control.

Chuck lunged forward with his left hand and made a grab through Stroker's boxer shorts; however, he was so skinny that Chuck ended up with a handful of skin and bone in his grasp. Stroker screamed though, as Chuck dug his nails in while Forsyth closed the front door to prevent the neighbours hearing.

"You little cunt," growled Chuck. "You're up to your neck in serious shit here, and I'm going to see to it that you are remanded tomorrow morning without bail." He squeezed harder and Stroker could only nod frantically, his eyes rolling now as he desperately tried to take the pain and earn release through compliance. In the end, it had been the mention of prison that instigated the tears.

Chuck let him collapse onto the floor in a heap, sobbing, before giving Forsyth a wink. "Oh Alby, where are you?"

Just then, Dudley appeared from the living room door, still in his bizarre underwear but also wearing a plastic toy spaceman helmet now. Through its visor, he was smoking a roll-up cigarette. "Leave it out," he said to them. "That there is a cod fisherman's great grandson," he added, pointing at his snivelling flatmate who was still in a foetal position at Chuck's feet.

"This is Alby Dudley," smiled Chuck, amused at this old lunatic. "He is completely demented like Gollum here, but with fewer of the ego parasites chewing away at his soul," Chuck explained. "They both like kiddies, don't you girls?" Chuck gave Stroker a somewhat restrained probe with his foot. "Stroker here likes them at around 14 to 20, as they are easier to control, while Alby likes them somewhat younger and has no preference for gender," he said, as if describing their preferred holiday destinations.

"Who else is here?" asked Forsyth, and Stroker whined, "Nobody, I promise," in reply.

""Right, both of you, in the living room now," snarled Chuck before giving Forsyth the nod to check the little flat over. When Forsyth entered the lounge a few minutes later, he gave Chuck a shake of his head.

"Right, take that bloody helmet off, Alby, and both of you listen to me," Chuck demanded of them while Forsyth leaned across the doorway and scanned the room.

It was a small flat and the lounge window overlooked Musselburgh's pebble beach. Forsyth looked around and noted a TV with hundreds of computer games and a couple of control pads, kids' sweets such as jelly babies and cola bottles on plates on the floor, toy cars, and a stuffed Garfield cat on a shelf. There were weird drawings of rainbows and what Forsyth could only describe as shadow figures all over the walls. He knew a sexy shrink who would probably understand all of this, mind.

Above the TV was an old poster of Morrissey and a Cadbury chocolate bar which had been blu-tacked onto the wall. Forsyth saw that there were obviously a few things going on here, but he cared not about them really. To his left, an old 'Look Again' magazine poster of a male with outrageous new romantic hair was pinned to the wall. It had '*Pat Sharp*' signed across the bottom of it. Then there were kids' toys and some old board games beneath it. Forsyth couldn't help thinking that he was in some sort of play zone.

Sensing his colleague's confusion, Chuck explained.

"Oh, this is all part of what the shrinks call the '*Chitty Chitty Bang Bang*' syndrome."

Both Stroker and Dudley looked up at him now with obvious interest.

"There is a guitar room through there with Floyd and Beatles albums," Chuck raised his thumb behind him and Forsyth nodded, as he had seen it.

"They use that and other things, to attract the stoners down, which makes them feel cool, and also convinces them that they have cool friends. In reality, though, they are just two wankers whose only friends are those who use this place as a weed harem for a short while, before going back to normality," he explained.

"While these two are riding 'A Saucerful of Secrets' full time," Forsyth nodded in empathy.

"Then there's this play room here," Chuck smirked now. "It's a kiddie trap, but all a mirage, like the sweet-bearing carriage of the child catcher from *Chitty Chitty Bang Bang*, eh lads?" he nudged Dudley's leg with his shoe. "All a mirage isn't it," he sighed.

"Now, one at a time, go with this officer and very quickly get dressed as you're both nicked for your antics with young Stacey, and for whatever drugs you're hiding here," he gave a knowing nod towards the soil scattered all over the floor. Forsyth then reached out and grabbed Stroker by his arm.

"You first, *Gollum,*" he said.

Stroker decided to drag his feet in the process, out of defiance and in order to keep up his tough guy bravado for Dudley's benefit, so Forsyth booted him up the arse and out of the door.

"Don't tap-dance with me pal, you're not hard and you're not cool either. You're a silly wee wanker," he ordered the now-limping Stroker to give up the charade.

As they entered Stroker's bedroom, Forsyth noticed that it was surprisingly tidy, with a neatly-placed lineup of shoes along a wall. The bed was a mattress on the floor with a quilt and two pillows, but he was unexpectedly drawn to a noise coming from a small cheap piano that was pressed up against the foot of the bed. There it was again... like a scratch?

"What's that noise?" he growled as he began to suspect an animal was stuck inside the piano.

"It's just the cat, she gets put in there when she pisses in the house," replied Stroker.

Forsyth lifted the lid and out popped a skinny black cat which immediately bolted out of the door and into the kitchen to hide from the madness of her oppressor.

"You disgusting little beast," hissed Forsyth, fighting back the irresistible urge to smack this creature a right hook across what would likely be a glass chin.

"It's only for a minute or two, to deter her," pleaded Stroker whilst sensing the threat. He began cringing again and took two steps back from Forsyth.

"Absolute pish, Stroker," growled Forsyth. "We just woke you up; that bloody cat has been in there since you went to bed, you evil little toad. And it pisses because you're in bed all day and never let it out!" He was shouting now and could be heard in the toy room, where Dudley was attempting to play the mentally ill card by giggling. Chuck, just stared hard at him in disgust.

A couple of minutes later Forsyth returned with the now-clothed Stroker, whom he had by his shirt collar. He then shoved him back onto the sofa.

"Right Alby, go and get dressed now," Chuck ordered Dudley. The latter got up, still giggling, and went out with Forsyth.

As they entered Dudley's room, they had to crouch under the home-made bunk bed which took up most of the cramped space. Suddenly the noise of Stroker yelling from the lounge filtered through, but it quickly went quiet again. Dudley looked up at Forsyth, who shook his head and told him to hurry up or expect much of the same. This seemed to do the trick, and less than a minute later Forsyth pushed him back into the play room, wearing a Watford football shirt and a pair of ripped flared jeans that had scribbled writing in felt-tip pen all over them. When he noticed Forsyth reading it, he piped up; "Nigel Callaghan," he offered cheerily.

"Is that your boyfriend then?" Forsyth knew who the former footballer was but was bemused by the fact his name was penned all over a grown man's jeans. Dudley straightened up at this tone but sat down on the sofa quietly and did not respond.

Stroker was now sitting holding his eye, but he removed his hand to show Forsyth that it was bruised. "*Gollum* just tripped over that big plant pot there," Chuck pointed at the dying Yucca plant.

"Silly Billy," said Forsyth.

"Reckon they hid something in there, Detective Sergeant?" Chuck asked Forsyth, raising an eyebrow. "Take a look, will you?"

Forsyth went over and had a little look around the soil. As per the cat, the plant was neglected and he could see the tunnelling marks through the dehydrated soil. He poked his finger in and fiddled around, then stood back up and walked in front of the sofa with a small see-through plastic bag the size of a credit card and full of white powder, which he dangled as he might a mouse by its tail.

"Well, well, well, Chrissy, what the fuck have we got here then?" Chuck put on a primary one classroom teacher's slow, babying tone.

Both Stroker and Dudley looked up, stunned, then Stroker immediately protested in a whining tone, "That's not ours; you just planted that!"

"Yeah, that is like a total..." Dudley was flicking his gaze between all three men, "Like a total... oh, fucking hell man! What do you want from us?" Chuck had been hoping for such a crumbling of resolve at this point but he knew it was the loathsome Stroker he really needed to break in order to get anywhere here.

Sharon Adams had spoken to Forsyth first thing whilst he was out running his brown Labrador, and had confirmed much of what Chuck already knew on Stroker. She also informed them that Dudley had recently been cautioned for bothering a local Musselburgh female whom he had shared a joint with on the beach. They had arranged to meet for a drink, and the female had introduced him to her friends as a hip, dope smoking 40-something musician with a Paul Weller haircut. This had been a mistake on her part, because Dudley was in fact a sociopath who hid behind a pretension that he was an insane musical genius. His personality disorder soon became evident to the younger group; and the fact that he didn't do social drinking, at least outwith his own cave, distanced him further – so she told him to fuck off and not to contact them again.

Sadly, Dudley, who had a real flutter in his stomach for the female, did not stop texting. He even found out her address and started sitting at the bus stop across the road, playing his guitar whilst wearing earphones.

"He learned this from Stroker?" Forsyth had considered.

187

Police had been called, and Dudley obtained a formal warning which then developed into a caution a few days later.

"Or vice versa?" had been Chucks reply.

Chuck knew that Dudley and Stroker were both weasels who were terrified of most things, particularly prison, so when briefed by Forsyth that morning, he had lost no time in working out a scam that involved Forsyth nipping back up to his flat and filling up a small bag with talcum powder for this purpose.

Forsyth then had both men stand up and handcuffed them before giving the room the once-over for effect, and lo and behold, he came across the Tupperware container full of weed under the sofa. "Guv," he showed it to Chuck, who winked at him,

"Oh dear, Chrissy," he said.

"Oh dear, guv," Forsyth played along.

"That looks like an ounce of Charlie and a fair whack of weed, too," Chuck told the pair of them.

"With your previous conviction for cultivation, Irvine, I reckon if we have a word with the Fiscal about your dark history on both sides of the border regarding young females, we can persuade a sheriff to give you at least a year in prison."

"That is a plant, and the grass is personal so I'll tell the judge the truth and see that you're sacked, you bully!" Stroker snapped now, unable to control his temper.

"Once again, your ego has taken over your senses, you nasty little shit," growled Forsyth, "Who the hell do you think a sheriff is going to believe, you or a Fiscal?" Forsyth shook his head in mock despondency, "Come on Irvine, don't be so naïve."

Stroker tried a different tack, once the reality of his predicament had had time to hit home. "Well, how can you prove that it's mine and not Alby's?"

Dudley looked at him desperately, "Fuck off, it's not mine. I can't afford tobacco, never mind cocaine," he whined.

"Most folk who get pinched for intent to supply use the 'I'm unemployed and broke' card as a defence in court. Arguing that they cannot afford to buy coke. I'm afraid it never helps them, though," assured Forsyth.

Stroker gazed down at the dirty carpet and attempted to locate some kind of rational way out of this jam, his face distorted as if in haemorrhoidal discomfort in the process. Eventually he released an illicit groan as he touched his bruise with his finger. Chuck reckoned he was beginning to feel sorry for himself now. He decided to turn the fear factor dial up a little bit higher however.

"If one of you takes the Derry[18]," Chuck paused a second to suggest that he was deep in thought, "Hmm, perhaps the Fiscal may accept that and let the other one of you walk; however, if neither of you admit to owning this Charlie, you'll likely both be convicted... at least, you shall, Irvine," he told the cowardly Stroker who was looking straight at him now with obvious concern in his watery eyes.

"But it was planted!" he howled before bursting into tears and falling to his knees.

Time now for Chuck to reveal himself as Stroker's only hope of salvation. "You have spent your whole life taking cover, Irvine; indeed, it could be said that you are an expert in avoiding punishment, so get up onto the sofa and listen. I can give you an opportunity to save your hide," he demanded. Stroker jumped up like a schoolboy threatened with the cane and sat on the sofa with his skinny knees together.

"Right," Chuck took a breath and paused. This was it, this was match point now. "If you don't grasp this opportunity, I swear to you that you will be remanded in custody on a full committal tomorrow morning, with months to wait till the trial," he assured them.

"Then, as soon as you're both up in Saughton, you can be sure that I will let it be known to every hall that you are a grass and a paedophile, Irvine. Nasty things might happen to you then. You'll probably go onto a 24-hour protection watch. And that means shut up in a peter[19] with only ten minutes supervised exercise per day." Chuck shook his head gravely in mock sadness at the thought of such a miserable scenario.

"But, you're only protected by a door, mind," added Forsyth. "The cleaners and food servers will remind you of your vulnerability all through the day. That's the only interaction you will get," he warned grimly.

"Then, at night you'll have to lie on your bed and listen to the rest of the hall shouting threats at you and the other beasts on your landing," Chuck forecast.

"Your food will be spat on by the passman delivering it, and maybe even by the screws supervising him," continued Forsyth for good measure.

---

[18] 'Taking the Derry' is a slang term used in the Leith and east Edinburgh neighbourhoods, referring to the Walls of Derry, wall rhyming with fall. Meaning: 'Take the fall'.

[19] 'Peter' is a slang term referring to the late actor Peter Sellers, whose name partially rhymes with 'cell'.

Dudley looked at Stroker for a reaction, and when there was none except a few more tears, he spoke to him. "I'd kill myself, Irvine," he blubbered, their eyes met briefly with identical looks of horror before Dudley began to now sob uncontrollably too.

"Right, shut up the pair of you!" Chuck adopted a firmer tone despite also finding it difficult not to grin, but he persevered. He sat down on a seat facing the two of them and played his hand: "Or you can give me some information and we can forget about everything," he said.

Stroker looked up at both cops and gradually stopped sobbing, though with stubborn reluctance.

"What do you want from us, then?" he hissed through clenched teeth, his Terry Thomas gap producing a windy whistle.

"Your landlord Leo Frazer was murdered two days ago," Chuck said.

"We know; it has been all over the news," Dudley put in.

"Well, we know that you have been sharing your desire for young females with Frazer, Irvine," Chuck told him. Stroker dropped his gaze and slowly ran his fingers through his hair, but did not reply. Dudley, on the other hand, looked at his flat mate, then at both cops before turning back to Stroker as if he expected him to suddenly jump up and deal with this threat.

"We know you gifted him young Stacey Williamson," added Chuck.

"What do you want to know?" Dudley was fidgeting on the sofa, scratching his arms and nudging Stroker with his elbows, which confirmed that Stroker could indeed provide information if he chose to do so.

Stroker then looked up at Chuck to hear the price of his freedom.

"I'm not interested in anything other than who else Frazer hung out with." Chuck told him slowly.

"He was a brief and he owned flats like this." Stroker looked around him, "He never let me hang out with his snobby mates. What do you mean, and how can I help you?" he protested.

"Who he brought here with him. Who owns that cottage out by Straiton that Stacey got taken to, and who else in his world likes to fuck teeny weeny pussy?" snarled Forsyth, and pointed a finger straight at him.

"It's fine Chris. If he doesn't want to play ball, we'll follow the letter of the law and take him in right now," Chuck smiled and promptly stood up.

"OK, OK, for fuck's sake," Stroker hissed.

Chuck sat down again. "Right, this really is your last chance. I'm running late, son."

190

Stroker sighed, rubbed his face again, and said, "I have only ever seen one other man with him, and that was in his car. Lionel told me he owned a place out in the sticks where he had set up some pretty mad orgies."

"And?" Forsyth prompted.

"And over a period of about a year, Lionel offered me cash to find girls he could take there for his friend," Stroker told them. "I found two 18-year olds who agreed to do it for cash, and that way I made a quid or two out of it."

"No underage girls, then?" Chuck asked doubtfully.

"No, honestly. No. Lionel asked me to try and get kids, but I didn't want to do it. I got him two 18-year olds," insisted Stroker. Dudley looked terrified; not at Stroker's confession, but at the imagined possibility of what Forsyth might do to them both, judging by his reddening face and clenched fists.

"Who was the man in the car?" Chuck calmly asked.

"I don't know his name, but I've seen him on the local news before. I think he works in education." Stroker appeared to be genuinely trying to rack his brains for information to give them.

"His name, Irvine, or we have no deal," insisted Chuck.

"He was on the news trying to explain why that kid had died in the school in Gilmerton." Stroker was clutching at straws now, but his vague words switched a light on within Chuck's head.

"I remember, Chrissy," he turned to Forsyth and clicked his fingers. "It was the council getting the blame for a classroom ceiling collapsing or something. Ring the school and ask them who it was that got interviewed on TV at the time," Chuck said.

Forsyth got out his phone and searched online for the number, which he then called. He soon got through to an overly informative female in the school office called Dorothy who had obviously memorised all the reports of the incident. She was so helpful that Forsyth had to hang up to get rid of her in the end.

"She reckons it was either a Garry Welsh from the council or the head teacher, Rudy Gibson." Forsyth was already googling these names now.

"What else can you tell me, Irvine?" Chuck asked.

"Only that Lionel brought the guy in the car one day to pick up the two girls and that was it. Honestly, I swear there is nothing else," Stroker was almost crying again in desperation, his eyes wide with fear and pleading for leniency.

At that moment, Forsyth stuck his phone with the image of a man on the screen under Stroker's face: "Is that him?"

Stroker shook his head and began crying again.

"Where did you find the girls? Were they customers in your mini cab?" Chuck demanded.

"No, I lost my licence years ago, and trained as a chef," Stroker said proudly now.

"He's really good at it," Dudley put in.

"Shut it," Forsyth growled at him without looking up from his phone.

"Names and addresses for the girls?" Chuck prompted of Stroker.

"They were both in St James Women's Hostel on the Cowgate," Stroker replied. "I met them a few times through Facebook. Wendy Allen and Yvonne Kidd." He sighed and shook his head as though to express his concern in them being dragged into this shit-storm.

"Is this him?" Forsyth stuck his phone in Stroker's face again. Stroker took one look at the image of the grey bearded, wig-wearing man holding an apple pie outside a bakery as part of a PR stunt.

"That's him."

Forsyth then looked at Chuck. "Garry Welsh, Executive Director of Midlothian Regional Council," he said, showing him the image.

Chuck nodded, and addressed Stroker. "Fine. I might need a statement later but in the meanwhile, if you tell anyone about this, I'll make absolutely sure not only that that the pair of you go to jail for as long as possible, but also that the entire city knows that you are beasts and informants, understand?"

Both men nodded frantically and Chuck threw them back the container of weed before he moved swiftly out of the door. Back in the car, Chuck told Forsyth to ring Sharon Adams for intel on the two girls; and then to call the freelance photographer Johnny Dewar, who often did work for the squad, to find out if he was available to 'stalk' a target for 48 hours. Chuck was offering him £300 to sit and photograph all those who entered or left Collysdean Golf Course, which Dewar was only too happy to accept.

Forsyth rang Dewar first, then turned to Chuck, "That young Dewar's going to be bird-watching the golf course within the hour," he told him. Eventually he came off the phone to Sharon Adams. "We have an address for an Yvonne Kidd in Meadowbank, as she's been nicked for shop lifting, guv; but nought on Wendy Allen," he said as he chucked the bag with the talcum powder out of his window.

Yvonne Kidd lived in a flat with her mother on Queens Park Avenue. When they arrived at her door, they found the mother barely able to stand up straight and reeking of booze. She told them that Yvonne worked from 5am as a cleaner in town and often did not get home until after 1 pm. She asked who they were, but Chuck lied so as not to panic the girl or her mother and said they were from the council tax registration department. The old woman was too pickled to think about it and staggered back into her room.

"We can pop back later today," Chuck said to Forsyth as they descended the stairs.

At the loch car park opposite Trevelen's house at the opposite side of the park, they found Gav and Joe sitting in their car smoking cigarettes. "Anything?" Chuck asked them.

"Went to dinner at a French place off the Royal Mile last night guv, and was seen hugging a guy who I then followed to this address." Gav handed Chuck a piece of paper with Irvine Stroker's Musselburgh address on it.

"What?" Chuck gasped before handing it to Forsyth.

"I followed him; I just thought they looked too cosy, guv," replied Caine.

"You did right Gav, we have just hit this address this morning," Forsyth laughed.

After Chuck filled them in on Stroker, Gav explained that he had followed him in a taxi to Musselburgh as the hugs and cases of wine had alerted his interest. Joe added that there had been no more activity after Trevelen had returned home.

"Well, we need to keep an eye on the loch side of the house too, as he has a boat and could just bugger off to the Prestonfield side," Chuck said before tapping the car roof. "Right, get home to bed. Joe, when you go past Collysdean Golf Course, ring young Dewar who should be pitched up somewhere and watching the place, and check up on him. I want to know that the bugger is earning his coin."

"And be back here by 7 pm, guys," added Forsyth.

As they sat in the car, watching the boat house through a gap in a hedgerow which had starlings tweeting from somewhere within it, the car radio was playing a breakfast show from London discussing the pending Scottish referendum. Both men listened silently as a representative from an English-owned bank predicted gloom and doom should Scotland vote Yes in the coming referendum. A monetary expert speaking via phone from Singapore was poking holes in the banker's logic.

"This is all doing my head in, guv," Forsyth yawned.

Chuck smiled, "It's taking over everything, you're right. Do you think it's unpatriotic to abstain and just hope it all goes away?" he joked.

"Depends who's judging you, guv," said Forsyth. "Personally, I think it's something we could all do without. Me and the Mrs fell out about it last night and we still weren't speaking this morning," he yawned.

"I saw a tenement window in Leith the other day," mused Chuck. "One side had a Yes poster, the other a Union Jack with a big No written across it," he recalled with amusement. "Then underneath was another sheet of paper with 'We don't talk much anymore' written on it!" Both men laughed at this. After a moment or two, they listened to the DJ talking about the SLP and the dominance of the so-called 'Forbenistas' at the head of the party.

"Let's hear what Colin Anderson-Forbes, the new darling of those Scottish right wing zealots, the SLP, has to say on the matter whilst on the campaign trail," the well-known English presenter said.

"I'm delighted to be back here in Aviemore, where I had a fabulous holiday in the Coylumbridge hotel as a child," Forbes told a female journalist who had a Highland accent.

"It's important to me to come here and meet people who are working within the tourist industry and who are, regrettably, not adequately recognised by their overseas employers. What we have now is a deindustrialising population which relies more and more upon a service industry that works harder than some, but which receives less income than most. In an independent Scotland with the SLP in government, I would personally ensure that new legislation regarding a new Scottish minimum wage be approved by Holyrood, to provide these workers with the respect they deserve." He paused for breath, but just as the journalist started to ask a question, he continued confidently.

"The SLP are committed to instilling a sense of purpose within local authorities, to ensure that safe, warm accommodation is always financially feasible to those working their backsides off; not only in the service industries, but also in other low income employment. For economic inequality and perhaps a lack of caring in some communities, sadly come hand-in-hand and must be addressed. I shall set out a plan to address this alongside continued investment in local health services; leading, I believe, to greater social respect and mobility."

When it became clear that the speech had finished, the young female cheerily asked him, "So is it fair, then, to compare your current mantra on crime as another social fault, with echoes of Tony Blair's '*Tough on crime, tough on the causes of crime*'?"

"Yes Kirsty, you could argue that crime is partly down to social variation and that there is a habit of accepting economic inequality as the norm." Forbes took in a deep breath. "What I would say, however, is that this is going to be the start of something wonderful, something the Scottish people have waited generations for. Indeed, this is the birth of a new generation of Scots, wherein we will be free to make proper and righteous adjustments to the so-called norm. The SLP are proposing to act as the people's party for this new golden era."

Forsyth leaned over and turned it off, "He's a lying racist bastard who loves the sound of his own voice."

Chuck had been listening to it, but he said nothing and merely nodded slowly. They sat for a while, perhaps ten minutes, just watching the boathouse before Forsyth spoke again. "What the fuck was Stroker doing meeting Trevelen in a French restaurant last night?"

"We will drop in on him again later today, Chris; it might be another late one for us again but Stroker is getting another visit for sure." Chuck sighed. He had been considering the same question himself; was Trevelen screwing Stroker?

"Stroker is a snake, Chris," he went on, "We should suspect the worst, as he is our one and only connection between Trevelen and Frazer who can support the bar staff witnesses at the Sheep's Heid."

Just then, Trevelen appeared at his front door, carrying a briefcase and wearing a blue shirt, cap, and a white cricket sweater. He then jumped into the Land Rover and pulled out of his driveway.

"We'll tail along and see what he is up to." Chuck started up the engine.

Trevelen drove out the park, into Newington and then to the Meadows. Chuck was an excellent surveillance driver and kept a couple of vehicles behind, remaining innocuous while also keeping him within view. As they tailed him down Lothian Road and onto Queensferry Road, it dawned on Chuck that Trevelen might be heading over to Fife to his Bramble mansion. He shared this possibility with Forsyth just as Forsyth's mobile rang; it was Joe, saying he had met up with Dewar, who had made a den and was now photographing the comings and goings. Chuck arranged for Joe to get the registration numbers and photos later on from Dewar, on his way back in.

Trevelen was driving out towards the Forth Road Bridge and presumably across it to Fife. Chuck did not consider slowing down and letting him go, regardless of Fife being well outwith his jurisdiction.

"How do you know about the bramble estate guv, and what about the Fife cops?" Forsyth asked.

"Did some online reading last night and we are on a deniable operation, Chrissy. So as long as we are just intelligence-gathering, the Fife constabulary are irrelevant, aren't they?"

The two of them both felt themselves relax a little as they crossed the Forth; the roads in Fife are ten times better than in Edinburgh, the traffic is ten times lighter and the country scenery a sight for city-sore eyes.

"Not a pot-hole or a cobble within miles, Chris; it's a pleasant place to drive right enough."

Trevelen took a newish motorway, the A92, which cut through the kingdom's endless green fields and through valleys situated between Dunfermline and Kirkcaldy. From his position on the road, five or six cars behind the Land Rover, Chuck could see Trevelen flicking ash out of his window. Adams had provided Forsyth with a pretty useless update on him earlier, which had included his mobile phone number. Chuck knew that if they rang it, the cocky bugger would pick up his phone and answer it, and could then be pulled over and growled at, but it was wiser to gather more intel on him before making any kind of move like that.

At the outskirts of Kirkcaldy, the A92 turned north for a few miles before skirting down the eastern border of Glenrothes, where it then developed into a thin single lane for several miles north into the glorious countryside of northern Fife. As they drove through the golden, green and brown fields, the occasional sparrowhawk and buzzard were to be seen; sitting on walls and signs along the way, watching for road kill and rodents in the long grass. Chuck felt that there was something of a French feel to the landscape. The country fields with ponies and hilly little apple orchards with their ancient stone bridges across running streams, soon completely smoothed out into a vast flat plain of green farmland and forestry beyond the hamlet of Freuchie.

Forsyth broke the comfortable silence between the two men by mentioning that the local women were all up for "the new Sheriff in town," and Chuck laughed.

"How would you know?" he eventually responded as he kept his eye on the Land Rover about a mile ahead.

"I played footie over here, mind," Forsyth reminded him.

"That was Raith Rovers in Kirkcaldy, though," Chuck laughed a little more.

"Yeah, but all these country birds head into the towns at the weekends looking for WAG targets."

"WAG targets, eh? On Raith Rovers wages?" Chuck continued to chuckle at this as they were suddenly shadowed on either side of the road by exceptionally tall Scots and Corsican pine trees.

"Wow, this is like something out of *Hansel and Gretel*," Forsyth said.

"Yep, was just thinking it's like the woods they escaped into in *The Great Escape* or something."

For the next few miles Chuck gave Forsyth some background on Trevelen and his business, explaining that it was all internet research, rather

196

than mentioning his angelic source. Forsyth then searched online for details on the layout of the Melville estate.

"Says here the house was a Royal Navy hospital and rehabilitation centre during WW1 guv, and that after 1940 it was a Special Forces base for Polish Auxiliary Commandos. There were 78 of them there in the face of an almost certain belief that Hitler was about to invade, apparently." The two men exchanged glances.

"Also says they built tunnels for living in after the expected invasion, then… oh, then it just goes on about the bramble wine business," Forsyth replaced his phone in his pocket.

"Well, there is certainly enough land to keep an army," Chuck pointed out as the Land Rover turned into an opening that had obviously once been the old coach track up to the house. A sign that identified the estate and the fruit wine was visible as they slowly continued past.

"What now, guv? Do we find somewhere to park and take a nosey wee trek up through the estate woods?" he pointed at the woodland that walled the track and swallowed up the estate.

"Let's drive around," Chuck said, continuing along the A92 for a mile or so. After a while, both men could see the large mansion off to their right across some grain fields which were ripe for harvesting. The woodland snaked up to it and thus enclosed the long drive, but from the grain fields the place was viewable at a stretch.

"Let's find somewhere to park and go spy on the place for a little while, Chris," Chuck suggested as he put his foot down.

When they arrived at another tiny hamlet named Letham, which had appeared on their left-hand side, Chuck turned in and drove through it. There were perhaps ten houses and a tiny little post office. Chuck thought it resembled a set from an Agatha Christie drama. There were no people to be seen except a green-haired punk rocker chick standing in an old-fashioned bus shelter, alongside which was a lane and a sign reading 'Monimail Road'. It obviously ran towards the estate, so Chuck took it. It was a curving road with horseshit scattered all along it. Bramble was held over old stone walls that penned sheep in hilly, grassy land.

When they came to a sizeable parish church and graveyard, Chuck crawled into the gravel drive and quickly saw that the church had a large rusty padlock on its grand black door. He parked and they sat silently for a moment, looking at the stained-glass windows upon the kirk.

"There are age-old gravestones there, by the looks of it," Forsyth nodded towards the small graveyard. There was a rubble wall running alongside it for about ten yards or so, before bushes and hedgerow obscured the view and carried on around the roadside border where they were sitting.

"I doubt anyone's likely to turn up to lay flowers," he added, pointing at a gravestone close by, dated 1804. The stones were all old; one or two were grand, in Roman classical designs.

"Let's go over that," Chuck pointed over at the wall. "And through the field, so we can get a wee spy at the Melville place," he turned to Forsyth and smiled enthusiastically.

"Bring your phone for filming and snapping," Chuck added as Forsyth opened his door with a grin.

They climbed over the 5 ft. drystone wall which had probably been created by farmers for the kirk many years previously. On the other side was the golden harvest field as far as the A92 to the south and Lethem village to the east. They stayed by the wall and headed west for a few minutes until there was no wall, only thick tree branches hanging over the path, providing shadowy cover from the farm buildings to the south. After another five minutes' walk the trees turned into brambles and the little line they had walked upon became muddier as the soil deepened slightly.

"Fucking shoes are going to be goosed, by the way," moaned Forsyth.

"Sssh... what's that?" Chuck whispered and pointed into the brambles a few feet away.

"What?" Forsyth's jaw dropped as he looked up and saw an old cow shelter covered in bramble and weeds. He had been too busy dealing with the soft earth to notice it.

"Cowshed, guv," he whispered as he crept into it slowly, glad to be out of the field and onto firmer terrain. Chuck followed, soon seeing that it was a perfectly camouflaged little pen with gaps in the old walls. The ground was a mixture of grass, rubble and old wooden pallets.

"This hasn't been a cow pen in years," Chuck moved over to look through a gap in one wall.

"More a shagging den for randy farmers, I reckon," Forsyth said, noticing a couple of empty wine bottles and roll-up cigarette butts lying around on the floor.

Through the gap, Chuck found that he had a clear view down onto the estate and the five-level Palladian mansion below their hidden position. The entrance of the grand house, with its impressive Corinthian pillars, sat to their immediate right.

"Got to be around 20 bedrooms, that," Forsyth whispered while looking down from another gap beside Chuck.

There were about 15 acres of gardens and grounds around the place. The house itself was approached by an impressive winding drive which led through parkland to their right. To the north was an expanse of grass which looked like a cricket pitch with a green wooden pavilion on it. Adjacent to the drive were two large concrete buildings with a few people walking in and out, and three lorries parked outside. On the front of one lorry was a sign with the wine logo on it. To the far west appeared to be miles and miles of brambles, and a forklift was coming from that direction with boxes, heading for the concrete buildings.

To the south of the house, the original forecourt garden was now a series of lawns with a circular path enclosing the central lawn. To the east of the house, adjacent to buildings that may once have either been stables or a coach house, was a walled garden and a couple of over-grown tennis courts that looked as if they had not been used since the thirties. Then, there was the woodland coach drive to the south that led back to the A92, which Trevelen had entered from. There were four cars in the car park and a Ford Transit van with the wine logo also upon it.

"Need the registration numbers," Forsyth said.

Just then, a wine-coloured Jaguar came down the winding drive to their right and into the car park. A fat female with short, greyish-brown hair, wearing a blue pinstripe trouser suit got out, carrying a handbag the same colour as the Jag. Trevelen appeared from the Corinthian pillars to greet her, and at the entrance another, older man then appeared, wearing a cream linen summer suit and wearing a light blue Panama hat. He walked out to shake the woman's hand too and seemingly to welcome her, before walking over to a silver Lexus, taking a laptop from its boot, and then returning to the house.

Forsyth had a top-of-the-range phone with him, while Chuck had taken a cheap one for this mission, "I've got the reg numbers guv, but not the best of pics of the two players," he said disappointedly.

"Are you game for creeping in and trying to see if we can get anything else?" Chuck asked with the mischievous grin back upon his face.

Forsyth was about to reply when they heard a stone being moved behind them. Instinctively they both turned around, Chuck reaching into his pocket and Forsyth clenching his fists.

"Oh, I don't think you want to do that, gents," said the tall, well-built man behind them with a dark beard and a thick east Fife accent. He was wearing a green tweed jacket and leather boots. His eyes were dark and deep, and his teeth looked as though they had just been whitened. He took a step closer to find better footing on the rubble, and slowly produced a meat cleaver from his jacket pocket with his right hand.

"Put that down right now," snapped Forsyth, and both officers instinctively produced their detective badges and flashed them at the brute.

"Police… you're under arrest, pal," Chuck said softly but firmly for effect.

The man nodded knowingly. "Oh, I detected the odour of law enforcement from the stream beyond the tree house. You are sadly mistaken, and I'm now going to hack you to death," he told them almost playfully before taking a step toward Forsyth, with the cleaver raised ready to strike.

"Stop!" shouted Forsyth before moving his body onto his left foot, a football shimmy which sold the man a dummy and fooled him into moving his weight onto his right side. Forsyth quickly moved onto his right foot, knelt, grabbed a half brick, and launched it through the air at his would-be attacker, but his strike was slightly out and it only clipped the man's ear. The blow had sufficient force however, to spin him around and back into the brambles.

"Get him!" shouted Chuck, and they both launched themselves across the rubble at him.

The man recovered quicker than either of them had anticipated, and instantly launched an Olympic-class karate kick with one extraordinary long leg. It caught Forsyth clean in the face, knocking him across the rubble and against the wall, which he then bounced off, into a pile of palates before lying still in a crumpled heap. The man then jumped out of the brambles and swung his cleaver towards Chuck, who moved quickly backwards before falling over a boulder. The attacker was upon him when he pressed the finger print switch on the ball launcher Dai had given him, but it swiftly cut clean through his neck without Chuck feeling any bone contact.

"Where did you get that, then?" a voice then demanded to know.

Chuck flicked the hairy head from its shoulders and with a bit of effort slid the body off his stomach. He was soaked in warm blood and needed to get onto his feet pronto. He looked up to see another figure standing at the entrance. This one was tall, well-built with a grey beard, wax jacket, and bonnet. He had dark hair and quizzical dark eyes, "Well?" he demanded without moving.

As Chuck got to his feet he heard a hissing noise coming from the slain man's carcass. It then began to dissolve into some sort of steamy evaporation right before Chuck's eyes.

"He is departing thanks to your toy; who gave you it?" the new guy snapped again.

"Who or what are you?" Chuck asked, breathing heavily with one eye on the steam hissing around him.

"You're human. Why and how did you come about that weapon?" the man demanded once again.

"Come and try to take it off me, you bastard!" Chuck snarled at him. When the man stayed still, Chuck charged at him, swinging the ball launcher at him. His opponent swiftly retreated into the outside field and began sprinting away towards the estate hedge row.

"I'll kill you for that!" he shouted back at.

Chuck pursued him down the edge of the field, yet his quarry distanced himself at great speed, before leaping across the hedge like a gymnast, and out of sight. Chuck put the brakes on and jogged back up the field to the old cow pen where Forsyth appeared with blood all over his face and a brick in each hand.

"What happened?" he gasped as Chuck returned the launcher to pocket-size and replaced it in his small pocket.

"Tell you in the car. First, go and check in there to see you have your phone," Chuck replied breathlessly.

Forsyth dropped the bricks and located his phone in his pocket, undamaged, before nipping back inside, looking around and seeing nothing but rubble, not even a trace of blood, and rejoining Chuck in the field.

"Anything?" Chuck was terrified of the answer.

"Nought guv, but I think my back is bruised to buggery," chuckled Forsyth.

He asked Chuck about what had happened when he had been knocked out as they hurriedly made their way back to the car. Forsyth had blacked out for a minute or two while Chuck had beheaded the foe, and had missed the appearance of the other guy. Chuck was still shaking and fighting a strong desire to vomit. Obviously, if that body had not vanished in a skoosh of steam as it had apparently done, then he would be calling the local Fife cops and trying to wing his way out of rather a serious mess. Yet the fact that it had suggested to him that the man had not been human at all – either that, or Chuck was losing his marbles under the stress of this investigation.

"Did you see how fast that big bastard moved when he kung-fu-kicked me, guv?" Forsyth was gibbering now, and Chuck thought he might have a concussion.

"You banged your head against the wall, Chris; do you think you're alright, mate?" he asked.

"I'm OK, let's just get back across the bridge before uniform gives us a pull," Forsyth replied, as he received a hand lift from Chuck and heaved himself up and over the wall.

On the drive back, Forsyth stared out of the window at his wing mirror in anticipation of company as they floored it out of Letham and back onto the A92. Chuck could feel his heart beating and beads of sweat trickling down his cheeks. He opened his window and kept the foot down. After a while, Forsyth suddenly turned to him and asked: "why on earth are you covered in blood, guv?"

"He was bleeding like a pig from when you skelped him with that bloody brick!" Chuck lied.

"I hope to Christ that he doesn't die." Forsyth seemed worried, for obvious reasons.

"I'm pretty sure he's fine, Chris; he could run like Linford Christie afterwards, so don't worry. He won't cause any bother either – after all, he made the first move to start the fight and tried to kill us." Chuck tried to calm his DS' concerns. The two officers had established a strong bond – an enduring one – in their time working together, but Chuck did not feel authorised to relay all that he knew to him, nor did he have the time to do so even if he were allowed. Dai could make the point in a minute flat if necessary. Anyway, how did he know that Forsyth would not freak out on him and refuse to accept God's involvement in the events? If he did so, he would be at odds with his wing-man and even worse, Forsyth might tell Adams, or even Wong, that Chuck had banged his head back there and was now losing the plot himself. Not that Chuck thought he would, just that few people believe anything without hard evidence, as he perhaps had. He kept his foot on the gas as they entered the plain of Freuchie.

When they had both calmed down again and stopped talking about the 'Olympian' who had attacked them, they fell quiet for a while. They continued to watch their respective mirrors, though, whilst Chuck did two laps around each of the large roundabouts which interrupt the flow of the A92.

"One thing's for sure guv, our man must be super-rich to own that place," Forsyth said, breaking the silence.

"Trevelen is a schemer, Chris; he is dirty and I feel it even more after that drama back there."

"Yep, and he has got to be one of our TIC men, but is the cunt going to lead us to them, or do we go all in and drag him in for questioning at the last minute?"

"Chris, I just don't know how it will pan out but I think you're right, this guy is TIC hierarchy if I'm being asked to call it, and whoever the hell that was that attacked us back there was one of his pets; so, it would be attempted murder that we would be tugging the bastard in for, that's for sure." Chuck was angry now, thinking of the danger they had recently been exposed to.

"And more to the point, what are they hiding there that warranted such a fucking mental assault, guv?"

"Haven't got a clue, but that can wait, as it is way out of our jurisdiction and it would be risking everything to involve the Fife Constabulary in our suspicions. After all, there's a chance that they might be in on it," Chuck insisted, and Forsyth nodded and leaned back, closing his eyes. Chuck saw that it was midday, so he put on the radio, looking for news. A clipped, posh female BBC voice spoke out:

"And while the Scottish Labour leader was discussing how he supported the SNP's plan for post-independence legislation that will assure ethical behaviour within the financial sector, here is what SLP Leader Colin Anderson-Forbes had to say about suggestions by Labour that the SLP is lifting its skirt to the North Sea Gas and Oil sector in return for dirty jobs it can tout in its election campaign next year…

'Well, Linda, Labour have attacked everything we have proposed over the last couple of years, so it is not exactly a surprise that they have done so again. They refuse to change their ways and help boost the nation and the people of Scotland because they are puppets of Westminster and seek to maintain the union. Consequently, the SLP will not take lectures from a party who almost bankrupted the UK due to mismanagement, and their puppet party, who were found both wanting and corrupt in Scotland when they too held power. So, frankly, they have zero credibility as a consequence of their own dirtiness.'" Forbes' voice had the usual brisk manner to it and there were several children shouting and laughing in the background of the interview.

He went on, "an independent Scotland under SLP leadership will not only address the tax amnesties put in place by Labour and continued by the SNP, but it will also provide further wealth to the state by ending quantitative easing."

"Linda Muircroft with Colin Anderson-Forbes there at St Martin's primary school in St Andrews," the presenter said.

Chuck turned it off again and put one of Kim's CDs on instead. The first track to come on was the Stones' '*Devil Song*', which he loved.

"Tune," said Forsyth, still resting with eyes shut.

Twenty-five minutes later they were back in town and headed for Chuck's place. "We'll go to mine, get cleaned up, then go and give Stroker a hard tug, right?" As he spoke, they hit Blackhall and then took the Telford Road eastwards.

"Sure, but what about Trevelen? We could go and take a look around his Duddingston house as it might be empty just now, guv?"

"Let's see if Stroker can help fill in the gaps with that, then, Chris," Chuck said, tightening his grip on the steering wheel and gritting his teeth.

Ten

"The line dividing good and evil cuts through the heart of every human being. And who is willing to destroy a piece of his own heart?"

Aleksandr Solzhenitsyn

"Wong wants an update from me this afternoon," said an anxious-sounding Adams down the phone. Chuck had just burned his bloodied clothes on the barbeque in his garden and had been about to wash his hands when she rang. Forsyth's hands had been in worse state, however. He must have used them to protect his head, upon landing on the rubble. Nothing that a wash, Savlon and a plaster or two wouldn't sort out, although he was shaken too. After quick showers the two men had ravenously devoured lunch. *It was surprising*, Chuck thought, *how much appetite a morning of mortal danger gave you.*

"OK, tell him we have a suspect and are working furiously on his associates today and expect to give him an update in 48 hours, but it is as hard as we originally feared," he said, hoping to buy time.

"Right, on that note, Joe sent me these number plates from your golf course spy." Chuck could hear her shuffling some paper down the line.

"The better intel, if any, should come in the evening when Joe checks in again with him," said Chuck.

"Only two cars, both staff: a Magda Dabrowski, cleaner and receptionist, and one Clive Ogilvy, who's the Assistant Manager," Adams slowly read out.

"Can you look at Ogilvy for me?" he asked.

"Sure, send over the evening intel and I'll get onto that too. I'll try to get the registration numbers Chris sent in back to you this afternoon also," she said cheerily.

Chuck and Chris finished their large lunches and headed down to Musselburgh to work on Stroker. En route, Chuck's phone received a text from Adams. He clumsily fumbled around with it whilst he drove, before handing it to Forsyth to sort out.

"It's from Sharon, guv; she says there is nothing much on Ogilvy other than an apparent known history in bar and hotel work. Former employer was the Barnton Hotel three years ago, where he was a police witness in a bar brawl case."

"OK, well, let us see what young Dewar comes across throughout the day," Chuck was quite optimistic, having used the young photographer in the past.

"Do you think Stroker will be home, guv?" asked Forsyth.

"Yes, he will have been sitting, getting stoned, from the minute we left, Chris," assured Chuck.

"He might not answer the door," considered Forsyth.

"Then I'll boot the bloody thing in, Chris, I shit you not mate!" Chuck was coldly convincing and Forsyth forced a nervous chuckle at the thought of further career-threatening antics. Christopher Kenneth Forsyth was as game as they came, and his loyalty to Chuck, both as a friend and colleague, was almost strong enough to see him behave like a criminal, but it was his inner sense of mental hygiene, that propelled him past the Rubicon now[20].

"Let's just make sure the fucker's in though, guv, as it's a busy stair," he smiled diplomatically.

Luckily, just as they arrived at Stroker's door, the man himself appeared, his coat on and carrying a rucksack.

"Ah… ah… ah," Chuck waved a finger at him to warn him not to close the door behind him. Stroker's face went white as a sheet and his eyes expanded to the size of golf balls.

"Erm, what?" he gasped, as Chuck pushed him back through the doorway and into the flat. Forsyth followed again and closed the door behind him.

"Shut up. Where's your boyfriend?" Chuck could hear classical music coming from the kitchen.

"In the kitchen." Stroker's head dropped and his frail body went semi-limp as he exhaled.

"Who else is in?" Forsyth asked nicely.

"Just us, I'm going to be late for work."

"Forget that, go get him," Chuck turned and nodded to Forsyth, who went off to find Dudley. Chuck dragged Stroker back into the toy room and told him to sit down and shut up while they waited on Forsyth. When

---

[20] The Rubicon: A river in northern Italy that Julius Caesar was ordered by the Roman Senate of 49BC not to cross. When he duly did, he uttered the eternal comment, "The die is cast."

Forsyth duly retrieved a stoned-looking Dudley, who was carrying a guitar in one hand and a joint in the other, he was moaning but smiling. "Leave it out, there is no need for this; I was about to make some soup with the peas from the garden," he said, putting the joint in his mouth and producing a couple of what looked like furry peapods.

"Those aren't peas, you idiot. So sit down, shut up, and put that fucking joint out," Forsyth snapped at him. Dudley quickly obeyed thereafter.

"I've told him that," Stroker had to add, earning himself a slap across the face from Chuck.

"Shut it! Both of you!" he shouted at them.

Stroker began cringing again now, and Dudley froze like a corpse.

"How do you know Philip Trevelen?" Chuck snarled at Stroker while looking directly down into Dudley's eyes for recognition, but finding none.

"He is my boss' friend," came the muffled and strained response from Stroker, who was hiding his face with an arm.

"Bollocks," Chuck lunged down, pulled him up by the collar and held him up while drawing his fist back. "Tell me right now, Irvine, or I'll smash your face, then charge you with possession and intent to supply, plus police assault," he snarled at the cringing beast before him.

Stroker immediately crumbled and scrunched up his face and eyelids while trying to cover them with his hands. "OK, OK, I met him through Leo Frazer," he squealed.

Chuck lowered his fist and shoved him back onto the sofa. "Better. Now tell me everything or I swear that you're going down for possession of twenty ounces of heroin with intent to supply, and I have the fucking dirty brown shit in the car, by the way," he barked down at him.

"And prison won't be an escape, Irvine," he added, slightly more calmly, "You must understand the power and reach of a Drug Squad Inspector, or are you such an ego-worshipping nut that you think you could play with fire?"

Stroker remained silent.

"You have heard of the Cattaneo family?" Chuck asked. He knew Stroker would find it impossible to deny a link to the well-known Scottish-Italian ice cream family who had controlled the ice cream industry in Edinburgh since the turn of the last century. Some of them had become involved in saunas and nightclubs back in the 1970s before a branch of them went into heroin supplying in the 1980s, and the occasional murder to go with it. Today they owned a couple of small private casinos and had their own law firm, Rodgers & Gough, who boasted celebrity clients. Chuck knew that most wannabe gangsters professed a connection to the family, and that Stroker would be no exception to that rule.

"Yes, I know one or two; the guy who had the yacht with the heroin on the TV a few years ago." Stroker was struggling, so Chuck took out his phone.

"Well, in this phone I have the number of a guy who stabs and slashes for them in their heroin distribution enterprise," Chuck assured, "and he will make a call within a minute of getting a text from me, to whatever prison hall you're in; and trust me, after he does, even the warders will be out to get you!" Chuck displayed a chillingly convincing gaze that made Stroker lower his head a moment before he broke.

"OK, what do you want to know?" he raised his hands in defeat and then looked up with utter submission.

"Everything."

"Leo introduced us at a party in a flat on East Claremont Street," Stroker groaned.

"Whose flat?" snapped Forsyth.

"I don't know. Some guy who worked in the media somewhere. I went with Leo because he wanted me to bring that Yvonne bird, that's the only reason I was there. It was all rich bastards and a few randy student birds."

"And?" Chuck had little patience left.

"There was one girl, probably in her mid-twenties. She had a shirt and tie on and wore jodhpurs and riding boots. You can imagine that she looked quite bizarre to me."

"Bit old for you, Irvine?" said Forsyth humorously, but Chuck continued to frown.

Stroker was offended but checked himself and kept his head down.

"I thought she was another interesting snobby eccentric; her hair was bobbed and she was smoking from one of those things," he told them.

"What was she smoking?"

"Fags, mainly, but there was an upstairs room, all glass panels with long velvet curtains. People were smoking hash and grass up there."

"Coke, pills?" Forsyth was relentless.

"Everything," Stroker nodded.

"Get on with it, Irvine," Chuck warned him.

"Yeah, so you swooned her with your bit of rough charm?" smirked Forsyth.

"What happened to your nose, officer?" Dudley suddenly asked.

"Shut it, Alby," snarled Chuck.

"Anyway, she was a bit dirty, I thought," Stroker shrugged his shoulders. "And I had a foursome with her and three other guys, but none of the guys touched each other, it was just her," he insisted.

"And?" Chuck wanted the intel without the fantasy.

"Philip Trevelen was one of the other guys."

"And?"

"We became mates from then on. I was invited to another party at a swish pad on Royal Terrace through Leo, but I think that was because Philip told him to bring me. It was a posh place and there was a group of young lassies there who I had never met before."

"Liar…" snarled Chuck, but he let him go on. Stroker looked at him nervously and paused, but then seemed to figure that it was best to keep talking.

"The owner was an old bloke with balding grey hair who had been at the earlier party. I remembered him, as he had a young boy of maybe 16 in tow," Stroker said.

"So, the 16-year old boy was more a 14-year old boy that you probably supplied because Leo fucking Frazer ordered him for the old bastard? How about that? And at the second party, you supplied the underage girls too; am I getting closer to the truth Irvine?"

"Nope, not the case. Anyway," he went on, "at the Royal Terrace bash I got talking to Philip and he let me fish on his loch a few times after," Stroker revealed.

"So, you two are friends?" Forsyth asked.

"Yes, I'd say we are mates," Stroker seemed like he was convincing himself.

"Been in his house?" Chuck asked.

"Nope, nothing like that. He has helped me sort my life out to some extent. He got me a job in a French restaurant as a dishwasher," revealed Stroker.

"Where?" asked Chuck.

"In the Marine Hotel first for a few months, then I trained as a commis chef. Then last Christmas he got me into the Bistro de L'oulette up at the Royal Mile where I'm now training as a chef de partie."

"So, you're a chef now?" Chuck was weary.

"Surprised he doesn't tell people that he is the head chef or owner," Forsyth offered contemptuously.

"He does, sometimes," piped up Dudley in amusement, earning himself a scunner of a look from Stroker.

"Shut it, Alby," said Forsyth.

"Anyway, that's all there is to it." Stroker was poker faced now.

"Why did you not just tell us all of this at the start?" Forsyth asked.

"Didn't want to lose my job because of you," Stroker admitted, and Chuck sensed he was now playing fair to some extent.

"Alby, do not tell anyone that we have visited. Nor that we discussed any of this. Nor that Irvine is coming with us to assist us today," Chuck told Dudley, who nodded his agreement.

"Cos if you do, you're getting nicked, jailed and tarred as a grass and a child molester, right?" shouted Forsyth like a Sergeant Major on parade. He was so effective that even Chuck almost jumped in surprise. Dudley, however, nodded frantically and promised to stay at home and "watch Bargain Hunt on TV".

"Right, Irvine, you're working for me today." Chuck pulled him up by his hood.

"Will I be coming home later?" Stroker asked with a terrified expression, as he realised that he was being shanghaied.

"Yes, if you play my way," Chuck confirmed.

In the car, Stroker asked where they were headed. "Show me the flats where the two parties were, then we can discuss how you're going to help me nail Philip Trevelen as a paedophile," Chuck replied as he started up the Volvo.

"And then what?"

"Then I'll let you go, give you £1000 for your trouble, and never bother you again."

"Well, that sounds fine to me," Stroker said before looking out of the window, towards his flat.

"What can you tell me about the jodhpur girl?" Chuck asked.

"Fuck all, she was studying Japanese or something like that, and was just another yah."

"No name?" Forsyth asked.

"Never asked, and never heard anyone call her anything other than 'Darling'."

"When was the last time you saw Yvonne?" Chuck wanted to know.

"Ages ago, honestly, I don't know anything about her," maintained Stroker.

"And that bloke from the council that turned up with Leo?" Chuck asked.

"I told you the truth about that," Stroker replied adamantly.

"Right, East Claremont Street it is," Chuck said, as they drove over to the old cobbled Georgian Street.

"Can't remember exactly where, but I think it's next door to the Territorial Army building." Stroker pointed at a Victorian sandstone building with a union jack flying from it when they arrived on the street.

"Top flat?" Forsyth asked.

"Yep... erm... that one there," Stroker seemed to recall and pointed to a Georgian block of six with large bay windows and a big black wooden door numbered 14.

"Right, phone the guvnor and get a name for the top flat occupants," Chuck told Forsyth.

They then drove over to Royal Terrace and Stroker asked Chuck to slow down, then to pull over beside a stunning Georgian building. "That one," he confirmed by leaning forward between them and pointing.

"Used to be the old Carriage Club casino," said Chuck. "Anyway, text Sharon again and get this house looked at too," he told Forsyth. They then headed down towards Holyrood and the Queens Park again.

"Where are we going now?" Stroker asked.

"To see Yvonne," replied Chuck.

As they passed the Scottish Parliament, the NO campaigners were hanging about flying Union Jack flags. Over on the grassy section, nationalists were throwing eggs and even the odd stone at them. Police were arriving as the Volvo took the bend at the palace, and all three of them were alarmed to see a scuffle break out, involving two females on the roundabout at Queens Drive.

"Are you not supposed to stop that?" crowed Stroker, thinking he was onto something.

"Uniform are on it, so you can shut up," Forsyth turned around and eyeballed him.

"It's split the country, this bloody vote," Stroker said as he turned to look out of the rear window.

"Shut it!" ordered Chuck as he turned the radio on. It was the news, and a Scottish Socialist bloke with a Glaswegian accent was arguing about the amount of oil left in the North Sea with a pro-unionist woman from the Labour Party, who sounded Dundonian. Chuck quickly turned it to another station and the voice of Forbes was transmitted into the car once again. Chuck hesitated.

"Cracking down on corruption is key, yes, Janet. However, it is important also to note that since all the regional forces in Scotland were merged into one entity, Police Scotland, violent crime has been reduced from our streets. And, the SLP were major supporters and instigators in that

211

transformation," he said with considerable engine traffic in the background of the broadcast.

"And why is that exactly?" Janet asked him.

"Well, the fact that intelligence has been easier to access on a national level has been a big contributor to the reduction in serious crime," Forbes told her.

"And that would not have been possible without devolution, then?" she asked.

"Well, no; we just need to look at England to see this. But this type of change, for the better, is an example of what self-rule can achieve, and highlights the competence of us Scots. I would go much further and make changes within the judiciary too; as well as cracking down on crime, I would target criminal assets abroad. That would produce extra finance which could then be used to improve public services which are, as you know, Janet, currently bearing the brunt of Westminster's austerity measures. The situation we are now in is partly a consequence of Labour's wars in Iraq and Afghanistan, which the Scottish people wanted nothing to do with."

Chuck turned it off. He had had enough of the bloody referendum, and wanted instead to talk shop.

"Right, you're coming up with us," he told Stroker, as he pulled into Yvonne's street at the edge of the Royal Park.

Stroker looked surprised, then grinned, perhaps as an indication of his secret desire to see her.

"Look at him," Chuck motioned Forsyth.

"Yep, he has mentally screwed her too, haven't you?" Forsyth turned and faced him.

"I have done nothing to that girl," Stroker insisted as he looked out of the window at a couple heading into the park with a red setter. Then, as if he had gathered his defence, he turned back to Forsyth with a piercing glare, and continued, "It's just that I know her for a wee dirty slag and I also know that she knows that; so she can't look in my eyes," he grinned.

"So, you torture her whenever you see her? She knocked you back, I take it?" Chuck guessed, and smiling in a manner which provoked Stroker to defend himself and assert his alpha-maleness. He was cautious though, and forced himself to ignore the bait. He then said nothing from then on, even as they entered the clean, tiled interior of the fancy old tenement building and began climbing the endless stairs to Yvonne's flat. Forsyth spoke quietly to Chuck about smelling dope from somewhere.

"Probably this fucker here?" offered Forsyth jokingly.

When Yvonne opened her flat door, she was surprised to see Stroker standing between the two official-looking men. Then she looked at Chuck and gasped, "Yes?"

"Hi, is it Yvonne?" Chuck asked her without bothering to look at Stroker, who was trying to stand on one leg, all cool but casual. Forsyth noticed this and assumed that he probably fancied Yvonne.

"Yes, and you are?" *Well, she was polite enough*, Chuck thought. She was small with creamy skin and a shapely figure. Her face was pleasant rather than beautiful, and there was a well-worn shine to her blue eyes and Slavic features. Her brown hair was probably dyed, Chuck guessed by her darker eyebrows, and her voice had a trace of an early-twenties smoker about it.

"Police," Forsyth flashed his badge in the tried and tested manner, which Yvonne bought instantly.

"OK," she looked worried, all three men were relieved to note.

"We popped up earlier. Don't worry, you're not in any trouble. We just need to ask you a couple of questions which we can either do here, or down at the station," Chuck lied.

Yvonne looked at Stroker, then back at Chuck. "Why is he here?" she had the boldness and savvy to enquire.

"He, like you, is helping us with our enquiries," Chuck assured.

"Right, you'd better come in, then. My neighbours are nosey buggers," she sighed.

They followed her through to a small green lounge with one of the old council-issued gas fires as the centrepiece. There was a budgie in a cage next to a large window with a stunning view out over the Queens Drive, all the way back to Holyrood itself. "Sit down," she motioned at a green settee. "My mum is terminally ill and is in her bed; she won't bother us but give me a sec to go and close her door," she said.

As they waited, they did not speak between themselves and instead vaguely watched the TV in the room for a minute or two, with the volume off. Yvonne returned with a purple plastic tray with three glasses of ice and a chilled bottle of Italian sparkling water, which she duly poured into the three glasses. She gave one each to Chuck and Forsyth and kept one for herself, before sitting down in an armchair.

"Do I not get a drink, then?" Stroker smugly asked her.

"No, because you're a prick," she said coolly before sipping her own.

"Here," Chuck handed his untouched glass over, which Stroker gladly took. Yvonne got up and went out for a few seconds before returning with another glass of ice, which she duly filled and handed to Chuck. Stroker chuckled.

"Thank you. I want to ask you about your connection to Leo Frazer, who died recently," Chuck asked her before taking a sip.

Yvonne appeared to freeze at these words. Her mouth, which she had opened to sip some water, remained ajar a little longer than she had intended, before she composed herself. "I take it Irvine has told you that I went to a couple of parties with Leo and his friends, then?"

"Told him everything, Yvonne," Stroker said with a sneaky grin.

"So, what is it you want?" she asked, looking only at Chuck.

"You don't appear surprised that Leo has died?" Chuck grinned at her. She shuffled her position and placed her glass back upon the tray, which rested upon a small, scratched mahogany coffee table.

"I saw it on the news so no, I'm not surprised, and I'm certainly not sorry about it; as he was a using paedo," she hissed contemptuously.

"He says you went to a party at East Claremont Street a while back with him?" Chuck nudged Stroker.

"Yes, I've been to a few 'parties' in my time, officer," she said with some sarcasm in her tone.

"And did you have underage sex with friends of Leo Frazer at any of them?" Chuck quickly came to the point.

"Why do you ask?"

"We need to know who they were so we can prevent it from continuing."

At Chuck's reply, Yvonne laughed aloud. It was a strange laugh, like a seal in distress. "Let me tell you, officer," she insisted once she had composed herself, "that the people who Leo had in his group of friends could have you walking the beat again in no time, or out of the force altogether, so you might want to stay away from them."

"Were they powerful enough to have him killed?" Chuck asked playfully.

"Moving on…" she sighed.

"No," Chuck snapped, "I want names."

Just then there was a knock on the front door. "It's a courier delivering a new budgie cage from eBay, I'm expecting it this afternoon," she smiled coldly and got up.

"Fine," Chuck said, taking a larger swig of his drink as she went out into the hall, pulling the lounge door closed behind her.

"She is fucking cocky, isn't she?" whispered Forsyth. Chuck grinned and nodded.

"Where did she get that confidence from, talking about this kind of filth?" Chuck nodded because he was thinking likewise.

"Maybe she is still entertaining the TIC mob?" Forsyth said, then wished he hadn't.

"TIC?" Stroker was onto it.

"Shut up, you silly little cunt," Forsyth told him.

"Look where she is living. Classy property yes, but look at the furniture and TV," Chuck said, gesturing towards the ancient television set with its wooden veneer. "Nah, they struggle by, I think," mused Chuck.

Just then he received a text from Kim to say she had witnessed a Labour MSP and his associates being shouted out, pushed and then brawling with a group of young chavs claiming to be Yes voters. Chuck thought about asking if she was ok, but she obviously was and had no time to exchange texts for the next half hour with her.

Instead, he decided to go and see what was keeping her. When he did, he got the fright of his life. Her body was lying face down in the hallway with the front door wide open. "Chris," he whispered as loudly as he could.

She was bleeding, and when he kneeled to check her pulse, he heard the ground floor door slam shut. "Fuck, is she OK?" Forsyth gasped.

"Nope, she's dead," Chuck said, after failing to find her pulse. He was stunned but instinctively rolled her over to reveal a large puncture wound above her left breast which was spouting out blood. Then he returned her into the position he had discovered her in. Her throat was also slashed deeply and was gushing blood at an incredible rate. "Stab wound to the heart has done it almost instantly," he guessed.

He carefully got back up and avoided the two spongey puddles forming on the carpet. "Get the fucking glasses and let's get the fuck out of here," he urged. When Stroker appeared, Chuck made him remove his coat, which he took from him and quickly dipped in the blood. The three of them then moved quickly down the flights of stairs, each man hoping that no one would open a door or come into the stairway and see them.

Back at the car, Chuck carefully put Stroker's coat in a carrier bag and placed it in the boot of the Volvo. "What the fuck just happened there?" panted Forsyth.

"She was murdered, obviously," snapped Chuck, his heart beating, his groin sweating and the air he was gulping getting hotter and hotter. The sweat was running down the three of them as they drove off. All of them looked up at the building's windows to see if anyone was watching them, but they saw no one.

"But who the fuck?"

"And why did you put blood on my coat, you bastard?" Stroker was beginning to fume and was considering trying to force the car into a crash to get more cops on the scene.

"Only as insurance that you won't fuck us over, Irvine; because we need to stick together and we need to stick to our story, which is that we were never here, right?" Chuck told him as they sat in the lights at Jock's Lodge. It was not until they reached Portobello that Chuck let Forsyth jump out and chuck all the glasses into the nearest bin.

"We could go and figure this out over a cup of tea at mine?" suggested Stroker.

"Will Alby be there?" Chuck asked, watching Stroker via the rear-view mirror.

"He will be on a train to Broughty Ferry to borrow money from his parents by now; he lied about 'Bargain Hunt'. He'll probably be back later tonight, so we have a bit of time," Stroker said knowingly.

"Alby can't ever know about this, Irvine," Chuck warned.

"No way, don't worry about that; he might use it against me," Stroker agreed.

They headed to Stroker's place then. Once it was confirmed that it was empty, Chuck had everyone take their gear off and made Stroker put a boiling hot wash on, in case any minute blood spots had managed to get onto their clothing. All three men sat in their underwear on the orange leather sofa in considerable discomfort. Stroker eventually put on some other clothes and made coffee. After a while he also put on some chips to fry, which he burned but tried to eat regardless.

"I burned them intentionally," he insisted before finally giving in and taking them back into the kitchen and slinging them in the sink, then returning with a peanut butter sandwich instead.

"Mind if I smoke?" he lifted his weed box up towards Chuck. Chuck simply nodded that he could if he wished. So Stroker made a joint, lit it, and sat back into the sofa beside Forsyth; who took the spliff off him and had a quick puff himself.

"No, thanks," Chuck shook his head when it was offered to him and supped at his coffee instead. "What the fucking hell happened back there, Chrissy?" he asked.

"All we know is that someone killed her while we sat in the lounge, guv, and that they did it quickly and quietly."

"An experienced hit?" Chuck asked.

"Well the stab wound to the heart area looked precise, and the cut throat may have been a way of making sure?" Forsyth suggested.

"Trevelen?" Chuck speculated aloud.

"After what happened earlier in the cow shed it's possible, but evidence-wise, a bit far-fetched?" Forsyth replied.

"Same cunts what killed Leo, I bet you," offered Stroker.

Chuck's phone buzzed. It was a text message from Adams:

"Update: The four vehicle registration numbers Chris sent earlier today. First car was a Hertz hired vehicle out of Gatwick airport and is rented out to a Darren Reid, 39, of Stockbridge, Edinburgh, not known. Another two are owned by a Derek McCracken, 42, of Luthrie in Fife, not known, and a Sean Kidd, 61, of Newburgh in Fife, known for speeding 1982, and for losing a publican's licence of the Covenanter Arms in St Andrews due to a conviction of reset in 1990. The other motor, the Jag, is registered to the Head Coroner for Lothian and Borders, Dr Esther Faulkner. Car's registered at 16A Abercorn Mews, Haddington, East Lothian." Chuck showed Forsyth.

"So, what was the head coroner for Lothian doing at Trevelen's estate in Fife?" considered Forsyth.

Stroker was lounging, but was still overcome with worry. "What about the blood on my coat?" he asked softly.

"It will be safe; I'm going to stash it well, but don't try and fuck us over or I'll bury you, Irvine," Chuck warned him. Stroker just shut his eyes and nodded slowly as the dope kicked in.

"The question is, did the murderer know we were there?" asked Forsyth.

"Perhaps, Chris, but I doubt anyone would do a front door hit like that without coming in and being at least a little discreet about it. After all, it was always going to be a gamble given that any of the neighbours might appear."

"Either way, this is a fucking mess, guv. Maybe we're better off cutting our losses and getting out of it now," Forsyth half-suggested.

"No, they know we are onto their scent, so I think they'll probably come after us regardless of whether we walk away or not. On that basis, we have nothing much to lose by pressing on with the hunt."

Stroker eventually reached out with a remote control and turned the TV on; it was an American news network, reporting from somewhere in Scotland.

"And as Colin Anderson-Forbes arrived for his fleeting tour of the Western Isles here at Portree harbour on Skye, he spent the afternoon out on a fishing boat catching langoustines," said the Glaswegian reporter.

"And so, while the leaders of the other parties concentrate on attending Holyrood, Mr Anderson-Forbes has been out on a mini tour of the Scottish islands, campaigning to sway the population into a YES vote, David?" the female studio host asked him.

"Yes, absolutely, Brooke. As we know, Colin Anderson-Forbes is a very energetic and dynamic politician and he's here on Skye, engaging local businesses and trying to reassure people that a YES vote would be beneficial to their livelihood," the man on the scene confirmed in front of a small fishing boat, the crew of which were unloading their catch with Forbes trying to assist them. Several photos were then taken of him holding a langoustine and carrying crates of fish, of course.

Stroker turned it over to a local news station to hear if there was anything about the murder, but he had missed the news part as the weather report was on.

"What if a neighbour got the car reg?" he then asked somewhat dopily.

"My phone would ring, and it has been an hour now, so relax," Chuck winked to reassure him.

"Yeah, make us another brew, Irvine?" Forsyth gave him a little nudge so he got up, took their cups and went through. Forsyth followed and Chuck closed his eyes and rubbed his head.

He sat thinking about the situation, now that the adrenaline had subsided and he could consider things more rationally. The investigation had certainly turned into a shit-storm of extreme proportions. In one day, he knew he had probably killed a sub-human Nephilim, and been present at the site of another murder, of a key witness no less, which looked to be the work of either an experienced hit man or another of those bastards. Not to mention Lionel Frazer's hit, which had professional written all over it, so things probably couldn't get much hotter. There were no prints at Yvonne's place, he was confident of that, but her steamer of a mother had spoken to them earlier and could, regardless of her habit, possibly identify them. It was doubtful that she was capable of that though, and besides, a murder squad officer would have no reason to show her photos of him or Forsyth. All that said, it was still a gamble not calling Yvonne's murder in. Well, he was not rushing into a decision without his clothes on, so he sat and continued to think.

His phone rang. Adams spoke again,

"I've had a DI Kinnaird from the West End on the phone now," she gave him one of her infuriated performances. "He's leading the murder squad on the Lionel Frazer hit and has learned that our squad were chin-wagging with him prior to his being released from custody."

"He wanted to know why we were interested in Frazer and said that he was only interested in discovering whether or not the reason was of any interest to his investigation."

"What did you say?" he asked.

"Told him we were only responding to him being charged with the cocaine in his car, and that we are interested in his client, Leslie Cairns," she replied.

"And?"

"He said he still seeks a sit-down with the investigating officers, but I told him one is on holiday and the other, his partner, is off sick. I asked if he wanted your emails or addresses and he said he already had them, but that he would contact us here again soon."

"I bet him and the duty inspector at St Leonards at the time are all handshaked up," Chuck said with the bitterness Adams had come to know existed within him, regardless of his best efforts to hide it.

"Don't worry, he seemed happy with that, but I'm going to mention it to Wong anyway, OK?"

"Yes, good idea, just in case this guy Kinnaird is dirty too. Sharon, this is one hell of a wicked web we are in to here, but I'll get a brief with you shortly, mate." Chuck's voice betrayed that he was concerned and she couldn't help feeling worried about something, although she was not sure exactly what that was.

"Clothes won't be long, guv," said Forsyth as both he and Stroker returned, bearing coffee.

Chuck was about to say something in code about Adams' call to Forsyth, but his phone rang again. This time the number was withheld.

"Hello?"

"It's Dai here," the angel said warmly.

Chuck took a breath and scanned the faces of the other two men. Forsyth was going through his text messages, and Stroker was busy making another joint.

"… Yes?" he said slowly, feeling a surge of optimism from the traces of wellbeing that Dai seemed to ignite inside him.

"Don't worry, I simply wanted to reassure you. Chuck, relax. The murderer of that woman did not know you three were in the other room," he said with such certainty and truth that Chuck actually did relax a little in the knowledge that the TIC, or whoever, was not trying to frame him or follow him.

"Who were they?" he asked instinctively, causing the other two men to look up.

"Only men. And we shall discuss this morning's drama in Fife later, you need to know that you were not seen and nor was the Volvo," Dai told him in the way a mother might reassure a child. "You need to stay focused on Trevelen; he is still in Fife at present," the angel added, before hanging up.

"Anything wrong?" Forsyth shrugged his shoulders.

"No, just the wife saying she had two Mormons at the door and she had to slam it shut," Chuck instinctively replied, but before Forsyth could tell his own humorous story about Mormons, Chuck's phone rang again.

"Hello?"

"Not a good example. Meter Reader or courier would have sufficed!" Dai chuckled at him before hanging up.

Chuck was stunned and leaned over towards Stroker. "Give me a shot of that!" He pointed at the almost-made joint. Stroker then began to think and plot at this point in the proceedings.

After a while the clothes were dry. Chuck put his on and smoothed them out as best he could. The important thing was that they had been boiled and made foolproof; after all, mistakes at this stage could bring a lot of trouble, and they had to stay in the game.

"Don't worry about the Yvonne situation, chaps." Chuck looked out of the window towards the small pebbly beach below. To the left was Musselburgh harbour with a few private yachts bobbing serenely around it as the sea became a little choppy. He thought it might rain later. A couple of basset hounds on leads trailed behind a girl of about fifteen, who was walking slowly, trying to keep her footing on the beach track while she texted from her phone.

"That is all going to be fine. They won't be looking for us as there's no connection to us being there, so take the secret to your graves," he told them.

"How do you know?" Stroker asked reservedly.

"I just do, right?" Chuck growled, though quietly enough to half-convince the nervous Stroker that he knew what the outcome would be.

"How do you know, though?" Forsyth asked because he was stoned now.

Chuck turned to face them both, "I swear to you, I just know."

Stroker looked up and studied his face for a while, then grinned and turned away.

"Do you doubt it, Irvine?" asked a voice from the chair beside the door. All three of them turned instantly, like antelopes upon catching the scent of an approaching lioness.

Stroker looked at Dai and screamed in exclamation, leaning back into Forsyth who had almost lost control of his bowels. Forsyth was also looking back and forth from Dai to Chuck, who had jumped back against the window to try and adopt a more relaxed posture. He was surprised, if not quite startled.

"This is Dai. He is our friend. Don't be scared, and don't swear, whatever you do," Chuck explained, tense but, he thought, in an even tone of voice.

Dai smiled as he stood up and raised his right hand for Chuck to allow him to explain. "I am an angel of God. I was not planning to be here among you, but there have been developments, one of which, Chuck…" he looked at Chuck now and shrugged a shoulder, pausing to rephrase what he had been about to say, "You're losing this one." Dai then gazed directly down at Stroker, who was frozen stiff with mouth open, unsure whether to scream or not.

"Even now you're trying to rationalise how this just happened, aren't you?" He winked at Stroker, who relaxed and felt all his tension depart as the warmth of goodness massaged him. He knew instantly that this suddenly-arrived person did not wish to hurt him, which always helped.

"The last time you felt goodness was from your mother as a child, am I right?" he caringly inquired of Stroker; who nodded, his eyes wide open.

"Well, he was not meant to be saved," Dai looked back to Chuck. "I was not meant to come here and do what I am about to do Chuck, but things have quickly developed since I rang you, and I have had to obtain special permission to come here now," Dai's explanation as always, seemed sincere.

"To do what, Dai?" Chuck asked.

"I am to give these two men a lucky ticket," Dai smirked, clearly amused at things.

"You're an angel?" Forsyth asked very slowly.

"Quite. And I am now going to do something to convince you both of the facts. Chuck, you're coming too." Dai smiled fondly and reached out his hand for Chuck to take. It is difficult to speculate just what the three different personalities felt at that precise moment. A respectful vibe now replaced the previous fear and competitiveness with feelings of respect and affection. This was slightly similar, as the three men instantly respected and trusted this being, but they also knew instinctively not to mess with him too.

"Everyone, I ask that you indulge me please. Hold hands in a circle and grant me two minutes of your life as we are about to travel through a spiritual doorway and into another type of reality, and then I shall return you to this exact room with renewed faith in my authority," Dai said so kindly. "Hold tight then, and do not let go of one another."

Eleven

"Power is the great aphrodisiac"

Henry Kissinger

Forbes was nervous about Scottish midges, having once endured a vicious assault as a 10-year-old boy scout hiking along the West Highland Way. His patrol, 'the Magpies', had been placed in the rear guard behind the main body of scouts, when they were bitten severely for two hours by the mini-mosquitos, an experience which still made him flinch when he had occasion to recall it.

His PA and spin paramedic, John Logan, who had worked on the last-minute trip to the Western Isles had been warned to organise anti-midge sprays and protective head gear. Ewan Lawrenson had, as unofficial head of strategy, suggested that Forbes undertake a three-day trip throughout the islands to try to establish the party in the hearts of the inhabitants. Forbes was to be portrayed as someone who cared about the islands, and who could potentially challenge the 'NO THANKS' leaners who usually voted SNP, but who were still unsure about separation from the Union.

Arriving on Skye after 3 pm, the tour coach carried Forbes and his mini-mafia of Logan, Col's Dolls, his adviser Vernon Keith and Keith's wife Pamela; who specialised in media law, but was giving more volunteer time to the party's all round Indyref campaign. Three burly security men, provided by the same firm which protected Akadion's interests in Scotland, sat among them. They had been chatty enough with everyone, making brews for all and sundry, yet they appeared more like thugs than ex-military men. Lawrenson told an ex-cop named Sandy from Glasgow to go and check out the accommodation Logan had sourced beforehand, because of several death threats against Forbes during the referendum campaign. Sandy, who was 51, had once been a third-degree brown belt in karate and would be in the room next to Forbes in said hotels for the duration of the trip. Forbes was aware of this, but chose to keep it from the rest of his team.

The itinerary included a short trip out on a local fishing boat to fish for langoustines. This was particularly poignant because the SLP's shadow environmental minister had jumped ship previously to join the Greens. Despite replacing him with Justin Burke, who had jumped ship from Labour to the SLP himself a couple of years previously, and whose father had been a whaler; Lawrenson now felt that Forbes should be seen to take a special interest in the fishing concerns of the islanders, whose industry was under threat by proposals to close water zones around the Western Isles.

The little crab boat and its two-man crew were waiting for Forbes as he arrived with Logan creeping alongside him, filming the trip, in a role in which he quite fancied himself as a documentary cameraman. The stunt went well enough, as the salty larders ensured that when the boat returned, the SLP leader could step onto dry land; filmed by Logan and posing like Agamemnon when he stepped onto the beach at Troy; holding a crab, crayfish and even a couple of lobsters. Logan then climbed up onto the coach and rang one of his television news desk chums in Glasgow to sell her Forbes as Agamemnon.

"Oh, it's fabulous Lydia, Col's out there like Captain Pugwash, holding genuine Scottish crayfish in his hand whilst chewing the fat with the ship's captain about their dependency upon the industry and nature tourism. Oh, and he is holding the crayfish too!"

"Get it over to us pronto then and we'll see if it can go out on the six o'clock news," Lydia had urged.

The film did go out at 6 pm in Scotland, headlined '*Anderson-Forbes attempts to charm the Western Islanders whilst fishing for west coast treasures, as the rest of the field focus upon Scotland's eastern treasure at Holyrood today, North Sea Oil*'.

Afterwards, a tired and hungry Forbes was driven to a hotel in Portree, where the entire party were staying that evening. Local police had parked along the street for the remainder of the evening. One of the local bobbies jested to his female colleague that they might turn a blind eye, should anyone try to kill the SLP leader. WPC Kirk, however, was a supporter of the party, and began what eventually turned into a 3-hour political debate with her colleague, that only ended when she got out, slammed the door, and went and sat on a bench until her shift ended. When Forbes heard about his police guard, he had lobster sandwiches and cups of tea sent out to them with his regards. He ate alone in a double room which overlooked the sea and as he was exhausted from the day of travel across Scotland, went to bed at an early hour.

The journey from St Andrews to Skye had taken several hours through the beautiful and emotion-stirring landscape which was no better reflected by the multiple colours flashing by, thanks to short bursts of seasonal rain and sunshine. The drive had been unpleasant for Forbes because he had argued bitterly over the phone for much of it with Lawrenson about decriminalizing marijuana and Lawrenson's pet idea for instigating government-run heroin-shooting galleries.

"If you move now to state that weed will be decriminalized in an independent Scotland under an SLP government, we can really use that as our economic safety net, Colin."

"No, I'm not making it morally acceptable to take drugs."

"OK, well, think of the Dutch example, then think of the economics before you just write it off," Lawrenson added, persistently.

"No Ewan, I have friends and former friends who smoke it, and they are all lazy, brain-dead wasters. That to me completely undermines our dream of perfection for Scotland and her people."

Lawrenson had kept the issue going and tried throwing figures at him, before eventually swearing at him and hanging up.

"It could swing us another half a mill in the referendum Colin, not to mention the national election that will follow independence," Lawrenson tried again afterwards when he had called back.

"Let me think about it Ewan. I'll consider your points and get back to you after this little trip."

"And the shooting galleries?" Lawrenson pressed the full mile.

He heard a long sigh at Forbes' end. "Don't tell me all the junkies will actually get out of their beds and go and vote Ewan! Look, I'll think about the weed thing and give you my final answer soon, alright?"

His throat had been sore and his tongue ached as he hung up and he soon felt himself begin to drift off. Impatient for the vote, he fought the need for sleep a while longer; trying to imagine himself as Prime Minister of an independent Scotland.

In the morning, he had porridge and coffee in a local café, bright and early with Logan.

"The king of the junkies," Logan teased as Forbes arrived and took a pew.

"El president de la jakeballs, actually," smirked Forbes as he spooned honey onto his porridge.

Logan smiled and handed him a newspaper. The front page had a snap of him holding the crayfish on the boat and a headline of '*Anderson-Forbes promises to protect fishing for Scotland's islanders*'.

"Could be worse," Forbes smiled sardonically as he read. Then his phone began ringing; it was Lawrenson.

The party headed south to Iona by chartered helicopter straight after breakfast while the coach took the ferry to the island of Lewis. They were headed initially to Iona for a brief photo shoot and interview with Pollock Hamilton's glossy magazine, *Manifesto*. Forbes was all prepared to champion Iona's unique green and white marble, which lies around her coastline. A short, sharp script had been prepared on how the marble would be used firstly to improve the Scottish parliament building at Holyrood, remoulding it away from its 'Catalan disaster', followed by something about how the material can be used more in art and architecture, thus creating employment and beauty within an independent Scotland. The only problems with this were that, like the oil on the east coast of Scotland, there was little left to plunder, and that Iona's reputation was of a place of quiet contemplation, not industry.

The Dolls were on standby to mention to any irritating journalists who may raise these points afterward, that following independence, the SLP would make it an election pledge to investigate this. If it turned out that there was insufficient marble, then the uniqueness of it would be displayed in a national monument of independence on Arthur's Seat in Edinburgh, and any quarrying costs would be small.

As they flew south through the two and a half miles of sea between the Islands of Rum and Eigg, one of the girls enthused, "It's like the Caribbean from up here – the blue sea and those green peaks!"

Logan thought of Odysseus being pinballed around the Greek islands. "Or the Aegean, even," he said thoughtfully.

"Yes, I was thinking precisely that, and then half-expecting to see Muslim refugees crossing the strait below on lilos and coconut rafts," Forbes added with a smirk.

"What would you do about this refugee crisis when you become El Presidente?" asked Logan.

"Recommend to our neighbours in Europe that they stop them from coming in," Forbes was clearly contemptuous of the subject. "If we bar entry in Greece and stop rescuing the boats heading for Sicily, then we stop the problem," he said firmly.

"By making them swim back?" grinned Logan.

"No, but we could round them up on the beaches and then put them on humanitarian ships that all EU members fund. We could sail them around and dump them in Africa; I'm sure that the South Africans could be persuaded one way or another to set up camps for them, that we help to fund, until they can go home. More importantly, the ones who are already here in Scotland can all be sent to camps like the ones the Australians have created offshore on Nauru, to keep them all in one place," he added, pointing out of his window and over towards Rum.

"But boss, the Australians are getting some terrible press about the conditions of their offshore detention camps as well as claims of staff violence; there's even been child rape allegations by whistle-blowers," one doll warned with genuine concern.

"Yes, but the skippies just passed a new law stating that any social worker or medical worker who discusses these matters again, will be liable to serve two years in prison; simple and effective. So as bad as things may be on Nauru, they have successfully stopped the boats heading to Australia, haven't they?" Forbes pointed out. "And the bad press has also been dealt with," he smirked.

The toadies all nodded in agreement but Logan looked out at the islands, "Or, just refuse them all benefits and then they won't come anymore. Besides, which island would you put them on?" he asked.

"Muck seems suitable, no?" They all sniggered at this wit.

Vernon Keith, who had been quiet for most of the flight, spoke again, "And then Scotland may face a global backlash for doing so."

"Isolationism?" Forbes asked him, and got a poker-faced nod in reply.

"Well, our home policy, if we come to power under my leadership, Vernon, will be one of Scottish-ism, and our foreign policy will not be one of globalism anyway," he assured.

"Still?" Keith smiled at him and shrugged his shoulders.

"We only have to look at how badly-run the Australian offshore camps are, and then note how the world have simply accepted it. This is why we shall be able to do something similar Vernon, but on a more humane scale," Forbes pointed out before gazing out to sea again.

For the rest of the airborne jolly, most of the passengers read emails and news updates on their phones and tablets whilst Forbes closed his eyes and thought initially about both his upcoming meeting with Bill Garneau and then of the pending House of Commons report into arms export contracts. In particular, he pondered the said report's focus upon HM government potentially having issued licences to certain companies alleged to have produced arms for states regarded as abusers of human rights. Yet he knew he must at least explore what Garneau was offering, because if things went pear-shaped in London, Logan would have a safety net prepared for the party and they could not be penalised for listening. The decision over whether or not to get into bed with these guys, could come after he listened to them then.

Iona was a short stop. Two 4x4s were on hand to rush them to the location for the shoot. There was a huge, golden, sandy beach, where they met the marine archaeologist, the *Manifesto* journalist and a couple of local marble craftsmen. The archaeologist swam out a little in a wet suit and returned with a grey stone that one of the craftsmen then split in half with a mallet to reveal the impressive green and white marble.

It was here that Forbes gave a romantically moving interview with the glossy about how his Scotland would create new monuments and buildings from this unique marble.

"On a day like today, these islands are a paradise for us standing here. Each island is breathtaking with its own unique personality, crying out for tourism. An independent Scotland would be able draw a new wave of tourism for these beautiful islands by promoting these scattered gems out there," he thumbed out to the sea behind him, whilst holding a handful of marbled chips from the stone the craftsman had smashed.

A mere 34 minutes later, they were back in the sky and heading for Tobermory on nearby Mull. Pamela Keith took the chair directly opposite Forbes and gave him another smile. She had been doing a lot of that lately, and thus the gesture was becoming a discreet one. He had caught the scent, but then it was regularly there anyway and quite varied at that, so hardly an exciting distraction for him. He observed her now however; she was perhaps not beautiful but far from ugly. She was wearing a trouser suit and a Royal Stewart tartan shawl. She opened her legs a couple of times to display her best assets; her body and well-shaped legs and the crease of her crotch, which he couldn't help but glance at. Forbes remembered that she had pulled her trousers up as they had all approached the helipad, so this was probably a deliberate display. However, he had other matters to think about, rather than some slutty married lawyer.

Looking out of his window as they approached the southern cape of Mull, Forbes watched as dark green and brown Iona, the Torran Rocks, and the anchorages at Bulls Hole were replaced by the light green rocky landscape of Mull with her inlets and lochs. He thought a bit about the drug question and went over the pros and cons of things a little. If the numbers were there, and more votes were going to be the prize, then to hell with morality. He mimicked his father's voice in his mind to convince himself. "President Anderson-Forbes," he tried out the name so silently that nobody else could hear, though if they had looked they may have seen his breath evident upon his window, and should anyone have placed a hand upon his chest, a very fast heart beat would have been detected.

"About this TV question and answer thing tomorrow, boss," Vernon Keith raised his head from his tablet and interrupted the fantasy.

Forbes leaned forward and took a slow drink from a bottle of spring water, hoping that no one would see how this prospect irked him. He was up against the pro-unionist MP Johnny Bett, a Lewis-born lefty and former Labour party MP who now sat as an independent in Birmingham. Bett was a clever politician who liked women too much and had been hounded by the tabloids as a result. However, he possessed a quite excellent understanding of political matters and an often sharp-witted debating style. Forbes feared him more than anyone, and had suggested that his opponent was ineligible to debate during the referendum due to his London 'soap-opera life'.

"Yep?"

"Darren has just asked whether you mind sitting next to Johnny Bett, as the other debater is deaf in one ear." Keith shrugged his shoulders and shook his head.

"No. Tell them I am not sitting next to that red bastard."

Tobermory was as lovely as always when the Forbes mafia arrived and marched along the busy seafront with its colourful shops and houses. It was a fine day with a very light breeze, and out beyond the immediate noise of passing car engines and tourists, the sound of jet skis and the odd seaplane could be heard. The party headed out past a packed little beach to a stone pier, where the owners of working boats were busying about. There they met a *Mercury* photographer and journalist wearing a tweed cap, a local radio journalist, and a three-man TV Crew who by now had latched onto the Forbes island trip. Marine archaeologist Martha Rooney was on hand with a little boat run by Cambridge University. She waved them all on board and briefed them over some cold apple juice, before motoring out beyond the harbour.

The cameras caught her ambitious waffle about the existence of ships from the Spanish Armada wrecked in the area. She was learned enough and gave a good argument, at least from an academic perspective, but there was of course little evidence.

"Well, the proof shall be in the pudding presumably, and because we know that at least one Spanish ship, the San Francisco, came here to escape the English fleet, and moored to resupply, it seems to me to be a national duty to investigate whether or not sunken Spanish ships do lie here," Forbes said to the camera before the little boat turned back to harbour.

"So, if you were to be elected as First Minister, are you saying you would search for what some experts believe are Spanish galleons filled with gold?" asked one of the TV interviewers.

Forbes laughed at this and shuffled his position, leaning on the metal rim around the side of the boat. "I think it would be more realistic to presume that an investigation of this size and financial output would be best done by an independent Scotland, whose new leadership is supportive of the nation exploring itself through such projects," he smiled at the camera.

"It is doubtful whether we would find anything, never mind treasure, but it would be wonderful to create a visitor centre here on Mull, and raising a wreck would be a great part of that process," he elaborated further while thoughtfully looking out to sea. "So, it seems to me to be important that we investigate the matter" he surmised.

When they returned to the stone pier and had some photos done with Rooney, Forbes gave the local radio reporter a ten-minute interview on the Armada subject and gave a decent performance in showing that he cared about the island's economy, even going as far as to lie and say that the SLP had initial plans drawn up for the Armada project that may provide "a considerable amount of employment to the island".

As they departed the pier, a scooter appeared to slow down then beep its horn, before the female rider shouted out "fuck off you racist prick!" as she passed.

Forbes shook his head and walked on regardless. "No need to behave like a hooligan," he said. "One must always keep one's dignity, guys," he told the team before striding on at the front.

Afterwards, when they had covered the mile or so back to the helipad, mostly lost in their own thoughts, they quickly departed for the next island stop. On the flight to Lewis, Lawrenson rang Forbes to try to persuade him to emphasise his meritocratic personal political history whilst on the campaign trail, and to bury any sense of wealth or privilege. The call was prompted by an article in a New York daily about Forbes' poshness and "estuary accent that all English public schoolboys possessed".

"Don't worry, everyone is on it and the rag will be making an apology shortly Colin – no doubt on page 42, as always – but in the meantime, let's focus on the working man and his vote here, old chap."

"Well I'm staying in shitty guest houses and living on ale and chips, if that is any good to you, squire," replied Forbes contemptuously.

"And do you regret doing so?" teased Lawrenson.

"*Je ne regrette rien*," smirked Forbes who, when the call ended, turned to Logan and told him to arrange for fish and chips after the debate.

That night they all stayed in a cosy little hotel in Stornoway. The dolls doubled up and the Vernons were next door to Logan. The security boys all took a room down the corridor and the unofficial security, like at Skye, had the room next door to Forbes. After the debate, in which Johnny Bett had performed particularly well, Forbes, Logan and the security men sat in the hotel bar and had a few drinks. The consensus was that Forbes had done well enough against the wily old red, particularly when Bett tried to argue that all Scots were alike in sharing a common tongue, culture and history. Forbes had pointed out that in Fife they called a popular cake a custard slice, but that in Edinburgh, the same cake was known as a vanilla slice.

"Scots are more diverse than you say, Johnny, particularly in class terms," he had told Bett. "Take religion, music, and politics for instance; these are changed days from when you and your father preached socialist unity through resentment and poverty." Here, he had tried to twist the subject onto an attack upon Bett's socialist history, but his adversary concentrated upon the referendum in reply. In the end, Bett had performed well enough in favour of the union and Forbes came away thinking he might have done better.

"That was an off showing," he told Logan however. "I'll pick up the performance for Edinburgh," he added, as if to convince himself, on the way back to the hotel.

There were a couple of local fiddlers playing in the bar, so they all sat longer, drank more than they had intended and foot-tapped away until late, as the Indyref was forgotten for a while. The following morning, as they turned out for the famous Lewis carnival, Forbes was wearing sunglasses and carrying a bottle of Irn Bru, known for its anti-hangover properties. Logan had arranged for him to volunteer for a couple of hours on a stall selling local products. The stall was run by a farmer named Mike, who was an SLP supporter.

"So, this lovely chutney that I'm enjoying here Mike, do you make this on your farm?" Forbes asked as Logan filmed and the security men scanned the busy crowd.

When Mike confirmed that the mixed fruit chutney was indeed made by his daughter Sam, who just happened to be the busty teenager standing beside them in a Barbour jacket with a mischievous smirk, Forbes turned and smiled at her.

"And not just a pretty face then," he offered casually while continuing to nibble at a home-made pork pie with some of the delicious chutney on it.

The girl smiled but said nothing. "Do you enjoy working on the farm?" Forbes pressed her.

"I'm a student in Glasgow and only get involved when I come home for the festival," Sam nonchalantly replied.

Sensing that Mike was uncomfortable, Forbes turned around and smiled at him and returned to the subject of chutney.

The two hours at the carnival passed quickly, mainly due to the marvellous floats which passed throughout and the brass and highland bands which marched up and down creating a party atmosphere. When the time was right, Forbes was walked into the crowd by his team and began shaking hands and instigating conversations with couples and families about the referendum, playing the investigative reporter at first but soon changing tack and taking a soap box tone in addressing those who gathered around to listen and take snaps of him on their phones.

"And what is going to happen to all the North Sea oil once we agree to separate from the union?" shouted an older gent.

"Well, I can tell you one thing," quipped Forbes as he deployed his endearing smile, "it won't be crossing Hadrian's Wall until the Scottish government has renegotiated the price," he roared to an appreciative crowd. Logan took some more pictures of the barnstorming performance in front of maybe 180 people. Some cheered him, some asked questions about how much oil was left, while others shouted in favour of the union.

"If Scotland votes for independence, the SLP shall campaign in the following national elections. I intend to win, and govern with a mandate to rejuvenate these magnificent islands and their economies by nurturing a tourist industry which will rival the visitor numbers of the Canary Islands," he lied to them.

"How?" asked a journalist pretending to be Joe Public.

Forbes paused to look around at the growing crowd with that smile, "I believe that our stunningly varied and unique islands, with their welcoming ways, stunning scenery and beaches straight out of a Hollywood movie, could and should attract a greater number of visitors, but have been neglected by London over the last thirty years." He looked around them all again with a confused expression.

"Where are the major hotel investments, golf resorts and visitor attractions, I ask you?" he went on playing with them.

"There's nothing here, not even a casino or a club," shouted one young guy amongst a group of men in their twenties, to Forbes' right.

"And that's because no money has been made available here," Forbes argued. "But that will all change if we vote for independence and self-rule," he promised them.

Some just stared and thought about his logic, others applauded and some even shouted "Yes. Yes. Yes!" but no-one booed or attacked his darker political ideology. That is, until a man in his fifties shouted out.

"We fought a war against racism, son, and we bloody won! What makes you think we'll let a wee racist bugger like you into government?" He was immediately drowned out by the continued chants of "Yes," however.

Thirty minutes later, they were all aboard the tour bus and heading south along the A859 to the village of Balallan on Loch Erisort. Forbes raised his head a while to look out at the countryside, and set eyes on a large SLP billboard that Ewan had splattered across the islands as well as the mainland. It displayed the Lion Rampant with a paw pointed at the reader, in an echo of Kitchener's WWI, "Your Country Needs You."

The text read:

"These are not ordinary times and this is not an ordinary vote. I need your help and I need your hand."

Could it really happen? Could Scotland free herself from this union? Forbes pondered on this, as they drove on toward a quick meeting with Andrea 'Andy' Friggieri; the millionaire owner of Alba, a low-cost airline; and Bill Garneau, who had been fishing on Loch Erisort whilst staying at Friggieri's villa. Lawrenson had arranged the meet, and Forbes was under the impression that it would be a coffee or two with further discussion about his party using his Alba Airlines.

"Loch Erisort is a Viking name, boss, and the Callanish Stones are only half an hour away; they were erected in the late Neolithic era and look very Stonehenge-y," Forbes snapped out of it as one of the dolls passed him her phone with a photo of a circle of stones, which were indeed Stonehenge-y. He was impressed.

"Right, good call, Katie," he smiled at her. "After this meeting, which shouldn't take longer than half an hour or so, we shall stop there for a quick photoshoot on our way back to the ferry. Then get the pics uploaded to the Mercury under suggested a title of, *'Anything England can do, we can do better and older'.*" Forbes winked at her. They were staying on the coach and catching the last ferry to Ullapool on the mainland, then planning to drive straight down to Edinburgh for the Ingleston event. They were booked into the nearby Norton House Hotel, where the rest of the party would be awaiting.

Both Keith and Logan took peeks at the phone too, and then at its owner, in surprise that they had not thought of this first. "OK," said Keith crisply, "I'll try and get the *Mercury* to go with one of the photos and a headline along the lines of *"Anything England can do, we can do better."* He raised a hopeful set of eyebrows at everyone.

"No, let me see if we can argue that our Stonehenge came before the English one," Logan said, putting his hand on Forbes' wrist and then quickly removing it when Forbes shook his head.

"Let's stop off at the Lewis war memorial, as that has been closed to the public since 1975. We will look into that instead, John, and see if we can pledge to reopen it or something," he told them.

Forbes considered that the country just might vote for independence now, having always been pessimistic about change in that direction. The majority of Scots were too conservative and scared of change, he often thought. But this was different, this was spreading like a virus among the population and may not be containable. If she did decide to go solo and run herself, Scotland would require a national election, and if things were played properly, Labour and the Liberals were there for the taking, he reckoned. The SLP could become the second biggest party in the land and the main opposition party at Holyrood.

Coalition meant ideas being pushed through; yes, they would force Salmond's hand in the elections next year. He smiled and went back to his emails.

Shortly before they reached Balallan, the coach turned down a lane leading to a crofter's farm, with some impressive villas out on the hillside to their right, which looked out onto the loch itself. One isolated house, large and creamy with several vehicles outside it, and a helicopter on a little grassy ledge about the size of a tennis court, stood out. Friggieri had inherited the place from his maternal grandmother, and used it in summer when he wanted to get away from London. It had apparently been the location for a reality musical TV show in the past, as the creator was a mate of Friggieri's singer girlfriend.

Forbes disembarked the bus with the security men and Logan, and noticed one or two other security men loitering around outside, prompting him to wonder what was going on. Forbes clapped the old iron doorknocker that was carved in the shape of a dragon.

The door opened and there stood the 40-something Friggieri wearing a t-shirt, shorts and slippers. It was a grand property with large glass windows, displaying a still loch outside and a little boardwalk with a couple of small rowing boats moored to them.

"Hey Colin, good to see you again, dude!" said the annoyingly hip Friggieri.

"Hi Andy, pleasure to have been asked," Forbes smiled warmly. "These chaps are my minders," he half joked and Friggieri nodded in understanding.

"They can go in the kitchen, plenty of food and beers for them in there," Friggieri motioned toward a large white-tiled open plan kitchen off to the left where one or two other burly blokes were smoking. Forbes' security men went through to join them.

Forbes nodded and followed Friggieri through to a spacious reception room and then through to a lounge where several people were seated, supping at drinks. Forbes immediately recognised Pollock Hamilton, who was seated by a redundant fire place, eating peanuts and drinking whisky. The two men nodded to each other.

Graeme De Sailes was sitting beside Bill Garneau and another man whom Forbes didn't recognise. Beside them sat three other men on single leather chairs, all drinking. In fact, the man beside De Sailes and Garneau was the only one not drinking whisky; instead, he had a cup of tea neatly sitting upon his knees.

"This is Major General Drew Fraser-Hunter, General Officer Scotland Command, based at Edinburgh," Friggieri said as he introduced Forbes to the fat, cold-faced old man with the cup of tea.

"I know you know these guys," he added, as he waved a hand at De Sailes and then Garneau, who in turn, toasted their glasses at Forbes with toothy grins.

"You know Pollock, of course. Oh yes, and this is a computer man, Brian Robertson of Mega-Ram," he gestured to one of the three unknowns, a fat, curly-haired, spectacle-wearing slob in a *Star Wars* t-shirt.

"Hi there, pleasure to meet you," offered Robertson as they shook hands. Forbes knew who he was only from his chain of computer parts shops across the UK and having read about his successful breakthrough into Silicon Valley with his venture-financed software company, Mega Technologies.

"Pleasure," Forbes lied.

"And this is Calum Thomson," said Friggieri and he gestured to a tall, balding gent with a black moustache, who did not smile when he offered his hand, "the Chief Constable of Police, and this is his deputy Nigel Sharpe." He let them shake hands before turning to point at a small man in his fifties, who was smoking a pipe by the sliding doors that led out to the boardwalk.

"And this is Ryan Ross, the Lord President and Lord Justice General of the High Court of the Judiciary," said Friggieri, as if presenting royalty.

Forbes walked over and shook the little pipe smoker's hand. "The head of the Scottish judicial system himself, and to what do I owe this pleasure?" he said, turning to ask his host.

"Well, it is us who are honoured, Colin, but first, please," Friggieri gestured for him to take a rather expensive-looking seat, "what will you have to drink?"

"Gin and tonic, thanks."

While Friggieri went off to fetch the drink, De Sailes asked Forbes how his trip was going. Forbes noted a couple of large Persian rugs and a large cactus plant; which gave the place too much of a colonial vibe, he rather thought. On one wood-panelled wall hung a large portrait of red-coated and tartan-wearing soldiers and cavalrymen fighting blue-coated Frenchmen. Forbes looked up at it, noting that all the cavalry rode grey horses, and that one rider was depicted reaching out to seize a French Eagle standard.

"Scots Greys smashing the Frogs at..."

"Waterloo," Forbes cut the Major General off without lifting his gaze from the painting.

"Are you military-educated, Mr Anderson-Forbes?" asked the Chief Constable, knowing quite well that he was not.

"No, I just saw the old movie and recall the scene when Bonaparte refers to their charge as 'terrifying'," Forbes said with a smile. The cop stared at him for a moment, then turned away towards the Major General.

Friggieri returned and served Forbes his drink, which he drank from thirstily, then slouched back in anticipation of an explanation of what all this was about, from his host. However, it was Pollock Hamilton who took the stage.

"I expect you are wondering why we are all gathered here, Colin, and why the secrecy?" he asked with a big fake grin which revealed whitened teeth.

Forbes played it cool by shrugging a shoulder, while in fact, the excitement at what may be on offer had set off butterflies in his stomach.

"Colin, I shall come to the point if I may," Hamilton continued. "We represent a wider group of friends, some who wish to remain anonymous for the time being, who share your political aspirations as well as your ideology."

"We like what you talk about, and genuinely feel that you care for this country with the same passion that we also do," he said in a measured tone, which sounded as though it had been carefully rehearsed.

"Where do you feel the SLP will be by the time Salmond calls an election?" he asked Forbes straight out.

"We are growing more and more popular amongst the lower classes and we feel we shall soon overtake Labour and the Libs in the battle for the middle classes," Forbes told them.

"So, you believe that you might well challenge the SNP for government?" De Sailes piped in now, but the nationalist within Forbes felt concerned about this foreigner's presence in a discussion about his party strategy and inspirations.

"Perhaps, or at least challenge by creating a coalition as an alternative with either the Tories or the Greens, or both," smirked Forbes with that outstanding confidence which made them all consider him for a moment. He was certainly confident, sharp, good-looking and game for the challenge. He was either playing this very well or he was naturally good at it, considered the experienced Garneau.

"What is your interest anyway, Graeme?" Forbes suddenly turned and smugly inquired of De Sailes.

"I represent the money," came the curt reply as De Sailes caught Garneau's eye.

"All of us here, and others, have an interest in you being the first elected leader of an independent Scotland, Colin," Hamilton stated.

"We have the power to commit to ensuring that the SLP electoral campaign, following a successful referendum, has more financial, media and online support than any of the other parties – perhaps all of them combined." Hamilton was getting to it now.

"And we shall either push you over the line ahead of Salmond, or into a coalition government with other parties at the very least; even the SNP if required."

"A coalition would not allow me to promise you the perks you would presumably be seeking," Forbes questioned their logic.

"What do you think we are seeking, Colin?" Hamilton softly asked him.

Forbes slowly looked around them all, smiling, as he took a further sip of his drink, before replacing it on the little glass table in front of him.

"Well, there is currently £1.8 billion in arms trade coming out of Scotland, and this provides 12,000 jobs." Forbes looked thoughtfully before continuing. "I'd hazard a guess that Akadion want tax relief, an invitation to expand rapidly, and quite possibly the right to drive the creation of our new Scottish Defence Force; kicking off massive naval projects both on Clydeside and at Rosyth in the long run?"

No one replied straight away. Forbes was warming to his subject, his natural confidence bolstered by the gin.

"Then there is your company, Graeme," he smiled at De Sailes, pausing for dramatic effect.

"You'll be after tax relief too and the overall control of the remainder of our oil and gas?"

De Sailes grinned. "Well, if we can agree certain things in principle here, Colin, we can all get started on making you king of this castle. Your first deposit of three £15,000,000 payments shall be placed into any account of your choice tomorrow morning," he said, as cool as a cucumber, before adding, "Preferably a Swiss account."

Forbes shuffled in his seat now. He could feel his cock hardening and the butterflies in his stomach giving way to fireworks.

"And what say you?" he coolly asked Robertson.

"I have people I work with in America who would like me to instigate a new Silicon Valley in Valleyfield in Fife. Which would be inside the EU single market, and which would provide for all of Scotland's needs and potentially work alongside any neighbouring Rosyth projects, as you mentioned just now." Robertson gave a seemingly honest response, to which Forbes nodded.

"We would have to begin discussions on that and come to terms on exactly what it is you are proposing. However, if it does contribute to the state's economy and it works for all of us, then in essence that sounds exciting," Forbes nodded.

"So obviously, lots to talk about Colin, but initially there is the first £15,000,000 which is ready for you now, based on our close analysis of what you plan to do. Then another £15,000,000 before next year's election and the final payment thereafter. If we fail at the pending elections then the deal is off, but you may keep the initial two payments," Hamilton said slowly, to be quite clear. "It goes without saying that we do expect complete discretion from you, and your word that you will take this matter to your grave," he added.

"Naturally. But, if the SLP do gain power through a coalition with the SNP or whomever, how do you propose I push your mandate through Holyrood then? We won't be calling all the shots in such a scenario." Forbes was tempted to take the initial payment but needed to confirm that this lot would all walk away, should he not do as well as they hoped in the election.

"In a scenario like that," assured Pollock, "the coalition partner would suddenly die of natural causes, and you would be sworn in as leader, having stepped up from your position of Deputy Prime Minister," he said chillingly.

Forbes took a second or two to take these words in; after all, the suggestion here was murder and perhaps potential treason.

"You would murder Salmond if I became his deputy within a coalition?" he asked quietly as they all studied his reaction.

"Obviously, we would not be directly responsible for a... murder, as you so directly put it, Mr Forbes – but the law would support your elevation if something like that should happen," offered the little Lord Justice General, standing now by the fireplace, which dwarfed his diminutive frame.

"And the law would be enforced if challenged," concurred the Chief Constable.

"Aye, and if they can't handle things, I will personally lead a squadron of Scottish and Irish Yeomanry in to occupy Holyrood and the Palace area while sending Royal Dragoons and Jackal armoured vehicles from Leuchars, to sort out any protests elsewhere," the Major General assured, and the Chief Constable gave him a grave yet knowing nod.

"We are powerful, Mr Anderson-Forbes, and if you come together with us here today, we can talk about how the SLP will storm next year's election through an online social media strategy that myself and some associates have thought out for you," urged Robertson.

"So, Colin, shall we shake hands on an initial commitment to being friends who help each other, and start talking things through?" Hamilton smiled hopefully and reached out his bony hand.

Forbes considered them for a while, and his instinct was that they were dangerously forward. Indeed, he envied them their boldness. He also grudged them their collective supremacy. Who did they think they were? Beliefs, and his innate cautiousness and political antennae aside, an inner darkness deep inside him saw the opportunity, and urged him to play along until they made him king. At which point they could be dealt with. His personal brand of fascism had provided his vision of ethics within the party and a projection of morality to the people. Yet something far stronger drew him toward this conspiracy.

The act of murder was irrelevant if one could get away with it, he reminded himself. Especially if it put him in Bute House, as leader of an independent Scotland. Besides, where was the harm in taking the money for indulging these self-important crooks, in a simple discussion? They didn't seem to need any guarantees. There was no conflict of ethics here either, since the SLP could decide on the terms of any deals. Then there was also the distinct possibility that this lot might also have considered arranging an accident for himself, should he not agree to play along at this point. The potential of him broadcasting their proposition would obviously place him in a very unsafe position now that they had shown him their hand. So what if they were powerful, he would take them all down a peg when he got himself on the throne; starting with a new Lord Justice General, he smirked to himself. A man had to put himself before others if one were to succeed, he also reminded himself.

"A man's a man for a' that[21]," he then beamed a huge smile, leaned over, and shook Hamilton's hand, causing the others to clap loudly.

---

[21] 1795 poem by Robert Burns, otherwise known as 'Is there for honest poverty'.

Twelve

"When men stop believing in God they do not believe in nothing, they believe in anything"

G.K. Chesterton

The early evening breeze was welcomed by the residents of Jerusalem in 30 AD. For the Samarian Auxiliaries at the Antonia fortress it signalled the impending changing of the guard after a long day spent pacing the royal portico. The air often became chilly soon afterwards, but as the three men crossed the portal and stepped on to the eastern city wall, their backs to the city below, they gasped it into their lungs with wonder as they viewed the beautiful brown-beige mound of olives, and the olive trees sprinkled across it. As they gazed out, the sky was a bright blue streaked with burnt orange clouds, and the three men each instinctively raised a hand to shade their eyes from the light. It was a truly beautiful view, although they also noticed the bright red cloaks of a Roman army group, and the blue robes of some merchant slaves, dotted among the groves.

Chuck knew that the energy flow, which they had just passed through here was something material science could not hope to quantify, as it was smoother than electricity or magnetism and the process of departure and entry from one realm to another, had taken two seconds at most. Stroker looked down upon the Kidron Valley to the Gihon spring, where many pilgrims were encamped. He half-recognised their Arab-esque clothing from biblical movie scenes but was still confused about where he was. Chuck looked down at the Romans and the carts full of firewood that they appeared to be guarding whilst the slaves picked olives. It was certainly a long way down and he felt scared. Their feet seemed secure, but Dai warned them as the breeze picked up:

"Watch your footing, gents. If you fall you will be saved, but do not fall, OK?" he laughed.

Stroker was not convinced. "Where is this?" He was shivering, and felt tears dripping from his eyes. However, with a great deal of effort, he maintained control of himself and wiped them dry.

"We are on the Eastern Wall of the city of Jerusalem, in the year of our Lord 30 AD," Dai told them.

"Oh, my God, please don't let me fall, I beg you." Forsyth began crying out like a child.

"That out there is the Mount of Olives, where Jesus of Nazareth preached," Dai revealed to them with his gloriously radiant smile, which naturally comforted them. "This, gentlemen, is a rare gift. It shall last only a short while before we return home."

"Have no fear," he went on. "You are safe with me, so simply try your best to relax and enjoy the experience. Start by turning around slowly," he told them with such love and poise that none of them doubted him.

Indeed, none of the men could even begin to comprehend the power at work here, and that included Chuck. They had an idea of what was happening well enough, but how it was possible remained beyond them at this point. Chuck remembered the Christian story about Jesus approaching a reviled but rich tax collector, and advising him to drop everything and simply follow him instead; the tax collector apparently did so. Chuck considered it must be a similar magic at work here, as the men now turned around and gazed down upon Roman-administered Jerusalem.

Stroker felt his knees buckle as more tears flowed, but Dai stretched out a hand and touched the back of his neck, causing him to immediately straighten up.

"Thank you," he mumbled. His anger, envy, bitterness and self-pity cringed for cover within him now from this dazzling realisation.

Chuck and Forsyth stood rooted in amazement. Forsyth was still weeping while Chuck wiped his own eyes, just in case. Straight below the thirty-foot wall lay a Roman hippodrome and the old city of David, to the right. Stroker looked down at small square buildings with people dotted on their flat rooftops, cooking and sitting on carpets. 'Shaloms' could be heard as neighbours acknowledged one another. Above these homes, on a steeper mound, another residential area was visible; with what, Chuck supposed, must be Roman villas and porticoes.

Further south were various steep paved streets, packed with people and the odd camel, and also featuring many archways. Most of the streets appeared to run towards a large souk further along. In the distance to Chuck's right, he thought he could make out a Roman forum and a large palace complex. The breeze brought up smells of cinnamon, bread and lentils from hundreds of ovens and stoves upon the rooftops below, where women prepared the evening meals. These little houses and courtyards, some with *mikvah* baths in them, also rang out the odd psalm.

"Is this the time of Jesus?" asked Stroker now. "It is, isn't it?" He wanted it to be. He dearly sought purification now. Perhaps that was half the battle?

Dai looked at him with benign tolerance, and softly replied, "You have said well, Irvine, but everyone, look to your right now," he urged.

They all turned to their right and looked along the wall.

"Behold, the holy temple of the Lord," Dai said. "Further south is the road to the Jordan," he added, smiling gently at the idea of being a tour guide.

"It's beautiful," Chuck thought out loud. He was drawn to it, as they all were. It was a vast, magnificent complex lined with enormous pillars.

"Follow me along this wall until we come to the temple complex, then stop," Dai instructed them gently before walking off to lead the way.

Chuck couldn't take his eyes from the glorious structure, which grew in scale and grandeur as they approached.

"The year is 30 AD, gentlemen, and the feast of Tabernacles is approaching, which is why the streets are congested below us. This is also why so many pilgrims are encamped in the Kidron Valley to our right, and up on the Mound of Olives beyond," explained Dai.

Chuck usually hated heights, but he had faith that if he fell Dai would catch him, so he was conscious that his usual fear of falling was not engulfing him as it usually might. He then proceeded with a mysterious confidence along the wall.

"Oh, my God, forgive me my sins, please forgive me," Stroker muttered every few feet; whilst Forsyth knew that he would never again turn his back on God after this, if he lived through it.

"Are we here at the time Jesus comes to Jerusalem and is arrested by the priests?" Chuck asked Dai as they walked.

"The Pharisees, not priests," Dai corrected him. "That occurs a few months from now at the Feast of Passover," he explained. "He is here now with his disciples, seeking what some call debate and what others call confrontation."

"Oh, my God, are we going to see him? Oh, my God!" The tears continued to pour down Forsyth's face.

"Yes, he is in the temple now, gentlemen," Dai chuckled at them as the north breeze brought the pleasant smell of the sizzling evening sacrifices from the temple, then blew away towards the Judean wilderness beyond the olive hill.

"Are we in trouble? Please don't hurt me, I'm so sorry for my life," Stroker cried out in fear now, though he continued to proceed slowly and carefully.

"Fear not. I am with you, and I swear to you, you have nothing to fear now," Dai reassured them all again.

As they continued, Stroker dried his eyes a little and stared at Dai ahead of him. Whoever or whatever this good and mysterious being might be – he was dressed casually, almost raggedly, in jeans, boots and a hooded coat that could have been a ski-jacket. His clothes looked old and worn but there was a splendour about them, a sort of glow and cut which hinted at a cloth completely superior to that which they were all wearing. Stroker realised that Dai must be an angel, and instantly felt love and loyalty toward him. The sure knowledge that he would worship God after this caused him to break down again, and he attempted to pray and beg for mercy as he continued along. This caused Dai to grin to himself again.

"Never fear young Irvine, for you are not the only fool to have rejected God. Think how easy it was to begin using terms such as 'wicked' in place of 'good', and 'killer' in place of 'great,'" Dai told him. Stroker knew plenty of Scots who had embraced this new vocabulary. "Like I say, Irvine", smiled Dai as he continued along the wall, "You're one among many, but you have a chance now to change your situation; follow on then, in joy".

Chuck looked down into the city, a stream of sweat by now running down his spine, in the warmth of the still-hot evening sun. Suddenly, a waft of urine made the three of them jerk their necks in surprise.

"Just a large laundry, gents; they use urine here to clean the sheets," explained Dai without stopping.

The place was buzzing, not only because of the evening meals being prepared on the rooftops, but also because, as Dai explained, "There is a general excitement for the coming feast tomorrow. This is the finest city on earth, and this is one of several special occasions for the Israelites."

The visiting party were simultaneously awestruck, humbled, emotional, elated and apprehensive by this point, but Dai helped them to overcome their fears and to appreciate the experience. His gentle love now prevented them from embracing such human instincts as fear or hesitation.

"I have brought you here to kick-start your faith. Do not concern yourselves with thoughts about how we travelled here, for the answers are beyond your comprehension," he told them.

"You are simply here, reliving something that has passed in time, because it is necessary. So please watch and listen to this rare gift from the boss."

As they reached the temple's southern wall, Dai lifted them upwards with a gentle yet firm gush of energy and air, seemingly generated from a command of his wrist. Up and over the higher wall they went, and then slowly down and onto the smooth stone flooring beneath the royal porch. It was a large complex inside and they stood in a shadow between two of the great pillars which lined the Court of the Gentiles. There, several men, wearing worn robes and mantles with tassels hanging from them, were chatting. Others were tidying up some timber benches and wooden bird cages, and a small timber-framed goat pen lined with straw was being filled up with sheep and goats, which seemed to have escaped and roamed free.

Dai motioned the men to follow him beneath Solomon's porch, through a gateway and across the middle courtyard that was warm from the sun and to where a group of around two hundred men were gathered at the foot of some large stone steps with porticoes.

"The court of the woman," said Dai, but they saw that there were no women around. They went through the Nicanor gate and into another large courtyard, where several bearded men with black and mustard coloured robes, and white mantels with blue stripes stitched along them, stood at the top of some steps.

"Pharisees," said Dai as they approached the large and noisy crowd at the foot of the stairs.

Many spectators were observing this group of men from other nooks and crannies, Chuck noted with his policeman's vigilance. Some of them were soon shouting and waving their fists angrily. The Pharisees, in turn, were barking back at the men. One even appeared to be calling in the temple guards, who came running down some steps from the Western Wall; thirty of them armed with swords, holding shields and wearing leather tunics. Chuck couldn't believe what he was witnessing; it was utterly amazing, so real, yet quite surreal too; like a huge historic film set, except that he knew that everything he could see was real, and not staged. He even pinched himself.

"So, you dare to display such arrogance here in the house of the Lord?" Suddenly, Chuck could make out what one of the Pharisees was shouting down at the crowd.

Some men nearby laughed and Chuck realised that these people couldn't see him. Nor, strangely enough, did any of them walk or come anywhere near him as the three of them loitered around Dai, listening to the crowd who were shouting in an unknown language that, nevertheless, was as clear and understandable to them as English.

"Who does he think he is? He's nothing more than a country bumpkin!" came one cry.

"A Galilean teacher, apparently?" offered an old man.

"But he heals everyone; how can that not be good?" another voice roared as the guards waded through what was slowly developing into a mob.

"Kill him! He has the devil in him!" came another cry.

"Enosh, Enosh, come quickly, there is a blasphemer who heals on the Sabbath and who claims he has a right to do so because his father told him to," a youth ran out of the crowd to inform a friend who was newly arrived from outside.

"Some nutter from Nazareth supposedly?" another voice was followed by laughter.

"Is he the one they say heals lepers?" roared one fat bearded man, and several other men around him gesticulated, nodded, and retorted that they had witnessed him doing so.

"Is he a Pharisee?" asked someone else.

"Who is his father, that he claims has given him the authority to heal on the Sabbath?" snarled another, darker, Pharisee.

"Is his father a Roman?" asked someone near Chuck.

"Yes teacher, do tell us who your father is?" an old Pharisee chortled down at the crowd.

Dai spoke gently to his group now, "See how they try to take his life by tricking him."

"Which is worse?" A bald, bearded man who was one of the Galilean's followers shouted back up at the Pharisees. "To heal on the Sabbath as the teacher does, or to conspire to convict and murder on the Sabbath, as you do, you hypocrites?"

"You there, you shut your mouth!" screamed a Pharisee before calling for the guard again.

The guards had ceased their advance however, as whatever it was they were targeting somehow seemed beyond them. Now they stood watching the spectacle in a state of amazement similar to Chuck, Forsyth and Stroker.

"How do you presume the authority to preach to us?" another relentless Pharisee shouted down the stairs, bitterly at the crowd.

"No, Rabbi, do not take their bait!" Chuck heard someone say.

"Let's get him out of here!" shouted another.

Chuck half expected to see an arrest, or the guards starting to attack the inner crowd where Jesus was obviously being surrounded by his friends.

"They won't arrest him now, for he does not wish to be arrested today," said Dai, sensing their joint concern.

"Stone him!" shouted someone in the crowd.

From among the gathered crowd, one set of eyes looked upon them, a man's knowing eyes that darted over at the three of them. He had shoulder-length brown hair and compassionate eyes and spoke loudly and confidently while his companions quickly ushered him away.

"You unbelieving and perverse generation, I tell you; do you not think that if a man owns one hundred sheep, and one of them wanders away, he will not leave the other 99 on the hills while he goes to look for his lost sheep?" The man continued to stare at the three of them as he spoke despite being moved along by his group. All three impulsively fell to their knees, lowered their heads and wept as he passed them. Dai, meanwhile, bowed to him and then nodded with love and affection.

"For I tell you, you will not see me again until you accept that blessed is he who comes in the name of the Lord," he continued. "If you believe, you will receive anything you ask for in prayer."

They all prayed there and then, for forgiveness and guidance. More precisely, Stroker begged for it. Moments later they were all back up upon the wall walking west along it. "Beyond your view is the city of Joppa and the sea," Dai pointed out as he once again led the way.

Far from being stunned at this sudden transfer, by what appeared to be another powerful fusion of energy and air, on to the wall again, they were all alert and obedient.

"Holy, holy, holy is the Lord most holy," he sang cheerily now as he skipped along like a professional ballet dancer, apparently defying the laws of gravity.

"You lot don't try this," he chuckled back at them, but they were not as joyful. They were instead emotionally buzzing, yet they walked in complete silence, only sniffs and one or two sighs to be heard from them.

They then found themselves down in the city, on a rooftop where a family sat together on old sheets. The pool of Siloam was near, and despite the time, the sound of splashing could just be made out from where they stood. There were clay amphorae of oil, water and wine near them, and a young girl was mixing some of the wine with what appeared to be honey in a clay bowl. She handed the bowl to an old woman, who was sitting in a corner, sewing some cloth together.

Dai told them to observe this family, because they were a family with real faith. Two other women were busy preparing food around a fire while three children sat listening to an elderly man singing the praises of the Lord.

"See your king comes to you, gentle and riding upon a donkey," he read to them the words of old.

The women also listened, one cutting vegetables for her stew and the other making flatbreads. Two other men sat, sipping wine and discussing the drama at the temple that day.

"He is the Lamb of God, brother, I saw him heal a cripple earlier, and saw the goodness on his face. I'm sure he is," one said to the other excitedly.

"You sound like that man John who was baptising everyone down at the Jordan River," smiled the other man.

"I tell you, the fact that John called him this should convince you, brother," the first man insisted.

The elder bearded brother, nodded his head at that. "He certainly is not satanic or anything like what the Pharisees are claiming, I'll grant you that, brother. Although he does tend to speak in riddles, and this frustrates simple men."

"Nonsense, he speaks with the intelligence of an academic, unlike the other country bumpkins from Galilee. No, there is more to him, and I am inclined to believe that he might well be the Messiah. Praise be to the living God."

"I heard he was from Nazareth? That may prove to be another obstruction for any would-be Messiah," the older, darker of the two surmised.

Just then, on a neighbouring rooftop, a voice called over:

"You shouldn't be here!" it barked; but only Dai, Chuck and his two contemporaries heard it. They all turned to look, Dai with grave eyes.

They saw a man who stood under 6 ft. but who was, bizarrely, wearing modern black motorbike leathers and boots. His head was hairless and his eyes were the colour of emeralds.

"Move on!" Dai bellowed back at him.

"It is you who should not be here, and nor should your pet monkeys," the man declared as he pointed a long-nailed finger at them.

"If I have to tell you again, you'll regret it."

"I doubt that," he smirked contemptuously, without shifting the stare of his bright green eyes from the three men.

Chuck was on edge; butterflies were loose again in his gut and he instinctively reached for the ball thrower and pressed the button. When Stroker and Forsyth saw it they both took a step backwards. Forsyth was about to ask him what it was, but the man spoke again whilst eyeballing Chuck.

"I see they have forged a toy for you, monkey?" he smirked. Dai said nothing, but continued to return his glare.

When he received no response, the man turned and looked down into the street below where passers-by were debating and shouting about the disturbance at the temple. He laughed at them, and they looked up but did not see him. "I see you brought your pets here to observe the son being ejected from the father's house, as I often do," he chortled.

Stroker gave Dai a sharp look; one of extreme concern, then looked around for a means of escape. To hang and fall from the side of the house was out of the question; it was at least an 18 ft. drop onto the stone street below, which was full of pilgrims heading for supper. Just then, the woman who had been making the bread lit a lantern and Forsyth heard hooves clip-clopping in the street and an animal's bellow, probably a donkey's.

"It's like a good movie, how about that for an analogy?" the leather-clad man looked at Chuck again. Forsyth thought he resembled a character from one of the Mad Max films.

"Who is he?" Chuck whispered to Dai.

"Like a real classic that you will always return to watch on a rainy day…" The thing pointed at Chuck now,

" *'Godfather Part II'*," he added after a short pause, staring him in the eye. Chuck glanced at Dai as the theme tune to the film began to ring out, as though broadcast from a hidden speaker.

"Or *'Papillion'*, even." Now the man pointed at Forsyth, who looked down while the sound of waves battering against rocks echoed everywhere.

"Or *'Terms of Endearment'*…" He then pointed at Stroker before turning to Dai and bursting into barnstorming laughter at this. "Who the fuck is into *'Terms of Endearment'*? Oh wait, is it because you crave women to give you their sympathy?" he asked Stroker mockingly.

"Let us end this little dance now," Dai said before leaping from one roof to the other. In response, the being screamed like a distressed fox, turned, ran and jumped down onto the street below. Dai walked over to the edge and saw him, now in a Roman prefect's uniform, melting into a group of Roman soldiers who were jogging up towards the hippodrome.

"Hurry up lads, we have much work to do," he shouted at them in the gutter Latin of the army.

"What on earth was he?" asked Chuck.

"A fallen one," replied Dai.

"As in a fallen angel?" Stroker looked like he was about to vomit. "Oh, that's just great dude, we are going to get done over by that nasty looking bastard, what the fu…"

"Don't swear in my presence, Irvine, please." Dai raised a finger to stop him mid-profanity, then smiled at him again. "Irvine, I assure you that he can't bother you, because you're working for the boss now, and if you're lucky, he might forgive you your sins."

"Are you always going to be around to protect us, like?" Stroker snapped now.

"Shut it, Stroker," growled Chuck, weapon still out, but Dai waved at him to let it go.

"But where has he gone?" asked Forsyth.

"To attend to his own talking monkeys, as he likes to put it," smiled Dai. "The Pharisees."

"Can we get one of them?" Forsyth impulsively gestured to Chuck's weapon.

Dai turned and smiled at him. "Perhaps, if you ever find the heart to offer a dog in need of rescue a home, Christopher," he replied humorously. "Come, take hands again and we shall go from here back to the doorway," he added.

They then all held hands again and he lead them through a portal and back into Stroker's living room again. The three men looked at each other before Stroker fell to his knees, while Forsyth became emotional and sunk into the ugly orange sofa as if he had just climbed a mountain.

"Chuck will lead you both now, we have placed our faith in him, and he has placed his in you," said Dai as he gently raised Stroker up without touching him.

"Now, Irvine," he opened his spectacularly reflective eyes at him, and considered the fragile little person for a second or two. "You were fortunate to be given this great opportunity, so do not sin again, and do not let Chuck down," he told him firmly.

"But Sir, please, can I just ask you what the hell is…" Stroker had so much to ask but found himself tongue-tied.

"Chuck can fill you in; just don't waste this very, very special opportunity to do good with your life," said Dai, cutting him off. Then he nodded at Chuck, raised a hand at them all and said softly, "Talk a while, and try to understand the nature of the game in which you now find yourselves."

"Thanks for that," Chuck said, glad to have Forsyth fully briefed, as it were.

"You need him, and he is not a bad man, though his repertoire of football banter is quite excruciating. Irvine on the other hand, was almost lost." Dai turned to look at Stroker, who looked down before falling back upon his knees.

Chuck nodded in understanding as Dai gave him an inconspicuous twinkle of his eyes while walking out of the door. A moment later they heard the front door close, followed by a few more moments which passed in silence before Stroker spoke, "I will need you to stop at a book shop so I can pick up a Bible," he said slowly to Chuck, to the latter's surprise.

"Yeah, me too, guv," added Forsyth.

"It will be easier to find bloody drugs than to find a Bible these days," sighed Chuck.

"But not snakes like that freaky fallen angel guy, what if he can travel here too," Stroker looked scared now.

"Don't worry," put in Forsyth. "Snakes no longer hiss these days, they call you 'mate' instead."

"Right, I'll put a quick brew on, then. Stroker, don't move." Chuck ordered before heading through to the kitchen.

Stroker went straight to a corner, fell on his knees, and began silently praying. Forsyth watched him for a while, wanting to join him but not quite knowing how to. Instead, he leaned back and decided to replay the whole experience in his mind.

"I think we might need some crucifixes too; just in case that big fucker in the biker gear does turn up again." he said to himself.

Thirteen
"The colour of the cat doesn't matter so long as it catches the rat"
Deng Xiaoping

The men spent an hour or so discussing the experience. Chuck struggled to trust or like Stroker. They had gone so far beyond even the most benign pleasantries, that being in some form of covenant with the man felt impractical. Yet at the same time, Chuck could see that Stroker was somehow changed, and he felt a tolerance emerging towards him. He may give him a fairer crack of the whip now, as long as the conceited little prick helped him to pinch this high-end paedophile ring. If God decided to partially forgive him for the service, well, that was another matter and no skin off Chuck's back.

In contrast to his boss, Forsyth still eyed Stroker like an abused dog which was undergoing training and social therapy, and which in the meanwhile should be kept muzzled and firmly on the lead. That aside, they had all experienced a very beautiful thing and were all still buzzing. Smiles between them, open ears, and a new shared desire from all sides for Stroker to improve his pathetic life, were already emerging. This, of course, was a considerable change to the previously overwhelming instinct shared by both Chuck and Forsyth to simply kick Stroker's arse every time they saw him. Time would tell, but if he was changed at heart, and could help, then maybe.

They went over it all again, giving their opinions in what at times seemed like a university tutorial on theology. Chuck found himself pretending to have to phone Kim, just so he could nip outside and sit in the car for a few minutes, to find some solitude and release the built up emotional appreciation of the incident he had experienced. His realisation of things, of the facts, were still developing, but at the core of it all was a new-found faith. Today he had experienced excitement, then sadness, before the terror of the threat upon the rooftop. He felt stupid now for not realising the truth before, but he put that down to having ignored his instinct, as opposed to completely rejecting it. All these sentiments had been activated today, so Chuck allowed himself a wee cry.

On top of all that, there was the constant urgency of the investigation and serious concern caused by Yvonne's death. That feeling of a tense weight and pressure on his shoulders had not deserted him since he had discovered God. Sure, he had masked his feelings much more effectively than the other two back in Jerusalem, but then again perhaps that was why he had been asked to lead this frantic undertaking?

He initially ignored the inevitable tears by Googling images of the old temple as he sat in the car. He noted a strong sense building within him, which urged him to believe that Stroker would not betray them now. He then fished out Stroker's bloody jacket and decided to return it to him as a goodwill gesture. Then, he thought about the face of the man who had stared at them today within the ancient temple. The only face within the temple who had seen them, perhaps. It had been as though he had been talking to them directly, as opposed to the crowd around him or the Pharisees on the steps above him.

That man had a plain-looking Jewish or Turkish face with dark brown curly hair and a short, unkempt dark beard. Chuck had not considered him handsome, not like Dai. Indeed, he was quite simple by comparison, and yet there was a pureness and beauty in knowing who he was without any of them having to ask. Chuck prayed a while and asked God for nothing, only telling him that his appreciation for the things he had be noted. He felt that he was praying to the father himself, and it seemed natural. Afterwards, he prayed to the Son and offered his intention to worship him too. He did not know how to pray properly; but thinking back, he could remember the Jesus of Nazareth TV film with Robert Powell as Christ, and in particular the scene on the mound when Jesus tells everyone how to read the Lord's Prayer. Chuck knew the Lord's Prayer and went with that, before allowing himself to shed more tears as he sat there in the car. He then went back up to the flat, feeling a little better for having released some of his pent-up emotions. He immediately handed Stroker his coat.

"Put that on the BBQ, Irvine."

Stroker had been praying, as had Forsyth, but he looked up, smiled and quickly did as he was told, soaking the thing in lighter fuel, then incinerating it. Then, after more chat about what had recently happened, Chuck briefed them both on his previous contact with Dai and his instructions.

"Something in your bloodline maybe, guv?" Forsyth suggested having heard all about Chuck's family history and the often-retold events at the Somme. "Why else would they have singled you out?" he reasoned.

"And they gave you the ball catcher, didn't they?" Stroker pointed out.

"Keep your eyes off that, Stroker; it gives cancer to anyone other than me, apparently," Chuck lied.

"What next?" Stroker inquired with a schoolboy inquisitiveness.

Chuck begun considering this himself. The next move was key to any success they might achieve, and he knew they couldn't take their eyes off Trevelen as Dai had insisted. It would have been handy if they had been able to put a tail on this mate of Leo Frazer's, the so called Executive Director of Midlothian Regional Council – Garry Welsh, but there simply wasn't the manpower. It was never going to happen, with eyes focused upon Trevelen at all hours, which required a minimum of two officers. Bugger it then. Welsh would be the last resort, but they could look into whether he owned a woodland cottage, out in the sticks near Straiton.

The prize was Trevelen, but how? Chuck knew that he had to make progress now, or by tomorrow at the latest. Then, Stroker suggested that they could wiretap Trevelen's conversations with his boss at the restaurant he worked in. He explained that Trevelen would eat once or twice a week at the restaurant, usually at the same table:

"He always sits at Table two next to the bar with my boss, and they talk and eat for an hour or so. He often pops into the kitchen to say hello too as he is leaving," he told them.

"Does he book?" asked Chuck.

"No, but he regularly comes in to eat and he supplies wine to us, so he we can expect him at least twice a week."

"Right, then tomorrow can you set up the device under the table if we show you how?"

"With pleasure." Stroker gave an eager nod, enjoying his new role.

Maybe this would be the breakthrough Chuck was searching for. "OK, look," Chuck checked his watch – 4:30 pm. "You stay here and come to terms with everything, Irvine, and we'll go do some errands and pick up a wire. We'll come around in the morning and plot the operation," he said, feeling sure that he could now trust Stroker not to betray them, and that he would not dare tell Dudley about events. Ten minutes later, Stroker, who had managed to tap one of his downstairs neighbours for a loan of a King James Bible, locked his room door and was flat out on his bed, reading it thereafter.

Chuck and Forsyth drove in silence until they reached the car park at Duddingston Loch opposite Trevelen's house. His car was not in the driveway, so they sat there and waited, watching the golden sun retreating over the trout-filled loch, causing the ripples to shimmer yellow and blue.

"Do you think those fuckers in Fife were Nephilim, guv?"

Chuck sighed, "Probably, but I'll need to see what Dai has to say about all that stuff."

"I say we break in," Forsyth was looking over at Trevelen's house as he spoke.

"Too risky Chris, he'll have alarms and cameras." Chuck had already considered it.

"Do you think we will have to kill one of those fuckers, then?" Forsyth asked.

It was a fair question considering they had done so earlier that day. "Yes, I do," replied Chuck.

"Then I need a weapon, guv."

"I'll get you something as soon as I talk to Sharon," Chuck started to say just as Joe drove his car onto the gravel space beside them.

"Got these number plates and couple of decent photos from Dewar, guv," Joe told them when he and Gav got into the back seat of the Volvo. "I texted the file over to the DI already."

"Sound, lads. Let's just wait on her call, then, before we plan anything," urged Chuck.

When Adams rang a few minutes later, she told him that there was nothing more on the golf course staff, but that she had 18 car registrations and owners' addresses from the Dewar intel. "He got some good photos of people coming and leaving the club, one of whom I recognised as my own bloody dentist!" She gave a half-hearted laugh at that.

"Anyone else we know?"

"One guy has a record for bank fraud, a Ronnie Shaw from Barnton," she said despondently. "Was extradited from Australia after stealing half a million from the RBS, did a deal and got six years, which he served. Been out four and a half years now and runs several black cabs."

"No problem getting a licence for them, then? Must be one of the good ol' boys," Chuck mused derisively.

"For sure. Remember your old gaffer at the Cab Office, the now-retired Inspector Herriot, of 122 Colinton Road?" Adams knew Chuck's history with Herriot; who in the Druggies didn't?

"Well, well, well," Chuck smiled now. "Keep a note of that Shaw guy, and keep a note of Gary Welsh, the head of the council. Consider them both to be hotter than hell Sharon. I'll have a think about that old bastard Herriot, and get back to you."

"OK, and of course we're still working on the photos to see who the passengers are. I'm also checking up on some of the other vehicle owners," she advised.

"Thanks a lot. Can you really help me out and check into whether any of them own, or have any connection to any properties – particularly cottages – south of the city bypass?" he asked delicately, as a child might ask for money to go to the ice cream van.

"You're kicking the arse out of it now, sunshine," she half joked. "That will be a nightmare and I'm busy as hell here while you lot are away. I'll try and find time tomorrow when I'm not stalling our guvnor or a bloody murder squad who want to talk to you," she forced a laugh without humour, but made her point regardless.

"As always, I appreciate your support," he teased her.

"Who's paying your wee pal Mr Dewar?" she changed the subject.

"I'll sort him out. Can you text me the names you have, and I'll see if any of them stand out to me?" he asked. "I also need a wiretap with up to six hours recording space for under a table. Can you get me one of the little box ones from downstairs and I'll meet you in Stockbridge somewhere tomorrow morning?"

It was after 6 pm when Chuck dropped Forsyth off, politely declining the pleading invite to come in for a drink. "Mind, Chris," Chuck looked up at him as he leaned back into the car at the kerbstone, "best you don't try and convince the Mrs yet, bud, but if you feel the need to later, I'll come up and support you," he promised.

"What, about the referendum?" he gawked.

"No the bloody time travel and angel stuff" Chuck shook his head.

Forsyth nodded and slowly headed upstairs, sucking in a deep breath and forcing a mask of normality back across his face for the benefit of his partner, with whom he so wanted to share his new-found faith. Chuck drove home. The evening air was still warm; it smothered him, as the Volvo felt like an oven. He too wanted to share things with Kim, but he knew he couldn't yet. He also knew that he and his team were going head-to-head with something far more dangerous than he had ever dared to believe existed.

As he passed Giuliano's restaurant at Leith shore, he could smell the garlic on the warm breeze. He saw a few couples in their summer evening gear heading there, or to the Turkish place next door; which he and Kim kept meaning to try. He envied them somewhat. A large glass of chilled rosé and a nice supper should be what he was enjoying in these temperatures. The last time he had eaten out had been with Forsyth, for heaven's sake. It was a wonder Kim hadn't had an affair, unless perhaps she had?

Then, as he passed the large bronze statue of Robert Burns that looked up Constitution Street at the junction with Baltic and Bernard, he saw two young females women brawling on the pavement whilst a group of onlookers stood by and watched. The city itself was presently a powder keg of raw emotions, perhaps partly due to resentment towards mass immigration, and Islamophobia? Long-term resentment towards the policies established by Blair, such as wars based upon lies, and the massive benefit culture which had fuelled class division, made people lazy, and, Chuck believed, had increased Scottish youth delinquency. Hell, the country even had its own term for these hoodie-wearing thugs – 'Neds'.

He pondered how a social media culture had developed and caused the benefit-dependent masses to crave luxurious lifestyles? Chuck connected this with grumbling, drinking and an increase in social drug-taking, including new highs such as cocaine and crack. The middle classes were also increasingly resentful and unhappy, mainly because they felt that they were the donkeys slaving away and paying their taxes to fund the underclasses. Consequently, Chuck had seen with his own eyes that violence was increasing within the city lately, particularly in the summer months when more people were drunk in the streets. In winter, fraud and theft increased as the low-life villains chased a better Christmas than they deserved, and after the New Year celebrations, murders rose as the whole country came down from the festive jollies.

A large percentage of the population had been easily convinced that these bubbling concerns were all down to the union. People believe what they wish to believe, Chuck knew well enough, but if anyone thinks that all this resentment and unhappiness will somehow dissolve after the referendum, they don't deserve a bloody vote, he thought. A promised utopia within an independent state which would somehow morph everyone's lives back to the good old days, was exactly what that prick Anderson-Forbes was selling to the plebs. A misplaced hope that was contagious, however, he knew. Even his neighbours were leaning towards Forbes and this alarmed him, when he took the time to dwell on it. He sighed now at the sight of the brawl and drove on, noting with relief a 'Better Together' billboard with a young couple and two kids upon it, promoting the 'NO THANKS, we love families' position.

When he parked outside his home fifteen minutes later, he noticed a scruffy gent, perhaps a beggar, watching him reverse park. Two other men were also gawking at him from across the road, but this was hardly unusual on his street, which ran down to the busy beach. So, he did not give them any further thought. As he was about to open his door, his phone rang. It was Sharon Adams.

"Benny Latif has been done for murdering his common-law wife, and is in St Leonards with the CID, being interviewed. I'm now going up with Gary Duffy to try and push our beaks into things and see if we can get Latif to help us with Les Cairns," she declared quite cheerily.

Chuck recalled who she was talking about. Babar 'Benny' Latif part-owned an Indian Restaurant in Penicuik called 'The Jehangir' with a couple of his brothers who were legit businessmen. Benny, on the other hand, was a vicious murdering bastard who had received a 'Not Guilty' verdict on a murder rap years previously at the High Court. Everyone knew that Benny had killed a Granton drug dealer and night club extortioner by walking into his flat one afternoon and shooting him dead, but the Crown had struggled with the case. Three witnesses had placed him in the street, and one in the flat stairwell after the shooting, but nobody saw him pull the trigger.

Latif was not seen on the victim's landing, and those who had seen him downstairs had not seen a gun. He had also been spotted walking away as though he was out for a stroll and without any sign of urgency. No search of his home or cars could conjure up residue from a gun, never mind the gun itself. And, worst of all from the prosecution's perspective, he had an alibi, which was that he had gone to visit a friend who lived on the first floor. The friend had no criminal record, worked in the care industry, and was PVG registered. A pillar of community honesty, and so on, his defence had spun the jury. After the trial, said friend bought a new flat in upmarket Morningside and treated herself to a new car. No one ever considered how a £14,500 a year carer living in a council flat alone with her 8-year-old son had managed that. If she had been asked where her mortgage deposit had come from, she would have said that she had been on the game and had won in the casinos.

Since beating the rap, 'Benny' boy had been enforcing for Les Cairns, unofficially managing a couple of strip joints for him, as well as running the security. He was additionally wanted by Dutch police in relation to an ongoing enquiry into the armed robbery of a jeweller's in Rotterdam however, so there was obviously going to be a few other departments interested, now that he was in custody. Chuck remembered a fair bit of detail about the man and his nefarious history.

"When he got his two-stretch for ecstasy back in '97 he had sung like a canary apparently, so he might agree to give us Cairns?" he suggested.

"That's what I'm thinking. It's whether or not the CID will get in our way," Adams sounded slightly anxious at the prospect.

"What's the background to this turn of events?"

"Not sure; apparently, he went for his partner at a BBQ somewhere and now she's a goner. Other guests rang the police and they turned up in full force like SAS warriors, all armed and ready, but he complied and they took him to St Leonards."

Chuck smirked at the image of disappointment on the Rambo brigade's faces as this well-known thug complied fully and meekly gave himself up. "Call his lawyers, let them know we are open to deals and that he should request to see you and I, just in case CID are batting for the other side. I'll meet you there in twenty minutes."

He was tired and felt his bones ache as he was taken downstairs at St Leonards by a burly wannabe Navy Seal – a turnkey with a fat neck and a US Marine Corps sergeant's shaved flat-top haircut. Adams smirked at Chuck as they and DC Duffy all walked along behind this warrior jailer. He had even called her 'Ma'am' when she arrived, which had tickled her.

The CID had offices upstairs and the turnkey showed them into a room that faced out onto Arthur's Seat. There were three desks, and three shirts and ties sitting at computers behind each.

"Well, well, what are the Druggies wanting to interview our man about then?" the leading detective, a DI Whyte, asked them as they entered.

He was a fat bald man in his late fifties and unknown to any of them. "Apart from the fact that he is well-known to us, runs coke through at least two clubs and has done time for supply, nothing of interest to you," Adams was curt with him.

"Nought to do with your interest in his boss, Les Cairns, then?" Whyte asked cockily.

This told Chuck all he needed to know about this guy, which was that if he knew and mentioned the Cairns connection, he was shady and therefore to be brushed off. This drained the room of what little air there was and made any professional courtesy unlikely. "Now, you know why we're here, shall we just get on with it?" Chuck urged.

"Don't you want to know anything about our case against him?" fat arse asked.

"Only where you're at with it," Adams prompted.

Fat Arse shuffled his backside a little. He was an accomplished liar but the other CID men, writing up their paperwork, suggested that Latif had already been charged. "He is charged with murder," he eventually smiled. "Paki bastard has been seeing the victim for years; a white lassie named Barbara Riggs. They were over at her sister's for a barbeque tonight, and he didn't like some snarky comments she made about him being a shitty father, so he punched the shit out of her right there and then. She fell into a coma, then died in hospital two hours later."

"Easy on the racism there, Buck," smiled Adams.

"He has kids with her?" asked Chuck.

"Three girls: 5, 8 and 10."

"You know, he also has a Pakistani wife with a daughter who lives at Lochend?" Adams asked him.

"Yes, but he lives… lived… with Riggs at a swanky villa in Colinton," responded fat arse with obvious contempt.

"And have you notified Interpol?" Chuck wanted to know.

"Not yet, but I will do that before I send the report over to the Fiscal."

"OK chaps, let's go and see if Mr Latif can tell us anything about cocaine in our nightclubs, eh?" smiled Adams.

"Two DIs on a fishing expedition, that's rare," smirked Fat Arse.

"Well, we Druggies don't have your vast resources, mate," Adams said as she exited behind Chuck and Duffy. "We'll find our own way back downstairs, thanks."

So, Chuck and Adams knew that the arresting CID were at the report stage of their case and were unlikely to object to the Druggies interviewing Latif. "He's bang to rights, another scumbag off the streets and that's all that fat radge is interested in," offered Duffy, who should know nothing about Chuck's investigation. Adams and Chuck shared a quick glance which suggested the contrary. The little bit of banter about Cairns told Chuck that either Fat Arse had been on the dark force, or was just another puppet of theirs, otherwise why would he ask about Cairns, and how did he know anything about their interest in him?

"What kind of deal can you offer me?" asked Benny Latif, a 6 ft. body builder-type with a goatee beard and short dark hair, as he shrugged his shoulders at them.

"Who says we are offering you anything, Benny?" asked Adams.

"My solicitor said it was in my interest to talk to you. Why else are you here? Do you think I'm grassing on anyone just because I'm looking at a life sentence?"

"How about, what do you have to offer?" Adams was playing hardball and it showed early on.

"Plenty," Latif eyeballed her.

"Did you offer anything to the arresting officers or the CID?" Chuck asked.

"Not yet, waiting on my brief arriving."

"Well, make us the offer then. We have the power to haul in the Fiscal and the Chief Constable, Benny," Chuck offered a fake but warm smile.

"Can you make the charge go away?" He made his play.

"That's a tough ask, lad," Chuck shrugged his shoulders. "You have a garden full of witnesses apparently."

"Yeah, her parents and a few more besides," Benny nodded with regret; he was clearly a liability to the public if he were to obtain his liberty.

"Well then, the Fiscal is going to shy away from letting anyone walk from a bang to rights murder case, when there are plenty of witnesses to start raising concerns. I would suggest a plea deal though, Benny," Chuck shook his head at him.

"How long?"

"Well, let's face facts. You're potentially looking at 20 to 25 years once a judge sees your previous records and your background is revealed. The fact that it was the mother of your children means you'll be tagged as a beast, both once you're inside and in judicial thinking, so you can expect a heavy hit from a judge. If they did anything else, there would be an outcry," Adams added as Duffy nodded at her.

"And if it's a female judge, well then, it's good night altogether for you," Chuck pointed out.

"Where are your kids now?" Adams asked.

"Haven't got a clue, probably at my sister's." He paused, and the sides of his mouth turned downwards. "She was there – in the garden. With her husband, who... er... I also punched."

"But you're not charged with that?" Duffy asked him, and Benny shook his head to confirm that he was not.

"Well, I'll tell you what. If you can help us nail Les Cairns, maybe a guilty plea could get a recommendation of 6 years, and that way you'd serve 3 and a bit," Chuck offered gamely.

"And most of that time would be served in an open clink based on the Fiscal deal," Adams added, playing along without the foggiest idea as to what Latif had to offer or whether any Fiscal would even be remotely interested in any deals.

There was an eerie silence for a moment while the nightmare reality of his situation sank in for Latif. Until now, he had not contemplated any of this. The truth was that he simply couldn't handle drink or drugs and was, like all thugs, a bully who imagined something that had not occurred

261

between his partner and his brother-in-law. He lacked any self-awareness, and now he only had a dim memory of what he had done.

"I can give you Les Cairns on conspiracy to murder, and some useful info on his drugs business," he finally looked up and told them. "It's all in various voice and video recordings on a mobile phone I happen to have stashed."

"Will it convict him?" Adams asked, knowing that Benny knew what was required by law, which was why he had curated this particular collection.

"It will see him charged, but as you and I both know, there's no way of telling whether he would be convicted in court."

"Need to see it?" Chuck pressed.

"No." Benny shook his head at them. "This is how I need it to happen. You get the offer from the Fiscal to my brief before I appear at court in the morning, and I'll send you to the phone then plead guilty tomorrow," he said firmly.

"OK, Benny," sighed Adams. "Don't talk to another soul and we'll speak to you again in a while."

Latif nodded.

The three Druggies reconvened in a staff room down the corridor while the wannabe Navy Seal took Benny back to his cell.

"Pop off and fetch us all a brew please, Gary," Adams told Duffy.

"Well?" she grinned at Chuck once he had closed the door behind him.

"I could do with cracking on with Cairns over the next day or two, so I can produce a decisive result on schedule, and the best way to do this would be to lie to Latif about any deal." Chuck met her gaze with hope in his eyes.

"Well I'm not convinced that the Fiscal would offer him anything anyway, considering he is bang to rights. And, if we tell the Fiscal that Latif can finger Cairns, it might alert whomever murdered Lionel Frazer?" said Adams, partly thinking aloud.

"If the phone has enough on it, we can bust Cairns on that basis and then tell Latif to go chase himself." Chuck urged her to concur.

"What about his brief?" she naturally queried.

"We can tell Latif that we spoke to the Fiscal and that the deal will be set in stone at court tomorrow morning. We can also tell Latif's lawyer this if he is getting an agent visit here in custody today that is, otherwise Latif will just have to take our word on the deal and give us the lowdown on this phone of his," agreed Chuck.

"Right, tell Gary the truth but leave out my mission, and I'll go and see if Latif's brief is getting a visit or not," he added before quickly heading along the squeaky-floored corridor in search of the custody sergeant.

Ten minutes later, he learned that no lawyer's visit would be taking place until he is transferred to court in the morning. The three Druggies were soon necking cups of tea in the interview room then, while the wannabe fetched Latif back from his cell. The place stank of disinfectant and every now and then, despite sitting quietly with their drinks, they would catch each other's gaze and smile at the echoed expletives shouted from the holding cells next door.

Chuck wondered about the murder squad being assembled to investigate Yvonne's murder, because her body would be undergoing the pathologic process and a squad would be all over her stairwell by now. Then there was this pending interview with the separate squad who were running the Leo Frazer murder investigation. He supped his coffee and rubbed the back of his neck.

When Latif returned, Chuck assessed that he was still within that smoky haze period between being charged and sitting down with his lawyer at court, when dreams about unrealistic deals are swirling around and hope swamps the mind. Any optimism soon sunk however, when it was explained to him that the Fiscal had shown no interest in dropping the charges because he wasn't interested enough in Cairns to be offering any deals. But, Latif was then told that after plenty of to-ing and fro-ing, Adams had persuaded the Fiscal to agree to a plea bargain of 6 years with most it spent in an open nick up in Angus region.

"Will I need to plead guilty in the morning, then?"

"Yes, and you'll be up in Forfar within the month, mate," promised Chuck.

"And my lawyer, when does he confirm this to me?" He was not so dumb, this guy.

"At court in the morning, but we need the phone tonight."

"No chance, soon as the deal is done, you'll get your phone."

"No dice, Benny, the Fiscal wants to see it first thing and we need to see it before we even think about embarrassing ourselves in the Fiscal's office tomorrow, pal. So, phone right now, or no deal and we'll see you in twenty years." Chuck went all in, and slowly the three cops got up and moved toward the door. Chuck was about to call the turnkey.

"Alright, alright," Latif suddenly realised that he had little to play with and no leverage. "Fine, but if you fuck me over on this, I won't be a witness and will say the content of the phone is all drama rehearsals," he grimaced, and both Chuck and Adams smiled back at him. Duffy felt like he was being left out so remained poker-faced but curious.

The phone was stashed in a dog poo bag, inside a bag of compost in an allotment shed off Pirniefield place in Leith. Adams and Chuck climbed the 5 ft. gate at the west entrance and walked around a pathway lined with young saplings until they found the little hut with the mint-painted door, which had been described to them. Benny had been as good as his word and the lock opened to the combination number he gave them. Chuck and Adams sat on some upside-down ceramic pots, helped themselves to a couple of little glass bottles from a crate of Coca Cola, and watched the contents on the phone.

There were lots of pictures of little interest, with Cairns in a few beside a kids' football team. "Benny said something about there being a drugs connection with the kids in the photos?" Chuck said, thinking.

One image had Cairns with the head of Midlothian council, Gary Welsh, at a sports awards ceremony involving schoolboys. Another image was a photo of a boys' team wearing red and yellow striped strips with 'The Cunning Fox' across their chests.

"The Cunning Fox is a Leith boozer, and Cairns' sister owns it," said Chuck thoughtfully.

"More like she is the licensee, but Cairns owns it," scoffed Adams.

Chuck froze, then argued with himself mentally a moment before blurting out a guess. "Bet he is sponsoring a boys team and providing buses to take them overseas to tournaments on the continent," he turned to look at Adams, whose jaw had dropped slightly.

"And stashing dope on the bus or even on the kids somehow?" he added.

Adams nodded, "Why else did Benny say there were some drug-related images?"

However, as promised, they soon found three videos of sit-down conversations between Cairns and Latif. Latif said that he had filmed them with a secret camera inside a pen bought on eBay and then stored on this phone as 'a safety net' against both Cairns and the police.

The first video showed Cairns handing over cash in a McDonald's bag and ordering the murder of a 'Franny McGowan'. The next was similar but in it, Cairns talked more about the planning of a murder of a Vicky Hewitt for grassing, and instructed Latif to leave some pound coins in her mouth after she had been slain, "as a message to any other wee grassing cunt out there."

The video then showed Cairns handing over "£50,000" to Latif, or at least to his hands in the video. Chuck and Adams were thrilled by these two videos and Chuck now felt confident that he had Cairns. The third recording was of Cairns offering Latif a contract hit on an unnamed politician in the future, which would pay "1.2 million." Cairns then added, "You can start arranging a crew to do the job probably next year at some point. There will be a cancellation payment of thirty grand if it is aborted."

Latif replied that he would consider anything but would wait to hear who it was and what the situation was in due course.

"Vicky Hewitt was that bird found in the Firth of Forth, who was tied to the hash supplier Steve Fleming," Chuck remembered. Fleming had been supplying the Parkhead area with hash for a while and the Druggies were interested in him, but he had been relatively small-scale. When his fuck-buddy (and former shoplifting champion) Vicky Hewitt was hauled out of the sea underneath the Forth Rail Bridge, tied up with Fleming; Adams had focused on Flemings' little enterprise for a while before concluding that as they had thought, he had just been a small-scale supplier of hash only.

"Franny McGowan is not a name I know," Chuck shrugged.

Adams called into Fettes and did a person check on the name alone. They quickly learned that a Francis James McGowan of Bishopbriggs, who was known and had served time for serious assault and an armed robbery upon a pub in Burnley, had been found dead from stab wounds in a flat in the west end of Glasgow two years previously. He was regarded as a thug and as a gypsy traveller. It had to be the Franny McGowan mentioned.

"Let's lift Cairns, Sharon," Chuck instinctively sensed the end game approaching now.

Adams felt it too but wanted to wait. "OK, but let's do it at 9 am tomorrow, Chuck. That way I can sort out rooms for the interview and do a bit of digging on this football team stuff beforehand," she urged. "It's great news and Cairns might deliver for us, but we need to be on form and play it right," she argued reasonably well.

Chuck knew she was right and felt indescribably tired at that moment. "OK, I'll hang on to the phone tonight then?" he nodded as they parted.

As Chuck drove home with the phone in his pocket, he felt for the first time in this whole operation that real progress had been achieved. Cairns was pretty much bang to rights on two conspiracy to murder charges. That and anything else which might come from Latif's subtle hints at drugs being tied to the kids' football team might force Cairns to sing his heart out tomorrow. Then, he considered, what if Cairns pending arrest were to bring in the TIC and strings start getting pulled? We should all be armed and prepared for the shit to hit the fan then, he decided. He found himself hoping that Dai would appear before he got home, if only to go over everything from the fight in Fife until now. "Where are you?"

As he pulled into his street, he noted that his neighbour had a large blue-and-white 'YES' poster upon their front-facing lounge window. He shook his head and smiled in mock confusion, since he was not really confused as to why his Bristolian neighbours would support Scottish independence. He knew well enough that people followed the fashion and this was just another amusing example of it. He found a parking space and sat a moment in the hope that Dai would show up, but there was no sign.

After a while he opened the driver's door and got out. Instantaneously, the beggar who had been hanging around earlier approached him at a fast pace and then was right beside him, producing a machete. With a murderous look on his scruffy face, he swung it towards Chuck, who ducked then skipped backward out of danger for a moment. "What the…?" He then produced the ball thrower, pressed it and noted two men also walking fast towards him from across the street.

"Give me the phone!" demanded the beggar, but Chuck waved his weapon at him but remained back a foot or so, out of reach of the danger. As the two other men arrived, Chuck saw that they resembled the men in Fife by appearance but when they both suddenly produced what appeared to be short glowing swords and moved towards him, he broke and ran for the stairway next door to his house. The door was locked so he crashed it open with his shoulder as the two men pursued him. As soon as he was in the stairway, Chuck turned in the doorway and slashed out at the two Nephilim. The two creatures stepped back and then forward again, jabbing their swords at him as he prevented them from entering the doorway with desperate criss-cross slashes of his weapon. This diagonal cross movement was keeping them back as it was damn near impossible to get around or through the doorway, but he knew it could only last until his arm tired and slowed down, and then he would be able to do little more.

"ENOUGH!" roared a voice from the pavement. The combatants all stopped to look at the originator of this demand, who was a black-suited man with dark hair tied back in a ponytail. He was impressive, like a model but tough-looking at the same time. He too produced a sword that appeared to glow. "Stand aside, cretins!" he ordered the two Nephilim, and they lowered their heads and did as he commanded.

"That is a fine weapon they have given you; I may use it to kill your wife," the man then grinned over at Chuck.

"Come and take it then, you fucker," gasped Chuck who was also considering a sneaky slash at one of the Nephilim, while their heads and weapons were lowered and despite the gut-turning terror now pumping throughout his body.

The man then leaped from the pavement and onto the path with lightning speed, and stabbed Chuck through his left shoulder blade. He yelled in the most horrendous agony before automatically falling back into the stairwell and onto his hands and knees. The man took a step towards him before crashing into the wall and then back out onto the path. Chuck looked up to see Dai and three other angels, including the one who had been introduced to him as his guardian angel, setting about his attacker and the Nephilim.

The howls they made were like that of a fox in distress, and they echoed loudly down the quiet street. There was blood everywhere, sprayed upon cars and dripping from hedges, but it was already beginning to quickly evaporate as it had done before. The guardian angel approached him and leaned down until his amazingly smooth and beautiful face was next to Chuck's, and assured him, "He is dead. I will reverse this wound, so unbutton your shirt," which Chuck did in considerable pain. The wound was small but deep, and he could see that he was bleeding profusely. The angel touched the wound with something from a small miniature glass bottle. Within a second or two the wound had gone, and the pain had disappeared; only the blood on his clothes remained. "Job done. You may meet me again," the angel winked at him.

Then Dai shouted, "Are you OK?" Chuck turned to look, lost for words, before turning back to find that his guardian angel had disappeared. The other angel had also departed and any traces of the four dead enemies had vanished also.

Dai stared out at the spot where Baal had been slain and thought back to when he had first confronted this Lord of the Flies back in May 1941, with America still several months away from joining the war. Back then the course of the war had been very much in the balance. Had Britain fallen after the Dunkirk evacuation, or had Egypt been captured and held by Erwin Rommel, the game may have been over much sooner in Europe. First Yugoslavia had fallen to the Third Reich and then Greece followed. The Royal Navy had evacuated Commonwealth troops, British and Greek officials, including the King of Greece, from the mainland, to Crete. From there, many had been taken by Royal Navy-controlled sea routes across the Levant to Alexandria and then on to Cairo.

Dai vividly remembered that the garrison on Crete had included some very brave Greek infantry who had fought well on the Bulgarian Metaxas line the previous year, against the same German division who would play a part of the Crete invasion. There were also upwards of 25,000 British and Commonwealth troops from Australia, New Zealand, Palestine and Cyprus. Initially, the Luftwaffe had blitzed the island with long-range and dive bombers, sinking Royal Navy cruisers and destroyers. The few serviceable RAF aircraft in the area were outgunned, and those which survived the air attacks upon Cretan airfields were soon forced to withdraw from the island on 19th May, leaving a garrison to fight on against an air invasion without any air support. This had been the first time in military history that such odds had been played out.

Most of the sea supply line was also under considerable siege while the Germans began landing in gliders and parachuting from Junker 52s. Initially, the invaders had been given a bloody nose and a black eye by the defenders, particularly from the New Zealanders, who bayonet-charged the crash-landed enemy eight times across Maleme airfield, both on the strip itself and at the nearby beach.

At Canea, the British troops defending the main route into the port of Suda Bay were surprised and overcome by 1,800 gliders carrying German paratroopers. However, the New Zealanders then came to the rescue by defeating and capturing the majority of the German force. Even north of Canea, another German invasion force was smashed by British forces, to keep the Suda Bay supply line open. Suda Bay was where the British had their first maritime supply line to Egypt, and Heraklion, the largest city on the island, was where they had their second. The problem here, Dai recalled, was that with a lack of RAF support, it would only be a matter of time until the Germans bombed both ports and the convoys coming in at night from Egypt would cease. In fact, there was soon only a three-hour unloading period at Heraklion throughout the night before the Luftwaffe would appear on the horizon again. Sadly, of the 27,000 tons of supplies sent out by the Cairo station, only around 2700 tons arrived.

Dai knew at the time that Hitler would order more German troops, land armoured vehicles and jeeps, as opposed to just giving up on the plan, despite the casualties and captured parachutists he had suffered. It simply was not in the nature of the man to go elsewhere now that his mentors had convinced him of his greatness. Dai had been granted permission to remove the Warlock in possession of a senior British military officer in Egypt – Jumbo Barling. Instead of following the demands of Winston Churchill, who had warned Cairo that if Crete were to fall into Nazi hands, Cyprus and Egypt would be under air siege from the Luftwaffe, Jumbo had been all set to sabotage the island's defence.

In response to the need for armour, troops and aircraft, the Middle Eastern high command had sent a military band and some boot polish instead. Dai appeared while Jumbo was sleeping alone in his residence, the famous Shepherds Hotel in Cairo; which was preferred by the high command, Americans with fat wallets and war correspondents. The sounds of the evening call to prayer echoed throughout the six-story building which had some poor views over to the railroad and to Cook's tourist office building, which still did a roaring trade despite the war.

Jumbo was soon to be awakened by one of his batsmen, who worked for him as his valet and secretary, in order to meet with other senior officers and Churchill's loyal lieutenant, Anthony Eden, at a gathering on the veranda of the American First Secretary's house. Apparently, meeting the Brits inside his home might have compromised the pretence of American impartiality. Dai knew that he needed to act before these men met to discuss the Crete situation.

"Up!" he demanded as he entered the dark room, lit only by the moonlight outside and cool due to a ceiling fan swooshing along above the bed.

Jumbo was a man in his late fifties, overweight, and bald with a white moustache. He had been sleeping under a mosquito net in his underpants and string vest.

"What the devil?" he pushed himself up to see who it was that was barking orders at him.

"Up!" Dai snarled now as he took a step closer.

The man stood up and faced him.

"Ahh, so you have come to fight?" he asked mischievously in old Phoenician.

His eyes appeared to be rolling before tears formed and began trickling slowly down his rounded cheeks and into his moustache.

At that instant, a being stepped out of Jumbo's body as if exiting a shower and Jumbo collapsed into a sweating heap on the floor.

"Well?" growled this creature, Baal.

Dai considered the Warlock for a brief moment before attacking him with his hands, grabbing him by his thin throat and squeezing it exceptionally hard. Baal hit him across his head twice but when this failed to dislodge Dai, he drew his sword.

Dai then quickly released him and took a step back. "Fine, then today you will lose your head," he warned as he produced his own glowing sword.

At that, Baal burst past him, breaking one of the four posts on Jumbo's bed as he did so, and glided out of the open window into the night. "You're too late. Crete will fall and Rommel will soon occupy this hotel," he screamed back before disappearing into the city.

Dai pulled Jumbo to his feet.

"What the hell?" asked a now-gasping Jumbo.

"Precisely," smiled Dai. "Now listen. You were possessed by an evil entity who has been influencing your thoughts and orders regarding the Cretan affair," he told him.

Jumbo, still sweating but full of relief, nodded in understanding.

"I am an angel who was sent to remove it. I have done so, and now I command you to rectify your errors in Crete."

"What have I done?" Jumbo began to cry again.

"You have delayed sending aircraft and troops to the defenders, and the supplies that have got through by ship are of little use," explained Dai. "Do not dwell on this. You are now free of that thing. I promise you it won't return and that I shall help you, but you must shower and get dressed now. You are due at the American First Secretary's home shortly, where you will urge your superiors to cease worrying about Rommel's advance and send as many aircraft as possible, plus as many commandos as they can muster, to Crete," Dai urged him.

As things turned out, a paltry nine aircraft and 500 commandos were available, but they were sent to Crete within 24 hours of this incident. Dai's recollection, which had crossed his mind in an instant, ceased and he looked down to Chuck now, in the present, or what passed for it.

"It is finished," Dai said as he lifted Chuck to his feet.

"Who…?" Chuck was in shock. The pain he had experienced had been excruciating, like nothing he had ever gone through before, and it had completely disabled him. He remembered that there had been nothing he could do but await execution for seconds which seemed like hours, before the apparent divine intervention which had saved his life. The adrenaline which had come, prompted his initial gameness in defending himself. It had not quite been extinguished yet, but was diluted by a physical sensation of extreme comfort, flowing slowly as honey does from the spoon; from the healed wound, out across his body.

"What you're experiencing is the ambrosia that was applied to the wound. It has completely relaxed you, body and soul, so we can talk tomorrow young Chuck, but rest assured that you are doing well and that the situation is looking better than before," Dai smiled, then smelled the evening breeze coming in from the street.

"Who were they, and who were the guys in Fife?"

"All Nephilim and disciples of hell. Apart from the one who stabbed you. He was a fallen angel, and I have killed him," Dai said sadly.

"And what now?" Chuck whispered, fearing the worst.

"Well, this incident has what you might call 'diplomatic consequences', but he attacked you so it was he who crossed the Rubicon." explained Dai.

"What, so you only get involved when they do, and I'm on my own with these demented Nephilim bastards?"

Dai allowed the language to go but Chuck knew not to push it. "So, by crossing the Rubicon, do you mean that this is the first time that an angel has killed a fallen angel?" he asked softly.

Dai turned and smiled at him again, "No, that began elsewhere in another place, so do not fret."

"I almost died tonight, didn't I?"

"Everything you are doing is right, Chuck. The pincer movement against your old Inspector Herriot, that you're thinking, and the tapping of Trevelen's restaurant table, are the right steps to take. Also, you are quite correct to sense closure now, so chin up and stay strong," Dai assured him. "Cairns may be brought to the point of no return tomorrow so you are leading well and progressing neatly," beamed Dai, ignoring the question but making Chuck feel less concerned and somewhat more relaxed.

"Is the phone safe?" he asked him softly.

Chuck felt for it and it was. He nodded.

"I suggest you go home and make a copy of the data, then get some sleep. Know also that I and others are protecting your home tonight. The same applies to your wife until the game ends."

"A game?" Chuck was being contentious as usual when someone offered him the bright side of things, it was a delaying weakness that he knew he must give over; then it was not every day that he was forced to play murder for fun.

"Don't be facetious, try appreciative instead. Now, we shall talk tomorrow, go and rest Chuck." Dai told him.

Chuck then watched him walk away but had to ask, "Why do their blood and bodies evaporate?"

"Because they are neither flesh nor blood, and shall not pollute the earth," Dai nodded for him to go inside now.

Chuck burned the contents of the phone onto a disc as soon as he got in, then hid the phone in a bag of frozen sweetcorn in the freezer before going to bed exhausted and dopey from the ambrosia. Even so, his sleep that night was fitful.

Fourteen

*"Nothing is secret that shall not be known and come to light, take care
then how you hear"*

Luke 8:17-18

It had gone 5 am by the time Chuck got out of the shower and began making breakfast. The newspaper had arrived, so he sat down at the kitchen table to sup his coffee and read a little of the ongoing referendum crap. He could hardly avoid it; it was in all the headlines. Apparently, there was going to be an American-style televised debate between 'Yes' and 'No' politicians next week and the hacks were either on about that or attacking the Tories and the SNP for their future economic projections. A quick flick at the back pages revealed much of the same, with football pundits getting behind each of the two sides. He put it down and yawned again. He had spent most of the night awake, holding his ball launcher, listening to Kim sleeping and freezing at every little noise outside. At that moment, Dai appeared and grabbed a pew.

"Still not reading scripture, then?" he relaxed and leaned back with his arms behind his head.

"When have I had a chance?"

"Well, you find time to read those lies, don't you?" Dai nodded toward the paper.

"Sssh," Chuck raised his finger to his lips. "If Kim hears she will come through."

"She won't, she's still sleeping. I checked on her just now," Dai smiled knowingly.

"Besides, this is relaxation before the storm for me," Chuck claimed.

"Some relaxation, when you can't stand to read it?"

"OK, OK." Chuck gave in.

"You're tired and worrying that you won't have the energy for your plans for today and tonight," Dai sighed. "But if you read, say, *Isaiah* 40:29-31, you might know that your God will give you what you need, and not…"

he pointed at a packet of Pro-plus caffeine pills above the fridge "…that stuff."

"Point taken. I know you told me to sleep but it's not every day I am attacked by the spawn of Satan and his merry men."

Dai chuckled at this and helped himself to a piece of the toast. "Romans 8:31: '*If God is with us then who can be against us*'," he winked as he took a bite, then replaced it upon the plate.

"Oh, only evil fucking demons who stab you with swords to steal police evidence," Chuck hissed contemptuously, but Dai knew it was just tiredness and bravado, so he let it go.

Laughing at this controlled tantrum, Dai smiled. "But we saved you, and they are dead now."

Chuck couldn't argue with that, so said nothing and instead got up to make some more coffee.

"You sense that you are closer to cracking your case, do you not?" Dai asked him.

Chuck shrugged his shoulders.

"Oh come, come, Chuck. I can't abide huffs. You are doing well and the news about Cairns has improved things. Though I must confess that your strategy regarding Herriot and Trevelen is also looking quite good."

"You already know my plan to force the issue with old Herriot, then?" Chuck stirred his mug.

"Yes. I think it is strategically sound – a pincer movement raking in both men."

"And Yvonne?"

"She was killed because of what and who she knew. They will cover up her death."

"Stroker?"

"He was not supposed to be saved. But you were losing him. I saw his thoughts, he was leaning toward a police complaint against you and Christopher. He was also close to texting Trevelen," explained Dai.

"And now?" Chuck sat down again at the table.

"And now he is repenting and can be regarded as loyal to your crusade."

"My crusade?" Chuck looked up from his mug at him.

"Like I said before, Chuck, you are stumbling into a much larger game, and today it will reveal itself to you. You must, as the Scots say, go canny with it," Dai smiled at him knowingly.

"With Cairns?"

"Yes and no. Just be ready and cunning, and don't panic or slip; because if you do, rest assured that Cairns will call out to his friends while in custody."

"And?" Chuck had deeply feared this scenario: would the TIC's shadowy membership pull strings to spring Cairns? Would the phone evidence vanish from the evidence room at St Leonards? After all, that was the entire case against him. Would the murder squads who investigated the murders discussed on the phone messages now be directed to take over the investigation from the Druggies? These scenarios were all quite possible and would leave Chuck and his team high and dry.

"You were well chosen for this game, Chuck, for you are unquestionably a talented player. You have got this far and have produced a fine performance to date. So, keep on playing to the best of your ability for the next day or so and then let us see where we are." Dai's assuring nod and wink was highly convincing and all that Chuck needed to hear under the circumstances.

"You always make it sound like some sort of game. I mean, lives and careers are on the line here, Dai."

"Quite. And many, many more than you think, Chuck."

"So, that is why those monsters tried to kill me out there last night?"

Dai nodded and smiled. He was considering the simplicity of the man seated opposite him. He knew nothing, just like Job[22], yet there was enough evidence to alert him to the fact that he should listen. Yet, Chuck was struggling with faith in the mission. The hour was late now, and this may have seemed cute to some angels, but Dai knew that it would soon become tiresome to him.

"The hour is late my friend; shall we focus on success, as opposed to the inconvenience of it all?" he suggested with a chuckle.

"What's so funny? Is it not true? I'm a hunted man because you have involved me in your games."

"It would be considerably worse if I were not supporting you, Chuck."

"How so?"

"I can't say. What I can confirm is that we only intervened yesterday because another of my kind became involved in your brawl with the three Nephilim. If he had not, it would have been down to you, though your

_____

[22] Job is the central character in the Book of Job in the Bible. We are told that he was a good and prosperous family man beset by horrendous disasters that took away all that he held dear, including his offspring, his health and his property. He struggled to understand his situation.

guardian angel may well have stepped in. I can't really say. But call for help in future to speed things up," Dai nodded at him.

"So, you only fight for men when they are attacked by fallen angels?" Chuck shrugged contemptuously. "Three half-angels with obvious supernatural speed and strength attack me in broad daylight, outside my home, where my family live, all because of this game?" he exaggerated the effort he was putting into controlling his temper. "And you won't jump in because they are only half-angels?" he raised both eyebrows at Dai.

"Kim is safe, and your boy is married and living away from here, so spare me the commotion, Chuck," Dai pointed out. "Anyway, I gave you a weapon to use in an emergency. The abomination you chased through the fields in Fife with it showed you its value."

"And you call it a game. It is me who is on the line here. Why did you lot have to get involved in mankind's world?" he said bitterly because he knew Dai cared about him. He sensed this, and he was sure that Dai wouldn't hurt him, not for a little bit of contemptuous bravado.

"Yes, but you would have had greater problems in the long term if I had not been sent to help."

"A hunted man," Chuck repeated to himself very quietly.

"What danger threatens a great reputation?" Dai asked. Chuck looked up at him in confusion.

"Plutarch." explained Dai as he reached over and helped himself to another nibble of toast.

"Who was that guy who stabbed me?" Chuck locked his gaze on him to press for an answer.

Dai sighed by response and replaced the toast again. "His name is Baal, though he was once called Hamon and before that, Meltaad."

"Did you know him?" Chuck asked thoughtfully. He could remember the intense pain, and his ears ached as he did so.

"Yes. Your kind knows little of him, though some men still sacrifice to him as Baal, a Phoenician deity, upon the tiny island of Sancti Petri, off Cadiz," revealed Dai.

"But he is a fallen angel, not a god?"

"Correct. Jewish scholars have given him the title of 'Lord of the Flies'. But that is meant as an insult, implying that he is dung and his disciples, the three who attacked you outside, are the flies," Dai explained.

"And the other guy we saw on the rooftop in Jerusalem?"

"Just another pile of dung," Dai winked again, and his celestial poise radiated upon Chuck, who accordingly felt a little better about things almost instantaneously.

275

"These conflicts have gone on for a long time, Chuck. As far back as the blood-soaked plain of Troy, where guardian angels were forced to observe the carnage of ambition. For at Troy, as both primitive forces slogged it out, the fallen lords dared to do battle with angels. In the end our side was forced to withdraw from the field at Troy."

"As in the Trojan War?" Chuck knew a little from films and stories of Achilles and Hector.

"The very one," chuckled Dai.

"Always thought that was mythology, like Jason and the Argonauts," Chuck smiled.

"Luciferic influence has seen to it that most religions owe more to a misinterpretation of basic truths than anything else. History is written by the winners, Chuck. Differences are amplified and erased. The differences are regarded as more important to the followers of such creeds than the common ties between them – all because of a pollution of the same fundamental knowledge," Dai clarified for him.

"All the world's major religions are pagan-influenced, but equally, they have all gradually moved their sights further and further towards where the truth lies. It is the same with legend and myth; stories of events passed down from father to son until they become something else entirely and come to be regarded as mythology or old wives' tales." Dai nodded to assure Chuck of his earnestness.

They both looked at one another for a moment.

"And, don't consider this to be a game as in the concept of sport or recreation," Dai waved his hand. "It is so much more than a game. It is the Kertamen; a contest and tactical trial between right and wrong, my friend."

"To me, it seems like a cold war, Dai." Chuck could think of no other way to describe it.

"In a way, yes. And our motive is to prevent it from developing into a full-scale nuclear conflict," agreed Dai.

"It's all so emotionally demanding, Dai. I feel pretty exhausted when you aren't here to bolster my spirits. I appreciate the proof and shall worship God for the rest of my life, I can assure you of that, but I'm just not strong enough to keep this up much longer. Particularly the supernatural fighting," Chuck shrugged back and this delighted Dai enough to make him sit up, clap and laugh out loud.

"Here," he replied, leaning over with a little glass bottle similar to that which Chuck's guardian angel had used to heal his wound. "Drink this for energy and sharpness of mind." Dai dropped two small beads of the same syrupy lotion into the coffee.

"What is it?" Chuck asked as he slowly raised the mug to his lips.

"Ambrosia. It's a sort of booster, but a little bit more special," Dai smiled again as Chuck consumed the beverage. The latter tasted of nothing other than coffee, but he was instantly alert, feeling energetic, on the ball and confident. He felt as if he had just been for a short walk in the crisp air – wide-eyed, alert and rejuvenated.

"Good. Now go get 'em, tiger, and remember I'm always close," Dai patted his hand and then was gone. Chuck sat and finished his coffee and thought about where he had left his black gaffer tape.

Thirty minutes later, he arrived alone at Stroker's flat. Stroker let him in.

"Where's Alby?"

"Crashed out in his bed. I've been up all night reading the Bible," Stroker said as he left the door open and walked back through to the lounge, where he had been sitting; drinking coffee and reading.

Chuck followed him through and took a deep breath. "Can I trust you?" he asked him with a hard stare.

"Whether you feel you can or you can't, I will never betray you or DS Forsyth." Stroker met the stare and Chuck detected trustworthiness deep within this normally dishonest man's eyes. It was as if the ambrosia had boosted his senses too.

"OK," Chuck said, handed him the small recorder, pointed to the on/off switch, and then gave him the gaffer tape. "We can record for ten hours on our receiver. Tape this under Trevelen's table when you go to work, and switch it on. What time do you finish tonight?"

"11-ish."

"Fine, I'll pick you up, and then we have a mission," Chuck told him.

Stroker looked excited again, "Doing what?" he asked enthusiastically.

"Tell you later, here is my number." Chuck handed him a piece of paper. "Text me if and when Trevelen comes in. If he doesn't, we can try again tomorrow, but I'll pick you up when you finish work tonight, OK?"

Stroker examined the little microphone and wire as though he was an expert. "OK, boss," he nodded.

"Don't call me that."

"Cool. But I won't let you down."

"If you betray me, I'll fu..." Chuck stopped short.

"Naturally. I won't, though. Just you wait and see." Stroker nodded and looked straight into Chuck's eyes again.

Chuck drove over to where Joe and Gav were stalking Trevelen's house. He was early, so he leaned in their window and told them to go home but to go and take a sniff at another address en route. He handed them Herriot's Lanark Road address on another scrap of paper. "We might be trying to get inside, or blowing either chloroform or that volatile anaesthetic stuff through the letter box later, as this guy is an ex-cop with suspected ties to our TIC crew."

"But what are we going to do once we are in, and why do we want them asleep, guv?" Gav was obviously concerned by the unauthorised madness being proposed.

"To persuade the old bastard to wear a wire in the golf club where he was meeting with one or two individuals who we think are in our TIC child abuse circle," Chuck told him. Gav nodded uneasily. He was thinking about how they were being so dismissive of the laws they had sworn to uphold.

"We need evidence fast, before Wong calls off this investigation. If we get Herriot to wear a wire, the truth might become clearer and we might get to the evidence-gathering stage," Chuck reminded them.

They were silent for a moment and the radio in the car broadcasted a discussion about the cold war. "Laws are silent in time of war," said an older female voice to a group of women.

The other women laughed and then one asked, "Who said that, Rosie?"

"Cicero, I think." More laughter.

Joe and Chuck smiled while Gav nodded in appreciation of the point before then turning the radio off.

Chuck then got back in the Volvo and thanked God for that little bit of persuasive assistance.

Fifteen

"We cannot keep the good news to ourselves any longer, time is running out"

Angus Buchan

Forsyth did not sleep well due to him thinking about the creation process as well as the obvious; niggling concerns about safety and self-preservation, yet he felt quite alert and prepared when Chuck picked him up early doors. "I feel guilty about the fact that I still don't trust Stroker, guv," was his only grumble as they drove back along Seafield to Portobello.

They were driving to Chuck's house to meet Adams and would then all move on to arrest Cairns from there. Chuck was also concerned about the magnitude of the quest, but he sensed now that they were roller coasting along toward the kill now; so he too was ready and focused upon another demanding day ahead.

"You don't have to trust him; just give him a chance to assist us against these bastards."

"Still an untrustworthy Russian rodent," Forsyth said, firmly.

"Russian?" This was a new one to Chuck.

"Or German, or wherever his name is from?" Forsyth said.

"Where did you come up with that?" Chuck was glad to break focus for a moment and to reignite their usual banter.

"Well, wasn't there an East German left-back named Stroker?" grinned Forsyth.

"Anyway..." Chuck dragged himself back into work by proceeding to explain all about the attack on him by the fallen angel outside his home the previous evening. "I was lucky to survive, Chrissy."

Forsyth was shocked but also disgusted by this news.

"We need to annihilate every one of those Nephilim cunts, guv," he hissed angrily.

"Might be a good idea if you and your Mrs came and stayed with us for a while, mate," suggested Chuck. "At least until we know that this heat is cooling down."

"I'll ask her and get back to you on that, guv." Forsyth knew he would have to think up a crafty lie to ensure an easy process with his Mrs, and right now he simply couldn't think about that as they had Cairns in their sights and she was in a bad enough mood right now regarding the referendum. "Could do with one of those ball-launcher things though," he suggested again.

"Don't know why; it didn't help me with that master swordsman, mate," Chuck recalled with a hint of alarm. He also knew that there was no question that either of them could tell their partners the truth until Dai gave the go-ahead, sadly. "You can tell the Mrs that it is Cairns and his contractors who are threatening your home etc., Chris," he suggested.

Forsyth said nothing, he would leave it until the last minute for sure.

When they eventually pulled up outside Chuck's house, Adams and Duffy were sitting, waiting in Duffy's SAAB convertible. "Bet he has the Miami Vice CD playing," jested Forsyth as they got out. Chuck and Adams met on the pavement for a chat; something Chuck was exceptionally weary about as he kept his hand on the ball-launcher in his pocket.

Forsyth eyed up and down the street and then, quite strangely, Duffy thought, the sky above them.

"I've looked into the footie team," Adams said with a sour expression which suggested that she had turned up zilch. "Nothing doing yet on the coaches or parents," she confirmed. "We can look at them again properly as soon as we deal with this murder stuff," she added.

"Yep, and we should look into the coach company involved in any European trips. Then we may learn of any pending trips," Chuck sighed because he knew this was all wishful thinking – there simply wouldn't be the time or resources to do anything other than shelve this lead, as Wong's deadline approached.

"There has also been a tip-off about a coke deal taking place in the next few days in a Travel Lodge car park at Swanston," she told him.

"Where is the intel from?" he asked.

"Liverpool Druggies, who assure us that it's from a good source. They have said that they currently have surveillance on the main player and will let us know when the courier is on the motorway. Wong will have read this intel too, because the Scousers emailed him in on it. Nightshift rang them up and got the details, then mailed just you and me," she said with a grin, indirectly scolding him for obviously not checking his emails.

"With this in the post, Wong could pull the plug on your deniable op, unless we produce something real soon," she sounded tired as well as frustrated as she said this. Chuck felt sorry for her and wished he could give her a hit of that ambrosia stuff too; for he now felt as sharp as a razor.

"OK, let's go hit Cairns then," he urged, wanting to get on with some practical action.

"I've ordered armed officers to do exactly that. He should be at St Leonards, detained under suspicion of conspiracy to murder," she gave him a cheeky tweak of her nose.

"Good girl. I have the phone, so let's go get a result."

Both cars made their way over to Newington. St Leonard's was busier than usual with several angry taxi drivers, who had been detained for brawling among themselves at the Rutland Place taxi rank in the West End. As the druggies weaved through the chaos and down the stairs toward the holding cells, one big, fat elderly female, with peroxide hair that should have been given up twenty-five years earlier, and a husky manly growl, started swinging blubber-shaking right hooks at one of the other drivers.

"Out the way, you silly fat radge," snarled an impatient Forsyth as he shouldered her into the arms of a little PC, who felt like he had been hit by a bus. He ended up flat on his back, with her tripping over his boots and into a tin rubbish bin that got crushed by the impact.

Two WPCs, both carrying batons, passed the Druggies as they headed along a corridor leading to the custody suite. A few seconds later, four male uniforms came charging past them and heading toward the chaotic reception area.

Chuck thought back to his cab-office days as they continued through more automatic doors. All those taxi drivers would be facing long suspensions if the current Cab Inspector was anywhere near as brutal as old Herriot had been. He then thought about Herriot and what was to be done about him. Chloroform or some other form of anaesthetic perhaps?

Back in the holding area a different custody team was on duty, and the sergeant had a bee in his bonnet about all the attention being lavished upon his latest prisoner – Leslie Cairns.

"I've got the press calling up already, not to mention more calls from individuals claiming to be the brass and then hanging up and withholding their numbers!" The moustached sergeant would much have preferred to have been back in the old uniform of shirt with rolled-up sleeves, and tie. He was clearly a moaner and a pretend-hater of his job.

"Won't be long, and I apologise about all the drama, Sergeant; frankly, he's a bad man," Adams said piously whilst batting her tired eyelids at him. He was not sure whether she was being sarcastic or genuine and did not know what to do next. "Set Cairns up in an interview room with tapes please, and be a dear and arrange four coffees for us," she added as she signed the relevant forms.

"Who might the concerned callers have been?" Forsyth said quietly as they sat in the interview room awaiting Cairns. The turnkeys had enquired as to whether they had preferred Cairns handcuffed or not; they preferred not.

Duffy had been told to sit in the custody office with several other cops waiting to interview or fingerprint their custodies. There was nothing new to this as there were two inspectors and a DS available, so Duffy was not suspicious; just disappointed that despite the car, white chinos and lack of socks, he was not portraying the Sonny Crocket[23] role he craved.

Cairns arrived in a t-shirt, the shorts he had been sleeping in, and bare feet. He had clearly been dragged from his bed by the O.K. Corral brigade and had a face like a Greek Cypriot at a Turkish military parade. He was large, muscular for his age, and ugly to go with it. He was well-tanned, doubtless due to frequent stays at his Spanish villa near Torremolinos, and there was a white tan mark around his neck where a necklace had been. "I'm flying to Florida with my family in a couple of days, so you better release me sharpish, or have enough to remand me with, arseholes," he snarled at them with a rough, nicotine-damaged growl.

Chuck was neither daunted nor impressed by this angry man who was used to getting what he wanted, for Chuck saw the anger for what it really was: a weakness.

"We have enough to throw away the key pal, so sit down, shut up and answer our questions. We aren't members of your little gang of crooks, we're the guvnors here, pal," he told Cairns coldly and without the slightest hint of aggression. Cairns felt real worry surface in his gut now for the first time since his dramatic arrest less than an hour ago; at the time, he had assumed he would be freed again that same morning.

"What have you got?" he demanded from them, more softly now.

"Three conspiracies to murder," beamed Chuck.

"Crap," Cairns beamed at them all quizzically.

Chuck took the phone out and showed him everything for ten minutes without anyone uttering a word. From time to time Cairns raised an eyebrow and looked down then back up when something struck a chord. When it was over, Adams informed him that Benny Latif was a sworn Crown witness to the three conspiracies, and lied further that Latif was

---

[23] James 'Sonny' Crocket was a fictional undercover vice cop from the TV series 'Miami Vice', played by Don Johnson.

down on tape and had signed statements. Cairns said nothing for a moment as this news set in. He would have known that Benny was lifted yesterday, Chuck suspected, but not much more at this stage as Latif would now have been transferred to the court and would not see his lawyer for at least another hour yet. The clock was ticking, but still on the druggies' side.

"The body was found with a mouthful of pound coins, too," Forsyth told Cairns what he already knew well enough.

"I need to make a phone call," Cairns finally said.

"No phone call. You're getting the book thrown at you and not a soul from your Fairmilehead brethren is getting a chance to do you any favours, because I'm charging you with all three counts of conspiracy to murder," Chuck snarled at him and slammed his hand on the desk.

Cairns growled, his teeth showing like a cornered fox. "Fuck you, that isn't me on your phone. Go on, charge me and see what happens to you."

"I plan to," replied Chuck, before standing up and leaving the room to call the turnkey.

"Not going to charge me first, Inspector?"

"We are not superheroes, Mr Cairns, we need to type up things first," Adams smiled as she too stood up.

"You'll get charged in your cell." Chuck turned and told him as the custody officer arrived.

Chuck walked down to Cairns cell five minutes later, opened the hatch and grinned in at him. "You're getting plenty of time, I promise you that. Goodbye, dickhead," he waved at him, then closed the hatch and returned to the interview room where Adams and Forsyth were discussing things.

"We have enough, guv, but we should go up to the court and put Latif on tape; then we can charge Cairns," suggested Forsyth.

"Not interested in charging him. We need him to spill the beans on who and where the paedo group are, Chris."

"I'm with you Chuck, but if we're not hugely careful here, we could get told to walk away from someone – and from the whole investigation," Adams felt required to point out.

"He'll crack first, and soon. He knows he is fucked, and that at best he might shake the conspiracy to murder a politician, but not the other two; because we have two dead bodies and Latif on board as a witness, stating that he murdered them for Cairns."

"But we haven't got Latif secured, guv." Forsyth insisted.

"Cairns doesn't know that yet, and he has no reason to think otherwise now that he knows that Latif made the recordings," Chuck winked at them both.

"Bet that phone call he asked for was to initiate a hit on Latif once he arrives in Saughton on remand later today," Adams suggested thoughtfully. It was clear to her that Chuck was on form here, so she sat waiting with Forsyth, letting him run things his way – fast and aggressive; she could play the good cop when he required.

Chuck told them both to wait a moment whilst he took a slow walk back down to Cairns cell, wherein he opened the hatch again, and coolly informed him that they were also in the process of investigating his sponsorship of a boys' football team, as well as bus trips abroad. Cairns scoffed at this but offered no other response, so the hatch was replaced. Chuck waited a moment before taking another peek through the eye hole, and much to his relief, there was Cairns sitting biting his nails, wide-eyed. As Chuck walked back along the corridors to the interview room, he realised that he was smirking.

"We need to get him back in, guv." Forsyth was tapping his knee with his fingers, clearly concerned about the time.

"Patience," urged Chuck.

The three of them sat for a while. Forsyth went out to see how Duffy was and walked right into a heated verbal debate between him and some uniform regarding the bloody referendum. He stopped in his tracks, turned and went back to the interview room, releasing nothing more than a sigh and a wave of his hand as both Chuck and Adams gave him quizzical looks.

A few more silent minutes passed, during which they all thought that the bluff might blow up in their faces at any moment. Then, Adams' personal mobile rang. "It's Wong," she whispered as if he could hear her, and took it outside.

"Good morning, Sir."

"Where's Chuck?" Wong sounded sharp and impatient.

"He is with me here at St Leonards, Sir."

There was a moment's silence. "Doing what?" Wong was interested enough to change his tone now.

"We have Leslie Cairns in custody based on evidence uncovered in the covert investigation," Adams said, in as calm and measured a tone as she could muster.

Wong paused, presumably to think for a moment. "Before we even get to that, can you tell me why the Procurator Fiscal has just complained to me that Chuck has promised one Babar Latif a reduced sentence in a murder case?" Wong was back on edge again. "And in the bloody Fiscal's name?"

"We learned that Latif was charged with murder, and, well Sir, he is Leslie Cairns enforcer and we were looking for solid intel," she tried to justify.

"So, you bullshitted Latif and got your info, and that's why Cairns is in custody now?" he snapped.

"Well… yes Sir, but there's more to it than that…."

"No!" he cut her off. "Why was I not updated on the progress with Latif? After all, it was achieved yesterday, was it not?"

"It was all systems go overnight with tracing all the intelligence discovered, Sir, and this resulted in Cairns' arrest this morning. We were literally just about to update you presently," she insisted.

"And why the hell are you involved? I was of the understanding that you were running the rest of the squad?"

"I am, Sir," she confirmed.

"A lead has come in regarding a new matter; I see from the shift change?" he asked. This meant he had been in the squad office speaking to people, she realised.

"So, Latif's lawyer is creating a shitstorm with the Fiscal and is complaining to me, Sharon."

"I'm sorry, Sir, but the intel gained was ground-breaking." She emphasised the success of the operation again.

"Which is?" he impatiently wanted to know.

"Three conspiracies to murder, Sir," she replied.

"Evidence?"

"Video evidence, and Latif is seen as the contract recipient."

"Is he offering Crown evidence against Cairns?"

"Yes, Sir, but we pressed Chuck's investigation as the priority and simply sought to push on with Cairns and press him for the lowdown on the child abuse group," she explained.

"Well, you've got a pile up of jobs here, not to mention this new intel regarding a drop-off. Then there is another new job, a guy arrested with an ounce and a half of coke in the Spiders Web bar last night by uniform. He needs to be interviewed by one of our lot," he pointed out. Adams stayed silent.

"I gave Chuck a week to look into this thing, but we are halfway through and there is nothing to date, am I correct?" he asked.

"Well, ask me that in an hour or so, Sir," she reminded him of the situation.

"Sharon, by your own acceptance nothing has come of the off-the-book investigation, other than the tangled web of the murder of Lionel Frazer, and a dubious confession or two regarding other murders, right?" he argued firmly.

"Well, I really think we could be on the brink of extracting some names regarding our child sex ring, as I said, Sir, and you did give us a week."

"Could and should are my least-liked words."

"Sir, if I can just…"

"We are not in the murder business. Sharon. Nor for that matter are we in the deniable operations business based on the say-so of a dead lawyer who might have claimed anything to save his jail-bound skin." Wong dissected the alternative argument well and Adams felt she had her hands tied as he was new in post, and they'd done well to get the secret op off the ground at all.

"And if Cairns did give you anything, do you think his word is going to carry through a conviction, or multiple convictions?" he asked her.

"Perhaps, Sir, especially if we locate the victims," she suggested.

"No, Sharon… I know you're keen to keep going but I really do need you all back and addressing this job pile up. The squad are stretched enough. With the new leads coming in, and Chuck's investigation is going nowhere, it's time for all hands on deck," he insisted.

"I wouldn't say it's going nowhere, Sir."

Wong was not budging, however. "Pass any intel over to the duty CID at St Leonards and get over here. If they choose to jail or release Cairns, then that will be their call. One thing is for sure, if Cairns is connected to any masonic or establishment conspiracy, they will all be aware of his arrest by now and Chuck's cover will be blown anyway, so stand down and give it to CID to form a murder investigation," he ordered.

"Yes, Sir."

"Good. I'll see the pair of you in my office within the hour," he added in a conclusive tone, then the phone went dead.

When Adams returned to the interview room she immediately relayed the conversation to them both, and received the expected groans and curses.

"I'm for just bashing on with Cairns, to see if we get a deal," Chuck said, not feeling inclined to concede defeat.

Adams was also minded to have a quick shot at it, but was less sure. "But if he isn't buying or prepared to give us names and locations within say…" she glanced at her white Casio which told her it was 10.05 am, "the next twenty minutes, we pull out and discuss later."

"Fine, but if we give CID the phone evidence, we are not only likely to find ourselves in the firing line, but it will most probably not be followed up if Cairns is connected to this TIC mob, guv," protested Forsyth.

Just then a blonde female turnkey knocked the door and entered the room, "Sorry to interrupt, officers. The prisoner Cairns is asking to speak to the DI from the drug squad. Do you want to have him brought up here, or just find out what he wants from his cell?" she asked.

"I'll go down," Chuck told her. He hesitated a moment to allow her to leave, then stood up. He winked at them both and whispered, "Bet he wants to play."

When he opened the cell hatch and peered in, he saw Cairns lying flat on his back on the thin blue mattress on the floor. The man had one wrist across his face, shading his eyes from the bright strip lights above him.

"C'mon then, what are you wanting? I'm busy trying to write out a charge here," he snarled.

Cairns removed his wrist from his eyes and sat up. "What did you pinch Benny for?"

"Nought to do with you. You can find out everything when you're on remand and the statements arrive in your cell," Chuck said, as he shook his head.

"Do you want a deal?" Cairns asked.

"Don't really need one, Les. You're fucked left, right and centre the way I see it, and it's murder this time, mate," Chuck said, coolly.

"The Fiscal will be offering a plea to one of the conspiracies, and to drop the other. As for the promise of another hit, one of a political nature, you can't charge me with that and you know it," Cairns pointed out confidently.

"Maybe. Not my problem. I'm charging you with all three and starting an intensive, probing investigation into your boys' football team sponsorship. If you get a deal from your mate the Fiscal, then good for you. Now, was that all?" Chuck smiled wryly at Cairns, who stood up and slowly approached the hatch.

Chuck did not flinch. He remained with his face at the hatch, wondering if Cairns might try to jab a fist at him or spit in his face.

Cairns stopped a foot from the hatch and asked quietly, "What would you want," he paused, taking a step closer, "to walk away from this long shot of yours?" He stepped up to the hatch to stare right into Chuck's eyes, as if to spot the twitch of a gambler.

Chuck looked into the cold eyes of a man who would think nothing of having Kim's nipples cut from her body and nailed to Chuck's forehead. The evil radiated out from Cairns like a radio wave, and Chuck read it easily. However, feeling on top of his game as an investigator, he also

287

realised that the beast before him was worried about the phone evidence, as well he should be.

"Give me the names, dates and locations of the little paedophile, drug-taking clique within your lodge." Chuck didn't flinch but smirked coolly at him. "That is your only out. Then we can talk, Leslie. Otherwise, I'm going to win this one and you will potentially die inside."

Cairns looked at the ground for a second. An angry smile appeared on his ugly face. "You're not asking for much pal, eh?" He then stepped back and leaned against the cell wall to think over his options.

"Bottom line." Chuck was showing his hand slightly by helping him along, but time was scarce and so he put needs first. "You're not one of them anyway, mate."

Cairns quickly turned to look and to try to find out what else Chuck knew.

"I know they only brought you in because you can provide muscle," Chuck told him, his gaze steady on his quarry. He paused to let this sink in, and then spoke again.

"They recognise your power within the criminal world, and preferred to put a collar and lead on you. Even your lawyer, Lionel Frazer, told me personally that he felt you were not the right sort for that lodge of Satan-worshipping cunts." He was throwing the kitchen sink at him now, trying to make that breakthrough.

Cairns was so far unmoved, but clearly listening.

"Bet Frazer took a fair whack from your savings too, am I right?"

Cairns gave him a quick glance to show he had possibly touched a nerve, but remained silent.

"They had you whack him, didn't they?"

No response.

"He was in custody, looking at time and a helluva lot of publicity, so they had him whacked," Chuck told him.

"What do you think they will do to you, Leslie?" Chuck urged. "Or are you the only muscle they have, mate?"

"They have Glasgow people, and some foreigners," Cairns said as he turned slowly and smirked. "No, I'm not the only tool in the box," he said softly so that none of the other cells would overhear.

"Well, I'm pretty sure they won't exercise any assets in order to spring you from this, Leslie. They will either let you rot, or hit you – which would you prefer?" Chuck raised his eyebrows and Cairns turned at this. Hello again, thinks Chuck, he fears them?

This was confirmed when Cairns looked up again. "What the fuck do you think they'll do if I grass any of them up for anything?" He raised his eyebrows to mirror Chuck.

A moment passed and Chuck felt his neck begin to hurt from leaning at the hatch.

"So, grass up my brothers, betray my oath, and live in a secret location somewhere under witness protection for the rest of my life? Is that the proposal?" Cairns sighed before lifting his head up to look at Chuck. "Or, face two murder or conspiracy to murder trials, if I stay alive on remand, and then probably get between 8 to 12 years at best. Some choice, Detective Inspector," he snarled coldly.

Chuck gave him a slow nod and then sighed to show that he was getting pissed off, waiting.

"What if I give you something just as large?"

"Such as?" Well, Chuck was first and foremost a druggie inspector.

"Plans for an assassination of a leading political figure and a government coup d'état?"

"I doubt you could prove those?" Chuck asked incredulously, but he did want to know. He was surprised at this, though because the third video on the phone had discussed a potential hit on a politician, it was obvious that Cairns might have a lot more details. But that did not automatically mean that a career criminal of Cairns' level was not playing him here, Chuck told himself, just as he was trying his best to play Cairns. The average liar will bullshit, but the craftsman of bullshit will feed meagre helpings of actuality in the hope of leading the cops up the garden path.

"I have had the contract offered and discussed. More importantly, I know a little about why and who," Cairns shrugged.

"What about the paedo ring?"

"Nah, fuck that; I'm not talking about stuff like that, and that's my final decision."

"OK, tell me what you have – and make it quick. Then I'll either think about it, or I'll walk away and come back shortly to charge you with a minimum two counts of conspiracy to murder, since you won't spill the beans about your Fairmilehead handshake brigade," Chuck told him firmly and with obvious impatience.

"You don't want to go down the road of all that, trust me, pal. You would be in way over your head very quickly the minute you made an enquiry. Your job, your life, even your family wouldn't be safe." Cairns shook his head.

"Are you scared of them, Les?"

"Not scared," Cairns shook his head. "But I know what they are and won't cross them."

"Why?"

"You wouldn't understand. There are things outwith your experience that I have seen, but only briefly, and even for me they have been hard to understand. Things even your wildest imagination could not help you to understand. Let's just leave it at that." He shook his head now, not in refusal, but in his lack of comprehension of his experiences with those people.

"Yet you provide them with children to abuse and coke to snort, so you have two or three uses to them. What are you so scared about, then?"

"Nothing can bring you away from the edge once you step in that direction, Inspector. Not morality, not wisdom, laws, science; not even God himself. It is utterly beyond your understanding," Cairns replied, sighing again softly.

They stared at each other momentarily before Cairns spoke again. "It is not fear."

"Are you really a Satanist, Les?" Chuck asked straight out.

"What do you think?"

"I think probably that at first you sought to join them for business reasons and protection from the law, but that gradually they gained favours from you, which may have meant unwittingly selling your soul to Old Nick. Am I getting warm?" Chuck smirked.

Cairns appeared slightly agitated by this and shook his head more urgently. "Bottom line, no can do pal!" he growled.

Just then, some other prisoners down the block began yelling at one another. The slow, exaggerated drawl of a junkie started to annoy the inhabitants of every other cell. He was shouting, asking for the occupants' names and places of abode. One reply was an aggressive order to shut it, so the pair of them went into a full, threatening square-up. A loony two cells down from Cairns began howling like a wolf while another, rougher voice promised to "batter every last one of you little bastards when we go on the bus to court in the morning." Chuck reckoned it was the voice of a man who could walk the walk too.

"Doubt we have a deal, then," he said, eyeballing Cairns disappointedly.

"I'll give you something bigger." Cairns spoke quietly but firmly as he raised his thick, greying eyebrows again.

"Well, come on then, sum it up quickly like I asked – you've got thirty seconds and I'm off." Chuck was eager to go and tell Adams that Cairns

290

was refusing to play ball, and to begin plotting the next move. And he was quite sure that one thing that would involve was handing over the phone evidence to that fat wanker upstairs in CID, who had nicked Benny Latif yesterday.

Cairns ducked his head back down to the hatch, "Salmond. Alex Salmond, he is the target," he whispered, then searched Chuck's face for a reaction. Chuck looked down at his own shoes while this sank in. Then, he looked hard into Cairns deep, cold, grey eyes.

"Go on?"

"The contractor reckons he is one of two or three strategies being set in place to take over control of the Scottish government shortly after the next election," Cairns went on.

"It might not have to take place if the election goes their way first, but if not, they will whack Salmond and I have been offered £1,000,000 to do the hit," he revealed with a modest nod.

"Who are 'they'? Who gave you the contract?"

"Leo Frazer offered me it, but he was acting for an anonymous wine dealer laird from the borders. But the real clients are the big oil companies; well, Leo suspected that anyway."

"So, with Leo dead, after you had him murdered, who is there to pinch on this offer of yours, and how would I go about doing so?" Chuck tried not to sound sarcastic, but he was not getting this yet.

"The wine dealer. I've met him once in the Maybury Casino, with Leo and others. He chatted a while and made it clear he appreciated my involvement in the contract. I don't know his name, but he was a posh guy in a nice suit, and was chatting to some guy who lectured at one of the universities. Looked a bit like Peter Bowles from that old TV series?" Cairns clicked his fingers but Chuck hadn't a clue who Peter Bowles was, so he shut the hatch and fired along the corridor to find Duffy, who was sitting, reading a tabloid newspaper in the office.

"Get me an image of Philip Trevelen on A4. Type in Melville Bramble Wine online then print it out and then cut and paste two images of similar looking blokes from Google images, and print them out too please, mate," he told him.

When he returned five minutes later with the three images Duffy looked as confused as ever, but Chuck simply thanked him and nipped off again back down the corridor to Cairns' block, where he opened his cell hatch again. "Any of these him?" he asked Cairns, who had thought he had been abandoned.

He took the pictures and looked at them. "That's him," he handed Chuck back the black and white image of Trevelen's face. "Peter Bowles," he grinned, revealing several gold fillings.

"Philip Trevelen," Chuck told him.

Cairns nodded and shrugged.

"The contract might be off, now that Leo is dead?" Chuck suggested.

"Nope," Cairns grinned. "He rang me after Leo bit the dust to establish contact and told me to continue with the assassination planning. He said he would arrange a meeting in a couple of months to go over things."

"Wasn't he upset about Leo being killed?"

"He didn't mention it as such. I remember he emphasised how important it was that we continue without him. He probably wasn't happy about making contact and withheld his number, but he certainly didn't suspect that I might have had anything to do with it – not that I'm saying I did, of course."

"What about your lodge? If Trevelen is one of the gang, then he must have known or been a part of the decision to give you the contract to kill Leo?" Chuck had decided to ask a sneaky question or two at this point, to see if Cairns could be goaded into making a revelation.

"He's not one of us," Cairns shook his head. "Just some mate of Leo's who was offering big coin for the job."

Chuck considered this for a moment. It was possible that Cairns was lying, but equally possible that he knew very little about things and was just a pawn in the bigger picture.

"You haven't met all the other members of the Fairmilehead lodge, though?" Chuck asked.

Cairns ignored the question. "His handshake was different. He was a Mason right enough, but not one of ours," he said firmly.

"So – I spring you, you won't tell anyone about our little deal, and will wear a wire next time you talk to Trevelen? Is that what you're offering me, Leslie?" Chuck chortled.

"The opportunity to prevent the assassination of the first leader of an independent Scotland? Yeah, I think that is a pretty rich deal for you," tutted Cairns.

"No deal. Give me the paedo ring, and the whole fucking cursed lodge membership list that you know about. Do that and I'll let you walk out of here a free man today."

"Nope, no deal." Cairns shook his head and turned his back on the hatch, then returned to the little plastic mattress on the floor.

Chuck shut the hatch and walked back along the block feeling deflated and thinking that catching these perverts under present circumstances was damn near impossible. Just as he thought that, he noticed some black marker pen scrawled in an open and unoccupied cell. This was rare, as prisoners rarely got through the detention process with pens these days. He stopped and for some reason took a closer look.

"Cui Bono," it simply read across the cell wall at an angle.

He did not understand Italian or whatever that was, and headed off to speak to Adams and Forsyth. As he did, he felt compelled to Google the translation on his phone.

"Cui Bono, Latin phrase for who stands, or stood, to gain from a crime, and so might have been responsible for it," he read on the screen.

Well, well, he thought to himself, and wondered whether he had just encountered a sign from Dai. Once back in the interview room with Adams and Forsyth, Chuck filled them in on the bad news and the strange offer. "You didn't deal?" Adams asked him.

"Nope, but interesting stuff about Trevelen, guys." They nodded in agreement.

Chuck's phone rang, and it was Joe. "Sniffed around your man Herriot's house, guv, and learned from his neighbour, who happened to be receiving a parcel for him and who was nattering loudly with the postie, that Herriot has a, and I quote here, 'posh camper van' that he has taken over to Crail in Fife for his holidays," he reported.

"OK, thanks Joe. You two get to your beds and meet me at Chris' flat at 6 pm. Oh, and Chris, ring and get that vehicle's details."

Chuck put his phone back in his pocket and looked round again at Adams. "Look, I don't want to just give this to CID." His eyes showed some desperation. He went on, talking quickly and intensely.

"This bastard might talk yet, and if not I want to charge him myself; and bugger what Wong says, Sharon," he urged her to agree with him.

"Let's go see him in the cell now, guv, and set about him?" Forsyth leaned forward on his chair and beamed confidently at him now. Adams looked at him to see if he was serious, but Chuck, with his gaze distant, refocused and changed tack.

"Time is short here, Sharon. We can hold him for around another 8 or 9 hours max, and if we charge him, we will have a much better chance of cracking him." Chuck knew he was clutching at straws and that she would realise this. However, he hoped that his obvious concerns were mutual and that she too, knew that something had to be done; and that Wong's orders to walk away were way off the mark.

"Suggestions?" she eventually sighed at them both.

"We could pray?" Forsyth suggested, while Adams studied him with even more interest now, as Chuck watched her for her reaction.

"I have wire taps on Trevelen ongoing tonight, and am led to believe that he is likely to turn up," Chuck told her.

Adams turned to Chuck and nodded slowly as she returned to the strategic options fluttering around her mind.

"And, I hope to have Herriot wearing one in a car with that guy Welsh from the council, as well as installing a tap in the golf club itself by tomorrow, or the next day at the latest," he added.

Again, she nodded soberly. "Not asking how you propose to get him to do that, exactly," she smiled. "But if he does, that might be fruitful, I agree," she said, her brow furrowing as she thought this play through.

"But Chuck – we just wouldn't have time to wait, if your pincer moves end up failing to produce evidence of who the bastards are," she pointed out.

"I know – but I think it's the best option we have. If you're with me, I'll keep on it until the day after tomorrow," he urged. "And if nothing by then, we'll walk away. Deal?"

"OK, deal. And I'll try to get through whatever jobs Wong has deemed urgent, without him knowing where you are. I'll need Chris back and, say, Gav. You can have Joe."

"Well, tonight I need them all, so you can have them tomorrow," Chuck told her and she smiled ruefully while shaking her head.

"And what about Cairns? He could cause a shitstorm if CID let him go."

"Well, let's go and see Wong as he wanted. I'll tell him I've passed everything on to CID, then nip back and work on Cairns. If I don't get anywhere with him, I'll pass him over to CID and tell them I have the phone backed up and am forwarding to the Lord Advocate because there was mention of an attack on whoever is in government after next year's Scottish elections." Chuck winked at them having said this. "That way, the fuckers will think twice about losing the evidence, and we will still have Cairns by the short and curlies."

"And we can always come back to him and charge him," Forsyth grinned as he saw the plan forming.

"Right, Chris, stay here with Cairns and make out to all the eyes and ears that we are still questioning him on narcotics matters, and that he will remain detained until we decide otherwise. I'll not be too long, hopefully. Sharon – I suggest that you and I go and take Duffy with us." He got up and led the way. Adams sighed, nodded at Forsyth who appeared unmoved by this, then got up and followed.

Duffy sat in the back but did not speak. Neither did Adams or Chuck. They passed a crowd of students at the Pleasance who were heading off on a confusing pro-green, pro-independence march to Holyrood. "Yes or No, then?" Adams nodded her head at them as she leaned around and smiled at Duffy, who shrugged his shoulders.

"Don't really know, guv. But my wife is voting Yes and has fallen out with her Mum, pals and almost myself, and I'm a bloody natural so far," the younger DC smiled.

"Yes." Adams turned back around lazily. "It's certainly creating a lot of tension," she sighed.

"And that will scare off some voters who will lean towards No," offered Chuck, as they made surprisingly fast progress up St Mary's Street and across onto Jeffrey Street.

"I agree. It is becoming crude, actually, and I see that Labour guy was threatened while on tour in Dundee the other day. It will be good when it's over." Adams turned the radio on and mucked around with it until she found some Boney M. Thereafter, the three of them listened in stony silence to 'Rasputin' as they headed from the Old into the New Town.

At Fettes, Chuck told Duffy to find a vehicle and drive over to the Maybury Casino to find out how often Trevelen used the place, and who signed him in or whom he signed in etc. Then, he and Adams walked in the other direction towards Wong's office upstairs.

"I'm going to tell him that myself and the boys have not slept in almost 40 hours, to buy us some sleeping time," Chuck whispered as they passed open office doors.

"Great, that'll have him off my back until at least tomorrow," she replied.

They knocked on the oak door, with Wong's gold nameplate stating his title upon it.

"Come in." He sounded expectant.

Wong gestured politely for them to sit down before returning to his window to water a couple of small plants.

"Lesley Cairns is care-of CID now, I take it?" he asked with his back to them.

"Hand-over taking place currently, Sir." replied Chuck.

"Any evidence on his drug business?"

"A good lead on the sponsorship of a youth football team that takes trips abroad. Potentially in a vehicle which they also use to bring drugs into the country," Adams told him.

Wong went back to his desk from the window, sat down, and quickly glanced at a memo from the Chief Constable. When he had finished doing so, he placed it to the right-hand side of his neatly arranged desk and nodded at them both individually. "Good morning, good morning," he said to each of them in turn.

"Now then, I'll come straight to the point. I'm afraid I must insist that you drop your investigation, Chuck, and focus upon squad business," he said, looking impartially at him.

"I had a look at what is becoming an alarming level of incoming jobs that remain neglected and one or two are of an urgent nature. I'm as alarmed as you are about any kind of claim involving sexual abuse, but the fact is, I can't put four officers on a deniable op while other work is flooding in. I'm sure you understand."

"Sure, Sir." Chuck nodded. "Can I strongly recommend that you bring in someone from the Met to investigate these serious claims?" he suggested in a professional tone.

Wong looked somewhat disturbed at this idea. "I don't have that kind of authority, Chuck. And besides, if we start shouting out that police officers on this force are somehow involved in crimes of this nature without any clear evidence; well, we'd be sabotaging our own careers," he said, point blank refusing Chuck's suggestion.

"Understood, Sir," Chuck lied efficiently.

"Sharon?" Wong then turned to Adams.

"It's your call, Sir, but in my opinion, at the very least, the squad should keep an eye and an ear open for new evidence, without compromising our own priorities through snouts, etcetera," she stated.

"Goes without saying," Wong nodded, and brought his hands together like a priest might, Chuck thought.

"I also think Chuck should get the credit for Cairns being collared for murder," Adams argued further.

"Noted; I shall give that some thought." Wong leaned towards each of them, gave them a nod, and added, "So now, please get onto the job pile-up and drop me an email tomorrow with updates. I'll see you the day after as I'm at a seminar in Glasgow tomorrow."

"Neither myself or the team have slept in two days, Sir," Chuck stood up. "We are going to get a few hours' sleep and freshen up, then we'll come in and take some jobs," Chuck lied.

"Fine, but see that you do." Wong had started reading the same memo over again and did not look up as they filed out in silence.

As they walked down the corridor, Adams looked behind her then whispered, "That's you really crossed the Rubicon now, babe, you'd better go and work fast," she smiled at him. "I'll deal with whatever he has got his knickers in a twist about. Send me Chris and one of the others tomorrow."

"Merci, Madame," he pecked her cheek and was quickly on his way.

As he drove back across the city, he pulled over at Stockbridge to take a call from Forsyth.

"Guv?"

"Yeh. I'm on my way back...."

"Guv," Forsyth sounded official.

"What is it?" he sensed something was up.

"They're saying Cairns is dead."

"Eh?"

"Dead. They're saying he slipped in his cell and banged his head." Forsyth sounded angry.

"What? Who found him?"

"Don't know. CID are arguing with some uniform wanker about the crime scene and the turnkey told me that a private ambulance was coming," Forsyth said. The sound of vehicles zooming past him could be heard in the background.

"Are you outside?"

"Sure. Couldn't talk in..."

"Never mind, get back inside and all over their crime scene, Chris. Don't let them move that body – if there is a dead body – and try get a look at it," Chuck snapped before chucking his phone on the seat and tearing off into the city.

"Bastards!" he shouted as he hit the pedal.

On Frederick Street, he sat at the lights, feeling absolutely gutted. Who the hell were these people, and how could they kill a man in cold blood inside a police station simply because he'd been pinched for murder? Also, how come they could find out and then act on it so quickly?

At the bus stop to his right-hand side were three large fliers for three different Festival shows. The first was in black and white and showed men in the trenches of WWI smoking and drinking at Christmas time. It was titled '*Chin Up*' and was being staged in the Assembly Rooms. The next was a comedy called '*Will B*', with a picture of a Bumble Bee. The third was of a choir playing at St Giles, titled '*Joyful and Triumphant*'. The picture was of an angelic choir and Chuck thought for a moment that he could see Dai's face amongst the choir members. Then the lights changed and an estate agent in her red mini beeped angrily, so he put his foot down again.

Sixteen

"If all men knew what others say of them, there would not be four friends in the world"

Blaise Pascal

The Bistro de L'oulette was busy with tourists as well as local couples within an hour of opening every day of the Fringe. Street shows were still in full flow at the top of the little cobbled lane, and every time a bill was paid and the waiters thought they might have time to breathe, another lot of customers drifted in, seeking a table.

Chuck sat in the Volvo with Forsyth, Gav and Joe. Stroker had texted him to say that he had learned that Trevelen was popping in at some point that evening, so they were waiting. Forsyth had his laptop on ready to record the transmission from the designated table when the target arrived. In the meantime, only the sounds of cutlery being set, footsteps, and occasional exclamations in Arabic French (somewhat old fashioned compared to modern European French) were coming through.

"Quatre plaques de bouillabaisse!" shouted a Scottish female, in French.

"Write it down," replied an East European male in English.

"Take four's garlic bread please, Omar," came another camp Scottish voice before the ever-familiar sound of broken glass.

"Merde," exclaimed a new female voice. "That stupid cow should be sacked!" she then declared in Canadian French.

"Grosse Conne," exclaimed another male.

"Bitchy bastards," offered Forsyth.

Gav was lounging in the back seat thinking that one of the females sounded quite sexy, and was mentally giving her a body and face. Joe was reading a back-page football article beside him while Forsyth sipped at a can of Lucozade he had bought to wash another Ibuprofen down with. He was nursing a black eye which had swollen up quite badly. Chuck had found him standing outside St Leonards hours earlier after hearing the news about Leslie Cairns death.

It turned out that Forsyth had attempted to get involved in the CID cover-up job by confronting the DI, a tall scar-faced thug by the name of Nisbet, who was busy wheeling Cairn's dead body out into a private ambulance. There were several suits involved and potentially two white-coated doctors. As they swarmed around the back exit to where the vehicle was being loaded, Forsyth had marched forward and been confronted by two of them. An argument developed, more uniform got involved when voices were raised, and then a Chief Inspector turned up with two other men whose identities Forsyth had been unable to establish due to being otherwise engaged in the receiving of several punches from at least four men. He gave as good as he got, mind, and one suit required stitches to his lower lip afterwards. In the end, Forsyth had no option but to allow himself to be escorted from the building by two uniformed constables, with the threat of further action ringing in his ears.

Chuck had tried to call Wong to persuade him to reconsider his command, but he couldn't get hold of him. Instead, he took Forsyth back to his Portobello house and composed and sent a long, concerned email to Wong in which he again urged him to bring an officer from the Met in to investigate what had now developed into a massive situation. He also spelled out his suspicions about Cairns' recent death and the melodramatic passage of the body to a potentially classified location. He then pointed out that a connection had been made between Trevelen and Head Coroner Dr Esther Faulkner, and went on to suggest that Cairns' body had been taken away to assure a suicide verdict. Lastly, as a courtesy, Chuck copied in Adams, Forsyth and Sheriff Mark Dailly – the former Procurator Fiscal who had subtly warned him about Masonic cops many years previously at the District Court.

Back in the car, however, the mission continued regardless of Wong. "The Frenchies know how to treat a man, you know?" smirked Gav as they continued to listen to the restaurant drama.

"How would you know?" asked Forsyth.

"Been to Paris a few times, actually," he boasted, and they all laughed him out.

Chuck had relayed Wong's stand-down order earlier on. He explained to the men that he wanted to push that little bit further against Trevelen, and then afterwards, against old Herriot in his fancy camper van in the East Neuk. "We shall truly be in an unauthorised position then, and could all be suspended if we continue," he had warned them.

He explained his crude but effective plan to persuade Herriot to comply, then went into how this was the only moral option open to them, in his opinion. He had not needed to bang on about how women and children depended upon them to protect their kids from evil, for they were all eager to have a quick go at it.

"If you want out, then you can walk away tonight with no bad feelings," he had promised each of them. Yet after only the usual questions, they all quickly agreed to press on, for it was one more night at any rate and a 24-hour covenant was made between them.

Thankfully, at about 9 pm Chuck received a text from Stroker informing him that Trevelen was in the restaurant, by dramatically coding this information into, "The eagle has landed, guv."

"I told you not to call me that, you madman," was Chuck's response.

A call from him followed seven minutes later. "He's at the table and has ordered Pastis," he was whispering but appeared to be edging himself ever closer to a fever of anxiety.

"Right, calm down, Irvine. We have him and you just get on with your shift as though nothing were amiss."

Stroker did as he was told.

Eventually, chair legs scraped the floor and Trevelen's hoity-toity voice came through loud and clear along with that of another male; older and very Marseilles. "Yes, I think I tried it in Lisbon. They sell thousands of those little custard tarts there at breakfast," Trevelen declared haughtily.

"So, I'll pass, thank you Louis. I'll have the pea soup as usual and then the lamb and pomegranate thing, thank you."

Louis now scraped his chair legs and gave the order to someone in French, before returning to the table and scraping them again.

Chuck wondered if the floorboards would now be marked as a consequence.

"So, how is Stroker progressing?" Trevelen inquired now, as the sound of the ice clinking loudly in his Pastis came over the radio between short sips.

"What is Pastis?" asked Joe.

"Like Pernod?" offered Gav.

"Ouzo or Sambuca, I think," said Forsyth.

"Shut it!" Chuck told them fiercely. So they listened.

"He improves and is good with pastries and desserts," came the reply in the thick accent of a northern Marseillais.

"Will he be ready to lead a kitchen in six months?"

"What can I say, Philip?"

"Yes or No?" Trevelen's tone was impatient.

"It will depend on the standard required at Bute House and the support or backstabbing provided by the assistant chefs," Louis considered as he swirled the ice in his glass around.

Eventually their food was served, and the men discussed an apparent investment in an orange grove on the Costa Blanca. Although they were talking about large figures, production and marketing, Chuck was thinking furiously about their references to placing Stroker in Bute House, the First Minister's residence. What on earth was all that be about?

Thankfully they returned to this point, when the degenerate gambler Louis; whose restaurant Chuck knew, made a tidy little profit, but who chucked much of it all back on the roulette tables; returned to the murky subject of finance. "Philip, when can I expect my end on the Stroker project, my friend?" He asked as casually as only the French can; Chuck almost sensed the accompanying shoulder shrug through the receiver.

"Sorry Louis, you get your forty." There was a pause, and Chuck and Forsyth exchanged looks. "When he gets the job at Bute House," insisted Trevelen.

"Are you sure you can place him in Bute House?" Louis asked between a mouthful of something crispy.

"There will be friendly interviewers and quite possibly a selected kitchen friend, but he must be able to cook. By the way, did he cook this?" Trevelen asked.

"Yes. Well, I can give him a cracking reference if need be," Louis pointed out.

"Yes, of course, and he will have references from two family friends as well, but at the end of the day he needs to operate as a head chef for up to three months," Trevelen stated.

"And what happens if the election goes your way and you don't need to dispose of the First Minister after all?" Louis sounded sceptical, as though they had discussed this previously.

"Then nothing." Trevelen was curt as his knife and fork clinked down on his plate.

"Well, what if…"

"Well, nothing." Trevelen cut Louis off. "Your council tax and business rates will be voided both here and at your home address. You won't ever have to worry about paying another parking ticket again, and I shall personally give you the second payment of forty grand after the election, regardless of the result," he told the old gambler.

"OK, then," Louis eventually laughed. He was not a greedy man, more a desperate gambler who still believed, like all desperate gamblers, that the answer to his desperation remained in the game. This arrangement cleared some stress and gave him the next chance of playing the game and winning all his losses back.

Outside, they could now hear wine being poured as they looked at one another in disbelief. "Stroker is the patsy, then?" said Joe, and Chuck nodded as he ran it all quickly through his mental processor again. "Yes, and it sounds like it's to be poisoning of the First Minister's food, assuming that the First Minister is not someone Trevelen desires to be in the post."

"That's conspiracy to murder right there, guv," snapped Forsyth, eager to nick the pair of them right away.

"Right, let's listen." Chuck put his index finger to his mouth so they sat and listened to another 48 minutes of chit-chat regarding orange production being the new wine production industry, and of all other things, fish. Nothing more of interest was said. Trevelen eventually left in a taxi at around 10.30 pm after Louis had paid him for some cases of his in-laws' wine.

"Well, we have Trevelen for manipulating the employer's rule handbook and we know from our intel from Leslie Cairns that more than one hit was being explored on the next First Minister," Chuck said.

When Chuck had briefed Gav and Joe earlier, Joe suggested that there might be enough to arrest Trevelen for conspiracy based upon this pending recording, but Chuck disagreed. "No, we needed Cairns for that, and that plan is now cream-crackered, Joe."

He thought for a moment and pointed out that "at least we know of two plots now. One, via the Bute House food chain, which most likely would involve a cover-up and either a dead or an incarcerated Stroker, and two, that Cairns was offered a contract to murder Salmond, should the SNP win the election next year."

"What, in 2015?" asked Gav.

"Yes, Gav. And only in a specific set of precise circumstances whereby the SNP had won the election."

"So, they might have a replacement ready, as in a Deputy First Minister?" asked Gav.

"Must have," shrugged Chuck. "Maybe they have a man in the Greens? In the case of Labour needing a coalition to prevent the SNP running away with it?" he suggested.

"The Green Party would be the smart cover choice?" Gav agreed, it was not so far-fetched really. "Everyone wants to do a deal with the Greens to beef up their chances."

"Why not just back an outright winner instead?" Forsyth suggested.

"Because the SNP are going to win," Chuck supposed, "and Salmond isn't for sale, as Donald Trump might be able to testify." He knew Salmond was not interested in wealth or glamour, simply from the man's words and actions. You did not have to agree with his ideology to determine that easily enough.

"What about the SNP Deputy First Minister, then?" Joe asked anyone.

"No way, she is Salmond's wee Jimmy Krankie," joked Forsyth, and they all laughed.

"I agree though, guv," offered Forsyth while zipping up the laptop in its holdall. "The most likely scenario would be to back a party and hope it could get in as a coalition government."

"Or they could simply back an in-your-face candidate such as Anderson-Forbes?" Chuck speculated aloud.

"We should nick the restauranteur – that Louis guy?" Forsyth urged. "Then we could get everything he knows, as he clearly knows a fair bit, guv."

"We'll need to put surveillance on him and have something to use first. So, with him and that Gary Welsh in line for tugs, we should best not create panic just yet. Instead, we will make Herriot work for us and then, hopefully, pinch Trevelen. Once we have him, the rest will all fall along into place," Chuck told them.

"Well in my brawl with CID at St Leonards, I might have let it be known that I thought they murdered Cairns, sorry," Forsyth looked out the window.

At this point in the discussion Gav farted, which was a real slap on the nose that caused much grumbling, and made them all exit the vehicle. Chuck leaned back against his door and considered things a moment further. He saw all the Fringe show fliers on the High Court wall. Then he saw a poster for the SNP. He looked at it for a while. An instinctive cop's guess came to mind, the party to back would be the SLP now. The SNP might consider a coalition with them and others, if it assured that they remain in power.

"They would use power, money and handshakes to get their person into power, but failing that, they would quite possibly murder whoever wins. Possibly even the whole cabinet," Chuck said, then realised it sounded an insane proposition. He let his train of thought continue aloud, though.

"And because these rodents are cunning, they will have back up contingencies, such as in the case of a close-run election, which would raise the likelihood of a coalition agreement," he turned to face his colleagues now.

"That could involve Labour and the SLP, or the SLP and the SNP. In that scenario, and mind, the forecasters are now saying that the SLP will be in contention. Regardless, if Salmond died, or the whole cabinet were murdered say, from poison contained in a lunch, the government would either collapse or at the very least wobble."

"And?" Forsyth asked.

"Then the opposition party would be asked to form a new government with the remainder of the SNP." Chuck was still trying to get this straight in his own head, as it was still such a tangled web of possibilities that in order to be sure of anything, further evidence was still required.

"Do you think they are that clever, guv? Do they have those kinds of resources to cover all the angles?" asked Gav

"Gav, these people do exactly this and have done it for years," Joe butted in.

"But who in their right mind works with such intricate and absurd planning guys?" Gav shook his head.

"People who are not in their right minds, Gav," smirked Chuck; and after a short pause, Gav relented and did so too.

They all got back into the car and waited for Stroker to finish his shift and join them. On the drive over to Fife, Stroker told them that Trevelen had brought some of the French wine along with some of his own bramble wine. "Doubt a penny changes hands," he offered.

"Let's ring HMRC on the bastard then, guv; hit them from every angle," snapped Gav.

"Ha ha, you're lethal Gav. Let's focus on Trevelen tonight though, eh," said Chuck jovially.

"Wouldn't want to be your enemy mate," Stroker, who was seated beside Gav in the rear, offered.

"Shut it, you," snarled Gav, offended by Stroker's mere presence. "I'm sick of Europeans coming here, dodging tax, getting benefits, pushing up rents and filling up the school places with their kids," he turned back to his sniggering colleagues.

"You sound like Anderson-Forbes," sighed Forsyth.

"Well, I'm going to vote for him next year," Gav said softly, and they were all silent a while as they crossed the River Forth towards the kingdom of Fife.

Chuck briefed them all on the situation by the time they had passed the little village of Dalmeny, with only a gasp or two and a little huff by Stroker to contend with in reply, but all had been finalised and everyone was up-to-date by the time they approached the North Queensferry side of the bridge.

"Right lads, quiet down a minute," Forsyth cut through the laughing. "If this is going to persuade the old steamer to do some good on our behalf, then we must seize the opportunity and be focused throughout," he said with straight face.

"It's not you who has to seize it though, is it officer?" Stroker protested again, despite having been shot down earlier by Chuck on the subject. This caused considerable amusement all round apart from Gav, who wanted to swat Stroker like a fly.

Nothing had been said to Stroker about the content of the recordings that night. When he asked how things had gone, Chuck simply changed the subject and asked whether he had brought the microphone back with him.

"It's all cool," he promised Chuck. "I'll pick it up at the start of my next shift tomorrow."

The Fife countryside lay in darkness as they headed along the coastal trail toward the East Neuk and their destination – Crail. The little seaside towns of St Monans, Pittenweam, Anstruther and Kilrenny appeared one by one on the dark horizon like Christmas card scenes; thanks to the moonlight which reflected down upon these old Augustinian towns. It was as though Van Gogh had painted the skyline and moonlit sea. Joe was the first to succumb to the silvery beauty of the sea below, which also provided a glittering view over the Edinburgh coast. He had apparently been at a Sea Scouts convention at St Monans way back when and went off on one about it. Gav spoke fondly of Pittenweam and of pushing his sister into the old outdoor pool there.

Chuck could have spoken about the award-winning fish and chip shop in Anstruther, or the outdoor pool at Cellerdyke, as he drove past the little fishing parish. Instead, he simply listened to the men chattering like tourists in their own childhoods, while he thought on the matter at hand. The windows were down, and the nostalgic, fired-up merriment, only required a hipflask of whisky to complete the scene. For Chuck, however, there was always the underlying sobriety and tense disposition of a law enforcement officer who was intent upon breaking the law. Indeed, he was aware, and constantly turning over in his mind, the fact that he was currently intent upon gambling with human life in the pursuit of righteousness.

Crail appeared at the head of golden wheat fields, which seemed a light lilac. The town was a rugged boomerang shape, a white nipple upon the breast of the East Neuk itself as it meets the North Sea. The dark purple waters of the estuary splashed against Crail's southern side, before meeting the rougher currents of the fiercely and often-dramatic sea. Down to the right sat the old harbour and the beach where the sea pressed gently, as if massaging the sand. The whole town was asleep too by the looks of it, despite the notice at the side of the road of a 'Musical Weekend' which was apparently taking place in some beach in nearby Kingsbarns; Chuck reckoned Herriot would be quite miffed about this and cracked a smile as a result.

Whitewashed houses in the Cornish fashion, with their curtains closed and little sign of light coming from the windows, were what they found. There were a few hippy stragglers with guitars and bongs hanging around outside the town's caravan park and campsite; which looked well-occupied due to being only a couple of miles from the event.

"What's that, guv?" Forsyth pointed in the direction of lights and noise coming from beyond a hedgerow to the car's right. Chuck stopped the car, got out and climbed up onto his toes upon the car door rim but could still barely see over the hedge. What he did see was a pleasant surprise, however, so he went around to the Volvo's rear and removed two spare number plates he had made for any upcoming druggie operations, and proceeded to change the plates on the car before then driving off again.

"It is a camp site in there," he said. "And there are a few campfire parties on the go and some generators."

"I thought I could hear a burger van engine or something?" chipped in Joe, who had been trying to figure out the chugging sound.

"So, we might not have any issue with running our engines for a wee while," smirked Forsyth in a timely tandem with Stroker's hushed groan.

Herriot's camper van took a while to locate, being away at the posher end. Chuck got the men all out on the deck walking around, doing recces of the site so that they could both locate the target vehicle and identify the best place to park the car while they carried out the deed. Back at the country lane where they had parked, it transpired that Joe had located Herriot and his position right beside the beach, a spot that was relatively tranquil.

"Right, where do we park, then?" Forsyth asked.

"There's a ditch and some woodland between his van and the wee lane, which is empty," said Joe. "We can park on the lane and run the hose through the ditch area, under the fence, and Bob's your uncle." He rubbed his hands together, enthusiastic to be pressing on. Chuck simply gave him a flicked salute, and they were all back in the car and off again around to this nearby lane.

It turned out to be a farmer's track with gravel, so there would be no danger of tyre marks. The farm was out of sight thankfully, with tall wheat covering the track from the little road, leading back up to a small kirk where they had come from. There was a line of woodland only around a few yards in width which separated them from the camper vans. When they all got out of the vehicle, the distant sound of Floyd's dreamy early Syd Barrett stuff was in the air from nearby Kingsbarns, and each of them felt the urge to hit the beach and sniff out narcotics – except Stroker of course, who was wondering how many young women would be out of it on the beach. Chuck had to smirk at the thought of how uncomfortable Herriot might be at such disturbances to his normally peaceful retreat.

Fortunately, there were one or two car engines and the odd generator on hand to allow them to start the Volvo's motor when the moment came. "Right, get stripped," Chuck snarled at Stroker to show that the laugh was over and that there would be no arguments from now on. Stroker began giggling at the command and when he finally did strip off upon the gravel track, he declined to protest.

Forsyth planted the extra-long hose pipe in the Volvo's exhaust while Chuck and Joe unrolled the rest of it through the wooded strip with the giggling Stroker scurrying alongside them, trying to cover himself like a woman needing to pee. "Cut the giggling out or I'll kick your arse," growled Joe as they all kneeled to go under the little fence and into the camper van zone.

Once at the vehicle, Chuck confirmed the registration number, and had a little sketch around the two adjoining vehicles, one of which had Sidney Devine blaring out of it, almost in retaliation to the Floyd event. There were a few rowdy west coast accents also coming from it, but the rest of the zone was still.

"Right, we need to move really quick here, guys," Chuck whispered to the pair of them. "Anyone could storm out of that campervan at any moment." He pointed over at the Sidney Devine camper. "So, do exactly as I say, and let's move. Right Joe, fit it!" he commanded.

Joe quickly stuck the end of the hose in the camper van's air vent while Chuck texted Forsyth to start the Volvo engine.

No one noticed the car engine and the light on Herriot's camper van did not come on. After ten minutes Joe removed the pipe just as Forsyth turned the engine off. Chuck slowly tried the camper door and found that it was locked, so he withdrew the skeleton keys he had taken from the squad offices, and picked it open very quickly. A great gust of exhaust fumes billowed out into the open air while Chuck and Stroker crouched back in the bushes, awaiting any movement. Joe took the hose back and let Gav rewind and stick it back in the boot, while he hurried back through the trees to crouch on one knee with Chuck. "Anything?" he whispered.

"No, let's hope he's still alive." Chuck got up and slowly led the way inside, with Stroker cowering behind him and Joe covering their rear.

Chuck, who was wearing gloves, could see Herriot lying on his back sound asleep while his wife lay beside him, snoring deeply with occasional coughs and splutters. Chuck opened all the windows to clear out the carbon monoxide. He had decided upon exhaust fumes rather than a chloroformed spray as he remembered Kim's pal from yoga once having had it done to her while driving across France and staying in her camper overnight at one of the 24-hour service stations. He shone a torch on Herriot, whose eyelids moved in the light but remained closed. He had really aged and was sporting a drinker's purple nose with a thick white moustache underneath. Chuck saw that they were both asleep on a double berth and had been hot, as they had a small fan running.

On the nearby table was an empty bottle of Grouse and five or six cans of Guinness. Chuck didn't know the couple were out due to the exhaust fumes or the booze, but he suspected both.

"Right, let's strip him," he whispered and they removed Herriot's brown and white pyjamas, pushed Mrs Herriot away, then laid him down on his back. He grunted once and farted, but apart from that he was well gone.

"Right, go on, do your stuff baby," Chuck urged the naked Stroker.

Joe put the lights on. Stroker, now a little more eager than they had expected, jumped up on the bed and mimed performing oral sex on Herriot. Chuck placed the whisky bottle and a couple of cans on the side, placed the black sunglasses he had brought, on Herriot's nose, and took several photographs with a phone, before ordering Stroker to quit. Herriot was redressed and his wife was positioned back, head upon pillow, then the lights went out, the door locked and they were away. They had not been interrupted. As they crawled back under the fence again, Chuck considered this to have been a successful operation; scrappy yes but successful regardless.

On the drive back, Gav went on a bit about what would have happened if the local Fife cops had happened along and how their careers would have been compromised. By the time Chuck had changed the plates and got them out of the place and onto the road home, everyone was laughing at the photos of Stroker, and optimism had soon united them all. Even Gav had to laugh at Stroker, who just wanted to be one of the lads.

Part one was now mission accomplished, Chuck knew as he cruised back along the coast and they all witnessed the morning sun appear over the Firth of Forth like a celestial intercession of the darkness.

Having dropped the other men off back in the city, Chuck then drove Forsyth home.

"You sure you don't want to stay with us, at least until this is over, Chris?" he offered again.

"Naw, I need my own bed guv, and besides, I'm not scared of those bastards."

"Fair enough. Call me if you need me." Chuck insisted as he dropped him off.

On the drive home, Chuck wondered if they would try to take the phone from him again. Or if they would try to take Forsyth's laptop from him. He instinctively felt for the ball thrower in his coin pocket and was glad when he felt it still snugly there. As he pulled up at a traffic light on Seafield Road, he suddenly realised that he was immensely tired; mentally as well as physically. This had been an intense few days and having been up all night, his eyes were now throbbing from the sunshine. He had not realised how much effort he was putting in to all this madness.

Suddenly the car doors unlocked and the passenger side opened as Dai stepped in, sat down and smiled that infectious smile of his. "Evening all," he teased.

"Where have you been?" Chuck demanded to know.

"If I told you, you would only be further confused and one question would develop into several – which I have no time for, Chuck," Dai continued to smile.

Chuck knew by now that it was impossible to be angry with him. "Cairns was murdered, I suspect," he said tiredly as the lights changed.

"Yes, I'm afraid he was," nodded Dai.

"He would have turned?" Chuck half asked him.

"He was certainly struggling with the thought of remand, never mind a trial and a long sentence to follow. So yes, he was weaker than both Latif and Frazer," Dai agreed.

"Wong pulled us out too early and they killed him in the gap." Chuck was seething now.

"Yes, I'm afraid so, and now they want you and your team sorted out," Dai warned.

"Because I now have Trevelen on conspiring to murder whoever is First, or Prime Minister, of an independent Scotland."

"Do you have him for that?" Dai raised his eyebrows to question this claim.

"The tape is strong evidence, no?" Chuck felt his heart sink.

"Depends on who the judge is." Dai shrugged.

310

"And nothing about the paedophile ring yet." Chuck was disappointed.

"No, but where you have exposed Trevelen's sloppiness, you may still do likewise through your little investment in Mr Herriot," Dai surmised optimistically.

"Time has virtually run out, Dai. My boss has pulled the plug on the investigation."

"Yes. But that won't stop you playing a covert long game, will it?" Dai gently pointed out.

"Meaning?" Chuck knew only too well what this meant, but he wanted to hear it.

"Wong is not under the thumb yet, Chuck. He instinctively senses the power gathering around him and he knows which way the wind is blowing. He's cautious, understandably."

"So, he's playing safe for self-preservation then?" Chuck reckoned he had sussed this much out himself already.

"Yes. But he can't ignore the weight of the evidence a willing-to-help Herriot can bring in."

"Well, at this stage the ship is still in port, Chuck. Herriot has not been approached by any investigation, nor has he reported the incident from last night, so chin up."

Chuck slowed down and looked at his passenger. "I was handcuffed as it was. I was working in the shadows while the TIC murder at will, and then cover up what they have done. The fact that they use Nephilim to do their dirty work; is by-the by Dai, but tell me, how am I to play this game any longer and hope to succeed?" he demanded to know.

"From an unauthorised position, and with my support," the angel winked at him confidently.

Chuck shook his head and sighed as he couldn't see it, but he was not giving in either.

"Rest assured that there is only going to be one winner in this fight – a struggle that began on the plains of Troy, and which will finish on the plain of Megiddo" Dai insisted with a wink.

"Look, put the TIC on the shelf for a minute and remember my original tip: to follow Trevelen. After all, you're now in possession of information regarding a potential conspiracy to execute a leading politician!" Dai reminded him, touching his arm as he did so. Chuck met his gaze and listened intently. "And you, Chuck, have dropped an explosive shell onto the bad guys' battleship. It might not sink them as you predict, but they are all hands on deck, addressing the issue even as we speak. Another direct hit will scuttle them completely, Chuck," Dai promised with that heart-warming and highly convincing vibe of his.

"Yes, but…"

"So, you need to focus on this planned assassination then and remember that there is more than one plan in progress. This group plans to kill their way to control of the state. Think about that, Chuck. What if Labour, and say the SLP, formed a coalition government to keep the SNP out next year?" Dai asked.

"Then they would whack leading figures internally within the coalition until their man was in the position to take up the leadership," Chuck growled, as a car in front of him indicated to go right then went left instead.

"Then, I advise you to follow that scent and not lose track of it. If you do, the other matter will resolve itself in within the process. And although I do not agree with your method in relation to Herriot, whose wife, incidentally, could have died of carbon monoxide poisoning; we did appreciate your high-tempo pressing and directness."

Chuck looked at him again but found only warm appreciation in those beautiful angelic eyes. "I just get frustrated at how they are using so much power to bump off witnesses, Dai," he sighed.

"Well, they have been allowed to gather and stock up on power for a long time, Chuck," Dai looked at him as if he were a child discovering how to write.

"Mankind has chosen to ignore the clues about the existence and origins of these people. They were allowed to gradually seize power from within a democracy, one step at a time," he went on.

"Clues that we missed?" he then asked after a moment's thought.

"Well, did you ever wonder why so many masons are employed within law enforcement? Or why the buses in Edinburgh are maroon and white instead of green and white?" Dai asked gently.

Chuck was silent.

"Or, why there are so many of what you may know as gargoyles, but that we know to be dragons, upon so many buildings around Edinburgh, hmmm…?" He shrugged as though he himself had no answer, but Chuck understood his meaning.

"Or of the interesting messages contained within the stonework of Roslyn Chapel?" Dai continued.

"OK. It is the establishment, then?" Chuck was fed up with the guessing.

"Sure," Dai turned to look out of his window as they passed the Cat and Dog home on Seafield.

"Well, I need more help from you lot then, Dai."

"And you shall receive it, my friend." Dai looked at him again and nodded.

"So, is the SLP guy, Anderson-Forbes, their man?" Chuck guessed.

"Look for the personification of change within Scottish politics, Chuck, not the individual man or woman," Dai told him. "The significance is the change that the person symbolises as opposed to any opportunistic individual who rides upon the coat tails of public dissatisfaction."

"How do you mean?"

"Follow Trevelen. Don't let the enemy get you down. This battle is far from over, and just because they will lower themselves to such depravities as murder, I must encourage you to continue to work against them, my friend. You are doing well, and you have achieved more than you realise already."

"Maybe, but that's easy for you to say. You are game enough to jump in when a fallen angel attacks me, but if a human or Nephilim wants to murder us, we are on our own, right?"

Dai did not answer this, but gazed ahead and thought about things a while before issuing a warning. "Be vigilant, for they are getting bolder with their violence. Keep your eyes open, don't take chances, and keep your finger on the ball-launcher; because I must tell you, they are likely to go for you or your team at any point now. I can't always be there when that happens. I am not an entirely free agent, Chuck."

Chuck pulled over on Portobello high street. "And my home?" he asked hopefully.

Dai nodded. "Your guardian angel will stand up to defend you if they try anything again at your house. All I'm saying is that you should be on your toes. They are panicking; you have one hand on their collars now, and they are running scared." Dai continued to smile as he opened his door to get out onto the pavement.

"And where will you be?"

Dai paused a moment and turned his head back to consider the man's simplicity again, "Abroad for an hour or so, but I shall talk to you again later this evening," he promised, before winking again and disappearing into a charity shop.

The lights changed ahead, so he pulled away again and turned on the car radio and hoped for a tune instead of any of the referendum stuff and a moment of peace while he drove.

U2's 'Acrobat' was on, and Chuck found himself focusing on the lyrics for some reason:

"Nothing makes sense, nothing seems to fit. I know you'd hit out if you
only knew who to hit.
And I'd join the movement
If there was one I could believe in
Yeah, I'd break bread and wine
If there was a church I could receive in.
'Cause I need it now.
To take the cup
To fill it up, to drink it slow.
I can't let you go. And I know that the tide is turning round,
So, don't let the bastards grind you down."

Chuck felt his confidence soaring, and as he turned into his street he was further lifted to find a vacant space right outside his house. When he got in, there was a note from Kim on the fridge saying she was out with her pal for supper and that there was some frozen food for him. He tossed it in the bin and took a few mouthfuls of cold milk from a carton that he was not allowed to do when she was in. He kicked off his shoes and lay down on the sofa. He held the ball-thrower in his right hand as he did so. He took some time to fully relax, but when he did he pondered over various arrest strategies for Trevelen under the current restricted circumstances. Before long, he had fallen into a light sleep where he dreamed of the faces of those who had attacked him outside.

"*Cui Bono?*" he could read upon the forehead of the beast who had stabbed him, and he remembered that this meant who would benefit. He realised with absolute clarity that it was his destiny to search out and destroy those who would benefit from the crimes Frazer had told him about.

"Hurrah!" smiled Dai at him now, "you are beginning to comprehend your *raison d'etre.*"

"My what?"

But then he awoke to the sound of his mobile phone ringing beside him. He sat up, launcher still in hand, stretched his back and arms up, and noted that the clock on the mantelpiece showed 3:40 pm. "Hello?" he asked into it without checking the caller's number beforehand.

"Guv, it's me." It was Joe, and he sounded as though he was driving. "I'm taking the Mrs over to the big Tesco and just drove past Herriot's gaff, what do you know: the campervan is only in the driveway," he revealed.

"Superb. Cheers, Joe, I shall speak to you in a bit."

So, it seemed like Herriot had limped home to figure out what had just happened to him and his wife. There was relief to hear that he was alive, well, no time like the present then; Chuck would deliver the knock-out blow right now. He stood up and grabbed his car keys. He wouldn't bother picking up Forsyth; this final gamble could be played without endangering any other officers, and besides, it shouldn't take long. He made a pit stop at an internet café in Newington run by a Turkish couple who turned a blind eye to blokes viewing hard-core porn in private booths, and whose printing machine was discreetly located behind these booths. He took a computer, and five minutes later had printed out all the relevant images he had taken of Herriot and Stroker on the phone, paid and headed outside.

There was a traffic warden in the process of booking the Volvo. Chuck flashed his badge at him and told him in no uncertain terms to go away. The East European male about-turned and moved on to a wedding car that was stopped outside a pharmacist momentarily. Chuck wondered who could do that particular job, and as anticipated he watched from his rear view mirror, as the bridesmaids all got out and started arguing with the warden.

It took Chuck a further fifteen minutes to drive over to Herriot's place. Once there, he parked around the corner and walked around to the house, up the driveway, and long press of the doorbell.

Herriot did not recognise his former employee upon opening the large red wooden door. "Yes?" he asked.

"Inspector Herriot, it's Inspector Charles Kean here from the Drug Squad," Chuck smiled at the old man, who looked quite scared.

The nervous quizzical frown morphed into a surprised beam now. "Chuck?" he asked with squinted eyes. He was obviously losing his memory for a face, Chuck considered.

"The very man," he grinned back in reply.

Herriot took a moment to consider all of this before grinning. "And they made you a DI now, then, eh?" he remarked, trying to sound merry.

"Indeed," Chuck smiled back.

"Come in, then, lad," said the old man, opening the door and leading the way through to a wide, old-fashioned farmhouse-style kitchen, "Sit," he motioned Chuck towards a table with chairs. Despite his apparent friendliness, no refreshment was offered.

"So, to what do I owe this unexpected pleasure then, Chuck?" Herriot asked as he took a chair and coughed deep from the chest.

"You took up smoking, Inspector?" Chuck enquired with mock concern.

"No." Herriot then cleared his throat and mouthed the content into a paper tissue which he then binned before washing his hands. "Actually, we were away in my camper van last night and somehow ended up at the wrong end of a bloody carbon monoxide leak," he replied.

"Carbon monoxide?"

"Yes, it's a nasty bugger. Bridget is away to the infirmary for a check-up as she was wheezing and we both had blinding headaches earlier." Herriot shook his head and rubbed it gently with his fingers as he retook his chair.

"Must have slept right through it last night, but I think I subconsciously realised something was amiss," he tapped his nose to show that he was a cunning cop at heart, "and so I got up and opened all the windows before passing out again."

"That's shocking, pal," replied Chuck before he produced the A4 images of Herriot and Stroker in action. He grinned as Herriot found his glasses and examined them closely. His eyes squinted at first but soon his face developed a deep purple shade which matched his drinker's nose.

"So, it was you, you cunt!" the old bastard snarled like a cornered fox.

"I'm afraid so," Chuck nodded with a confident but relaxed look.

"Why on earth...?"

"That particular photo," Chuck pointed at a perfectly staged image on one particular sheet, "would certainly stand out on the noticeboards and changing rooms of every cop-shop in Edinburgh with your name and old collar number written upon it," he assured his prey.

Herriot sat frozen. His bitter hatred for the man who now was occupying a seat at his dining table was abundantly obvious, even in the silence.

"It may also go to Collysdean Golf Club, and under the windscreen wipers of every car that turns up in every other golf course in Edinburgh too," Chuck remained relaxed, unthreatening by posture but convincingly chilling. Still, Herriot didn't reply and seemed frozen with rage.

"In your local chip shop, butchers and... oh, I think multi-dropped around Crail caravan park, just for good measure. Oh, do you guys drink in the local tavern there when you visit?" he toyed with Herriot further.

"I don't know how up you are on modern technology, but there are already Facebook and Twitter accounts just waiting for some images to promote; for which anyone and everyone whose opinions you value, from your GP to the person who does your MOT, will all receive an email link to these images," Chuck eyeballed him and nodded to assure him beyond any doubt that this threat was deadly serious.

"I see you enjoy watching kids' hockey?" Chuck pointed toward a framed image of Herriot and a young girl at a girls' hockey event.

"That's my granddaughter, Lilly. She's only 10, for pity's sake! What do you want from me?" Herriot spat.

"Well, all the adults involved at her club, including all the other kids' parents, will receive copies too. A long process, granted, but it will be done". Chuck let this kick in briefly. "My desire is to avoid all the unpleasantness I've just sketched out. To make this happen, you must agree to wear this wire." Chuck dropped a small microphone onto the table. "Every time you travel with and play golf with the council king, Garry Welsh," Chuck went back to grinning now.

"Gary Welsh?" Herriot was confused now and squinted his face to show it.

"Never mind why. Yes, Gary Welsh. As well as at least once a week within your lodge."

"My lodge?" Herriot instinctively played dumb.

"Uh huh. Now, don't even think about playing silly buggers or I'll walk straight out that door and destroy you, you Satanic bastard," snarled Chuck impatiently.

"Satanic?" Herriot took umbrage with that singular allegation more than the threat of blackmail.

"And if you try to cheat or restrict conversations, I'll walk away," Chuck promised him.

"Well, how bloody long do you want me to play the stool?" Herriot was playing ball now, almost.

"Until I get intel on the paedophile ring that operates among the leaders of certain institutions and others who frequent the Fairmilehead lodge," Chuck probed now.

"But they are bugger all to do with me or Gary!" Herriot continued to protest.

"Again, you don't need to understand why you're doing it, OK?"

Herriot ignored this and looked again at the images. "Dirty bastard, what the hell are you doing this for? I mean, this is attempted murder, you daft bastard. My wife is in A&E!"

"And this," Chuck then placed yet another microphone upon the table. Herriot looked up aghast now, jaw open, crooked and stained yellow teeth on full display.

"I want you to place that in the bar of the Collysdean clubhouse," Chuck demanded.

There was an uneasy silence during which Herriot barely controlled the desire to strangle Chuck. Eventually he took a deep breath, went over to the kitchen counter, and poured himself a large gin and lemonade.

"Well, deal or no deal, pal?" Chuck stood up and gathered the images from the table.

Herriot necked the booze and gasped.

"Well?"

"OK, I don't see what choice you give me. You have a deal," came the snarl. "But that's all I will do. I draw the line here. Don't think about adding anything more."

"Good. Here's a safe number to contact me on. I expect progress within 48 hours, and don't try to Judas me, pal, or I'll throw you to the wolves and take any backlash head-on. I promise you that," Chuck assured him before standing up and walking out.

Back in the city, the air was still warm from the early afternoon sunshine and Chuck was hungrily considering finding a Burger King drive-thru when his other phone rang. The number was blocked, so it could be the office. He answered without pulling over.

"Where are you, Chuck?" It was Wong, and he sounded under pressure.

"At my uncle's house in Bathgate, Sir, he is unwell and..." he instinctively lied, but was not sure why, only that he now trusted no one, least of all the man trying to pull the plug on his investigation.

"Well I need you to come in to my office straight away!"

There was a slight pause while Chuck considered why this might be. "I'm not sure I can right now – is everything OK, Sir?"

For five seconds or so, Chuck heard silence down the line...

"Look..." Wong sounded unsure as to whether to divulge anything else. "It is just that you are going to be subject to an internal investigation thanks to bloody Gavin Caine," Wong sounded pissed off now.

"Gav?"

"Look, don't you give me that." Wong turned now. "He has gone above my head to the Assistant Chief Constable and complained about having to work on the deniable op." Wong let that sink in and paused, listening for Chuck's reaction.

"And there's also the not insignificant matter of your assault on former Inspector bloody Herriot last night!" he shouted.

"I see, Sir." Gav had obviously sold them all down the river.

"Yes, you better had, Mr.," snapped Wong.

"Well, like I said Sir, I'm dealing with a personal matter and can come in a couple of hours." Chuck knew if Gav had talked, it would not be long until they went to speak to Herriot and when that old bastard had discovered that that the goal posts had moved again, he would sing like a canary too and prison may be on the cards now.

"And I have CID making a formal complaint to me about Forsyth, who they say provoked a bloody punch-up in the custody area at St Leonards?"

"I think the cover-up merchants actually assaulted DS Forsyth Sir, if you would care to examine his face."

"You weren't even there, so how the bloody hell can you know that?" Wong was on a roll.

"Look, I can be over in a couple of hours, Sir." Chuck had no time for the hairdryer phone treatment he was getting, and had a lot to do before facing Wong later.

"No, leave it now; it is getting on." Wong suddenly piped down a bit as he looked at his watch.

"9 am tomorrow morning will suffice. You will be formally suspended pending an investigation, which is likely to involve the Fife Constabulary; who may or may not see this as a big deal and charge you all with attempted murder!" Wong tried to scare him now.

"I'll be there, Sir," Chuck coolly replied.

"And you are suspended as from this moment. Is that clear, Detective Inspector Kean?" Wong went formal on him now.

"Crystal, Sir. May I ask who shall be heading the investigation?"

"You shall receive written notification of the procedure as you are no doubt aware, and of course you will be informed as to when you are required to make yourself available for interview." Wong clearly hadn't a clue about the details and was spitting out the formal crap, but Chuck knew only too well that it was likely to be a locally-chosen team, handpicked by the conspirators to keep matters cosy and in-house.

"Fine, Sir. I shall see you tomorrow morning." Chuck still wanted to go to Burger King, to eat and think.

"And there is also this matter regarding Babar Latif and the Fiscal who, as you also know, has complained to me via email; I think you can expect a written complaint in the post about that, too." Wong just would not let him slip away to gather his thoughts.

"That's fine, Sir, understood."

"And finally," Wong was obviously feeling little sympathy for his best detective's outlook, as his tone had chilled considerably. "That bloody murder squad who are on the Lionel Frazer case have emailed me complaining that you are not making yourself available for a chat. Is that correct?"

"That's a lot of crap, Sir. DI Adams told them I was busy because I was on an op and that I would see them in due course," Chuck protested.

"Fine. Well, I shall ring the DI up presently and tell them you will be available tomorrow after 11am. You're suspended, but you will have to talk to them. I don't expect to keep you longer than an hour," Wong told him.

"Roger that, Sir." Chuck just wanted away.

"Fine. I'm very disappointed with all this, but until tomorrow, goodbye," Wong said firmly.

Chuck hung up and headed for Forsyth's flat. At the Chesser junction with Gorgie, his phone rang again; this time, it was Adams.

"Just heard from Wong. Gav is a little bastard!"

"It's awkward, yep, but I'm going to email a few people, including a mate of mine in the Met, who can whisper in one or two ears." Chuck sounded defiant, with a decent bit of fight still left in him.

"Well, I've got to run. Just wanted to check on you. I've a meeting with Wong now but had to tell you that Alban Dudley recently dialled 999 to claim that he has discovered his flatmate Irvine Stroker dead from what he suspected to be a heroin overdose," she told him.

"Oh, Christ!" Chuck was shocked now. "Stroker was not a junkie."

"Was he not?"

"No." Chuck was sure of that.

"Look, I'll call you soon as I'm finished with Wong, hun," she said.

"Yeah, sure."

"Probably wants to tell me that Gav is acting DS while Forsyth is suspended," she said contemptuously.

"Probably. I'll speak to you soon," and he did not wait for the reply, switching his phone off and throwing it onto the passenger seat as he drove on in the direction of Stroker's place.

At Portobello, however, the need for a cold drink and some food forced him to pull over. The little grocery store there sold large bottles of mineral water and freshly-made baguettes, not quite the burger he craved, but he could stop briefly then get back on the road to Musselburgh straight away. If there were any cops at Stroker's place already, they would not be aware as yet that Chuck had been suspended and may either fill him in, or grant him access.

He came out of the shop to face a motorbike parked up with two people wearing helmets and sitting alongside the Volvo. They looked straight towards him but had helmets on with visors covering their faces. For a second he thought they were taking a selfie on the bike with one of those stick things, but he quickly realised he was wrong, as an orange explosion came out from where the camera should have been.

The pellets sprayed through the warm air like grape shot, simply tearing whatever they encountered apart. Chuck's chest, shoulder and upper rib cage took a considerable hit and by the time his face slammed down upon the concrete pavement, his lungs, heart and major arteries were all punctured. There was no saving him now. The Indian shopkeeper who had jumped down behind his counter shaking with terror knew, even without any first aid experience, that whoever had been in the line of that blast would be out of the game.

Chuck had seen the flash, and been blinded by it as the sheer force of it decked him like a punch from Mike Tyson. Then, everything had stopped. By the time the other side of his face had hit the pavement he had already been air-lifted out of his bodily vessel and was hovering over the scene at a height of around 15 ft.

He saw the shooter replace the sawn-off shotgun back into a black bag which was strapped around his neck, and the driver then tear off at such a ridiculous speed that Chuck was sure they would crash. Then, he was standing across the road outside the old watchmaker's shop, watching as the shopkeeper's head finally appeared at the grocery store window, with a phone to his ear.

Dai then appeared. "I'm so sorry, my friend," he said, his sad eyes focused downward now.

"So, am I dead?"

"Yes."

"Why?"

"I did not see it coming and could not intervene even if I had, and your guardian chose not to intervene."

"It's not really a matter of choice, though," said the guardian angel, who Chuck had encountered on the boat at the start of the matter, and who had appeared again just now.

He had spoken to Chuck, but was looking at Dai and shaking his head. "We are not authorised to intervene in the conflict between men, as Dai is well aware."

Dai shrugged and looked at Chuck, "I have done so in my time," he confessed.

"I can confirm that there was no foul play and that if anything, your man was not fully on his guard considering the threat," offered a new voice from a person who was darker than the other two.

"Who is this?" Chuck asked Dai.

"A Grigori; also known as a Watcher," replied Dai and he nodded at the entity, who then disappeared.

Chuck looked at himself now, feeling no pain at all. He was no longer flesh and bone, more like a quantum fluid which was shifting slowly within a pumping shape of sort; like a tranquil little whirlpool. He instantly realised that the bleeding vessel on the pavement across the road had been a hindrance compared to this new form.

"And Kim?" he suddenly asked telepathically.

"She will suffer your loss as you would no doubt expect she might. But she will be safe from violence. I can tell you that," Dai assured him with a heartening smile.

"Who was the shooter?"

"Just some young wannabe who took the contract from Frazer's so-called TIC."

"The same paedophiles who killed Frazer, Yvonne and Cairns, then?" Chuck asked.

"And Stroker too," replied Dai. "They will claim that he overdosed on heroin today." He shook his head.

"They were never junkies. Forsyth will see the truth," Chuck said.

"Chuck, we need to go. Come with me please, my friend." Dai drew him to somewhere new which seemed very much like a hospital at first.

They walked along a dark rubber-styled corridor, round in design, with fittings that Chuck might have imagined to find upon a space craft. Halfway along there was a beautiful marble desk with two figures. Chuck sensed that they were also angels. Dai gave them a nod, and said, "Charles Kean," then continued to proceed past them and with Chuck still in tow.

"Satisfaction lies in the effort, not in the attainment," Dai said to him.

"Gandhi said that, I think?" Chuck thought he knew the quote.

"Precisely," smiled Dai knowingly.

Another angel appeared at a large door that looked like it was flowing with some sort of liquid material Chuck had never seen before. The scent here, perhaps from beyond the door itself, was comforting.

"Chuck, this is Dagiel," said Dai.

This angel was also beautiful and was wearing a light blue toga and gold tunic. He had shoulder-length curly brown hair which gave him faint echoes of a British Civil War cavalier or a musketeer, Chuck thought.

"I am the being who plucked your great grandfather Hugh Kean from the jaws of hell in that trench at the Somme in 1915, Chuck," Dagiel smiled brilliantly at him.

"And again on the train?" Chuck felt himself compelled to ask, he knew the story so well.

"Yes, quite right. I remember I appeared to him when his nurse left him in the carriage for a moment. We selected him for his bloodline and were waiting for you to come of age," Dagiel said with an ongoing, gentle smile now.

Dai then spoke: "Chuck, I must leave now, but I shall return in a short while and hopefully escort you to a different place," he explained.

Chuck knew he was being honest, and gratefully accepted as Dagiel showed him into a small whitewashed stone room with a terracotta looking roof. It was a clean and somehow attractive space. It was warm and had a sort of tropical feel to it. There was a blue coloured window frame which looked out at a beautiful turquoise sea. A bright blue and pinkish sun warmed the room but not overly. There was a comfortable-looking modern bed with beautiful, crisp white sheets, and a marble table and stool.

"Rest here, my friend," said Dagiel.

"What happens now?" Chuck asked without much concern.

"Hopefully soon, there will be a lot of excited individuals waiting to see you. In the meanwhile, drink some of that to help you sleep" Dagiel indicated toward a green jug and glass on the table. "It will help you sleep" he smiled. "Is this heaven?" Chuck asked him.

"Not quite," the angel replied. "There are many different possibilities, but no, the heavens are above here. This is more of an assessment and processing centre, but there are worse places you could have ended up at this stage so rest easily Chuck" his manner was patient and understanding.

"Dai has gone to press your case to the boss and have you admitted into a Kingdom above," he explained. "You were well chosen, did a decent job and thus have nothing to preoccupy yourself with, my friend. Rest here, and I shall come for you soon to process your passing," he said before leaving and gently closing the wooden door behind him.

Chuck looked out at the large sun and poured some of the liquid in the jug into the glass. It was a light purple but had a citrus scent to it so he drank it. It was deliciously sweet, a cold wine he guessed. Then he laid himself down upon the bed and instantaneously succumbed to sleep.

Elsewhere, Dai spoke to Dagiel in their own tongue, "I'm sorry we lost him there, but he has earned his admission, I am confident of that."

"And now?" the long-haired angel asked.

"Plan B?" replied Dai.

"Plan B then," sighed Dagiel.